Gabriel's Great Perhaps

By: Deborah M. Young

This Book is a work of fiction. References to real people, events, establishments, organizations or locales are intended to provide a sense of authenticity and are used fictionally. All other characters, and all incidents and dialogues, are drawn from the author's imagination and are not to be construed as real.

For information contact Deborah Young @ www.gabrielsgreatperhaps.com.

First edition

Editor - Rachel Cooper www.rachelcooper.ca
Cover Design - Jeff Brown www.jeffbrowngraphics.com
Author Photo - Jeff Cook www.cookedphotography.com

ISBN 978-1-777-1033-0-9

Dedicated to all who dare to care for a better world

" I go to seek a great perhaps."- Last words of Francois Rabelais, April 9th, 1553. A humanist, physician, priest and writer who questioned the existence of an afterlife.

" Life is funny. Why should the afterlife be any different?"   -Nick Shamhart

" If I got rid of my demons, I'd lose my Angels."   -Tennessee Williams

Gabriel's Great Perhaps

Prologue

Gabriel was looking for the portal. Its location had not changed in all the centuries he had been coming here, but tonight he sensed a disturbance. He glanced at the sky; dusk would fall soon.

A solar eclipse was imminent, briefly interrupting the sun's dominance over the earth. Although he didn't need the eclipse, he appreciated its timing and, if he were honest, the drama. Ah, here it was. The path of the solar eclipse would pass directly over the portal.

Gabriel knew the eclipse was not the source of his unease. He had frequented this place many times during eclipses, both lunar and solar. He and his order knew what this energy was but had not discussed it. He frowned; they would need to discuss it. An unnamed problem sits in the dark and gains strength.

A purple streak of light sliced through the vermillion evening sky. He gave it barely a glance; his presence here was bound to create a light show.

As he stood in the middle of a freshly mown hayfield, Gabriel spread his arms. Spindly spruce trees were silhouetted against the darkening eastern sky. A flock of geese rose up beside him, and he launched himself into flight with them. They honked louder and their wings beat faster. He was still laughing when he landed a minute later and watched the geese circle and settle.

When he was told that the person he was to contact lived in this area, he was not surprised. People who lived here did not do anything extraordinary with their lives, yet each one played an essential role in this world and beyond. Although they did not know it, they protected this timeless portal through which angels and other magical beings came to earth.

A lineage of protectors, Gabriel mused, and not one of them is aware. Humans. Some inflate worthless qualities, but most live their lives unaware of their core majesty.

Neither Gabriel nor any others had approached anyone living here in centuries. For a moment, he felt a shift in the air around him. *Perhaps others have taken advantage of this solar eclipse and—.* Gabriel shook his head to clear the thought. Should he have changed his clothes? He could pass for any culture or a hybrid of cultures. Tall, dark haired with high cheekbones and almond-shaped eyes, Gabriel enjoyed his good looks. It made his job easier. People accepted him more readily because he appeared to belong to their tribe. But the long white tunic shirt and wide-legged pants were not standard apparel in these parts. He sighed. The trees swayed in the altered vibration.

Again, Gabriel felt the shift. He had to speak with Mrs. Potts before an Interloper broke through and found her first.

Across the front of the vivid chartreuse farmhouse with raspberry trim, a wide veranda sagged comfortably. As he walked up the long dirt driveway, Gabriel heard a quavering voice belting out a tune from the 1940s, accompanied by scratchy music from inside the house. The shaky vibrato was coming from a small figure in a nubby gray cardigan, rocking on the veranda and singing along with an ancient record player. Gabriel was grateful Mrs. Potts would be the narrator for this project and not part of the chorus.

He stepped into view. "Good evening, Mrs. Potts." He smiled his most charming smile and bowed slightly.

Mrs. Potts stopped singing. She brought the wicker rocker to a standstill and stared calmly at him.

"Are you here to take me away?"

"Mrs. Potts, allow me to introduce myself." Gabriel decided to keep on being charming.

"No need." She brushed away the first of many evening black flies.

"So, you know who I am?" He kept his gaze level with hers and sat on a wicker chair at the other end of the veranda.

"I have been expecting you. Didn't want to see you, but you're here now. Can I call someone to take my dog? I don't want her to see this, and I sure as hell don't want her wandering around unfed for days until some poor bastard finds my body." Mrs. Potts took a sip out of a bluebird-painted ceramic cup and put it down hard on the side table, liquid sloshing out. She looked at him defiantly.

"Mrs. Potts, who do you think I am?"

"The Angel of Death, I assume." She placed her shaking hands on her lap. "To be honest, I expected you or one of your kind years ago." She kept her gaze steady on Gabriel. "You're good looking, I'll give you that."

Without standing up, Gabriel was simply up and looking down on her. A breathless fear clotted her chest.

"Mrs. Potts, I expected more from you." His voice was soft. "Yes, I do guide people to appropriate realms. But that is not why I am here."

Mrs. Potts considered this and took a cautious sip. She shook out her shoulders and leaned forward in her chair. "What do you mean, appropriate realms?" Her dog ran up the steps, caught sight of Gabriel hovering, and ran back down with tail tucked, disappearing into the tall grass.

Gabriel raised his perfect eyebrows at this question. "The short answer? If you were Christian, you would be escorted to a realm that caters to Christians." He lowered himself into the chair and crossed his long legs.

"Interesting. Caters to Christians. I suppose that applies to Jews, Hindus, Buddhists and Muslims? What about those poor atheists?

And all those people who believe the universe was created for their pleasure?"

"I am assuming you mean New Agers. Your description is a bit unfair, Mrs. Potts. But, yes, the followers of any path are taken to a realm that best reflects their religion or beliefs."

"You didn't tell me what happens to those poor atheists." Now that she knew she was not about to die, Mrs. Potts was beginning to enjoy herself.

Gabriel slapped his knee. The porch swayed. Mrs. Potts reached for her cup to keep it from spilling.

"See, that is why we want you for this project. You care about the atheists and their experience of the afterlife." At this he swept his arm upward to include the vast expanse of the heavens. Venus was nearing the planet Jupiter, their combined brilliance dimming the other stars.

"I'm not sure I care that much. I was just curious. Those poor buggers don't seem to get enough sex. And don't you think they're angry? It seems to me anyone that angry doesn't get much sex."

"Well, there you have it! We do have a bit of fun with atheists when they die. One minute they are flying through the big void they had imagined, the next minute they are sitting around some great religious figure." Gabriel winked at her. "But where are my manners? Allow me to introduce myself. I am Gabriel. Not *the* Gabriel, mind you."

Mrs. Potts gave him a polite, cautious smile. "And you already know my name. I imagine you know a great deal about me, which makes me wonder why you want me."

Spring peepers were beginning their evening concert, and a lone crow flew low and fast, hurrying home for the night.

"You say you have a project for me. For the life of me, I can't imagine what. Can I refuse? Never mind. If I don't like the sound of it, I'll refuse. You can't kill me for that, can you?"

"Mrs. Potts! You shock me. No, I will not kill you—I am not capable of killing you or anyone. I will explain, but first may I have a cup of what you are drinking? It is gin, isn't it?"

Mrs. Potts stood up on wobbly legs, smoothed her dress and tottered into the house. Gabriel sat back. It was a pleasant night and he appreciated this rare pause. Hanging plants in need of watering hung along one end of the veranda. The house's lurid green siding somehow felt soothing. The screen door creaked open, and Mrs. Potts placed Gabriel's cup of gin on a nearby table before settling into the rocker.

"This is delicious, Mrs. Potts. Clear, direct and simple. Homemade, is it?" He took another sip and grimaced slightly. "Time for me to tell you what this project is all about."

"Before you begin, I have a question. It came to me while I was in the kitchen. How are you made? How did you come into existence? Is an angel born?"

"Brilliant question! Curious minds have benefited humankind more than you know." He beamed at her. "How does an angel come to be? Well, the color purple is important. Colliding nebulae, the birth of a new star, the death of an old star. So many factors, Mrs. Potts. Some of you believe that if your granny dies, she becomes your angel, but this is not true. She could become a guide, perhaps, if her credentials checked out. Is this enough of an explanation, Mrs. Potts? My time of departure is approaching and we have things to discuss."

Gabriel stretched out his legs and took another wary sip. "Why have you been chosen? It is simple. You are openly—and delightfully—curious. Curiosity is underrated by humans. If one is curious, assumptions and prejudices disappear. And, just as important, you live in this place. I am not sure if you are aware, but you live in an angel-protected entry zone. Only a few are scattered around the world, but this is the one I use." His brown eyes were warm. "And you write, Mrs. Potts. We need a writer."

Gabriel waited. The stars grew brighter in the night sky. The solar eclipse had passed, and the new moon was not yet visible. From the marsh beyond the house, the peepers sang more loudly.

When Mrs. Potts spoke, her tone had changed. The harsh edges were gone, replaced by a soft and sad whisper. "Yes, I had a feeling this place was special. An angel-protected zone, you say. Imagine!" Her eyes looked thoughtful. "I believe you, you know. Some part of me knew this place had a special connection." She paused and looked out into the endless darkness, where a world that could not exist in the light of day was coming to life.

"Gabriel, I gave up those sorry attempts at writing years ago, but I assume you know this. I wasn't very good. It is still painful for me to remember all the time I invested in it, one of my many great failures. I respectfully decline."

"I thought you might say something like that. And yet it is essential for this story to be told by you."

Gabriel stood and moved to the railing. He looked up at the dark heavens, then turned to face the small, straight figure in the rocker.

"You asked what happens to people of different faiths and traditions when they die. If you say yes, you will find out. Seven such beings have been brought to the same realm—a Christian, a Buddhist, a Jew, a Muslim, a Hindu, a New Ager and an atheist. The New Ager and the atheist come from the United States, but the others are from Germany, England, Canada, Australia and Italy. Their professional backgrounds are different. They are together now because of a situation that, if not corrected, could have dire consequences." He rubbed a hand over his face and took a breath. "Some in my realm accuse me of being dramatic. But even they agree the very existence of heaven and earth hangs in the balance. And I cannot begin to tell you what a challenge these seven are turning out to be. But these dear ones, these seven … well."

Gabriel leaned toward Mrs. Potts. She leaned farther back in her chair and drained the rest of her gin.

"Mrs. Potts, their story needs to be told. With our heaven-high hopes, it will open people's hearts a little wider. There is more, but …" He trailed off and listened to a sound only he could hear. Shaking his head and taking a sip of gin, he continued.

"Only someone like you can do this. Of course we know of your previous writing projects, but you have the heart to tell this story, and it has elements of a fantastic yarn as well as a global message. But even more important—," he stopped and listened. "You have loved well."

"You have got to be fucking kidding me." She dug into her pocket and fished out a cigarette.

"Please put that thing away. You are not scheduled to die for a while, and lighting up messes with our schedule."

Mrs. Potts tucked the cigarette back into her pocket. "You know I have not been pure of heart."

"Pure of heart? My dear, you have loved fearlessly. Those who love with open and courageous hearts often do not measure up to social conventions. We need you. Aren't you just a little curious? Think of what you will learn, what mysteries will be revealed to you."

Gabriel drained his cup and stood. Mrs. Potts had her eyes closed, hands folded on her lap. A wind picked up and dry leaves scraped and scattered on the walk. Mrs. Potts opened her eyes and grinned.

PART I: GABRIEL'S GREAT CHALLENGE

The interviews and invitations are not conducted for everyone, and Gabriel was quite exact in his descriptions of them. Now, most people who know me know I don't like following orders, and suggestions are just orders in fancy clothes. So when Gabriel gave me his notes and began to make suggestions, we had a little chat. Everything is okay now. We both gave a little. Gabriel has allowed me to add some descriptions as long as the message remains intact.

Before I forget, I should explain why Gabriel carries index cards. To be blunt, mistakes have been made. Gabriel is not the only one who has taken someone before their time, but the person is always returned. Changed, but returned. Yes, they come back to earth with strange ideas, but some of those ideas have been of great benefit. Of course, others have been just plain nutty. Anyways, before he leaves this realm, he is given the name of the person he is to touch. No one dies until they receive a touch from Gabriel. Most people miss feeling it, but the touch happens. So, just so you understand, to make sure that mistakes from the past are not repeated and he has the right person, Gabriel makes notes and writes them on index cards.

He also makes a practice of carrying a few blank cards. "You never know" is what he says. Now, that's creepy. ~ Mrs. Potts

Chapter 1: Joshua

Joshua didn't remember opening his eyes. He was lying in bed, the sage-green duvet cover with the binary code image down the center neatly folded over. He let out a breath, but there was no breath. His heartbeat should be keeping time with his rising anxiety, but there was no heartbeat. And yet the room looked the same as always. The Dali print he'd picked up in Chicago was on the wall opposite his bed. Fitness magazines were fanned out on the bedside table under the latest tech magazine with a cover shot of himself and Edison, his business partner. No Gillian, but this wasn't unusual—she was probably at her place.

Everything was so still. Then he heard it, a woman's voice chanting softly with faint sobs punctuating the cadence. Must be some wacky new neighbor. He decided to get up but was already up. Strange. A bluish light appeared by a chair near the window. Wait! Where was the window?

"Hi there, Joshua," said a voice that now belonged to the body sitting in his chair.

"What the hell is going on? Who the fuck are you? Wait a second, you're that grungy backpacker that sent me crashing to the sidewalk. Man, you could have hurt me! I mean, my clothes were messed up a bit. But …" He looked down at his spotless clothes, confused.

The backpacker sat there with a small smile. No backpack was in sight.

"Let me introduce myself, Joshua. I am your navigator, Gabriel."

My navigator? Hot panic thickened as Joshua realized his thoughts were being broadcast.

"My navigator?" Joshua repeated as the man sat smiling that smile.

"Yes," Gabriel said with more authority. *I hope he is not one of those,* he thought. Unlike Joshua, Gabriel could keep his thoughts private. "What else do you remember besides me crashing into you?" His clear voice seemed to fill the room.

Joshua began to recall the last few days but was rattled that his thoughts were being broadcast.

Gabriel sat forward, waving a hand to stop him. "Joshua, you have made transition. You have left your earthly body behind." His voice deepened and he talked more slowly, enunciating each word carefully.

"I've done what? Is this part of my marathon training?" Joshua asked hopefully.

"Joshua, you are now in spirit," Gabriel said.

"In the spirit of what?"

Gabriel was losing patience but remembered he was on probation for just this reason. "Joshua, you are dead," he said in as gentle a tone as he could muster.

Joshua began to laugh.

Well, I wasn't expecting this, thought Gabriel. He stood up and walked around the elegant but sterile bedroom.

"Okay, okay, who put you up to this? Was it that fat bastard Christian nutcase?" Joshua doubled over, hooting and wiping his eyes. "Or was it my mother? My crazy fucking father? Who?"

Gabriel sat down in an ergonomic chair.

"I mean, you see, I don't believe in life after ..." Joshua stopped laughing.

Without having stood up, Gabriel was standing. He liked to call it the Big Reveal, although it wasn't always necessary. Some people arrived and knew where they were. Sure, they sometimes needed to be assured they were not in hell. Politicians seemed to need that assurance more than anyone else. And some televangelists. And baseball players. Writers, yes; writers were the worst.

Gabriel fingered the index card in his pocket. He knew what was written on it by heart: it contained Joshua's identifying details to make sure Gabriel was helping the right person to transition. After some unfortunate blunders in past centuries, he had become diligent about writing and memorizing the small cards.

He ran over Joshua's description in his mind. Age: thirty-five. Appearance: 5'11", slim build, dark sandy hair, green eyes. Well-groomed and always well dressed. Has a scar on his left hand that extends from little finger diagonally to wrist. Occupation: Co-owner of a media relations company called Up & On. Religion: Atheist. Place of residence: Battery Park, New York City. Markings or quirks: Picks at imaginary dirt on his clothes. Talks on cell phone while walking; as a result, people constantly have to walk around him, or Joshua crashes into them.

"Joshua, you died." Gabriel sat back down and waited.

"But I'm here," Joshua said, waving his arms around his bedroom. "My art work, my magazines, my bed. All here."

"We like for people to feel comfortable when they first arrive, especially when," Gabriel imitated a cough, "it was, you know, sudden."

He looked hopefully at Joshua, waiting for him to remember on his own. And waited.

Then, "I don't fucking believe it! What happens now? I don't believe in any of this shit. God, heaven, angels—none of it," ranted Joshua. "This is fucking nuts." He took a step and floated. "If I'm fucking dead, then it's just my brain telling me wild stories as it shuts the fuck down. Forever. Nada. Nothing. The *big black!*" Joshua roared, throwing his arms above his head.

"You know, I am a big fan of the angel app you created. You did make a little mistake with Ariel, but it is actually pretty good," Gabriel said conversationally.

As though for the first time, Joshua looked at him. "So who are you supposed to be? Oh, wait, you are the 'navigator.'" He made air quotes. "What the fuck is a navigator? Wouldn't Angel of Death be more accurate? Forgot for a moment. That's one of those Christian constructs. 'The Angel of Death is just around the corner, kiddies.'"

Gabriel winced. "My mission is to help people cross over." His voice was suddenly sad, weary.

"Cross over? Cross over what? A river? The street?" Joshua started pacing. "So, if I'm dead, why am I not just floating around in darkness, 'cause that's what I believe. But, okay wait a minute, if the Christians got this right, where are the fat-assed angels? Where is this god of yours? Pearly fucking gates?" He kicked a rolled up yoga mat and floated sideways.

Gabriel was tired. He watched Joshua stomp/float around his room, hands balled into fists. Not long ago, he had talked with other angels, and they were feeling the same way. None had experienced this before, not in all the earth centuries. They were worried. Humans' seeming unwillingness to be kind and loving was wearing them down. But they had been through harsh, unkind times before. Howard—a friend of Gabriel's—had suggested that their fatigue might be due to humans being more disconnected from the cosmos.

"Even in ancient times, when humans could be especially cruel to one another, they were intimate with the earth and knew the skies. They would marvel at the heavens. This kept them more bound to us." Howard had a good point.

It was time to leave Joshua.

"We will be meeting with the others," Gabriel said.

"The others? Oh fuck, what others?" Joshua shouted as he reached to rub his forehead. He could not feel anything. Startled, he composed himself and asked more quietly, "And a meeting?"

"Lots to explain!" Gabriel said cheerfully. "You, Joshua are now part of a team. For now, let's just say that you and the others have some top-tier missions to accomplish." He pointed his index finger at Joshua, who had slumped onto the bed, head in hands. "As a matter of fact, I can even make you the project manager of this team. Would you like that?" He smiled. "See you later, then!"

And Gabriel was gone.

Joshua was alone. Again, he heard chanting, but this time there were no sobbing.

How well have you loved? He thought of Gillian, his mother, his father and his good buddy Edison. A deep, powerful love swept over Joshua for those he loved, even though they already felt very long ago. How could he feel such love and at the same time feel they were so distant? He couldn't even begin to think of how everything he believed did not appear to hold up. His belief of a non-existent afterlife was so firm while he was alive. He tried to recall scientific data he had read regarding brain activity after death.

That has to be it. Just all fucked-up dying brain matter.

Right now, though, his theories were not important. Maybe when he met the others, he could compare stories. He did not quite trust this Gabriel guy.

Okay, so my theories look a bit shaky, but there must be a nice, neat logical reason for this. But where am I? All he wanted was to explore these powerful feelings of love and tune out that damned chanting.

Chapter 2: Susan

Susan was trying to stay calm. In between chants, she recalled recent events. With the exception of the lack of windows, her bedroom looked the same. A shoe bag was peeking from under the bed, the protection masks she had bought from a Maori warrior were still arranged on the bookcase by the fireplace, and a massive fairy painting was hanging over her bed.

Okay, so let's try this again. Her serene inner voice did not reflect her frantic emotions. *Shining Spirits of the North, I humbly ask you for protection. Spirits of the East, I ask you to rise up and protect me. Guardians of the West, I ask for your assistance. Luminous Spirits of the South, protect me now in my hours of confusion.* She waited. Nothing.

Susan had already chanted what she remembered from her Level 11 Buddhist classes in Jersey City. It seemed like hours ago that she was doing protector chants she'd learned from a Saturday afternoon seminar on Navajo spiritual practices. By now, she was forgetting which ones she'd done and in what order.

When in great confusion, be silent. She remembered this wise counsel of her guru during a retreat when Susan had kept asking question after question. So she decided to be silent. Then she saw him.

"Are you an angel? Oh, I'm so sorry, you must be my spirit guide! Or my ..." she faltered. She sat on the edge of her bed twisting her hands.

Gabriel smiled what he hoped was his most reassuring smile and gave her a small bow. "Let me introduce myself. I am Gabriel." He slipped an index card from a concealed pocket to confirm what he already knew. Age sixty-two. She was a plump and sturdy 5'2", with unruly blond-gray hair and blue eyes.

He glanced back at Susan. *She looks exhausted and anxious. And that dress! Oh, here it is:* Wears long, loose dresses with lots of colors and patterns. These are fairy dresses of her own design and hard to miss, as the fairy pictured on the dress is a hand-painted picture of herself. Occupation: Artist and owner of Fairy-Fancy. Religion: New Age. Born and raised in San Diego, California. Now lives in Taos, New Mexico, and Seattle, Washington. Talks to her dog, Raj, using extravagant hand gestures (sometimes other body parts are involved.)

Gabriel tucked away the card and added an eye twinkle to his reassuring smile.

Susan jumped to her feet and backed away. *Gabriel? The Gabriel?* She was surprised to hear her thought as spoken words. Wide eyed, she waited.

Gabriel looked at her, trying to decide if she was naive or arrogant. Sometimes he found it difficult to tell the difference. "No, Susan," he said slowly. "I am not *the* Gabriel. *He* is a master; an old master but a master. Among his many tasks, he is charged with the sacred duty of assisting those who have died. I am one of his initiates, and he has allowed me to use the name 'Gabriel.' There are others, but ..." he tried to look modest. "I am one of his favorites."

He was about to continue when Susan interrupted in a harsh voice different from her earlier soft, whispery tone. "So I am dead."

"Yes." Gabriel looked around the bedroom.

I don't understand, she said to herself, again surprised that her thoughts were spoken words.

"What is it you don't understand?" Gabriel asked as patiently as he could.

"I am supposed to live to be very old, have great love in my life, travel more ..." she said as though repeating lines from a story.

"Why do you think that? And didn't you have great love in your life? Your daughters, for example?"

Susan felt she should be embarrassed but instead was angry. She knew this reaction wasn't spiritual, but she felt it just the same.

"I know, I know!" She tried unsuccessfully to steady her voice. "But I was told by my astrologer ... Oh, never mind." She plunked herself down on the high, soft bed, tossing off a red and orange pillow that had a Tao symbol stitched on the front.

"Lots of people come here holding onto stories of how they thought things should be," Gabriel said. "You know people do die in the middle of their stories sometimes."

"But what about all of this?" Susan said as she gestured around her bedroom. "Perhaps I'm still in the middle of a session with the shaman?" she said hopefully.

"No, Susan, you are dead." He pressed on. "You died with the shaman."

"So, where is he?" she asked. "I suppose he has a very special place."

"Oh, he is somewhere else. Special? You really don't need to know that. We have other plans for you."

Susan perked up and flashed what she hoped was a grateful smile at Gabriel, but then she gave a small start.

"Don't I know you? Wait a minute, were you at the Moments for Miracles workshop last fall? No, wait, it was more recent. My mother's funeral, you were—. No. That wasn't it, either." Susan paused. "It was on the flight!" she said, snapping her fingers.

She looked at her fingers, puzzled that they made no sound. "You were that handsome flight attendant. I remember your name tag said 'Navigator.' What were you doing? Do angels—that is what you are, right, an angel? Do they, I mean, do they stalk? I never thought of stalking angels." She shuddered.

"No!" His voice rose at the insult. "We do not stalk, as you call it, and yes, I am what you would call an angel. Before one of my cases is about to die, I make certain we have the right person. How would it look if I were to assist someone when it wasn't their time to make transition? It has happened, but ..." he glanced at Susan, "that was a long time ago and we were able to erase his memory. Most of it, anyway," he finished hurriedly.

Gabriel did not mean to be heard as he muttered, "He went on to become a great legend. After all this time, people still quote him. It's so annoying. Quite a few of his quotes came from *me*, inspired ideas that can only come from being in a place like this for a very long time." He stopped and smiled over-brightly and bowed again. "Sorry, Susan, I did not mean to share that. For the love of ..." He shook his head. *Can't people find new inspiration? It was the seventeenth century*, he finished, unaware that Susan had heard him. *And there were others; some recent and some that date back further than ...*, he stopped and looked slowly at Susan, who was on her feet again, eying him curiously.

"Oooh, this is fascinating. I can't wait to tell my group in ..." she looked down. "Are you sure I'm dead, Gabriel? If I could have just one more day, I could ..."

"'I hear that all the time, but here we are. And we have things to do." Seeing the look on her face, Gabriel added, "But there may be time to take some excursions."

"So, let me get this straight. You're an angel. I'm dead. And you have plans for me. Do I have this correct?" Susan stood with her arms folded. The scrunched fairy image on her flowing dress looked distressed.

Gabriel nodded. "But these plans are not mine. They come from a higher authority."

In a whispery, reverent tone, Susan asked, "You mean from—no, I cannot say it. Is it because of my level of spirituality? Do you choose people based on their higher frequency? Elevated vibration?" She released her grip on the fairy and was moving into a yoga pose.

"We will meet with the others soon. There is a little trouble with one, but I expect that to be straightened out soon."

"Others? What others?" Her reverent tone turned hard.

"We have a number of missions to accomplish, and we need people from a variety of backgrounds. You will play a valuable role."

Susan smiled. "So, you mean quest, don't you? I mean, 'mission' sounds so military." She gave Gabriel a small frown. "Is my mother here, or is *he* here?"

"Enough for today," Gabriel said crisply as he stood.

"But I have more questions! Will I be reborn, or am I considered one of the ascended ones? And where is Raj?" She suddenly remembered her dog, looking wildly around the room and under the bed.

The place where Gabriel had been standing was replaced by a bluish white light that spun faster and faster, pulling in a riot of vibrant colors until he exploded to form a fairy. Not just any fairy, but Susan's favorite of all time and the fairy painting she was most proud of. The fairy that depicted her mother.

"Thank you," she said.

He was gone.

Chapter 3: Sunita

Twisting the end of her azure silken scarf, Sunita sat at the very edge of her bed. She had no sense of time, simply a sense of being, but even this sense was flimsy, light. Jasmine and sandalwood. She could catch no scent of them, but she knew the room was filled with both. A lotus flower stood elegantly in a slim vase on a side table. In one corner, her elaborate altar with fresh offerings somehow no longer felt like hers. Should she be doing something? Sunita did not feel inspired to move.

Move? Does a spirit move? Or pray, or meditate? I know I am dead, but I did not think this was the way it would be.

"And how did you think it would be, Sunita?" Gabriel's voice filled the softly lit room. She looked up at him with curiosity but no surprise.

For Gabriel, this was like a hobby. He enjoyed hearing the variety of ways people envisioned heaven or, he corrected himself, this particular realm. Some stories were really quite creative; some were heartbreaking. He thought of himself as an ambassador whose job was to make each case feel at home and welcomed. As he had a tendency to overdo things, this sometimes got him into trouble.

Speaking of trouble, he quickly checked Sunita's index card for reassurance. Yes. Thirty-one years old, 5'4" with inky black shoulder-length hair and brown eyes. Wears glasses. Pretty. Gabriel glanced up. *Very pretty.* Occupation: Medical doctor. Religion: Hindu. Lives in Sydney, Australia, but considers Jaipur, India, her "heart's home." Markings and quirks: Wears saris all the time, and owns lots of them. She matches her outfits with a gemstone ring of the same color. Also wears a talisman or Yantra every day, even while she sleeps. Snores. *Snores?* In private, she practices Bollywood dance moves.

"Do you like your room?" Gabriel asked. The strange tiredness left his body. It would return, but for now he was grateful.

"Why yes, how could I not? It looks like my bedroom at home—" *Home?* She listened to her words, embarrassed. "But I did not have a lotus flower."

"You are aware you have died?"

"Yes, of course I am aware. I remember." Sunita spoke quietly, her words weighed down by sadness. She felt an unexpected rush of love and was astonished to see Gabriel become translucent and luminous for an instant. She smiled in wonder. "Thank you for that. I did not expect to feel sad about dying. It is completely natural, and I look forward to a good rebirth. But the way I died … What do I call you? Are you Yama?"

One of Gabriel's wings twitched; Yama was the Angel of Death. "No. I am Gabriel. Do you remember me?" His voice was hopeful. Another of his hobbies was working out the kind of character he would imitate when he made contact before escorting the person.

Sunita, still sitting on the edge of the bed but no longer twisting her scarf, looked at him with scorn. "How could I remember you? Before this life, I did not remember any of my other deaths, did I?"

As Gabriel's lips thinned with divine irritation, her eyes widened and she stood up. "You were the guard! I knew there was something different about you—you felt kind, but removed. Am I right? You were the guard?"

"Yes. Do you think it was a good disguise?"

"Well, I have nothing to compare it to, but yes, it was good. Should I thank you for helping me get here?"

"No, no, that is not necessary. You must have questions, though. I have been doing this for a long time, and people always have questions."

Sunita was intrigued. "How long have you been the Angel of D—?" Seeing the look on his face, she bit off her words and started again. "How long have been doing this, Gabriel?"

He let the slip pass. "Time in this realm cannot be measured against time on earth. Some scholarly angels have tried, and it just got them into trouble. They became so befuddled, they were sent to another realm for a spell."

"How could they get into trouble?" Frowning, Sunita absently touched the lotus flower, which shot up to the ceiling.

Gabriel gave her a puzzled look. "Have you forgotten where you are, Sunita?"

"But where am I exactly? Kamaloca?"

"My dear Sunita, it did not occur to me you would think you were in a realm where the spirit purifies or stays according to low spiritual vibration. I assure you, this is not Kamaloca. This realm is neither above nor below in terms of spiritual evolution. But you asked how an angel could get into trouble for trying to figure how time works in different realms. I'll tell you. Pride. Arrogance. One of our scholarly angels who tried to work out what we call 'realm times' became so convinced of her mind that she neglected her heart." He clasped his hands over his heart in what he hoped was a modern human gesture.

"Oh."

"I do have others to visit, so let us get on with your other questions."

"Yes, of course. Please tell me I was cremated. This is very, very important to me."

Gabriel steepled his fingers. "In good time, my dear." Sunita looked perplexed but continued her query.

"I do not really understand where I am. All my life I aimed to walk the sun's path and be with my favorite deity. But as I was dying, my dear mother and father were in my thoughts. Does this mean I will walk the moon's path and be with my ancestors? I would love that." Sunita sounded wistful.

"Ah, that is not my department. But I see no reason why you would not be given permission to walk the moon's path and be with your ancestors. This realm has many names, but my favorite is 'The Resolution Realm.' And we are within the orbit of the moon."

Sunita considered this. But the light on her pretty face dimmed as she asked, "Gabriel, are they disappointed with me? My parents. Will I see them again?"

"Oh, Sunita, they are not disappointed with you at all. They loved you as much as they loved all the gods and goddesses. If things turn out, you may visit them to make sure they are fine."

"A visit! That would be wonderful." More questions came out in a rush. "You mentioned, others. Who do you mean? And how long will I remain here in this realm? Or, I mean, this bedroom?"

"It won't be long before you meet the others. One is still missing, but I have it on good authority that he will be brought to this realm soon." Gabriel reached up and guided the lotus flower back down to its vase. "It is complicated. How long you and the others remain in this realm depends on many things. I will give you instructions. Although we do not use the concept of time here, we do understand that losing old frames of reference can be hard."

"Well then, when do we lose these frames of reference, as you call them? And what are the others like? Are they Hindu?"

In his most patient voice, the one he used for very frightened cases, he said, "You lose these frames of reference when you have fully accepted that your earthly life is over and you are ready to be what you always were on earth: a spirit. Dead stars. All humans come from the universe and are carefully and lovingly made from dead stars." He was pensive. "I do wish you humans could appreciate that little fact." After a moment, he added with an enigmatic smile, "You will see what the others are like, but no, they are not Hindu."

Sunita's brows drew together. That smile had mischief in it. *He is hiding something.* Her thought broadcast loudly, and she jumped.

"There is a vast difference between information and wisdom," Gabriel said. "Humans are forgetting this critical distinction. My dear Sunita, you simply do not have the foundational information to hear what I have to say with the required wisdom. *N'est-ce pas*?"

Sunita nodded. Slowly she unwrapped her scarf, revealing deep, raging red and purple bruises snaking around her slender neck.

"And what is the purpose of me and the others being in this place?" Her tone was business-like and her words were clipped.

"Sunita, you loved helping people when you were alive. That was one of the reasons you were selected." He bowed slightly and gave her a *namaste*.

Sunita was alone.

Chapter 4: Reinhardt

Reinhardt shifted on his meditation cushion. Frustrated, he tried not to be frustrated. He adjusted his kimono, took a sip of tea and returned to breath. There was no breath. And no tea. Instead he felt a lightness and nonbeing.

But this is not where I am supposed to be. He looked around. Yes, this was his bedroom and this was his shrine.

It must be a trick or a bardo—a gap of some kind. Reinhardt examined his legs and arms. He could still see his body, and clearly his awareness of himself and his surroundings was intact. Books on the environment, Buddhism and social consciousness were piled high on his nightstand. The newest book written by the Sakyong, the Earth Protector, was on top. A photo of him and Deborah on their last trip to Crete was barely visible behind the heap of books. They were standing by the Throne Room in Knossos Palace complex. A couple of French tourists had insisted on snapping their picture. Reinhardt smiled, remembering how Deborah hated to have her photo taken. He sighed, but no breath stirred. Remembering was not a good sign. After everything he had been taught, after years of practice, he should not be in whatever this place or realm was. *Maybe this is just a vivid dream.*

"No, you are not dreaming."

Reinhardt looked up from his cushion. "If I'm not dreaming, then I'm dead." He got up with an ease he had not felt in a long time.

"You are dead. You died of a heart attack while you were meditating." Gabriel said helpfully. Reinhardt's eyes widened with delight. This was an ideal way for a Buddhist to die, not the heart attack but while meditating.

Reinhardt bowed toward the painted silk thangka and turned to Gabriel. "Do you know where we are? Are you familiar with this place?"

"Oh yes, I know this place. I have been here a long time, according to how you keep time in the earth realm."

"That's unfortunate."

"Why unfortunate? I like it here."

"Don't you want to be enlightened? I'm not sure of where I am, but this doesn't seem to be a realm where that is achievable." Reinhardt frowned slightly and caught himself. "Of course, enlightenment is achievable anywhere and at any time."

"Enlightenment? My dear man, that is another thing altogether." Reinhardt was so calmly assured in his beliefs, so unshakably confident in his path, that for a moment Gabriel felt a queasy, irritating sense of inadequacy. He forced a smile and continued. "Some of us like to call this the Realm of Resolution. You will see what I mean soon. In the meantime, you may want to use this time to get used to things a bit."

"I have no intention of getting used to things here." Reinhardt's stance was rigid. He tucked in his elbows and stuck out his chin.

Gabriel regarded him thoughtfully. There was no doubt who this was. At sixty-four, Reinhardt was 6'1" with buzzed salt-and-pepper hair and hazel eyes. *Hazel eye*, Gabriel mentally corrected. A black eye patch with an Ashe symbol in the center covered Reinhardt's right eye. Until recently he had been overweight, but now he weighed 175 pounds. Occupation: Environmentalist. Religion: Buddhist. Place of residence: Hamburg, Germany. *Drives as though he is being chased; I could hardly keep up with him one night when I thought we had a meeting.* Likes practical jokes and cries easily. Usually wears a blazer, even in summer.

Gabriel recognized the Ashe symbol affixed to the wall opposite the bed as the same symbol on Reinhardt's eye patch. *These*

Buddhists. Not that we get many, but when they come here they want to get out as quickly as possible. Hoping to dispel Reinhardt's increasing anxiousness, he considered his words carefully. "I cannot reveal many details right now, but you and the others are here for good reasons."

"Others? What others?"

Not only Buddhist but a German Buddhist. Great. "You and some others have been selected to work as a group. Like you, most of them have died recently. All of you are needed to help with sensitive situations on earth. Reinhardt, while you were alive you demonstrated that you cared very much for the world. We are at a critical time. The world and the heavens are in peril." Gabriel kept emotion out of his voice.

Reinhardt relaxed his stance but stood up straighter. "I would be happy to help in any way I can. I assume you're aware of my work in social transformation groups?"

"Of course."

"But what if I receive a transcendental insight that moves me away from here before these sensitive situations, as you call them, are resolved?"

Gabriel sighed. The last thing he needed was to get into a prolonged discussion. He didn't want to give away sensitive details. "From what I have witnessed in the past, you will receive valuable insights that will be transcendental on some level. Will they be enough to take you away from here? No. Not until we have completed what needs to be completed. But be prepared, these insights will come from sources that may surprise you."

Reinhardt narrowed his eyes. "Don't I know you from somewhere? You look familiar. Did you go to seminary in Virginia in 1996?"

Gabriel had wondered how long it would take Reinhardt to recognize him.

"No, I did not go to seminary. Not in Virginia anyway."

"I don't remember names very well, but I'm good at faces," Reinhardt paused and then his face lit up. "You were that protester. The one who painted his face green and was naked except for the leaves." He chuckled. "That was great. We got some good press out of that. Thanks! What did they call you? Oh yes, Adam Green, like Adam from the Bible." Reinhardt laughed again.

"You are welcome." Gabriel bowed. "Any questions?" This German Buddhist seemed to be relaxing.

Reinhardt looked bemused. "Why am I in my bedroom?"

"We think it is best for you and the others be in familiar surroundings. It makes things more comfortable while you are here. Most importantly, it keeps you connected to the earth realm. Right now, we need you to maintain that connection."

To Gabriel's relief, Reinhardt agreed that made sense. "When do we get started?"

"As soon as everyone gets here. We are still missing one, but he should be along soon. Do you have everything you need?"

Reinhardt sat back down on his meditation cushion and for a time paid no attention to Gabriel. After a moment, he raised his head as if a thought had just occurred to him. "Do you know if I can taste anything?"

Gabriel had not been expecting this, but occasionally the question came up. "Some people do and some do not. Give it a try. Think of a food item and it will appear."

In an instant, a big rectangle of chocolate, a substantial chunk of Brie, and a fennel sausage sat on a tray beside Reinhardt. He grinned and bit into the chocolate. "Not quite the same, but not bad," he pronounced, breaking off another piece. "Before I forget, who are you? Or what will I call you?" His words were muffled as he concentrated on chewing.

At least he has not referred to me as the Angel of Death. "I am called Gabriel. I am not *the* Gabriel, but I am Gabriel. You might say I am part of an order."

Reinhardt nodded and reached for the Brie.

"I have a few duties, but the main one is to help the transitions of those who are ready to die. By the way, you transitioned very well. You appeared to know."

Reinhardt's chin dipped slightly in acknowledgment. "Not with certainty, but I had some insight. You could say I've been training a good part of my life for this. When I died, I simply followed the radiant clear light, and I was here. Not where I want to be but ..." Reinhardt took a bite of sausage, then put the food aside and settled more deeply into his meditation cushion.

The light surrounding Gabriel expanded. "Time to go." He nodded one last time at Reinhardt. "Ki ki," he said.

Reinhardt sat tall and replied strongly. "Ki ki so so, lha gyal lo." Victory to the gods.

Chapter 5: Emily

Gabriel was already in Emily's room to greet her. She had been only twenty-six when she died but seemed younger. A youth/women's counselor, she had trained as a social worker and was a devout Christian. Emily was a slim 5'5" with medium-length strawberry blond hair, sky-blue eyes, and freckles. Home was Charlottetown in Prince Edward Island, Canada. *She says "eh" a lot. Somewhat confusing.* Listens to ABBA. Will only sleep with her head pointing north. *What's that about?*

For Emily, he had decided to dress in his best angel-like finery. A long, flowing cloak of shimmering silvery white left a trail of tiny stars as he walked or floated. His dark, slightly curly hair was straightened and fell midway down his back. A large, silver Christian cross completed, Gabriel thought, the quintessential Christian angel image. He practiced looking beatific.

"Oh, Jesus!" Emily dived to her knees.

"No, no, I am not Jesus!" Gabriel shouted, waving his arms as a trail of stars swirled around him.

He didn't mean to shout. Shouting tended to cause problems, something to do with sound waves that travelled beyond this realm and reached the earth. The last time he shouted, there were disturbing reports of tidal waves in Lake Superior. Which, being a lake, had no tides to speak of.

Emily clasped her hands on her now-dead chest. "You are not Jesus? Who are you? Are you an angel? Is this a trick? What are you doing in my bedroom? What am *I* doing in my bedroom?" She became more agitated. "Wait. I was helping that old lady across the—. And then I was floating, I was flying through space, and there was this big white light, and then I saw a—." She stopped, and Gabriel saw her realization occur. It was a moment he knew well.

"Am I dead?" she asked in a small voice.

"Yes, you are." Gabriel said this as cheerily as he could.

"Oh, God, I mean, sorry if I insulted you. Whew, it's a lot to take in." She wrapped her arms around her chest as she sat down on the window seat, pushing off a tattered stuffed rabbit her father had given her when she was five, a time that was framed by a lifetime that no longer was. A breath in to begin, a breath out to end.

Old body habits used to self-comfort. Gabriel regarded Emily as she hugged her knees and sat without speaking.

"I don't remember any pain at all. The last thing I remember is—, okay, so I do recall bright lights and a feeling of blissful lightness. But there must be more." She looked up at Gabriel with hope in her eyes.

This is why I do not like being here when they arrive. Without exception, they all do this, recalling details around their death, trying to put it into some logical sequence. I know it is a big event, but still. He ran his fingers through his hair. Emily watched, fascinated, as tiny stars pirouetted in the air around his raised arm.

She collected her thoughts. "Okay, I need to ask some questions. Are you the, um, angel to ask? That is what you are, right? An angel?"

Gabriel walked/floated around the room, lightly touching the mantel, a picture, a lamp. Emily bit her lip, wondering when he would answer. She felt a strange mixture of fear and bliss.

"I didn't think it would be like this," she said softly.

"No one ever does." Gabriel sounded tired. "Now to answer your questions. That is why I am here. Yes, I am an angel."

"The Angel of Death?"

Gabriel gritted his teeth but continued in his most soothing voice. "No, I am not the Angel of Death. I am a facilitator type of angel, or a navigator, if you like. Do you remember seeing me before you died? When someone dies, I am there to ease their way and guide them to this realm. Assuming this is where the person is to be transported or spend time."

"Sounds like the Angel of Death to me," Emily muttered.

"Do you want me to answer your questions, or should I return at some other time?"

Emily shook her head vigorously. "No! Please don't leave me. If you would be so kind ..."

Gabriel stopped sweeping around the room and sat down on a royal blue chaise longue, draping his arms across the back. "Sir Winston Churchill," he said with a smile. "He was here, I mean in this realm, for a while. You know, he said he did not understand the purpose of a sitting room in a bedroom. 'Why sit when lying down is optimal?'" Gabriel chuckled. "We enjoyed him when he was here. But back to you, my dear. It is for your comfort that you are in your bedroom. You will not remain here, although for now you will stay before moving on. This beautiful realm has many bedrooms. You will see what the rest of it looks like when we have our first gathering." He sat up straight. "Almost forgot. While you are here, you will be joining a group."

"A group?" Emily was still holding her knees together.

"Yes, a group. Emily, you will like them. Most of them, anyway. Or some of them, at least."

She leaned forward, eager for his reply. "Why a group? Do I know any of them?"

"No. They are new, like you. Well, except for one, but he is not here yet." He sighed. "At this point, I cannot share with you why a group is essential. You will know more when we have our first meeting. I can say this, that everything you did and believed while you were alive will be essential to this group. Your work with people who have psychological challenges and resulting traumas, for example."

Not for the first time, Gabriel thought how strange, how contradictory, humans could be. Here was this young woman, a bit of an innocent, naive, who heard such horror stories from other people. In the stillness of her silence, Emily appeared even younger than her earth years. He continued to sit, allowing her this time of quiet.

Her voice, when she spoke, was tentative but calm. "Will I see him? Can I see him?"

"You mean Him, 'God the Father' Him?" Gabriel's perfect eyebrows arched high.

"No." She shook her head. "I mean, yes, that would be amazing, eh? But I wouldn't expect that. I mean, him, *my* father."

"To be clear, you mean your earthly father, not God the Father?"

"Yes. Is it possible?"

"Not right now. But if all goes well, you may be afforded a visit with your loved ones on earth." Gabriel thought for a moment. "We have to be careful about visits. We have had cases where the person who died stayed there. Sometimes for centuries! You call them ghosts; we call them stuck. We do our best to get them to move on and come back here, but some refuse. Offers of blissful, happy times are not enough for some of them. If they feel they have done some great wrong or are possessive about a loved one, they can be hard to budge."

He didn't mean to complain about his work. Something about Emily encouraged a kind of unloading, but he recalled this was in line with the work she had done.

Emily sat, nodding supportively, when her eyes widened. "You were the mechanic working on my car! I knew you didn't belong there. You seemed out of place, you know?"

Gabriel was a bit put out by her comment but said, "Yes, I was the mechanic."

Emily threw her head back and laughed, a surprisingly deep, hearty laugh with a few punctuating snorts. Gabriel frowned.

Looking more at ease she said, "Can we talk about people or spirits who get stuck, as you say, when they visit loved ones on earth? As a little girl, there were times when I thought I saw my father. Not my father who art in heaven, but my father. Sometimes I could smell him, and there was once when I swear I heard his voice. Is this possible? Could he visit me and not get stuck?"

"Yes, it is possible. Not easy, though. Think of it this way. Suppose you were allowed to be in contact with the most precious person, the one you loved above all else, and then you had to leave them? I mean, I haven't been human for so long …" Seeing the look on Emily's face, he paused. He had not meant to divulge that piece of history but continued, hoping she had not noticed. "Can you imagine the kind of love that is needed to do such a thing? Immense."

He turned his head, listening. "I need to leave now." His beautiful, shimmering robe gathered into a ball of silver and gold. "You may pray, if you want to." His voice was louder than he had intended.

Emily bowed her head. "Our Father who art in Heaven …"

Chapter 6: Khalid

"Everyone will taste the death, then unto us you shall be returned."

Khalid repeated this verse from the Holy Qur'an over and over again, yet nothing changed. He was still sitting on one of the battleship-gray folding chairs backstage. A forest of fake tropical plants was still covered in dusty neglect near the exit light. His laptop sat on a small wooden table near a jumble of sound equipment, and he could see one end of his rolled-up prayer rug sticking out of his backpack. He could almost hear his mother chastising him for this long practice.

Maybe I can post a video on YouTube, he thought with some bitterness. *My fans probably know by now that I'm dead. I wonder if there are any tributes. My parents, Oh Allah, please help them. They will blame the fame. What to do now? I'm clearly in some kind of trouble*, his brain reasoned. *I'm to be recreated in an image unknown to me, but here I am, the same. This isn't good.*

"I like your blue shirt. That is a kind of, what do they call it, *signature* color for you, isn't it?" Gabriel said. He touched the index card in his pocket but didn't need to look at it.

Khalid was twenty-eight. At 5'8", he was compact if a little chubby. Jade green eyes made a striking combination with his dark hair, and a small mole nestled by his left ear. Gabriel ran through the card in his head. Occupation: Comedian, stage name "Kaboom." Religion: Muslim. Place of residence: London, England. Despite being a performer, he was awkward. *Arms hang by his sides as though he has no idea what to do with them.* Walks around gripping his cell phone ready to record anything funny he sees or thinks of. When in public, he is always smiling, but in private is more serious. *Spends a lot of time practicing comedy routine in front of the mirror, I bet.*

Khalid looked up, surprised and scared. "Blue shirt? Yes, but how do you know? It is the spiritual color of Fez, Morocco, where my parents were born. I wear it to please them, but I became known for it. Are you Munkar or Nakeer?" Munkar and Nakeer are angels who test the faith of the dead in their graves.

Gabriel gave him a friendly smile. "As it happens, I am a big fan of yours."

"Really, a fan? So you are not a jinn then, or—?"

"No, I am not a jinn, nor am I one of the angels who stand by your grave, testing you. I am here to help you understand a few things."

"Azazel?"

"No, I am not the Angel of Death! I wish—oh, never mind." Gabriel swallowed his vexation. "I am Gabriel. Not the Gabriel who revealed the Holy Qur'an to your blessed Muhammad, peace be upon him, but I do know him. He is not in this realm, so I haven't seen him in a while."

Khalid was trying hard to listen but was still thinking about the fact that this angel had been a fan of his. *Wow, I knew I was well known, but I had no idea my fame was out of this world!* He laughed at his own joke, but then put his head in his hands. *That wasn't a good joke. Has my humor died with me?*

"We are happy you made people laugh. Laughter is important, even sacred. The gift of humor allows people to see neurotic parts of themselves in a way that feels safe. It is very healthy. Humans take themselves so seriously." Gabriel stood with his hands behind his back, wishing he had worn posher clothes. In jeans and a white T-shirt, he could pass for a stage hand. "Honestly, my colleagues and I find it exhausting to witness this seriousness—and it is getting worse. I will tell you a secret. When people laugh, angels and other higher beings feel the vibration, and we move closer to the source."

"Wait, you can read my thoughts? Wish I could have had that power! Hmm, also wish my family could have known that laughter is sacred." Khalid stood up fast. His head was fizzing.

"Yes, I can hear your thoughts. Khalid, this may not be a power you would really enjoy. The things you humans think sometimes! Your family loved you and were proud of what you accomplished. You know this to be true, but they had little laughter when they were young, so it was hard for them to understand. You also know this to be true."

Khalid nodded, his thoughts darting around. "So, I was spiraling through space, expecting some kind of paradise or at least a few visions of waterfalls and gardens, but here I am, backstage at my first big gig. I know I was not as observant as I could have been, but still. Backstage? Really?" Khalid stopped at the look on Gabriel's face.

Gabriel leaned closer. "Khalid, you tweeted once that the stage was like home to you. We thought it would be best if you and the others felt at home. Were we wrong in choosing this place for you?"

Khalid mumbled that, no, it was okay. "It's just ... I'm worried I will not go to paradise. This backstage is fine, but I don't wish to stay here until Judgment Day. I offered my sacred gift of humor. That has to count, right? And I gave to the poor as the Holy Qur'an instructs," he added hopefully.

"Khalid, you are not being punished. There are important reasons you are here. I promise, you will know more soon."

Khalid looked disappointed, and Gabriel noted that his energy field was dull and deflated. *If I remind him of his kindness, he will return to a happier state of spirit.*

"Khalid, you often said that your fans were part of your family. That was a nice thing to say."

Khalid slumped in the chair. At Gabriel's words, he looked up into Gabriel's face, searching for understanding. "I only said that to make people feel better. I'm not sure how much you know about our world right now, Gabriel, but a lot of people feel they don't belong, that they have no family. I think everyone needs to feel they fit in or belong to someone. I believe that's why I became so popular. You know what the Internet is like, you know Facebook—" He paused and looked enquiringly at Gabriel, who nodded. "It has become a cyber family for a lot of people, but it isn't enough. People feel even lonelier these days. Other comedians are funnier than me, but I wanted to create both a movement and community. People connected to this, even a few fundamentalist Christians. I wanted people to feel they mattered—you know, the way being part of a loving family can make you feel. I should have tried harder, with Allah's help, to make a difference."

Gabriel pulled up one of the folding chairs and sat down. "Khalid, you did make a difference. When people feel they matter, they are less fearful. When they are less fearful, they are not so angry, and when they are not so angry, they are able to love more. What you did was important. This is one reason you were chosen to be part of our group. And you will be of immeasurable benefit to it."

Khalid's face lit up at the praise. But then the word "group" leaped out at him, and his eyes narrowed. "Group? What kind of a group are you talking about?"

Gabriel couldn't conceal his excitement. "There will be seven of you. I wanted to call it the Group of Seven, but I hear that has been taken." He got to his feet and paced in the small space, raising dust as he brushed against the plastic plants. "Khalid, people often hold onto the naive hope of a happy ending, or even a tidy one. You know now"—he swept his arm around their dingy, cluttered surroundings—"that does not happen. As part of this group, some of you will get a chance to resolve matters that were, ah, meant to be resolved before you came here. Other members of the group will help you, and you will help them. The headliner, though," pleased with his pun, Gabriel winked at Khalid, "is current and upcoming global issues that can only be dealt with from this realm."

Khalid's eyes widened. "Has this ever been done before, or are we, this group of seven, the first?"

Gabriel cast his eye around the small room. He was beginning to regret having Khalid stay backstage. It really was quite bleak. And people thought being an entertainer was glamorous.

"We have done many missions in the past with the occasional human spirit but never with a group. At least, not a group like this. Our group is unique and very specific. We needed to have, as part of this group, people or spirits from different cultures, religious beliefs and career backgrounds." Gabriel shook his head and added, "You would not believe the logistics."

Sounds exciting! Khalid forgot he was dead and that Gabriel could hear his thoughts.

"Yes, it will be exciting. And challenging," Gabriel said.

"So, what can I possibly offer? Me, a Muslim comedian, okay a famous one, but a comedian?"

"Heavens to heavens, Khalid. You have talked about comedy being the art of protest. Do I have that right?"

Khalid raised his eyebrows and nodded. "Yes. One of my last television interviews was with "Conner Marches On." She, that is, Conner March, has a reputation for trapping people into saying things they wish they hadn't. In the interview, she was heading down the Muslim track, and I thought she needed a little education. So I talked about how in the past, black Americans called comedy the art of protest, and now Muslims are doing the same thing. We're using comedy to protest all the garbage."

Gabriel pushed himself away from the wall he'd been leaning on. "Thank you, dear Khalid. It is time for me to take my leave."

"Wait. Don't I know you from somewhere?" Khalid peered at Gabriel. "Did you go to my high school? No, wait, you couldn't have.

It was a madrasa, a Muslim school. Are you Arabic? Never mind, it doesn't matter. Oh! Were you a heckler at my last show?"

Gabriel struck a pose and pretended to click a camera.

Khalid laughed. "Good one! You were paparazzi. I knew you were different, somehow."

Gabriel, who had been looking behind curtains, turned around. "If you had that feeling, why did you not ask me more at the time?"

Khalid shrugged, his green eyes shining. "It was just a feeling."

Gabriel raised a finger and shook his head sadly. "Ah yes, ignoring intuition, even though it is one of our gifts to you humans. Tsk, tsk."

The backstage room began to fill with light. Lampshades of multicolored glass crowned ornate stems of gold. Delicate orchids, birds of paradise, calla lilies, Moroccan flowers, gingers and neon balloons with "Congratulations, Khalid" appeared. Thick, vibrantly colored Moroccan carpets with stories woven into the fine wool were draped over plush chairs. Khalid's heart was full. He recognized items from his childhood home.

"Thank you," he whispered. "You know my father wanted me to go on the next Hajj pilgrimage," he added, his voice tinged with regret.

Gabriel nodded. "Your father will offer up prayers for you, Khalid."

Khalid stood uncertainly, looking around the transformed room. His gaze lingered on the door that led to the stage and the darkened theater. He could hardly believe there would be no more performances.

Gabriel began to applaud. Khalid dipped his head, a small smile on his face, and bowed. Even after Gabriel had gone, he could still hear faint applause. He dug out his prayer rug from his backpack.

Gabriel's Great Perhaps by Deborah M. Young

"Allahu Akbar," he began.

Chapter 7: Alter

Alter could never remember having felt so angry in all his too-long life. He paced back and forth across the threadbare rugs.

"This is it!" he raged. "This is it! Am I, Alter, to spend time in Gehenna, where the wicked go? What have I done? I lived a righteous life. I gave to the poor, even though I had barely enough food. I studied the Torah. Where is my Hannah? Where is my Hannah? Or is this Kareit? Am I cut off from my Hannah forever? And from my sweet, humble mother? Where is my Savta, my dear grandmother who made me soup and wiped my forehead of the fever? This is too much for me to bear, God!" he wailed.

Gabriel clapped his hands over his ears. He could not stand this much longer. Poor Alter had been the subject of what he and the other angels called "The Great and Seemingly Never-ending Divine Search for Alter." The subtitle was "When I Get my Wings on that Stubborn Old Bastard."

And yet, he looked like an ordinary old man. At seventy-two, he had lived a good life, if a hard one, in the Jewish Ghetto of Venice, Italy, in the 1600s. As a young man he'd been tall and strong. Now he was a gaunt, slightly stooped 5'6" with scraggly white hair. Despite the stoop, he made an effort to stand straighter and not to shuffle his feet. Bushy eyebrows threatened to obscure his faded brown eyes. His narrow chin and thin cheeks were covered by a white beard. Alter was Jewish and a historian. Gabriel remembered what he had written down as Alter's quirks and looked at the old man with sympathy and wonder. *Talks to pigeons and his long dead wife. Reads and prays most of the day.*

Gabriel had been assigned the case. Had it been only a hundred and eight earth years? Seemed longer. It was a fluke Alter had even been found. Since his death, his spirit had drifted and at times soared through just about every astral plane there was. One report said that

Alter had even spent time in an astral plane no one had heard of. This was quickly dismissed as nonsense, but his reputation as a fugitive spirit grew with each passing earth year. Usually, when a spirit doesn't get through, he is pulled back to earth. But it seemed Alter did not want anything to do with earth.

Each spirit has a unique set of calibrated energies that are reset with every good or bad deed. At the time of passing, the spirit is magnetized toward a realm or plane of existence that is in accordance with its earthly energy patterns. This was so well known and elementary that Gabriel did not know why he was thinking of it.

Perhaps it was in his mind because of the upcoming review on Alter. While Gabriel felt proud to be part of the team that finally brought the old man in, he found it a wearisome challenge to appear humble. He uncovered his ears. Alter was still raging. Gabriel knew it was fear that kept Alter a fugitive spirit. It was time to meet him. Again.

Alter slowed his pacing when he caught sight of Gabriel reading one of his dusty texts. He stopped. "Who are you?" After all this time, his voice was still raspy from the dust.

In Gabriel's view, Alter's manners had not improved over the centuries. For each of his visits to the recently deceased, Gabriel made an effort to attire himself in clothing that would be familiar and acceptable to the guest. For Alter, he wore a long, dark cloak and one of the conical hats that Jewish men wore in seventeenth century Venice.

"I am here to welcome you and to answer any questions you may have," Gabriel began.

Alter hurried over and snatched away the text. "This text is for scholars. Are you Jewish, gentile or Moor?" He carefully placed the text on a teetering stack and settled into his favorite chair.

Gabriel looked at this legend, this thin, frail man, and replied in a strong voice, "I am all and none and more."

At first, this incensed Alter. Then he brightened and nodded. "That is a Jewish answer. Very good. But prove yourself. You said you are here to answer questions. Never mind about the welcome—I don't care about that. I feel as though I have been captured by the guards at the gates, but never mind. Is this Kareit? Where is my family?" As Alter continued sizing him up, Gabriel was happy he had appeared in a simple black cloak. *Less threatening*, he thought.

"Okay, no welcome. That is fine with me. You want to know where you are? Do you think you are in Gehenna?"

Alter opened his mouth to speak, but Gabriel held up a hand to stop him. "In a way, yes, and in a way, no. Alter, you were a righteous man, and this is not a place of punishment. But you will be here for as long as it takes to complete certain tasks," he said firmly and waited for Alter to absorb this.

Gabriel was under strict instructions with Alter. Although he did not want to humble him, he did want to make some things clear.

Settling more comfortably into the chair, Alter rested his chin on his chest, studying Gabriel from underneath his bushy eyebrows. *Was this a mal'akh, an angel? What could he know, this one?*

Gabriel had positioned himself near one of the many stacks of books and papers that touched the low ceiling of Alter's flat.

"My name is Gabriel, and I am an angel, or a *mal'akh*, as you say." He announced this proudly but then noticed the troubled look on the old man's face.

"You are the Angel of Justice?" Alter rasped.

Gabriel shook his head, and the conical hat tilted. He straightened it and said, "Alter, I understand you to be a great scholar of the Torah. You know Gabriel to be a great messenger, a mediator of the many dealings between heaven and earth. He is the great and wondrous angel who grants mercy and oversees all revelations, resurrection and, yes, death. I am not that Gabriel, although I am one of his protégés."

"Ah, I see. You are one of Gabriel's students," Alter said very slowly. "So tell me, Mr. Gabriel," he wagged a finger at him, "if this is the world to come, the afterlife, what am I doing, sitting here talking with you? You tell me that I have certain tasks to do before I am free to go on to another place. But will I, after all my years of suffering and waiting, be reunited with my Hannah, my family, when I am free? You must tell me for certain. If you cannot, then I will call on the mercy of Gabriel and God to grant me the right to stay in my flat for eternity."

Gabriel was taken aback but knew better than to argue with the old man. "I cannot tell you for certain, Alter. As a scholar, you know that both the Torah and the Talmud talk about the value of patience."

"Patience!" thundered Alter, struggling to his feet. "Patience," he repeated more quietly. "In Hebrew, the word, 'patience' also means tolerance. And from that same wretched word comes burden and suffering. So, I am to continue to be patient and carry the burden of this terrible suffering? Is that it? Is this what you and my God are asking?"

At that moment, Gabriel realized he had not secured the shield that protected him from absorbing pain and suffering. With some alarm, Alter said, "You are starting to fade. What is wrong with you?"

Gabriel could feel himself losing angel essence as the pain Alter had been carrying for centuries flooded into him. Despite his considerable powers, Gabriel knew that a heart that sits in dark, fearful places can, for a time, drain others who are either weakened or unusually empathic.

Regretting that he had to protect himself from Alter, Gabriel reset the shield and immediately felt an inflow of positive energy. "The tasks you are to perform are not simply to challenge you or the others," he said in a strong voice. "And they are not quests to test your righteousness. Alter, I will share with you something I have not shared with the others."

"What others?" demanded Alter.

"You lived a rather secluded life, only allowing those you knew well into your life. Now, it is time to broaden or expand."

"I don't know what you are talking about, young man, or *mal'akh*, or whatever you are!' Alter turned his back to Gabriel and stood as rigidly as his stooped frame allowed.

Gabriel pressed on and spoke to the back of the long, black, dusty coat. "You are needed, Alter. You are needed to be part of a group that we hope will heal and transform the world and ... well, if this doesn't happen, generations to come ... will ..." he trailed off.

Alter turned surprisingly quickly to look at Gabriel in puzzlement and irritation. "Are you talking about the curfew hours the gentiles have imposed at the gates to our Ghetto? I thought it was just one of the rumors my daughter, Sarah, heard from one of the other women. More limits to our life? Reducing the hours we can do business outside the gates? But what can we do about this?"

Gabriel paused. In his hurry to get this group together, and his sense of victory over finally bringing Alter in, he had momentarily forgotten that Alter had no concept of the world of the twenty-first century. He chose his words carefully. "My dear Alter, the world has changed beyond your imagination in the hundreds of years since you died. In some ways it is easier and kinder, but in others it is far more dangerous and sad. As we talk, the world is in danger more than ever, and this danger extends to the heavens. It was decided to form a group of people from different cultures, religions and work backgrounds, and this group is here in this realm now. As a matter of fact, you are the last to join it." Gabriel searched Alter's face for a reaction, but the old man just looked stolidly back at him. He went on, "This realm has many rooms, but I believe the room that will be of greatest interest to you is our glorious library. We are supremely proud of our library. It houses all the books ever written and even some unfinished books. A scholar's delight!" Gabriel stood waiting for some response. Alter gave no purchase. Gabriel pasted another smile on his face.

"Soon you will meet the rest of the group. And of course you will receive teachings on the world's history since your life in the Venice Ghetto."

Alter squinted at Gabriel as he eased himself back into the chair. "My eyes are bad, but you look familiar, Mr. Gabriel." He leaned forward until his nose almost touched his knees, peering at Gabriel. "You are that young man! God will not be pleased with you." He shook a crooked finger at Gabriel. "You were that disrespectful young man, picking your teeth with goose feathers. And I heard the way you spoke the Seven Blessings! These Blessings are sacred to our God!"

Gabriel laughed loudly. Back on earth, his laughter shook a few buildings in Seattle, resulting in false reports of an earthquake. He frowned for a moment and continued. "I heard from reliable sources that God actually loved it. Passion is a central motif in love's grand story, human or God! But let me repeat, the others in this group come from a very different place and time from you. Centuries of great and sometimes horrific change have passed since you died, my dear Alter."

Alter was about to interrupt, but Gabriel held up one of his long fingers to silence him. "I will be taking my leave now. There will be a gathering at the central courtyard, where you will meet the others and more details will be revealed. Until then, Alter, Shalom."

The Gabriel that Alter had been speaking to changed into the angel Gabriel Alter knew from paintings. "Shalom," said Alter absently. He picked up papers from beside his chair and began to read.

Chapter 8: The Invitations

The invitations were slipped under the doors of their rooms sometime during the night. Plain print on ordinary index cards. No gold embossing, no parchment paper, no florid writing, no inspired imagery, no frills of any kind. They were signed, "Gabriel, your Navigator." The words "Higher Vibrational Council" had been crossed out.

Appended to each invitation, Gabriel had written, "You are a miracle. Each one of you here and all the peoples left behind are miracles. The world is at a critical juncture, a threshold that must be crossed but at great peril. These invitations are simply that, invitations. No one is obligated to accept. Of course, it is encouraged. This is a noble moment."

Invitation to Joshua

You are invited to participate in what promises to be (" a once in a lifetime" was crossed out but still legible) an exciting opportunity for fun and adventure with interesting people. Joshua, we have noticed your talent for getting the message out to others. You certainly have a way with words. What is most remarkable is that you rarely let pesky emotions get in the way of your desired intent. How do you manage to do this? Once you determine your goals, nothing gets in your way. Your mission, or perhaps you prefer we call it your assignment, is to help spread messages that if you were alive you might not be terribly interested in conveying. This is of course your choice. Benefits will be outlined later. Also, you will be pleased to know that you are being considered for an additional position. You are, indeed a strong candidate.

Spiritual Path: Well, that is a bit of a stretch, right? Just kidding. We do enjoy people who engage in deconstruction. Corrosive cynicism, not so much. Yes, we are fully aware of your dauntless determination to remain a nonbeliever. We don't mind one bit. As a matter of fact, we see it as an asset. Somewhat. Joshua, if you choose to come on board our little adventure (and how can you possibly resist?), part of your role will be to test others' beliefs. Yes, you read correctly! We want you to use your relentless intensity as an atheist to ask people to consider and contemplate their chosen path. This will help them to ferret out what no longer serves them in their noble quest for spiritual salvation or redemption or enlightenment or … you get my drift.

Invitation to Susan

You are invited to participate in a truly unique mission, or quest, if you prefer. Due to your outstanding contributions to beauty and fantasy, you have been chosen (if you choose to accept) to help in an important matter that requires your considerable artistic skills and your spiritual background. Unencumbered by logic, you have created fantasies that have helped people believe in magic—*their* magic, Susan. And you are right in assuming that humans are imbued with magic. You have been often quoted as saying that beauty is everywhere, and again you are right! Sadly, people have forgotten. Susan, you are to open their eyes to beauty. If people can look at each other and the world around them, and the first thing they see is beauty, then the world will be a more loving place.

Spiritual Path: A little bit of that and a little bit of this, Susan? You have nipped some from one tradition and some from another and some from yet another. Each time something became uncomfortable for you, you simply moved on to another tradition. Now, it may sound as though we are criticizing you for this spiritual meandering, but that could not be further from the truth. Part of your mission (if you choose to accept) is to inspire wide-open curiosity in others who have become rigid in their ideas. Susan, you can help them explore other traditions and faiths.

Invitation to Sunita

You are invited to share your gifts of healing! We are so very pleased to have you here. We hope you accept our invitation. Sunita, you are a dedicated healer and have done your best to move people toward wellness. As we have witnessed, you have made considerable effort to increase people's awareness of the importance of good food and better care of the body. You know, we are seeing more and more people coming here who were not scheduled to arrive yet. Careless, I say. This disconnect from what the body naturally needs points to other disconnections. If we begin with the body, people can begin to heal other disconnections.

Spiritual Path: Yes, Sunita, come and celebrate! If you choose to take part, you will teach people the beauty and power of ritual, even if certain people are not religious or spiritual, as some are overly fond of saying. You know, we are honestly puzzled by the distinction some people make between religion and the spiritual. But before I get— how do you say it?—oh yes, sidetracked. Where was I? The importance of ritual cannot be overstated. Even something as mundane as washing your face in the morning can be dignified if you approach it as a ritual. Acting with dignity yourself, and being mindful of treating others with dignity, can do much for the world.

Invitation to Reinhardt

Cheerful welcome! You are invited to take part in a teaching that is designed to help humankind develop a more loving, heart-full relationship to the earth. We feel you are eminently qualified to offer these teachings. Reinhardt, we have watched you struggle to impart to people the importance of caring for the earth. We remain shocked at the arrogance and righteous ignorance humans have demonstrated in polluting it. You of all people know that what is happening cannot continue. It is, quite simply, unsustainable. If you choose to accept our offer to share your earth wisdom, you will find that time here is well suited to your penchant for sacred silence. Yes, we know some refer to this as loneliness, but back to your teachings. In this realm, actions can be taken without the usual obstructions, actions that will help to restore and heal your much wounded world. "Fragile." We love that song here. Do you like Sting? We love him.

Spiritual Path: Together with passion! Oh, how we love this. *Com* meaning together, and *passion*. Compassion. Now, we know you and some others talk about compassion a great deal. However, maybe it is me, but it feels as though compassion is talked about only as a concept. Make it real, Reinhardt. If you choose to share these teachings, we need you to make it real. You know how people are nowadays. They ask, "What's in it for me?" We are delighted to offer you the opportunity to transmute that attitude and replace it with loving compassion. And we know you know this, but it will be of great benefit to teach people to be compassionate with themselves.

Invitation to Emily

We are pleased to inform you that you have been selected to take part in a mission. We do not need to tell you how trauma holds the heart hostage. We have been keeping an eye on you and know you have been immersed in your work, helping to heal people's trauma. Yes, we know all humans experience trauma, but the people you worked with were quite wounded and as a result became detached from their hearts. Emily, while you are in this realm, you can contribute to healing or ridding some people of the painful burden of trauma that, given certain restrictions on earth, you were not able to accomplish. Easing their pain will help them to return to their hearts and keep them from doing harm to themselves and others. Imagine, Emily, being able to prevent harm and further trauma! If you choose to join this mission, you will be able to share your considerable gifts of care.

Spiritual Path: Devotion and service to others is a Christian ideal that you have practiced well. Yet these are not valued much in your world. An epidemic of narcissism is spreading. Emily, we want you to demonstrate that duty is sacred and the service and care of others creates a life full of joy. Naturally, and we hope you do not take offense, we prefer this be done without any holier-than-thou references. Beliefs are not as clear as you may think, Emily. Easy notions can become fixed ideas that narrow a spiritual experience. Using the old biblical stories as an unchanging source of wisdom does not allow for wisdom in Christianity.

Invitation to Khalid

You are invited to headline in a movement! Your enviable comedic talents have long been admired here, and this movement will let you showcase your talents in a unique environment. Khalid, the world is sad. We do not hear much laughter these days. Actually, this lack of humor is a bit of a crisis. In an interview you gave recently (yes, we listen to these things), you said that laughter eases tension and anxieties. We all applauded. What can I say? We enjoy a good laugh the same as anybody. Laughter expands the heart and can slice through prejudice and other neurosis. So, are you in? We will be pleased as punch if you join us. Benefits and other details will be explained later.

Spiritual Path: As a Muslim, you have been taught that words and deeds matter. Well a billion-plus Muslims cannot be wrong! Words have more power than people know. Words, cruelly and carelessly spoken, can harm generations. Spoken with compassion and care, they can heal generations. And, may we add, entire cultures. Khalid, if you choose to join this movement, you will be able to share this important message. Increasing awareness of the impact of word and deed will do much to help people, communities, countries and the world develop understanding. Not to be wildly optimistic, but perhaps even peace! Sorry, I am known to be a bit of a dreamer. Oh, and Khalid, the world has changed. The wisdom teachings of Muhammad are an invaluable guide. Drawing on these teachings are as crucial now as when they were first given. As you well know, Islam is about love and peace. It is not up to humans to decide who you share this love with.

Invitation to Alter

You lived a long time as a Jew and accumulated valued experience and knowledge. Alter, you learned and lived a life of resilience, patience and faith. The world has changed in ways you will initially find difficult to believe. We need you to teach people that they have the capacity to be resilient. Resilience is scarce these days. Your people have also learned about renewal. Alter, teach people to keep safe those seeds of renewal. Teach them it is their sacred obligation to look for opportunities to spread those seeds. And finally, Alter, teach people the value of history. We sift through the ashes of time to find the lessons of history; we do not use them to keep us in the past.

Spiritual Path: We ask you to show people of all races and beliefs the faults in the world and that these faults are to be celebrated as opportunities to grow. This is not an easy task. It is, in fact, a call to action.

Chapter 9: In the Beginning

"Everyone entrusted with a mission is an angel." Moses Maimonides said that. I like that quote. Guess it makes me an angel—at the moment, at least. Ha! If someone had told me I would have that thought, I'd have called them crazy. Anyways, we are just getting started.

Gabriel paced. The lights in the vast room brightened and dimmed with each step he took. Yellows, deeper yellows, oranges, deeper oranges, and the odd flash of a rebellious peacock blue scattered light across the walls and ceiling. His steps echoed.

He had argued long and hard with the Higher Vibrational Council for certain concessions. Such as smell. Smell was the most evocative of senses, and keeping a sense of smell would remind them of the moment of departure, of their death. In the end, the Council had relented, sort of. The seven new arrivals would have their sense of smell, but only when they ate in the kitchen.

Theory, Gabriel thought with exasperation. *They all operate from theory. Except maybe Howard. Just let them see how all that theory works in practice. Let them try it here for once.*

His pace quickened. *What do the Druids like to say? Ah, yes, "As above, so below." There is much at stake for everyone.* He reached into a deep pocket and flipped through the index cards. Alter's, on the bottom, was tissue thin. Gabriel left the cards where they were. There was no need to review them. All was in order. They were finally here.

Recollections of the last meeting of the Council quickened his step. He was fuming. More than nine hundred members sat on the Higher Vibrational Council, and not one had set foot in this realm.

Not one! The only thing they agreed on was how crucial this mission was to all. As above, so below. All beings, in all realms.

The interviews had gone well. *Perhaps I may be so bold as to say they went swimmingly.* Gabriel paused mid-stride, chuckling. He loved British expressions.

Interviews were his least favorite part of the job, though. He never knew what to expect. *And people today expect to live forever*, he thought with some amusement. True, they looked and acted younger than their predecessors. Some actually had their faces and bodies cut open and put back together to look younger. He had witnessed some crazy things over the centuries, but this trend had the whole realm laughing. One woman he'd met had seemed really, really surprised to see him, and he'd tried everything he could to reassure her. Turned out she'd had surgery that gave her a look of constant amazement. The other angels had teased him for days about that one.

Most of this group were okay. Some seemed to be in shock, but that was normal. For the most part, they were accepting. Perhaps the sensitivity sessions had paid off.

Gabriel flung himself into a chair and stretched his long legs over an ottoman. He had been reluctant to attend those sessions—*It's not like I am a newcomer*—but he had been reminded over and over how vital it was for this particular group to transition smoothly.

"Not to overstate or sensationalize this, Gabriel, but these are the most important missions we have undertaken in a long time," the current head of the Council had said. He'd shrugged but, despite some resentment, had gone to the sensitivity classes. And now the interviews were over, and they could move forward with an initiative that had never been tried before.

He half closed his eyes and reviewed the interviews in his head. Had he missed anything? He didn't think so. They would all get along … what was the word? Swimmingly. Yes. And with that being the case, they would be ready for the next step.

It was time.

Gabriel assessed his appearance. Except for the purple ribbon that held his glossy black hair in a neat pony tail, he was all in white. A crisp white tunic fell above wide-legged trousers. Dressing in white was the least he could do. It would help to shift their image of him from their interviews last night to one more closely aligned to his role on this realm. He had enjoyed the disguises, though. With this job, he took every chance for fun he could get.

He had arranged seven comfortable armchairs in a semicircle on a deeply piled, circular rug that was patterned in blue and gold. Two ottomans on casters sat in the middle of the semicircle, inviting visitors to put their feet up.

Each of the seven spirit people would descend a wide circular stairway from the upper level, where they were being housed for the duration of their stay. Every attempt was made so that each spirit person had their own room, but if some disaster befell earth, then single occupancy was not an option. When this was the case, the room reflected all people who occupied it. While this had led to some wild combinations, there had been few complaints thus far.

Twenty people could walk comfortably side by side down the expanse of the stairway which, if it were on earth, would take a person more than an hour to walk up. The steps were inlaid with gemstones from far reaches of the universe as well as from earth. All the gemstones were alive with their original energy, each one attuned to a particular vibration, which was why visitors were encouraged not to stand overlong on any one of them.

To the side of the stairway, suspended in mid-air, hung a prism that radiated colors too vivid for the human eye to process. Each color was encoded with a wisdom-emotion that could be sent to people on earth. Orange, for example, would be sent when compassion and caring were needed; a person feeling unloved and unloving might, out of the corner of their eye, see an orange glow. The prism's almond shape signified harmony.

At the bottom of the stairway a small wooden bridge, cloaked in translucent light, arched over a tiny stream that danced and gurgled. Gabriel appreciated the symbolism of the bridge. Bridges connect people, trade, and cultures. Sometimes they even help people lose their fear of the "other." Strange, this fear of the stranger. This small bridge served as a sacred transition. It raised a spirit person's vibrations so they could roam around the Great Unnamed Room, the library and all the other places in this realm. It also loosened attachments and rigidity and softened the ego.

Any step on the everlasting stairway gave a vast view of the Great Unnamed Room. Although the room was round, the space was so large that one could not grasp its shape at first. Walls of ancient red cedar and gold-veined marble stretched upward to a great domed ceiling that showed the heavens.

At the center of the room stood an elegant inner courtyard. Roman columns stood in a semicircle with large signposts pointing the way to the Wall of the Seven Heavens, the Room of Reflection, the kitchen, the library and to other rooms that appear when a spirit person needed to be alone. Buddhists in particular appreciated these rooms. In the courtyard, café tables were lit by small lanterns and decorated with single flowers in fluted vases.

Thickly cushioned benches in brightly colored patterns lined one massive wall. Suspended halfway between the stone floors and the domed ceilings, giant wind chimes rang with a sound that lulled babies and even some insomniacs to sleep on earth. The chimes were fashioned from a metal discovered by an order of angels who rarely came to this realm. At times, the wind chimes sent out lights that appeared on earth as rainbows. This was done when someone felt all was lost, but deep within held a small seed of hope.

At the center of the courtyard hung tall silver bird cages, home to the Ugly Brown Birds who sang songs that opened fragile human hearts. All human hearts are fragile, even the most disagreeable and wounded. The Ugly Brown Birds' songs were fearless, full of boundless hope and love. Some of their songs were sent to other realms, others were sent to musicians on earth. Some of these musicians were already famous, and many people were touched by the notes and inspired by the words. Others were still struggling, but when they shared the birds' music, the world soon took notice. At times, the birds sent their songs to people who were stuck deep in the darkness of their own shadows. Their breath no longer inhaled hope. If the song was sent while they were asleep, they awakened feeling renewed and ready to walk away from their sorrows. If the song was sent while they were awake, they simply felt lighter and more confident. The Ugly Brown Birds especially loved to send songs to a child or an old person who was not being well cared for.

All this was visible from the circular staircase. Gabriel stood facing the bridge with what he hoped was a cheery and welcoming smile.

A whistled rendition of "Knock, Knock, Knocking on Heaven's Door" was growing louder. Gabriel's smile was pained, but he rallied. "Welcome, welcome! You are the first one here!"

Joshua's whistling faltered when he saw the vast room, and he stepped back and pretended to examine the bridge. "What is the fucking point of this bridge?"

"Mostly symbolic, dear Joshua. Although it does serve to loosen attachments to one's former life. Please—have a seat." He waved toward the armchairs. "Sit wherever you like."

"What is this, a fucking therapy session for the newly departed? Can't wait to see what else my dying brain cells dream up. Did you like my tune? Sorry, bad joke. Proof my brain is dying. I'm usually much cleverer. And what is it with the everlasting stairway?" With an overcasual air, Joshua took the chair farthest away from Gabriel, at the center of the semicircle.

Hoping his smile was convincingly beatific, Gabriel squelched his outrage at Joshua's rudeness. He was used to being treated with reverence. He silently repeated a well-used mantra, maintaining his smile.

"You and the others will be given all the information you need for a comfortable and enjoyable stay after I give the welcoming address."

Joshua snorted. "Are you kidding me? A welcoming address like some convention? Fucked up, man."

Gabriel was about to make a stinging retort when he noticed Susan gliding off the bridge in one of her trademark diaphanous fairy dresses. A pillowy-bodied vision in a riot of turquoise, yellows and reds, she had the air of a glamorous Hestia, goddess of the hearth. At sight of her, Joshua groaned loudly and held his head. Gabriel flashed him a sharp look before turning a warm smile on Susan. "My dear Susan, you look both mystical and beautiful in that radiant dress. Please have a seat. Others will join us soon."

Susan beamed in gratitude but was unable to conceal the sorrow and fear in her eyes.

"Gabriel, thank you." Her voice was deep and soft. She bowed her best and deepest *namaste*.

"Actually, Susan, why don't you sit beside Joshua over there?" His glance at Joshua was wry.

Susan bustled over to Joshua, speaking in a rush. "Hello, Joshua. I love your name! One of the great biblical warriors, you know. Have you been here long? I expect to move on from 'here' soon." She made air quotes. "I've learned some of the great, if not the greatest, spiritual truths by the world's wisest and highly regarded spiritual masters. And of course," she paused and regarded him with a carefully constructed modesty, "I spent many hours in ashrams, monasteries and other sacred places. Who did you study with?"

Joshua leaned back in his chair. "Thanks for sharing your 'spiritual' credentials." His eyes rolled as he made his own air quotes. "But I do not believe in any fucking spiritual, religious, God, Buddha, Allah, Vishnu or any other sky-daddy crapola. So whatever you believed in while you were alive, whatever you believed in to keep you from feeling fucking alone, or whatever you believed in to imagine your life had purpose, I don't fucking care."

Susan's jaw dropped. She stumbled backward and clutched at Gabriel. "Why is he here?" she said in a small, scared whisper. "I thought this place was for those of us who had achieved a certain level of spiritual mastery." She looked around frantically.

"Please do not worry, dear Susan. We have a special quest for you. Relax and enjoy the enchantment of this beautiful room." As Gabriel escorted her back to her chair on Joshua's right, he glared at Joshua, who shrugged and grinned.

Reinhardt paused at the end of the bridge. He nodded at Gabriel and, out of habit, adjusted his eye patch. "I am not entirely sure this is not some kind of Bardo," he said with what he hoped was a casual tone.

Susan waved at him. "Oh, are you some kind of Buddhist? Come and sit by me." She patted the chair beside her. "I'm Susan."

"Reinhardt." He bowed slightly.

Joshua laughed. "Were you worried you were in some New Age hell, Susan? Relieved now that a bona fide 'spiritual' person has joined us?" He air quoted again.

Susan looked him up and down. "Why, yes, I am relieved that someone is here who's more enlightened than you." She glanced shyly at Reinhardt.

"Madam," Reinhardt said firmly, "I am not enlightened. Nor do I consider myself spiritual."

Susan flinched. But before she could ask questions that would confirm to her that Reinhardt was on the same level as she was, or at least someone of spiritual importance, she was distracted by a new arrival.

Khalid, handsome in a deep green shemagh—a traditional Middle Eastern desert head wrap—stood at the end of the bridge. Before Gabriel could announce him, he said, "I am Khalid and a direct descendant of the Prophet Muhammad, peace be upon him."

Joshua began to clap but quickly looked down at his hands. No sound. He continued to clap. Gabriel glared, then turned to Khalid and gave him a big smile.

"Welcome, Khalid! Please have a seat."

"Sorry, man." Joshua leaned across as Khalid sat down beside Reinhardt in the chair at the end of the semicircle. "Couldn't help myself. Just your act, proud Muslim man declaring your lineage and all that. Wow, I didn't know my fucked-up brain had so many stories."

Khalid stared at him in bafflement. "I *am* a proud Muslim. And you look like a typical arrogant American Christian."

"You got part of that right, man. I am an American and maybe a tad arrogant. Goes with being American, right? That's what you guys think. Am I right? The Christian bit is way off, though."

Khalid leaped to his feet and headed for Joshua. Susan put her hand out to touch his arm, and though he could not feel her touch, he understood the gesture.

"You have every right to be a proud Muslim. Most people," she looked pointedly at Joshua, "do not understand your peaceful religion. But in a workshop given by one of your imams after 9/11"—she lowered her voice as if embarrassed to mention 9/11—"we were told so many beautiful things about you Muslims."

Joshua threw up his hands. "Holy fucking everything! Peaceful? How the holy hell ...?"

In an even voice, Khalid said, "What or who do you believe in?"

Joshua stood up and executed a snappy bow. "Hello, my name is Joshua and I am an atheist. This means I do not kneel to some skinny, tortured figure on a cross, nor do I stick my ass in the air like you guys, worshiping some desert shepherd, nor do I—"

Khalid shot up and pointed a shaking finger at Joshua. "Show some respect! Why is this unbeliever here? Why is he not in hell?"

Khalid turned his chair away from Joshua and sat seething. Susan picked up her chair and joined him, arching a brow to Joshua.

"Well, Reinhardt," Joshua said. "Aren't you going to join them?"

Reinhardt grinned and shook his head. "I'm fine where I am. Besides, you look frightened. Perhaps I can help."

Joshua shifted in his seat. "No worries, man. I don't know what you Buddhists do, but sitting around on a cushion chanting stuff, staring into space, ringing fucking bells or whatever doesn't seem to do the world any good. I doubt it will do anything for me."

"Do you always direct your anger toward others?" Reinhardt said mildly.

After a moment, Khalid spoke. "Reinhardt, this hell-bound atheist has a point. What is it you Buddhists actually do?"

Susan swiveled to stare at Khalid. "You are agreeing with this disagreeable man?"

Khalid shrugged. "Just wondering."

Reinhardt adjusted his eye patch again and closed his eyes.

Susan was still staring at Khalid. "You're him!" She pointed a be-ringed and manicured finger inches from his face. "That comedian from England, the Muslim one! Oh my god, you're funny!" She turned to Joshua. "Have you seen him? He's amazing!" As she shook her head in wonder, her gray hair bounced around. "You're Khalid. Or do you go by Kaboom?"

Her smile faded as a thought struck her. "You … died?"

Laughter from any realm has a profound impact on the earth. With the exception of Susan, all including Gabriel laughed. The first wave of laughter activated the wind chimes; in San Francisco, a Buddhist nun thought it was time for morning chants. The lights on the prism grew more vibrant. South of Birmingham, England, a young woman hanging out her wash thought she saw a flash of lightning and grabbed the wash off the line.

Gabriel was happy. Laughter would ease their fears. Fear, after all, was the driving force behind prejudice.

"So, what fresh-from-the grave sap do we have here?" Joshua was watching a pretty young woman with reddish-blond hair step through the translucent light that surrounded the bridge.

"Please welcome Emily!" Gabriel announced.

Emily approached cautiously, eying the others. "Where should I sit?"

Before Gabriel could show her to a seat, Joshua jumped up. "You have a choice! You can sit across from the camel-riding, anti-women's rights Muslim, or the woman who has pillaged and plundered all the religious traditions throughout time, lumped them all together and thinks she has discovered some new bullshit, or the sit-on-a-cushion-all-fucking-day Buddhist. Or you can sit beside me, an atheist who, according to our peace-loving Muslim, will be roasty-toasty in hell for all time."

Khalid shot to his feet. "Too bloody right, you disrespectful bastard! And I'll bring the marshmallows!"

Nonplussed, Emily took a step back, stumbling at the edge of the bridge. Gabriel, without actually touching her, managed to catch her and direct her to the chair at the other end of the semicircle, across from Reinhardt.

"Looks like someone got up on the wrong side of the grave!" Gabriel threw back his head and laughed at his own joke. The Great Unnamed Room tilted a bit and then righted itself.

Emily laughed nervously and sat, casting a troubled look at Joshua.

"And what religion or spiritual path did you follow, dear?" Susan whispered loudly.

"I'm a Christian," Emily said. Susan's face fell, and she picked at the skirt of her fairy dress.

Joshua groaned theatrically. "Are you one of those born-again nut jobs?"

"I pray every night and go to church every Sunday, if that's what you mean. If I'd known of you when I was alive, I'd have prayed for your soul."

"No fucking thanks, sister. I am a devout atheist." Joshua liked tacking on that "devout." It confused the hell out of people.

Emily's cheeks grew pink. "Clearly, you were dead wrong. Look around you. It's not exactly what I expected but—"

Joshua fumed. "This is just some fucked-up dead brain stuff. Soon all of this will stop as my ever-so-smart brain cells sadly die off and I will be nothing. Ahh ... the big black."

"You're crazy! How can you possibly deny what's happening? How can you deny that we are someplace special? I'll pray for you after all, you arrogant twit!"

"Twit? How cruel! I am hurt and shocked. Is this the way a good Christian girl behaves?"

Emily turned her focus to Gabriel. Joshua shrugged.

Susan patted her hand. "I used to be a Christian, dear, but I learned there is more, much more ..."

"What do you mean, more? More what?" Emily's voice was thin with impatience. "Are you one of those New Age people?"

Assuming a mysterious look, Susan replied, "Yes, I'm proud to say I've learned some of the greatest spiritual secrets—truths that have been hidden by some of you Christians but by others as well ..."

"I find," Emily said quietly, "this New Age stuff insufferable and chock full of capital *Self*. There is an elitist vibe—am I using the right word, Susan? Vibe? This self-serving, narcissistic group who feel they are somehow above all other traditions are usually old hippies, or their spawn, who are drawn to the latest so-called spiritual high and have a childish need to be special. Somehow all this self-development has led to self-involvement."

"I think I love you," Joshua said with a laugh.

"Please don't," Emily said.

Sunita stood at the end of the bridge. She wore an aquamarine sari and silver scarf that made her skin glow. Gabriel pretended to clear his throat and bowed.

"Please welcome Sunita. Dear Sunita, you may take a seat across from the lovely lady in the fairy dress, but if you prefer to—" Sunita shook her head and settled gracefully into the chair across from Susan, next to Joshua.

Susan leaned forward eagerly. "Hello, Sunita. Are you from one of the upper castes of your mystical country?"

Sunita nodded. "And what is your name?"

"I am Susan. And despite all that has been so cruelly said here, I myself follow ancient and wise traditions including a few of your practices. Not all, mind you. I don't eat meat but have no objections to others eating beef. But tell me this, with so many of your fellow citizens starving and oh my so skinny, why are cows forbidden?"

Sunita adjusted her scarf. "Really, Susan, I find what you say to be quite simple-minded and, like most things said from ignorance, insulting. Hinduism is the oldest religion in the world. It is vast and multi-faceted. Cows? That is what you wish to speak about? For your information, we view cows as sacred nurturers, similar to mothers."

Joshua closed his eyes and wiped imaginary drool from his chin. "Oh man, I can't imagine life worth living without hamburgers or steak. Medium rare, please."

"Please, Joshua," Susan scolded, "show some respect for those of us who care for all of the great mother earth's creatures and all she creates."

"Oh my fucking fuck. My brain must have held onto every bit of spiritual crap it ever heard." Joshua tilted his head and slapped the side of it as if he had water in his ear. Then he stuck his pinky finger into the ear and wiggled it. "Now it's rewinding the worst of the worst. If I prayed like little Ms. Christian here, I would get down on my knees and pray very hard for the dark oblivion to come soon."

Emily rolled her eyes and caught Sunita doing the same. "Snap!" Sunita said with a grin.

"Just one more thing, dear," Susan said. "What about all those trinkets you Hindu people seem to love? Oh, and all those gods and goddesses. How many? Am I correct in remembering some ridiculous number like 330 lesser gods? This can't be true!"

"Madam, those trinkets are sacred and timeless. I like to call them divine reminders. As for all the gods, we believe God is so immense that all those lesser gods represent—"

"Thank you, dear," Susan interrupted her. "I think I know where you're heading with this."

Sunita sighed. Both Joshua and Emily laughed. When they caught each other's eye, they stopped abruptly and turned away.

And there he was. On the far side of the bridge, Alter stood at the foot of the stairway. Gabriel met his gaze without smiling. The other six stopped talking. With curiosity, they observed this frail old man wearing the red pointy hat. His long black coat, mottled with dust and ink, dragged on the floor. Alter's demeanor was both sad and fierce. He stood with an old man's stubbornness on the last step.

Gabriel bowed slightly. "Please welcome Alter," he said gently.

"Why is there a bridge here?" Alter's voice was raspy and just this side of peevish. "There is hardly enough water to need a stepping stone, never mind a bridge. Not like the canals."

Gabriel brightened. This was a question he could answer.

"My dear Alter, the bridge is mostly symbolic. But it moves you away from earthly bonds and raises your energy level. That is so you and the rest will find it easier to be in this great room. Nothing will happen when you cross this bridge, except that you will be joining the rest of us. You are the last." *It is certainly no surprise that he is the last.*

Alter moved one tattered shoe onto the bridge and then the other. He raised his bushy eyebrows and saw everyone looking at him. Step, step, he made his way across. Susan stood up and applauded, but she faltered when there was no sound.

Alter peered at her with mistrust and confusion. "What is your problem, lady? You look like an old fairy."

Joshua, to his surprise, felt a surge of protectiveness toward the old man.

Susan widened her eyes in mock surprise. "I am merely encouraging this lovely man. You are one of the Chosen People, are you not, Alter?"

"Are you for fucking real?" Joshua rolled his eyes at Emily. She gnawed her lip to stifle her laughter.

Alter caught sight of Khalid. "You there! Are you a Moor?"

"What century are you from, old man?" Khalid scoffed.

From somewhere in the Great Unnamed Room, a trumpet sounded. Gabriel directed Alter to the single empty chair, between Emily and Sunita, then strode back to the center of the space to address everyone.

"Welcome, welcome all! I am delighted you are here. Every single one of you. I know some of you may think there has been some kind of mix-up."

Susan waved her hand. "My astrologer said I had years and years left to live!" She looked around the group with an air of self-importance. "She did say that I'd be traveling to some rather interesting places and would receive transmissions of rare, esoteric teachings. Maybe this is the place."

Gabriel's smile slipped only briefly. "I will need your *silent* attention for the rest of my talk. But," he pointed a finger upwards, "you have been carefully selected to be here. I assure you that no mistakes have been made. Those days are long past," he said cheerily, patting his index cards. "Each one of you is meant to be here. I rather like that phrase 'meant to be here.' But some people feel it is so, so ..."

"Full of crap?" Joshua offered.

"You must be an Aries," Susan said. "Combative, argumentative—"

Joshua snorted. "I might have known. I don't believe in that starry-starry stuff, either."

"Silence!" Gabriel drew himself up to his full height.

From above the courtyard, in a tall silver cage hanging from nothing, Ugly Brown Birds stirred and flapped. Everyone craned their necks and gaped.

Gabriel sketched a salute to the birds, which settled and tucked their heads under their wings. He continued. "You are here not a moment too soon. As I was saying, each of you has been selected. You are to be part of a very special group. In all the realms, a great many discussions and late-night meetings, some of them quite heated, have wrestled with what do to about the current situation. The earth is at a critical stage. While a few people on earth are aware of this, most are either in denial or engaged with the never-ending search for this happiness thing." Gabriel shook his head slightly.

"After all these discussions it was agreed—and my good friends, agreement does not come easily here—." He pretended to suppress a chuckle. "It was agreed that we needed people from some of the major faiths, certain professional backgrounds and a variety of cultures to come together and contribute their unique gifts. You can appreciate the intricate timing and planning! First of all, be assured that each of you was scheduled to depart your earthly bodies when you did. I believe all of you remember me a day or so before you expired."

All of them were silent as Trappist monks, still as yogis. Gabriel met the eyes of each of them in turn. "You will be given three missions. All are important, but one particular mission is why you are here together on this realm. That mission is vital, not only for earth but for heaven as well. As above, so below." He searched their eyes. "Is this making sense to you?"

Reinhardt raised a hand, and Gabriel nodded in his direction.

"It makes complete sense. I am happy to contribute in any way I can. Am I to assume this has to do with the clear and present danger the world is facing in regard to the environment?" Reinhardt was eager to hear more about the missions. He had lived every minute of his adult life with purpose.

Joshua leaned toward him. "A German Buddhist? How the hell did that happen? Man, my brain. Wish I had written books or films or something."

"It is a simple story," Reinhardt said. "If you like, I will share it with you sometime."

"My dear ones," Gabriel continued. "Spirit people, we like to call you here. You will be given plenty of time to become acquainted with one another and to share your life stories. In fact, we encourage you to share them."

"Oh goody," Joshua muttered.

Gabriel stood tall, and his white garments gleamed. His eyes travelled the group and rested on Joshua. "We encourage this because it fosters trust," he said quietly. "I know this is a sensitive issue. Is that what you call it? An issue?"

Susan bobbed her head vigorously, her thick gray hair bouncing. "Yes, yes, that's what you call it, an issue. Joshua has an issue."

Joshua folded his arms across his chest. "Therapy, right? Ten or more years? Mommy *issues*?"

"Of course I've had therapy," Susan snapped. "I assume you haven't, which is a shame. It would have done you good."

Gabriel paced, hands clasped behind his back. The group fell silent.

"Now!" The overhead bird cage swayed. "Now," he said again in a normal voice. "You will be assigned positions. This will keep things nice and tidy. We do understand that humans like structure." He waved his arm about. "I know, I know, this has gotten you into trouble in the past. Too much or too little. Rules, laws, et cetera. Oh, heavens, the time." He continued in a rush. "I trust you've read your invitations. Remember, you are here in this magnificent realm to share the gifts that are particular to you, to your culture, and to the belief system you hold dear."

Khalid raised a hand. When Gabriel nodded, he pointed at Joshua. "What's he doing here, then? He's an atheist and should be burning in hell."

"Again, man? As you can clearly see, I am not roasting over any burning pit, designed by some psychopathic god or deranged angel. That belief is yours to deal with."

The Great Unnamed Room trembled. Gabriel vanished, and in his place appeared a circle of fire. Chairs tipped amid gasps as the group scrambled away.

"I knew it. He's a jinn after all." Khalid's quiet voice was gripped with fear.

And then Gabriel was back. "Sorry about that, folks. Just had to blow off a little steam. Everyone doing okay?"

Without a single dissenter, they nodded. *In unison,* Gabriel noted. *A good sign.* Chairs were righted, and the seven straggled back to their seats.

"As I was saying, there are positions to fill. Let's begin. Joshua, you are to be the Project Manager."

"Why him! He is not spiritually qualified!" Susan protested.

"Gabriel, I don't mean to be impertinent but is this, ah, morally …?" Emily wasn't sure she'd ever met an atheist before.

"Listen, I don't want this!" Joshua said. "It's all crazy, completely fucked up. Doesn't anyone see this?"

"It has been decided," Gabriel said evenly. "Joshua, please take these scrolls. Written on them are your positions, and those positions are not negotiable."

Joshua pushed out of his chair and reluctantly reached for the scrolls. He quickly checked the names, kept his own and handed out the rest. In gold writing and with great flourishes, this was what was written:

> **Susan,** *you are the artist. You will be Head of Beauty and Wonder.*

Emily, *you helped to ease and heal others' traumas. You will be Head of Trauma Healing.*

Reinhardt, *you endeavored to heal your gravely ill earth. You will be Protector of the Earth.*

Khalid, *you made people laugh and punctured their illusions. You will be Humorist/Satirist.*

Sunita, *you helped people heal from their physical wounds. You will be Head of Healthy Human Bodies.*

Alter, *dear Alter, you helped people remember and honor their past. You will be Teacher of the Past.*

Chapter 10: Inception

The group sat silent. From the courtyard, the Ugly Brown Birds crooned softly. Nearby, a grove of happy trees swayed gently without wind.

"Okay, if doing this moves me faster along to the big black sooner, I'm in," Joshua said at last. "How about the rest of you?"

Alter leaned forward, hands on his knees. "If this gets me closer to where my Hannah is, I will do my best to fulfill my duties as teacher."

"And I'll be happy to heal whoever I can—with the help of God," Emily said.

Alter nodded gravely to her. "You are a good girl, Emily."

"Thank you." Emily gave him a shy smile.

Khalid had been watching Alter and Emily with interest. "You know, the three of us belong to the same God. Our ancestor Abraham ties us together."

Alter nodded slowly. "It is difficult for this old man, Mr. Khalid. We Jews have been treated badly by both you Muslims and Christians."

"If my memory serves me well, and I am certain it does, you Jews did not treat us very well, either."

"Really, is there any point to this?" Emily pleaded.

"Jews killed your Christ, your beloved Son of God," Khalid said to her. "What do they call it? Deicide?"

"Drop it!" Emily said.

"Son, Mr. Khalid, Jesus was a Jew and lived the life of a pious Jew. It was Christians who decided he was no longer Jewish."

Khalid's response was cut off by Gabriel clapping his hands. The Great Unnamed Room shook. "Sorry about that," he said pleasantly. "I forget sometimes. I have other duties to attend to, and so do you."

Sunita leaned forward. "I realize this may not be an ideal time to ask questions, but could you indulge me?" Gabriel closed his eyes for a moment. Then his brown eyes met hers. "Yes, my dear Sunita. What questions do you have?"

Without hesitation or fear, Sunita said, "Why have I not gone through the Kamaloca?"

Susan's hand shot up. "Oh! Oh! I know what that is! Your ancient religion designated a place after death where you would purge your desires, so you could travel to higher heavens. Isn't that right, dear? Emily," Susan swung around in her chair, "this is similar to what you Christians, or at least Catholic Christians, call purgatory."

Sunita kept her focus on Gabriel. "If I did not go through the Kamaloca, how can I move to Devachan?"

"Sunita, I am happy you are asking this question. Susan, would you like to enlighten us on what Devachan is?" He cocked an eyebrow at her, but she became suddenly absorbed by one of the fairy wings on her billowing, gauzy dress.

"How can this be?" Joshua threw his head back and laughed. "My fucking world is shaken! The great New Age guru doesn't know the answer?"

"You are the meanest person I've ever had the displeasure of meeting." Emily inched her chair even farther away.

Gabriel ignored this exchange. He had places to go and people to see. "Devachan is the highest heaven." He gestured to include all of them. "For Sunita as for all of you, any realms or spheres you have been taught you would be transitioning through are best thought of, for now, as places in your future. However, depending on how we get along here in this glorious realm, you may not spend much if any time there. And Sunita, your Devachan awaits."

Sunita's face lit up, although she remained still. Gabriel noted her fierce calmness and was pleased she had been selected.

"By now," he continued, "you will have noticed some rather remarkable features in this Great Unnamed Room. These new scrolls I am giving you will explain these wonders and other features in this realm."

Emily raised her hand.

"May I remind you that you're not in school?" Joshua whispered.

She ignored him. "Gabriel, why is it called the Great Unnamed Room?"

"This is a long story, my dear one. The short version is that we have never been able to agree. Great thinkers, sages and so on who have passed this way had interesting suggestions, yet we could reach no consensus. As for me, I've grown fond of calling it the Great Unnamed Room. Now, if each of you would kindly come and receive your scrolls? As you can see, each is tied with a purple ribbon. I will share this with you: purple is my favorite color." He fingered the hair ribbon at the base of his neck.

With her fairy dress flowing behind her, Susan leaped forward. "I'm sure I'll come up with a name for this sacred place, a name that will be remembered for all time." She floated back to her chair, untying the scroll as she went.

"You may think I deserve to be screaming in everlasting pain over a massive pit of sulphur and fire, but you must agree that she" — Joshua jerked his thumb toward Susan—"is a bit much?"

Khalid laughed and picked up his scroll.

One by one, they took their scrolls. Alter shuffled up last.

"Hey, lookie here, a kitchen. Baffling! What the fuck else will my dying brain dial up? A kitchen in this so-called 'afterlife.'" Joshua sketched air quotes. "It says in the kitchen we can have whatever foods we used to eat. Susan, will that be tofu or spelt bread or quinoa or an eternity's worth of raw food?"

"I will love it all," Susan said defiantly.

'Oh, I'm sure you will. All that New Age food for the paisley and patchouli crowd. Ha ha! Love it!"

"Shut up."

"Well, that's not very spiritual of you!" Joshua sniffed and wiped an imaginary tear.

Emily laughed and kept on reading.

"What about you, Emily? Canadian, eh? Will you be chowing down on seal meat and maple syrup? Beaver tails?" Joshua asked in wide-eyed innocence.

Emily rolled her eyes and opened more of her scroll.

"I hope there is something kosher for you, Alter," Sunita commented.

Alter looked doubtful that anyone would go to the trouble of considering his needs.

"And Sunita. Pakoras? Curried something or other?" Joshua grinned.

"Really, Joshua. Of course those are part of my culture. I enjoy them as well as many other kinds of food. My mother used to call me 'the camel.' She swore she never saw anyone put away as much food as I do. Or did." She lapsed into a thoughtful silence.

Gabriel watched and listened. "Have you finished reading? Alter, we made sure yours was written in Yiddish. Reinhardt, I see you have not opened yours yet. Is there a problem?"

Reinhardt took a moment before answering. "I prefer to find things out for myself."

"Very well. I believe you will find the Great Green Sanctuary and the Room of Reflection of special interest to you." Gabriel spread his arms to encompass them all. "Okay, my dear ones, I will leave you to it. Again, welcome and congratulations! You have been chosen for special ... well, more on that later. For now, enjoy the enchantment. Oh, before I forget, please visit the kitchen. And since we feel that music complements any culinary experience, we invite you to take turns and choose your favorite music. But when you hear a bell, any kind of bell, please assemble in this part of the glorious Great Unnamed Room. I may appear as I am at this moment, or I may appear on a screen. Tally-ho. Cheers and blessings to you all."

Chapter 11: The Great Unnamed Room

The new scrolls explained all they'd already seen in the Great Unnamed Room and went on to describe the Wall of the Seven Heavens, the Great Green Sanctuary, the Room of Reflection, and the library. I'm not sure why I have to provide an intro to these scrolls but will do as requested. My ex-husband would have loved this compliant version of me! Come to think of it, my parents and friends and everyone else I've had a passing acquaintance with would have enjoyed this agreeable me. So here's some of what the seven, minus Reinhardt, read.

The Wall of the Seven Heavens is at the right of the stairway, at the far end. The entire wall on this end of the Great Unnamed Room has been dedicated to the holy and the sacred. On this space you will see a continuous series of scenes of the Seven Heavens. Khalid, you will be delighted and filled with wonder at the scene of Gabriel and al-Buraq, the heavenly steed ready to take Muhammad, peace be upon him, on his legendary trip through the heavens. Many have said they feel they are actually there.

The sacred symbolism of every religion, the infinite universe, ancient skies, new-born stars, glowing babies, planets, galaxies and all of nature's treasures are vividly depicted. The Seven Heavens, angels from all the orders, mystics and the delicate and fragile human are brilliantly featured with colors that the living human eye cannot see or process.

Artists throughout history have attempted to create a likeness. Some have come close, and it is rumored that those artists spent time in this realm. Each scene tells the full stories that human ears are not capable of hearing. You will encounter the numinous here. Humans who come to this or any realm come with their sacred struggles. Or, as you on earth call them, problems, troubles, worries and so on. Here you may gain clarity that these struggles were actually sacred and an essential part of your experience. Please note the warning sign posted nearby: "Too much glory. For your own safety, please stay here for only a short time."

Welcome to the Great Green Sanctuary! You will love what has been done here, Reinhardt! You really cannot call it a garden. Even the wildest garden with the most abundant array of trees, shrubs, vines, flowers and grasses would not come close to this green sanctuary. Here in this room, all the flora that have died out on earth have been saved and live here. This sanctuary is also becoming home to more and more bees, a situation which concerns us. Human survival depends on bees. Humans are precious in their own right, but they are also needed by the realms beyond the earth. Without humans, who will pray to us? Worship this deity or that deity? This realm, and for that matter its angels and other beings, cannot exist without humans.

If there were an accurate picture of the fabled Garden of Eden, then perhaps this would come close. It is our hope that in future your earth will be better able to support all the plants, trees, flowers—everything we are housing. When or if this happens, we will gently reintroduce them to a more caring world, one that nurtures. Just think what a surprise that will be. People will think they have discovered some rare plant or tree!

A sanctuary for our four-legged friends, winged creatures and aquatic animals who are on the edge of extinction is being worked on. Due to recent activity, this endeavor has intensified. It is our heaven-high hope to have this a part of our Great Unnamed Room very, very soon!

The Room of Reflection near the Great Green Sanctuary is a recent addition. Reinhardt, one of your teachers suggested we create this space. As you can see, the entrance to this room is an ordinary wooden door, the kind you might find in a modest home. The inside, however is anything but ordinary. Once you enter, you will find yourself in your chosen place of worship, whatever your faith or belief system. Feel free to go in anytime and pray, chant, and sing. This includes you, Joshua.

The library is also a recent addition, created in 1482. The style and form of architecture are lovely, outrageous and obvious Baroque! All books ever written and all books not finished are found here. Some of the unfinished books will open to their last page, waiting for their authors to return.

Wide, sweeping arches are festooned with gargoyles. Angels and mystical figures adorn the walls, hang from ceilings and stand sentry on floors. Passageways meander lazily, lined with more and more books. Baroque music plays throughout the library, including in the hundreds of passageways.

Tall candles stand as sentinels at the library's entrance. On a small table at the entryway lie three books. One is bound in rich red silk and is called *The History of Love*. The second is called *The History of Fear* and is bound in human skin. The last is a guest book and is bound in purple leather with gold embossed symbols. It is open to a page that has many signatures, but the last two are written in a color that is brighter than the others. "Had a great time. Happy I could help with those Ugly Brown Birds."—Elvis P. "We are all gifted. That is our inheritance."—Ethel W.

A new book will soon be added to those three on the table. It is called *The Book of Seven*.

Chapter 12: First Visit to Kitchen

With Gabriel's invitation to visit the kitchen still fresh in their minds, they agreed that a morning meal would be the most appropriate way to start. Reinhardt was the first one to enter the kitchen and was therefore entitled to choose the music. Standing at the doorway with the others crowded behind him, he announced, "Buena Vista Social Club."

The opening strains of Cuban guitar music had already begun as, one by one, they entered with caution and curiosity.

"This looks positively divine," Susan enthused.

As in so many homes on earth, the kitchen was the heart of the realm. The first feature they saw was an impressive stone fireplace, logs ablaze. The stones of the fireplace had been carefully and lovingly arranged in patterns, and each pattern told a story. A plaque beside the chimney explained that, a century earlier, a woman whose fight on earth included rights for women asked if she could tell stories of women throughout the ages. She was accustomed to telling stories in secret and had devised codes to communicate. It was said that if a woman touched a pattern, its story would be revealed to her.

Brightly polished copper pots and pans hung from low beams, and the spotless slate floor was strewn with baskets overflowing with the fruits of harvest. Candles burned in wall sconces, candelabras on sideboards, and candlesticks on the table. Three elegant bouquets of flowers graced the table.

And such a table!

In the center of the large kitchen sat a long, rough-hewn pine table that could seat fifty people. Deep into its surface were carved many initials; even after a person dies, the longing to be remembered is still strong.

At the near end of the table, seven places had been set with crystal and silver cutlery, and seven meals were already waiting. In the middle of the table between the set places, pitchers of water and juice, bowls of chilled fruit, baskets of toast and scones, and platters of eggs and meats were laid out.

"Plenty of granola and watery yogurt right here, Susan." Joshua pulled out her chair. "This must be yours." He scanned the table. "Ah, this must be where I sit. See, a nice, heaping plate of sausages and eggs over easy. Not bad at all. Thank you, dying brain cells!"

"I hope, as project manager, you will think about more than just your next meal." Susan sat down primly and patted the seat next to her, inviting Emily to join her.

"Before we eat, perhaps we can give thanks for this food? Grace?" Emily looked around.

Reinhardt's spoon was as big as a soup ladle. He paused mid-air and held it hovering over a large bowl of honeyed oatmeal. A large plate of cheeses, breads and jams sat ready to serve as his second course. "Good idea, Emily."

"And may I suggest that we take turn about? Each day, one person will assume the duty of offering thanks for the food." Emily smiled broadly at Reinhardt.

Joshua sat horrified. "Holy fuck, this just gets better and better."

"What does everyone else think?" Emily ignored Joshua.

Susan smiled. "Lovely. To honor the gods and goddesses, even here. Lovely. If only I had my drums."

Joshua pushed away from the table and dropped to his knees. He raised his head, closed his eyes and formed his hands as if in prayer.

Khalid laughed. "You are an asshole, Joshua, an atheist asshole."

"Just giving praise, man." Joshua got up from his knees and brushed his pants out of habit. Realizing what he was doing, he reddened and stopped.

"Shall we begin?" Emily sat with the poise of a dancer, her hands folded in prayer.

Everyone nodded. Joshua looked with interest at each one as they assumed their individual prayer poses. Reinhardt had his hands on his knees and was looking straight ahead. Alter and Khalid had their heads bowed. Sunita adjusted her scarf to cover more of her beautiful face and bowed her head in reverence. Susan leaned back in her chair, legs apart, which gave the fairy face on her dress a slightly maniacal look. Her head was tilted back and her outstretched arms reached upwards. Joshua clamped a hand over his mouth, choking back a laugh.

"Dear Lord in heaven, thank you for delivering us safely to this wondrous place," Emily said. "We offer our humble thanks for this food. And we ask that you show us how we can serve you better. In the name of the Father, the Son and the Holy Ghost. Amen."

Susan was on her feet, swaying and mumbling to herself.

"Time to eat, all," Joshua said. "Susan, by the looks of your food, I wouldn't go to a lot of trouble offering praise." Susan shot him a look, sat down and made an Oscar-worthy "Oh, yum!" face at the culinary delights before her.

"What Gabriel told us, and all of this"—Emily gestured around the room—"it's really a lot to take in," She bit into toast.

Reinhardt nodded and, between mouthfuls, said, "I suggest after we eat, it would be a good idea to fully explore the Great Unnamed Room. Some time spent in the Room of Reflections is recommended."

Sunita, rolling up a spiced vegetable pancake, nodded. "He is right. There is much to reflect on. I wonder when Gabriel will be back and if there is more for him to tell us besides these missions he speaks of."

Alter had not touched his food.

"What's wrong, old man?" Joshua's voice was tender. The others stopped eating and turned, surprised at his abrupt change of tone.

"This cannot all be for us! There is too much food." Alter looked desolate.

"Alter, old man, what is your problem?" Khalid asked. "You heard what Gabriel said. We would have food we'd enjoyed in life. It's okay."

Alter's head was down, and Khalid had to lean in to hear what he said. "How can I enjoy this plenitude when the poor Jews in Venice had so little to eat?"

"That was a very long time ago, Alter," Sunita said thoughtfully. "Sadly, it remains one of the world's great sorrows and failures that so many have so little food. Let's pray this will be a mission for us: to help feed those who do not have enough." She took a sip of tea.

"Well said, my dear." Susan said.

"While we're eating, perhaps we can get to know one another." Emily looked around the table.

"Why would we do that?" Joshua said. "As soon as the rest of my brain dies, you'll all disappear."

"Can you pretend or at least go along, Joshua?" Emily's voice was filled with exasperation.

Joshua shrugged and speared a sausage. "Doesn't fucking matter, I guess."

Emily rolled her eyes. "Thanks for your cheery cooperation, Mr. Project Manager. Anyone want to begin?"

Susan pushed her bowl away and stood up, wiping her chin with a flowered napkin. "If no one objects, I'll be happy to share my life story with all of you. I'm sure you'll be fascinated."

Joshua snickered. Khalid caught his eye and winked.

"Hey, aren't you supposed to hate my atheist guts?"

Khalid let that pass.

Alter looked puzzled. "I am not sure I understand. We are to talk about ourselves?"

"Yes, Alter. In the times you lived in, this would have been strange. But people talk about themselves all the time now. Many are rather obsessed with themselves." Emily avoided looking at Susan as she spoke.

"Thank you, Emily. This is indeed strange. I am not sure I can learn all these things. I am a very old man."

Emily smiled encouragingly at Alter. Sunita, who was sitting beside him, touched his hand.

Susan clapped her hands for attention, forgetting there would be no sound. She reached to the table and picked up a dainty dinner bell. Holding it over her head, she gave it a good shake. The tiny bell flew out of her hand when its ear-splitting ring was followed by a crack of thunder.

Reinhardt slapped his knee, threw back his big head and laughed. With the exception of Alter, who simply looked small and confused, everyone laughed.

Susan picked up the bell and placed it carefully on the table, then adjusted the fairy on her long, flowing dress. "Thank you for being here," she began.

Joshua stood up. "And what choice do we have? Okay, fine, we can get to know one another. Crazy getting to know hallucinations, but whatever. But," he jabbed a finger at Susan, "this particular hallucination has to keep it simple. Okay? Bullet points and then someone else gets up. Sound like a plan?"

"Okay, okay, I get your point!" Susan pulled herself up to her full five foot two and addressed the others. "Yes, I am Susan. I'm quite well known for my fairy paintings. I paint fairy depictions of people who are interested in their magical selves. My clients give me a brief personal history and their favorite picture of themselves so I can determine what element of fairy they belong to. You know—water, earth, fire or air. I include symbolism that reflects important turning points in their lives. I'm divorced with two daughters, who because of my family and ex-husband's influence, I rarely see. But," she waved her hand as if to dismiss the importance of this, "I am very happy. My life is rich and abundant thanks to my spiritual family and my spiritual practices. Of course," she cast her eyes down modestly, "I also have many, many fans."

Joshua continued eating. Sunita held her head in one of her elegant, hennaed hands. Alter looked sad. Khalid pushed his fork around his plate in circles. Reinhardt, eyes closed, nodded a silent encouragement.

Emily raised her hand.

"I remind you, this is not school, Miss Emily." Joshua was dunking a triangle of toast into an egg yolk.

Emily ignored him. "Is it appropriate to ask questions?"

Susan flung open her arms. "Yes! I'm delighted to answer questions about my life!" She placed her right hand over her very still heart.

"Okay." Joshua swallowed a bite. "How about we leave all the nitty-gritty details for another time? Anyone have any objection to what is probably the last sane thing my dying brain will think of?"

Reinhardt's hazel eye opened. "I concur with Joshua. I think it is a good thing to share our highlights at meals, but the details can come in a more natural, organic way."

"That's a wrap. At least for me." Crumpling his napkin, Joshua stood up and left the kitchen.

Chapter 13: What They Found in the Room of Reflection

The concept of time was more fluid in this realm than it was on earth. And although none of the seven could pinpoint exactly when they had first visited the Room of Reflection, or even if they had been awake at the time, it had made a profound impression on each of them.

Susan pushed hard on the door, but it didn't budge. For a moment, she stood with her nose touching it, wondering if she had the power to simply appear on the other side. Apparently not. Leaning all her weight on the door, she grunted with satisfaction as it opened just far enough for her to squeeze in past a tumble of meditation cushions. As she sidled through, pulling in her stomach and clutching her billowing dress close, she realized her body no longer had the capability to push anything.

Standing inside at last, she gasped with delight and astonishment. Here were icons from the many and various paths she had followed. Christian crosses of all sizes and styles dotted the walls. A nine-candled Hanukkah menorah glowed on a burnished walnut table. A laughing, golden Buddha that dominated the far end of the room reached the vaulted ceiling, while an imperious Shiva stood in one corner. Prominent on the left wall hung a pentacle, below which a large cauldron lay on its side. Incense wafted from ornate holders hanging from the ceiling beams, and bushels of sage lay on a low table to her right. Prayer rugs, yoga mats and meditation cushions were scattered throughout. Everywhere she looked were medicine wheels, drums and rattles, and candles of all colors burning yellow and orange. The brightness was extraordinary.

Susan, out of habit, shielded her eyes from the light. Every inch of wall was covered by an icon, deity or religious scene. Happily overwhelmed, she brought both her hands up to her chest and bowed a namaste to each sacred object.

She did not come out for some time.

Emily clasped her hands in delight when she opened the door.

Polished oak pews sat in serene rows, and a plush red carpet ran up the center aisle to the chancel. To her left, a large stained-glass window depicted Jesus in the Garden of Gethsemane, the colors so vibrant that Emily felt for a moment she was part of the scene. She could almost smell the fragrance of the trees, feel the cool Jerusalem night air touch her face. At the front, a magnificent pipe organ was flanked by three rows of chairs for the choir. A simple pulpit stood behind the altar, whose cloth, white as Gabriel's garments and thickly embossed with gold crosses, lay perfectly aligned.

But it was the large cross that dominated the room. Shining gold, it was the most beautiful that Emily had ever seen. She slipped into one of the pews and bowed her head.

Khalid took off his shoes and opened the door with hope. Two small fountains were spilling water into a basin, their soothing, burbling sound giving him comfort. Towels were neatly folded nearby, waiting to be used. The Holy Qur'an lay open on a small table. Khalid washed his face, hands and feet.

Tall, arching columns like those he had seen in the Great Mosque of Cordoba gave this sacred place a noble, vast feeling. Prayer rugs were scattered throughout the room, and Khalid was delighted to see his own rug at the front. The Minbar or pulpit was to the right of the Qibla wall that indicated the direction to Mecca. Facing the Mihrab prayer niche, Khalid focused on his intention and raised his hands to his ears. "Allahu Akbar ..."

Reinhardt knew he would be spending a good deal of time in the Room of Reflection. It was in his nature to enjoy not only meditation but also long periods of contemplation.

As he entered, he was pleased to see his own meditation cushion and a marble sculpture of Buddha. The Rigden, King of Shambhala, sat in royal ease, holding the sword of wisdom in his right hand and the flaming jewels of compassion in his left. An exquisitely painted Thangka Gesar of Ling hung in a place of sacred honor near the shrine. On the shrine itself stood a picture of Reinhardt's guru. Bells, gongs, dorje, scriptures and prayer beads were among the treasured items on the shrine. Juniper incense was burning, with its fragrant smoke curling up and up.

Reinhardt settled onto the cushion.

Sunita bowed as she entered the Room of Reflection. Bronze deities lined the walls, and a sculpture of Ganesh, the elephant-headed god, stood at the front of the room. Sunita had never seen such exquisite statues of Lord Shiva and of Parvati, goddess of love, fertility, devotion and divine strength. Centered above the altar of Parvati was a picture of Sunita's beloved Lakshmi, goddess of wealth, fortune and prosperity.

Sunita felt the radiance of her goddess clear away the sadness she had been carrying. Rich silk cloths were neatly placed on the shrine that held small bells, incense holders, a golden mala with rudraksha beads and, of course, the Vedas scriptures.

She smiled, feeling uplifted and comforted. The room dazzled with a warm golden light. Sunita brought her hands together and bowed again.

Joshua didn't have to lean on the door. As soon as he appeared in front of it, it swung open. He stepped through, and the door slammed shut behind him, which made him jump and spin around.

The inside of the door was the same featureless white as the door to his condominium apartment. Pushing past a sudden surge of nervousness, Joshua turned to face a bleak room.

Harsh blue light from overhead fluorescent tubes sizzled and flickered, revealing gray-white walls that were bare except for a poster of a book launch by Richard Dawkins and an old movie poster for Atlas Shrugged. *Near the door, a white plastic chair was tipped on its side, an empty Styrofoam cup on the worn linoleum floor beside it. From a shadowed alcove came the steady plink-plunk of dripping water.*

Joshua nudged the cup with his toe. "Anybody here?" His voice bounced off the walls. Unsure what to do, he stood around with his hands in his pockets. Then, hoping it was mealtime, he opened the door and left.

Alter did not understand why this Room of Reflection was necessary. He had spent countless hours, days, weeks and years praying and reflecting. But he entered anyway, touching his yarmulke and brushing nothing off his prayer shawl. Overcome with emotion, he stood small and still. Everything was in proper order.

Rows of wooden seats gleamed with polish. To the left was a small platform for the cantor. Ahead, to the east, a holy ark of acacia wood was positioned slightly under the Ner Tamid—the eternal light—which was suspended in space without support. Alter closed his eyes and pictured the Torah scrolls inside the ark. The parokhet, *the curtain covering the ark, was closed. He bowed his stooped body and sat down.*

Chapter 14: Susan's R.I.D.

After the morning meal, Joshua wandered around the Great Unnamed Room. He peeked into the Room of Reflection but quickly closed the door when he noticed Sunita watching him from her seat in the café. Alter had gone straight to the library and had not yet reappeared. Emily and Khalid were standing in front of the Wall of the Seven Heavens, their heads together, whispering. Occasionally, Joshua would cast a discreet glance in their direction. Reinhardt was leaning as far as he could over the silvery thread that acted as a protective barrier to the Great Green Sanctuary. Susan was bending down to examine etchings on the stone floor. Every once in a while she would straighten, sway her ample body and bow deeply.

Slowly, they all drifted to the café. His dark coat trailing, Alter emerged from the library wearing a look of disbelief. He staggered over to Sunita's table and sat down heavily beside her. Susan, after stretching her back, advanced with arms swinging toward Alter and Sunita. Reinhardt and Joshua's path intersected, and they walked together to join the others. Joshua glanced back from time to time at Emily and Khalid.

"Am I missing anything?" Emily called out as she hurried toward the gathering group at the café. Her steps were small and quick. Khalid sauntered behind her.

"No, no, dear. We're just beginning to gather. This is what the Spanish call a *juntarse*," Susan said breezily. Joshua groaned but sat down smartly beside Emily, almost colliding with Khalid.

"Pushy American tosser." Khalid muttered as he moved over to sit between Reinhardt and Susan. Susan reached out to him and said, "From what country does your family originate? Is it Saudi Arabia, or Jordan, or—"

"My parents immigrated to the UK from Morocco."

"Oh, I adore the rugs from there!"

Khalid smiled thinly.

Soon, they were all talking. Quiet pauses were filled with the songs of the Ugly Brown Birds, the swish of the swaying trees, and the ringing of the wind chimes in perfect C.

If there had been shadows, Gabriel would have stood in their dark comfort. Instead, he wandered over to where the birds were singing low and listened to the thoughts of the seven.

Oh, I've heard all this before.

Susan, thought Gabriel.

Stupid fucking stupid crap.

Joshua.

My grandmother used to tell me ghost stories where some of this would happen.

This must be the Bardo.

Emily and Reinhardt. Gabriel continued to stroll and began whistling the notes the birds were singing. One of the birds eyed him and squawked. He strolled away.

When will the testing be over?

How lovely to be an actual Deva.

I hoped to be a messenger, not playing games. But if this is what God wants ...

Khalid, Sunita, Alter.

And then Gabriel was with them. "Greetings, my dear ones. I trust you are becoming acquainted with our little realm." He looked around enquiringly, but all were silent. "I take that as a big yes! So, my dear ones, I have a surprise for all of you!"

"I can't handle any more of this!" Joshua muttered.

"What's your choice, mate?" Khalid whispered back.

"So now I'm 'mate,' not a burn-in-hell-for-eternity atheist?"

Khalid folded his arms. "Just trying to be friendly. Is being an arsehole part of being an atheist?"

Exasperation crept into Gabriel's tone. "My dear ones, it is time to set aside your differences. To accomplish our missions, with me as your navigator—"

"Navigator, my skinny white ass. Angel of Death is more fucking like it," Joshua whispered to Emily, who sat stone white, face frozen.

Gabriel seemed to grow larger, his face dark and angry. "DO YOU FORGET THAT I CAN HEAR YOU?" The voice boomed, filling every inch of the vast room. And he was gone.

All was quiet in the Great Unnamed Room. No Ugly Brown Birds sang, no swaying trees swished, no wind chimes moved.

Then Gabriel was back. "So, as I was saying before I was so rudely interrupted ..." he looked at Joshua. So did everyone else. Joshua examined a fingernail.

"There is one thing," Gabriel continued, "that was not included in your scrolls. That one thing, and I am thrilled to be able to offer this because it took some, how do you Americans say it, wrangling? Yes, that is it, *wrangling* to get others to agree to this concession, but I did it! Each and every one of you will get to view your R.I.D." Gabriel stood back and waited. No one moved or spoke.

"Are you not thrilled? Excited?"

Emily raised her hand. Gabriel nodded eagerly.

"What's an R.I.D.?"

Susan piped up, "I must have encountered this term before in my many spiritual journeys, but my mind can't recall. I'm sure I'll remember when you explain it, Gabriel." She smiled warmly, as though to a spiritual teammate.

Gabriel paced in front of the group as he collected his thoughts. "R.I.D. is an acronym for Ritual If Departing. On earth, you call it a funeral. So depressing! Well, sometimes there are laughs … Anyway, we prefer R.I.D., and each of you has the option of viewing yours. Again, this is a special privilege. Viewing your R.I.D., you can see all your loved ones gather to celebrate your life, weep over your loss, express regrets at how they treated you, and so on."

"And the purpose of this is?" Reinhardt said quietly.

Before Gabriel could answer, Susan spoke. "I completely see the point of the R.I.D. I put quite a lot of careful consideration and planning into my transition." She turned to the others.

"Transition means …?" Joshua said. "Oh, I get it. I'm sure we all get it, Susan. To whiten up the messy business of death, you use another word."

"As I was saying," Susan plowed on, "included in this careful planning, in part so my spirit would have just the right vibrations, I consulted my most trusted spiritual advisers, designers, city planners, caterers, lawyers, and my spiritual communities. And I put aside quite a bit of money to ensure my plans were carried out."

She added defensively, "I was quite well known. Many, many people loved and respected me. Well, not my nasty sister or her droopy husband or my ex-husband or ungrateful daughters, but others—others *loved* me. I'm sure of it." Susan pulled back her shoulders and looked directly at Gabriel. "I would like to view my R.I.D."

"*Wunderbar*," Gabriel exclaimed, tilting his head at Reinhardt for approval. "You may make your way to the benches along the wall."

"This should be worth the price of admission." Joshua snickered to Emily as they made their way to the bench cushions.

Emily stepped away from him. "Your snide remarks are becoming tiresome."

He reddened and looked away.

"And what would *your* R.I.D. look like?" Susan spoke in a huff after overhearing Joshua's comments.

"Good question, Old Fairy." Joshua settled into a cushion, picked up a smaller cushion and held it to his chest.

"Yes, Joshua what would an atheist funeral look like?" Khalid sat beside him but leaned over and winked at Emily. Joshua hugged his cushion more tightly and remained silent.

Gabriel stood near the center of the room. A large square, like shimmering water with tiny crystals twinkling, floated in front of the group. Thousands of midnight blue stars sparkled and disappeared. He threw his arms wide. "Here is our beloved Susan's R.I.D."

"Nice touch, Gabriel," Joshua said.

"It looks to be the work of some jinn," Alter added with deep worry in his voice.

Images began to emerge. Taps played as columns of military personnel lined a path. Thousands of grieving people stood behind them, respectfully watching six white horses pull a caisson with a flag-draped coffin on it.

"Hey, that looks like Arlington," Joshua said. "Were you in the military, Old Fairy?"

"No ..." Susan said slowly. "But my mother was." She sat mesmerized by the silvery screen. "Wait just one minute. This looks like President John F. Kennedy's funeral!"

"So sorry! Wrong one!" Gabriel fiddled with unseen controls. "I can just imagine who is behind this, but never mind. I will deal with this later." The images disappeared and new colors and images began to coalesce.

"Sail away, sail away, sail away," drifted up and around the room.

"Enya?" said Emily. Susan bobbed her head.

And then, "May it be an evening star shines down upon you." A lone rider on a white horse led the funeral procession. People lined the street, some holding signs that said, "Fairies go to Fairy Heaven" or "We love you Fairy Susan. R.I.P."

"Oh, look at that one," enthused Susan, wiping away tears that weren't there.

"Fairy-Heart, Merry-heart, we love you" was painted in rainbow colors with tiny fairies scattered throughout one sign held high by a gay couple hoping a TV camera would pan their way. Bored camera operators and reporters chatted, oblivious. The sun shone, but dark, swollen clouds were gathering.

"It looks like a festival in Jaipur," Sunita said excitedly. Loudspeakers continued to play Enya along the route.

"Susan, there are so many people wearing fairies on their dresses and T-shirts. Are they all your creations?" Emily said.

"Most are, my dear, but there are some rip-offs. A situation one of my lawyers was dealing with when I made transition."

"Died. You died, Susan." This from Joshua.

Groups of pale young women wearing long, flowing fairy dresses were dancing in circles, handing flowers to those who stood on the sidelines. A woman with curly blond hair hanging down to her waist was playing a small harp. She was seated on another white horse.

"How many white horses were used in this funeral performance?" Joshua asked innocently.

"Shhh. The best part is coming soon." Susan leaned forward.

The mayor of San Diego, looking uncomfortable but wearing a determined smile, walked behind a Native American whose massive drum had coyotes painted on the sides.

"Who is that man behind the drummer?" Emily hoped her tone was respectful.

"Oh, he is the mayor. I contributed to his campaign last year and asked that, in the unlikely event I transcended ..." Joshua looked heavenward but kept quiet. Susan narrowed her eyes. "In the unlikely event I transcended, would he take part in my transition ceremony? He happily agreed. I know all of you haven't had the invaluable experience of the rich and various traditions I've experienced, but if you notice the coyote that's painted on the side of that Indian's drum,"— her voice slowed dramatically—"he is a *trickster*. I believe death is a trickster."

Sunita turned to her. "What religion or tradition teaches that death is a trickster?"

"I made it up!" Susan smiled proudly.

"Too much!" Joshua said. "Not only do you pillage and plunder from all the sky-daddy religions out there, cherry-picking what will fit into your privileged, vacuous life, but now you're fucking making things up?"

"Ah, excuse me, but aren't you privileged as well?" Emily said.

"Comparatively, sure, but I don't go around adding more myths and lies to the myths and lies that have kept people on their everlasting fucking knees for eons."

Gabriel had paused Susan's R.I.D. He stood in perfect stillness.

Alter got slowly to his feet and stood before Joshua.

"Young man, I believe it is time for you to be quiet. I do not understand all of what you have been saying, but it sounds disrespectful. Be the good boy God wants you to be." He walked carefully back to his seat. Gabriel's eyes were warm as he watched the former fugitive.

"May we continue?" Susan's voice quavered.

Two people, one male and one female of unknown spiritual origins, walked on either side of a massive picture. A portrait of a younger and slimmer Susan was turning back and forth toward onlookers as the two walked down the street.

"You Americans! This is too much!" Khalid was snorting with laughter.

"This must have cost a great deal of money. Money that could have been well used by the poor." Sunita sat rigidly.

"'Come on baby, don't fear the reaper.' That song is so familiar!" Emily's blue eyes were dancing.

Reinhardt was making strange noises but managed to choke out, "It's 'Don't Fear the Reaper!'"

Susan gasped. "Oh, it must be some silly mistake. There're supposed to be bagpipes at this point in the processional playing 'The Skye Boat Song' followed by 'Amazing Grace.'"

Pipers came into view. As the skirling music grew louder, Joshua and Khalid doubled up with laughter, clutching each other for support. "Highway to Hell" followed by "Running with the Devil" played to stunned onlookers.

"What are they playing? What are they playing?" Susan was frantic. And then her face darkened. "I can't believe *she* would show her narrow, ugly horse face!" She stood shouting at the panel. A white, riderless horse trotted in front of the horse-drawn caisson that carried Susan's ashes. Richly colored cloths with Mayan, astrological, and Native American symbols and motifs were embroidered along the edge. Directly behind, pulling a small fluffy creature on a leash, walked Susan's sister and her sister's daughter.

"Is she smiling? That bitch!"

"May it be when darkness falls, your heart will be …" The ethereal sounds of Enya were drowned out by the pipers. Susan's sister assumed a look of shock, but something wasn't quite right as her face filled the large panel.

"She. Is. Smirking! She rigged this whole thing. Look at her with that stupid mutt of hers. Bringing it to my beautiful funeral. My perfect funeral!" Susan wailed.

Alter patted her knee and Emily put an arm around her shoulder. Joshua and Khalid were using every bit of willpower they had to suppress laughter that was threatening to erupt.

Reinhardt shook his head sadly. "She must be a very fearful, angry woman."

The caisson was nearing the end of Harritt Road which led to Lake Jennings on the outskirts of San Diego. Susan had obtained permission for her ashes to be scattered on the lake. A large flat-topped rock marked the entry point. Another harpist, a handsome, well-muscled and well-oiled young man, sat on the rock playing "Let it Be."

"There they are!" Susan pointed excitedly at her daughters. "See my beautiful girls? Oh my, I feel so sad. Look at them!"

Susan's daughters indeed looked sad but also very angry. Just as the caisson reached the lake, Susan's sister's dog broke away and ran toward the horses. Startled by the snapping bundle of fur, they reared. The coffin slid slowly and majestically onto the narrow bank of the lake, where it tipped drunkenly and hit a rock. The coffin lid popped open, and the urn tumbled out and cracked apart.

The harpist stopped playing. No one moved.

In the realm with Gabriel, no one moved either.

"Turn it off. Turn it off NOW!!!" Susan screamed and bolted for the stairway.

Quick-thinking bystanders settled the horses, but others from the crowd rushed the pipers and started punching them and grabbing the offending instruments. Still others linked arms and sang "In the Arms of an Angel." Meanwhile, the three spiritual people chosen to say final words and offer blessings were crouched at the edge of the lake, scooping ashes up from the mud and flinging them into the lake. They dumped the remaining contents of the urn into the water, rinsed their hands, and gave moving if hasty tributes. The screen flickered and vanished.

All of the watchers with Gabriel sat motionless.

Emily jumped up and faced the group, her face suffused with fury. "If any one of you, and I mean any single one of you," she pointed her finger at each of them in turn, "makes Susan feel worse than she already feels, I will hunt you down!" She dashed after Susan and followed her up the stairway.

"Well now." Gabriel brought his hands together. "Who would like to be the next to view their R.I.D.?"

In unison, five heads were shaking. Gabriel spun around so they would not see his radiant smile.

"This is going to go viral," Joshua said quietly.

Chapter 15: Contact Instructions

Susan had revenge in her heart.

The next morning, they were back in the kitchen having breakfast. All of them were being extra gentle with her. Even Joshua offered her some of his extra crispy bacon. When she declined, he joked, "Your watery yoghurt does look rather delicious."

Emily gave him a warm smile, acknowledging his attempt to be kind. The first to arrive, she had chosen the music. The strains of ABBA's greatest hits filled the room. "What do you think of this contact business?" Swaying her shoulders to "Dancing Queen," Emily tapped her finger on the scroll beside her plate. Beside everyone's plate sat a scroll, with *Contact Instructions* inscribed in gold lettering on the outside.

"I certainly will not entertain such nonsense. It is a trick of some jinns to be sure." Khalid speared a piece of meat and chewed loudly. "This music is too lively for breakfast."

"You mean too happy, eh?" Emily swiped a forkful of buckwheat pancake around the plate to capture the last of the maple syrup. "I thought we could stand something cheerful today."

Susan sat up straight and put down her fork. "Does anyone mind if I read the instructions aloud?" Without waiting for an answer, she stood up and unfurled her scroll. Her voice, after an initial wobble, was clear and strong.

Dear ones (Susan read), this scroll gives methods and instructions for making contact with your loved ones. Alter, I am sorry to say that you are on our no-contact list for the time being. However, you will be going with the rest on missions. You will pose no flight risk on these missions because you will be in a protective group-energy setting. Now, on to the instructions.

Standard Contact Methods, revised edition. Now commonly referred to as Method of Contact, or M.O.C.

Use your new, after-life vibration to affect tech devices! You can cause a favorite song shared by you and a loved one to play on radio stations or on what I think is called an iPod. Or you can post a mysterious message on Facebook or Twitter. Send a text! Of course, you may also turn on and off tech devices or create mysterious problems. One word of caution, though. Recent reports indicate that some have been a bit sloppy in aligning their vibration with tech devices. This has resulted in what is being called "computer viruses."

Smell is an easy and effective method for making contact with a loved one. Did you have a favorite flower or perfume? Did you smoke? Or did you have a particular scent that is recognizable by certain people? If so, simply emit smell! This is a gentle way of making contact, and people are generally not scared off by these smells. It doesn't even matter if the smell is pleasant or unpleasant. Emit away, I say!

Knock things about! This method requires skill and should be attempted only by those who have received proper instructions. If done with an overly heavy hand, it can result in light posts being toppled or massive chandeliers crashing to the floor and scaring cats. Really, the list is endless and causes much distress to loved ones. Too light a hand and nothing happens. The right touch, and it opens up the heart of your loved one to your presence. Please receive training and aim for small things, such as doors slamming, doorbells ringing, or overturned rabbit cages.

Missing items can also redirect your loved ones' thoughts to you, although this method can be a bit stressful to those left behind. But what isn't stressful to them these days?! Jewelry and car keys are common items to rearrange, but you may want to consider passports and favorite coffee cups. Often they will ask for your help to find the item you've tucked under the sofa. This will offer an opening for you to make contact. It also can provide fun while you watch them search for the item you have moved. You may use this on disgruntled relatives, friends who have betrayed you, teachers who gave you poor marks, or police officers who gave you traffic tickets or had your car towed.

Repeat numbers such as 11, 22 or 333 on digital clocks. You can use any combination of repeating numbers to grab their attention. Now this may seem overly obvious, but it does grab attention, and attention is increasingly short these days! At first, they may not know it is you. Usually there is a tendency to attribute this so-called coincidence to other beings, but if you persevere they will realize who is causing it. Some spirit-people use this method in combination with any of the other suggested methods.

Show up in their dreams! This method is fairly easy, even for novices, and it allows you to communicate freely and visit often. You may go back to a time with them that was mutually enjoyable. A shared picnic, perhaps, or that romantic walk on the beach. Or you may take them somewhere new. The list is endless. A practical suggestion is to take them somewhere you both wanted to go but did not get to. At this stage, you can easily align your vibration to roughly the same frequency as theirs while they are sleeping. Yes, my dear ones, the vibrations of spirit-people are similar to those of people in deep sleep. One word of caution, though. If they were drinking heavily before they fell asleep, their dream memory will be greatly distorted. Frankly, if you see them drinking before going to bed, it is a waste of your eternal time to visit.

Animals. This M.O.C. is especially effective and enjoyable for animal lovers. Naturally, cats and dogs are chosen most often, but you can choose horses, cows, goats, birds, giraffes—really any animal with which you or your loved one felt a kinship. Animals are much more aligned with this higher vibration than humans, which makes their behavior easy to influence. Some commonly used ways of making contact through an animal is having it focus intently in one direction for a prolonged period. This is particularly effective if a picture of you is nearby for the animal to fixate on. If it is normally sedentary, you might influence it to be hyperactive. Should you choose a household pet, have it sit in a chair that you used to sit on. Or if your loved one is finally getting around to clearing out your clothes, you can have the chosen animal sit stubbornly on a favorite sweater. If the animal happens to be a cat, this is an easy one for novices to try. Have fun with our four-legged brothers and sisters!

Send them a thought! Although most living people will dismiss a thought sent from you, it is still worth a go. Simply send whatever message you wish them to know. To help with believability, try sending a story or secret that only you and the receiver knows. For example, perhaps you are the only one who knows they cheated on their income tax. Do not worry, Alter, you do not need to know what this means. This is best done when the receiver is tired or feeling a bit hopeless.

Small coins. Now, I have asked around and no one I queried knows where this current afterlife contact idea originates. No matter, it is something that people are excited about and will respond to. So, leaving pennies and other small change around for your loved one to see will wake them up to your presence.

Cloud formations. These are fun! Arrange clouds to resemble your face. This is especially rewarding if they are staring idly out of an airplane window. This method does require skill and practice, but do not worry. If at first your cloud formations resemble an elephant or some deity, practice!

Physical manifestations. Please forget what you may have seen in movies. Alter, we are aware you do not know what a movie is. Some of you will be eager to try this, as it offers the most obvious way to let others know of your whereabouts. However, this method of making contact is the most difficult and necessitates direct instructions from a consulting angel.

Cheers and Blessings
Your Navigator
Gabriel

Susan rerolled her scroll and sat down, her filmy dress billowing slightly. Sinking a spoon into a bowl of fruit salad, she stopped with it halfway to her mouth, a thoughtful look on her face.

"So, what do you think?" Emily said to the group. "Is anyone thinking about making contact? With the exception of manifesting physically, it sounds straightforward."

Susan set the spoon down. "I would like to try first."

Reinhardt glanced up from his sausages. With his mouth half full, he said, "I do not like this idea of contact."

Emily ignored him and turned to Susan. "I think you should go first. How does everyone else feel about Susan making contact first?"

With the exception of Reinhardt and Khalid, the rest agreed. Sunita asked gently, "Who will you make contact with, Susan? Your beautiful daughters?"

"My sister." Susan took a sip of green tea.

Chapter 16: Susan Makes Contact

When they had walked through the Great Unnamed Room before breakfast, there had been no sign of Gabriel. Alter had remarked that maybe he had left them and, with grief in his voice, added that perhaps he would remain cut off forever from his Hannah.

"Oh I'm sure our Angel of Death will return," Joshua said. But as they re-entered the room now, there was still no sign of him. The Ugly Brown Birds sat quietly, staring at the group as they arrived.

Reinhardt walked purposely over to the cage; Reinhardt, in fact, walked purposely wherever he went. A scrap of parchment attached to the cage had three words scrawled in loopy letters.

"Press the button," Reinhardt read aloud.

"Press the button?" Alter croaked. "What does that mean?"

Sunita pointed. "Look! over there!" In the middle of a café table was an old-fashioned hotel buzzer. Sunita and Khalid got to it first.

Khalid crouched down to inspect it. "Guess this is what he means by button. But what if it's a trick? What if it's a jinn trying to create some terrible problem?"

"Oh yes," Susan said with a wise nod. "It could be the work of some lower astral entity."

Flashing her an irritated look, Joshua strode over and pressed the button.

The same shimmering panel that featured Susan's calamitous R.I.D. appeared. She flinched, but her brow cleared when she saw the handsome face of Gabriel on the screen. From what she could make out, he seemed to be dressed all in black. His eyes were lined with kohl and his nose was pierced with a gold ring.

"Greetings, my dear ones! Sorry I cannot join you, but I was called away on a bit of an emergency. Hope to be back soon. In the meantime, you are to watch the following for further instructions on how to make contact. Susan, I understand you want to go first. Please remember some of that love and light stuff you learned before coming here. The Council and I strongly discourage anyone from attempting physical contact until I am back."

A loud crack offscreen was followed by a thunderous roar. Gabriel squinted over his shoulder but quickly turned back to give them a cheery wave. "Cheers and blessings." The screen disappeared.

"God willing, if I am ever reunited with my friends and family, never will they believe me," Alter said.

Khalid laughed. "You are right on that one, old man. What was that? A bomb or an earthquake?"

Reinhardt rubbed thoughtfully at his eye patch. "The world is in a terrible mess. I am afraid we are entering a dark age from which we will take a very long time to emerge."

"You Buddhists are so glum, always focusing on suffering. I gave it a try, but it was too depressing," Susan said.

"What *didn't* you try?" said Joshua. At Emily's look, he made a show of throwing his hands in front of his face and backing away.

"Madam," Reinhardt said with more intensity than he intended, "I can safely say you do not understand Buddhism."

"So where are these instructions?" Joshua said.

"Let's press the button again," Sunita suggested as she leaned over the café table and pushed. The shimmering panel dropped down. Nine trumpets blared. The Ugly Brown Birds shrieked. Seven pairs of hands clapped over ears.

"So happy we got to keep our hearing," Khalid shouted. The music stopped, and a voice like Gabriel's, only much, much deeper, spoke. "Welcome, my dear ones, to our simple tutorial on making contact."

The only image was a rolling script the voice was reading. "We will cover all the methods save physical contact. I encourage you to practice by yourself and with others before making any actual attempt. A few on the Council thought Alter might still be a, how did they put it? Oh yes, a flight risk. I disagree, but who am I to say? Just because I have been here for centuries and centuries ..." The voice resumed with more enthusiasm.

"So. It is all very simple. Your vibrations are high. Without getting technical, this means with a little practice you can raise them a bit higher and away you'll go! You have the good luck to be in a room that makes this easy."

"Oh yeah, we're the luckiest bastards around," Joshua muttered. The others shushed him.

"And due to some inter-realm co-operation, we have made this easier than ever! Around your neck you will find a disc with a button."

They all looked down. A simple silver disc on a braided silver cord hung to the precise center of their hearts. In the center of the disc, a tiny bright blue button sparkled.

"I was only a kid in the eighties, but suddenly I feel like going to a disco," Joshua said.

Alter tentatively picked his up. "This would buy a lot of matzo. But if I cannot make contact, why waste it on me?"

"Lovely, aren't they? Alter, I am afraid yours does not work, but we did not want you to feel left out. Now, for the rest of you, we have only four rules. Rule one: You must take a companion on your contact adventure. Rule two: You may stay no longer than twenty-three minutes. Your button will flash a warning at precisely twenty minutes, and you must press it to return to this realm within a minute or two or you will be whisked away, which is a nasty experience. Rule three: You and your traveling companion are to press the button to enter and exit the contact experience at the same time. Rule four: To begin, you must follow five easy steps:

Step one: Sit quietly. Lotus position is ideal (Reinhardt, please explain this to Alter).

Step two: Choose your method of contact and focus on the person you wish to contact.

Step three: Recall a memory you shared with the person and summon as much emotional energy as you can about the shared memory.

Step four: Focus on the center of your forehead and use the energy located there to concentrate on the person's whereabouts.

Step five: Press the button. And that's it! A copy of these instructions is waiting for you in your rooms, but meanwhile we've left a scroll on the far side of the bird cage. Does anyone wish to volunteer to go with Susan? Or have you chosen someone you would like to accompany you?"

Reinhardt fetched the scroll and set it on the café table beside the button. Susan was already in the lotus position. She looked around the group. "My heart choice would be Emily, but I think it's time for Joshua to acquire some spiritual education."

"Oh, for fucking fuck's sake, why me? This is too much to ask. Way too much! I'm an atheist. This is all just fucked up brain chemistry crap happening!"

Susan gave him a sweet smile and said, "It will be an adventure, Joshua, a spiritual adventure. Aren't you curious? You remind me of an old boyfriend. He loved to tease. He was a bit of an ass but sharp as a tack. Where's your spirit of adventure?"

Joshua paced. "It died with me. Oh, what the hell. I'll go. But promise me you won't break into singing Kumbaya or recite Desiderata."

Susan laughed. "I promise. Ready?"

Joshua grabbed a cushion off the bench and assumed a lotus position opposite Susan. He grimaced but nodded. The rest stood back to watch.

"Should I share the memory with Joshua before we begin?"

The disembodied voice said hurriedly, "Yes, yes, sorry. Forgot to mention that."

All sound ceased. The Ugly Brown Birds held their breath.

"Guess we're on our own," Joshua said with a bit of a shake in his voice. "So where are we going?"

"San Diego. My sister and I were in our early teens. I'd just sold my first painting and spent the entire twenty dollars on a pair of suede hot-pants, and I was excited to wear them to school on picture day. But when I went to try them on, they were destroyed. My rotten fat bitch of a sister had worn them first, and she'd stretched the soft suede, ripped the seams and lost the brass buttons. And you know what she did? She laughed. She told me they were garbage anyway! My mother tried to calm things down, but my sister never apologized. That's the memory, Joshua. Sunita, dear, would you read out the steps? I want to make sure we get this good and right."

In a clear voice, Sunita read out each step. With each one, Joshua looked more and more nervous.

The sepia light in the room began to change, and blue lightning streaked up to the vaulted ceilings and down to the stone floor. The room's energy was intensifying. The soles of their feet tingled, and a high-pitched whine, just at the edge of their hearing, buzzed like cicadas in August. Sunita paused. It was time. "Step five. Press the button," she whispered.

Susan and Joshua pressed their buttons.

"Where are we?"

"It's the Castaway Café. It's a popular place for actors to meet." Susan looked around eagerly.

"Why are we here? Remember, twenty-three minutes."

"I know, I know. I used to meet my boyfriends here, way back when I wanted to become an actress. But you're right, let's get to my sister's house."

"This is definitely weird and kind of fun," Joshua said. "No one can see or hear us. Feels free and light, and I feel fearless. I don't remember ever feeling light or fearless."

A little girl was standing on her chair shouting, "Mommy, we can fly. All of us! We can fly!"

"Yes, with pixie dust," her mother replied, scrolling her phone.

"No, Mommy, no pixie dust. We need wings, and then we can fly!" She was flapping her arms to show her mother. Other patrons smiled. So did Joshua and Susan. "Mommy, I have to pee and poop. Mommy, do you see that old fairy lady and that man?"

"Oh my!" Susan clutched her chest. "I forgot that young children can sometimes see spirits more easily than—well, we better get going."

They floated through a harried waiter who was carrying a tray of drinks. Shivering, he looked around, dropped the tray and sent ice cubes flying. A young man managed to record it on his phone, but as he was laughing, Susan scooped up a few ice cubes and dumped them on his head.

The grass was so neatly landscaped, it looked as though each blade of grass was measured. Flowers were planted precisely two centimeters apart. Her sister's oversized white house sat in perfect order on the perfect lawn.

"Looks like she's preparing for a dinner party. This couldn't be better!" Susan whispered.

"Why are we whispering?" Joshua whispered back.

Catering trucks were arriving, and trays of food and cases of champagne were being carried inside. A florist's van had just pulled out of the circular driveway.

In a normal voice, Susan continued. "Her noodle husband is a political wannabe. He's been trying to make inroads for years. Elbows his way onto local TV news shows when a big story is breaking. You know, the know-it-all pundit. My sister has zero talent of her own, so she'd be thrilled to have her husband win a seat. We'd hear her bragging all the way up to our realm! No doubt she's invited the most influential people—people who can help her husband get elected. Come on, let's go inside."

"So fucking cool," Joshua said as they stood in the great room. "I don't mean this house. It's ordinary rich-white-person shit, but this feeling. Yeah, I said *feeling*."

Susan was not listening.

"There she is!" she whispered.

Susan's sister whipped her head around and yelled, "Has anyone left a window open? I feel a draft! We don't want our honored guests to get a chill." The galleried foyer was crowded with extra draped chairs.

"Minutes, Susan, minutes." Joshua tapped his wrist.

"I know. I'm going to get close to her and give her a big, nasty fart. I've been focusing on the garbage heaps outside of Mumbai, pig sties in Kansas, pulp and paper mills in Ontario. It's this combination I hope to emulate." She waggled her bottom.

Joshua raised his eyebrows and laughed. Susan went up to her sister and stuck out her tongue. She let one go.

"What in the name of all that is holy?!" her sister screamed. "Did something die?"

Flowers wilted. An elegant tray of exotic fruits rotted. Joshua bent over laughing. Susan winked at him. "Do you want to give it a try?"

"Don't need to ask twice!"

For the next few minutes, Susan and Joshua floated from room to room. Soon the entire house smelled like the garbage heaps of Mumbai, the pig sties of Kansas, the pulp and paper mills of Ontario.

Tears rolled down Susan's sister's face. "Someone, anyone, do something! They'll be here soon!"

Her husband walked in the door, then stepped smartly outside and slammed it behind him. The catering staff scrambled to their vans and spun away. Arriving guests backed away, silk scarves or elegant sleeves covering their faces. Even with doors and windows closed, smells were seeping out of the house. Neighbors, venturing over to inquire about the odors, dashed for home before they got half-way up the walk.

Susan's sister was devastated. "What did I ever do to deserve this?" she wailed.

Joshua and Susan laughed so hard they almost missed the flashing blue buttons.

"Angels farting! I never learned about this in any of my spiritual studies! Thank you, Joshua. This was perfect."

"Remember, we are not fuck—we are not angels. Okay, let's press our buttons and see what happens." Finger poised, Joshua said, "Susan, thank you."

They pressed the buttons.

Nothingness. No feeling, no thought, no body. Joshua and Susan were simply back in the room. Sunita and Emily looked crestfallen.

"It didn't work?" Emily cried.

Susan caught Joshua's eye, and they both started to laugh.

"It worked like a charm!"

"It was the fucking best!"

Sunita frowned. "You just left and now you are back. We have to assume nothing happened."

"Must be that time thing Gabriel talks about. A trick." Khalid sounded disappointed.

"The more plausible explanation is that time in this realm is simply different from time on earth." Reinhardt spoke as though to himself. "All of us have had the experience of falling asleep and then waking, thinking it's been hours, only to discover that only a few minutes have passed."

Susan was nodding. "Yes, time, frequencies, vibrations, the speed human eyes can see—"

Emily interrupted her. "Tell us what happened?"

Chapter 17: Who do you miss?

"Why don't we go back to the kitchen?" Reinhardt suggested. "Some *kuchen* may help your memory, Susan."

Alter shook his bony finger at Joshua and Susan. "I know for some strange reason you do not believe in God, my Joshua, but I prayed to him while you and Susan were gone. Now you are here, gone and back."

"Thank you, Alter. I feel fantastic," Joshua said. He turned and started for the kitchen, but Alter caught his arm.

"Let us walk together. My son, your name is very important in the Torah. Joshua was a great hero."

"Sorry, Alter. My mom and dad named me after the Joshua Tree, not the Biblical hero. They swore I was conceived under the stars in Joshua Tree National Park. Maybe it was my birth that transformed them from crazy, happy hippies to the neurotic messes I know so well. Knew. If it makes you feel better, my dad is very religious now."

Alter nodded as he trudged beside Joshua. "My son, I did not understand much of what you said, but I am happy, or as happy as this old man knows how to be, to hear your father is religious."

Assorted cakes, cookies and fruit were laid out on the long wooden table. Each of the seven took the same seat they had from the beginning. Susan reached for a tall piece of dark chocolate cake, but the cake wouldn't cooperate. She sighed and picked up a willing apple. Reinhardt bit into a ginger cookie.

"In Buddhism, we believe that any act of aggression comes from fear. Of course, Buddhists don't own this idea."

Susan put down her half-eaten apple. "Are you implying we acted aggressively? We just had a little fun." Joshua raised an eyebrow at her, opened his mouth and closed it again. "Besides, it was nothing compared to what that bitch did at my beautiful transition ceremony." She gave Reinhardt a dirty look and hitched her chair closer to the table.

"So what did you do?" Sunita said.

Joshua couldn't contain himself any longer. "It was fucking fantabulous!"

"Ahem." Susan cleared a throat that didn't need clearing. "I believe this is my story."

"You're right. Just got a little excited. If anyone wants me to come along with them to make contact, I'm in."

"I'll give it some thought," Emily said drily.

"Anyway, back to me and my story," Susan said, shooting Joshua a look. He saluted her and grabbed two chocolate cream donuts. Her eyes slid toward Reinhardt as she said haughtily, "As most of you are aware, this was not about resolution. It was simply making contact, and that is what Joshua and I did."

Susan told her story, adding embellishments about her sister's weight and the elegance of the flowers wilted by the stench. She acted out the part of her sister and enlisted Joshua to act the parts of staff, her brother-in-law and some of the neighbors. Joshua threw himself into the caricatures with happy abandon. Eyes streaming, Sunita pressed her hand to her mouth in a weak attempt to hide her laughter.

Khalid sat back and grinned. "That would make a fantastic skit."

Alter peered into the laughing faces one after another. The laughter puzzled him, but he was enjoying the feeling of community.

Reinhardt again spoke as though to himself. "Even though I feel this was quite aggressive, it is amusing. Deborah and I pulled off good practical jokes when we were together. I miss her."

Six heads swiveled in his direction. Up until this moment, the others had thought him wise but inscrutable.

Sunita looked across the table at Emily. "Who do you miss, Emily?"

"I guess I miss my fiancé."

Joshua leaned over. "You guess?"

"Oh come on, there are plenty of people I miss. I really loved him, you know …"

Joshua leaned back. "Well, my shrinking brain cells miss my Gillian. Strange though, I've been thinking about my business partner a lot. Wonder what he's up to? Poor bastard will be so fucking freaked out with me, ah, dying." He cast his eyes around the table. "Okay, let's go forward with our little enquiry. Khalid, my mysterious Muslim friend, who do you miss the most?"

Khalid shrugged.

"Really, man, you don't miss anyone?" Joshua slapped both hands on the table. They made no sound.

"Well, of course I miss my parents. They were very good parents."

"Wow, don't go all emotional on us, Khalid. Didn't you have a girlfriend? Good looking, successful—you got the goods, know what I mean? Or were you in some kind of arranged marriage thing?"

"On Prince Edward Island," Emily said pointedly, "we know when to allow others their privacy."

Joshua threw his hands up. "Just asking the guy some questions. Excuse me, Miss Perfect Canadian, eh?" He chortled at his own joke. "But Susan, what about you? Who do you miss the most?"

Happy to be noticed, Susan replied, "I didn't realize it until after I, you know—"

"Died," Reinhardt said.

"I believe it was I who was asked the question. I miss Raj terribly, of course."

Joshua clapped his hands. The room did not shake. "Now we're getting somewhere. An exotic Indian lover! Nice one, Susan but maybe not a total surprise. You old hippies always seem to go international."

"Raj was my dog, smartass. He was my most loyal ..." her chin quivered. "He accompanied me on so many spiritual journeys."

"Oh fucking Christ, a spiritual dog." Joshua checked to see if anyone else supported his faux outrage. Reinhardt laughed quietly. Alter listened intently, his thin, crooked hands in his lap.

Emily glared at Joshua and placed her hand over Susan's. "Go on. Some of us understand."

Susan bestowed what she hoped was a brave smile. "Throughout my life, I suffered so many betrayals. Love and loss. Even my own daughters." She paused. "Raj was far more than a dog. I mean, spell *dog* backwards. G-o-d."

Alter's face was shocked and pale. As he pushed his chair back, it fell sideways.

"Madam Susan." He shook his long gnarled finger at her. "Madam Susan." He walked out of the room.

Chapter 18: Sunita Makes Contact

"I want to go back. Khalid, would you be my guide?"

It was breakfast and Sunita was helping herself to a paratha with vegetable curry, curd and pickles.

"Sorry, my sister. I don't agree with this contact business." Khalid took a sip of his rich, dark coffee and popped a few dates into his mouth. In front of him, small plates and bowls contained fragrant cheeses, honey, helwa, fuhl, eggs and a stack of naan and chapati. Khalid was still amazed he had an appetite but was resigned to the idea it was another trick of Munkar and Nakeer.

Sunita sat back, regarding him. "Khalid, what do you think is happening here? Do you still think you are being tested?"

Khalid hoped if he showed great interest in his breakfast, she would move on to someone else. A quick sideways glance was met by her steady gaze. He swallowed.

"Sunita, I'm not sure. But my unsureness also can be a test."

Sunita didn't know why she wanted Khalid to accompany her, but it felt right and she trusted that feeling. She wished she had learned to trust her feelings more when she was alive.

"Khalid, what harm can it do? If you are being tested, what difference would one little excursion make?"

Susan tapped Sunita's shoulder. "My dear, I would be honored to join you on your sacred journey."

Khalid scoffed. "Susan, your contact was anything but sacred."

"That is unkind and unfair. I was seeking karmic balance, and I achieved it. That, my darlings, is sacred."

Sunita lifted a hennaed hand to rearrange her scarf, and Susan stepped back, brushing nonexistent crumbs from her dress before returning to her seat.

"I trust you, Khalid. There are people I really need to see. I may even be able to help them."

"You do know how much your people and my people have fought with each other? We are worlds apart in just about everything."

"Oh, but we inhabit the same world now." Sunita's voice was gentle.

Khalid looked to the others, but no one seemed inclined to save him.

"It may seem as though we're in the same world, but this too could be part of the test." Not for the first time, Khalid thought of his studies of the Holy Qur'an, the teachings of the Imam, his parents' devotion and help in furthering his understanding, and the teachings of the Prophet Muhammad, peace be upon him.

He was surprised to hear his thoughts spoken aloud. "I just can't make sense of this. Why would I be in my grave with an old Jew, a Buddhist, a Christian, a Hindu, a New Ager and an atheist?"

No one said anything. Khalid turned to Sunita. "So, where are we going?"

They were standing behind Sunita's secretary, who was scrolling through Facebook. The young woman shivered and pulled her sweater closer.

"I thought after my death she would find more worthwhile things to do."

"See there." Khalid pointed at the screen. "It's a memorial page dedicated to you by some man named Arun."

"I can't believe it! What does it say? Never mind. Let me see."

The secretary shivered again and looked around to see where the draft was coming from.

Sunita read aloud. "This page is dedicated to the beautiful and kind spirit of Sunita Gupta, who died on August twentieth. She is presumed drowned after falling from slippery rocks. Her body has yet to be found. Her beloved fiancé, Arun, lovingly dedicates this page to Sunita. Please perform Yagna."

Sunita and Khalid read quickly to the bottom. There were over 2,600 reactions and 1,800 comments. At the top of the page, a photo showed Arun and Sunita smiling.

Sunita was trembling.

"Sunita, you're shaking! In our current state, I didn't know this was possible. What's upsetting you?"

She moved away from Khalid and her assistant and performed the Vrikasana, the calming Tree Pose.

"What do you want to do? What can I do? Please tell me what's so upsetting."

Sunita brought her body back from the pose. "We have to get to Jaipur, Khalid. There is someone there who may be able to help find my body."

"But why not appear in a dream or vision to your parents?"

Sunita's grief was almost too much for Khalid to bear. "It would be too painful to appear to my wonderful parents." She stepped close to him, her eyes glinting with ferocity. "We will also bring my murderer to justice."

"You were murdered?! Yes, yes, of course we'll go to Jaipur. What does this wretched man look like?" Khalid's face was pale.

Sunita gestured at the screen. "The man who posted the loving tribute to me."

"Your fiancé?" Khalid did not try to hide his shock. "Okay, let's go to Jaipur."

"This is really lovely. I am so happy he has done well for himself." Sunita ran her graceful fingers over vases as she walked around a plain yet elegant bedroom. Khalid stood at the foot of a four-poster bed.

A tall young man walked in and sat on the edge of the bed. On a nightstand stood a photo of him and a kind-faced, pretty young woman.

"I think he is engaged to her," Sunita whispered to Khalid.

When the man picked up an iPad, Khalid leaned over to see it. "He's reading about your death, Sunita. Looks like he's read numerous articles about you. How do you know him?"

"I used to spend long holidays with my dadi—that's my grandmother. This is Jamal, and his mother was one of the cooks Dadi employed. They were from the Puppet Makers Slum. It is famous for its puppets, but it is still a slum. So Dadi forbade our relationship." Sunita's cheeks were wet. "I believe he was my destiny, Khalid. It is terrible karma to deny someone their destiny."

Jamal reached into the top drawer of the nightstand and rummaged until he retrieved a picture. He smoothed it out and stared at it.

No longer looking at Jamal, Khalid was transfixed by Sunita. "You look brighter—brighter and bigger. Sunita, your essence is filling the room! Is this what westerners call your aura?"

Sunita nodded. Khalid stood as a witness, watching without the resistance that fear and doubt generate.

Jamal kissed the photo of a young Sunita and Jamal sitting under an ancient Banyan tree. For a moment he held the picture to his heart before propping it against the bedside lamp. He sighed, pulled back the bedcovers and switched off the light.

The moment felt sacred and suspended. "Khalid, do you know the symbolism of the Banyan tree? It means immortality. And one leaf is said to be a resting place for Krishna."

As Jamal slipped into sleep, Sunita closed her eyes.

Jamal walked with Sunita along the edge of a wide river. They held hands, laughing and talking. His feet did not touch the uneven ground. Faster and faster they moved, not quite walking, not quite floating. When they reached a rocky cove, Sunita pointed.

"You are here, my darling. Come and see. This is where I am."

Jamal broke his gaze from Sunita's glowing face and looked down past an outcropping of rocks. Cobalt-blue fabric billowed with the flow of the river, and Sunita's beautiful head lay trapped between two rocks, her long, dark hair floating on the water as her sari billowed. "Jamal, my love, please tell them. Tell the Sydney police that Arun, my fiancé, did this. The police will know once they find my body. Tell them, Jamal." Sunita grew more luminous. "I love you, Jamal, and I know you love me. Take that love and add it to the love you feel toward your intended." For the briefest of moments she enveloped him in pure bliss.

In Jaipur, it was 3:11 a.m. Jamal shot up in bed, bathed in sweat and staring into the darkness. He knew what he had to do. Calming his breath, he picked up the phone.

"Sunita, we have to go." The medallions were flashing.

"Khalid, I want to see my parents."

"There's no time. Come, we have to go. Now!"

Through time that never really was, they flew. Through space that never really was, they returned.

Joshua and Reinhardt had pushed together café tables so the group could hear Sunita recount her experience. Emily leaned forward in her chair, not wanting to miss a word.

"It seems silly to have these café tables when we can't even drink or eat out here. What's the point?" Susan said.

"Well, one good reason is that we only have our sense of smell in the kitchen. Aren't you listening to Sunita?" asked Joshua.

"Of course I'm listening!"

"Oh, I get it. Sunita had a more 'spiritual' experience and you're jealous." Joshua laughed.

"Don't be foolish," Susan hissed. "I took a very enlightening three-day workshop on listening. And I'm most certainly not jealous. You have the insight of a two-year-old goat."

Joshua very, very quietly bleated.

Sunita's soft voice was even softer than usual. "You know, he lived a life of almosts. He was almost nice enough. Almost handsome enough. Almost convinced me to marry him. And he was almost smart enough to get away with my murder."

It was some time before anyone spoke. The amber light of the inner courtyard was deep and rich, holding their quiet contemplation.

Chapter 19: Emily's Mother Visits a Medium

The paved walkway was cracked and broken, with scrawny weeds finding places to poke through the cracks. Emily's mother picked her way carefully. The small house was clad in tired beige siding, now mottled by drizzle that had started as she pushed open the gate. From one corner, a trellis leaned so drunkenly that she wondered how it still stood. She rang the doorbell, brushing moisture from her jacket. *The angels are weeping. Maybe my daughter is one of them. What would Emily think of me going to this woman?*

The rain left Emily untouched as she watched her mother. Joshua tried to gauge her feelings. Determining others' feelings was not his forte, a failing that had sometimes gotten him into trouble.

"Are you okay?"

"Yeah, I guess. Come on, let's see what this woman has to say."

Joshua had volunteered to accompany Emily. His latest theory was that he was not actually dead but in a coma. He'd explained this theory to the others, adding that, when he woke up, he'd write a novel detailing all his wacky experiences. So, he reasoned, coming with Emily would give him plenty more material.

"What the fuck is your mother doing here?"

"Keep up, Joshua."

"Come in, come in." At the open door stood a woman wearing purple yoga pants, a sequined top and bubblegum-pink Crocs. Her legs were skinny but her waist was thick. A gold butterfly clip held down wispy orange hair. Through her legs and out the open door dashed a small wirehaired dog, barking. Emily's mother froze.

"Oh, Mr. Oxford won't hurt you, dear." Mr. Oxford skidded to a stop and sniffed the visitor's shoes. Then he raised his nose to the air, sniffed all around and let out a high-pitched yelp. "Don't be so foolish, Mr. Oxford. What's wrong with you today?" The woman scooped him up.

"What kind of dog is he?" Emily's mother reached to stroke his stiff fur. In her experience, dog owners softened when you showed interest in their pets.

"I tell people he's Canadian—a bit of this and a bit of that. Like most of us. Come in, dear. You didn't come to see my dog."

Emily's mother stepped through the door and adjusted her eyes to the dimness. The woman looked at her appraisingly and extended a plump hand. "I'm Hazel. I'm sorry for your loss, but you'll soon see that your daughter is still very much around you. Come this way." She guided Emily's mother down a hallway and opened a door.

"This is what I call my Room of Remembrances, but it's much more than memories, as you'll soon see. You may sit in this chair." Hazel cleared away a pile of magazines and deposited them on the floor.

Emily's mother sat. She was surprised to see a Bible on a side table. *Emily, dear, sweet Emily would approve.* Her eyes filled.

Hazel settled into a chair opposite her. "Did you bring some of your daughter's things?"

"Her name is Emily." She dug into her handbag, retrieving a small pearl necklace, a pair of earrings and a medal.

"Yes, Emily." Hazel half closed her eyes. "Let's pray." Both women bowed their heads. Hazel's voice deepened. "Oh merciful Father, lead us to the spirit of dear departed Emily. If you cannot, please ask one of your great angels to assist us. Amen."

"Is this what I think it is? This scammy witch is going to pretend to connect with your so-called spirit?"

Emily moved closer to Hazel. "Don't judge, Joshua. Let's hear what she has to say."

Joshua rolled his eyes. "Did I just roll my eyes? I miss being able to tell."

"I'm not looking at you. Shhh … listen!"

Hazel leaned her head back. Her voice was a loud whisper. "I feel her close by."

"I think I'm rolling eyes again."

"Hush! I don't care!"

In the same loud whisper, Hazel added, "Yes, your daughter is here with us, and I believe she has brought someone with her."

Emily threw an "I told you so" smirk to Joshua.

"Do you know who's with her?" Emily's mother's voice held a tinge of panic. "Is this person good or evil?"

Hazel spoke with care. "I'm sure this other spirit is okay. Their vibration keeps fading out, though. It's as though they're not on the same frequency, a lower or lesser being. Did Emily own a cat?"

Emily guffawed.

Joshua scowled. "I still don't believe in this hocus pocus bullshit. It's yet another crazy story my poor brain in a coma is amusing itself with."

"Emily was allergic to cats," her mother said.

"Strange. This entity feels angry and male but not dangerous in any way."

Her mother's eyes widened as Hazel picked up the small necklace and fingered it reverently. Hazel's voice was hushed. "How old was Emily when you gave her this necklace?"

Her mother cleared her throat. "I didn't give it to her. Her father did when she was four years old. Emily treasured it. She treasured everything her father gave her. He could do no wrong in her eyes. Me, on the other hand …" She looked suddenly weary. "Perhaps I should explain. Emily's father died in a car accident when she was five. The night he died, Emily dreamed she was holding her father's hand, walking down a bright tunnel. According to Emily, her father was looking straight ahead and told her she had to go back. In the morning his car was found in a ditch with a tape of Emily singing 'You Are My Sunshine' playing over and over."

Emily could sense Joshua looking at her with intense sympathy. She gnawed her lip and kept her eyes on her mother.

Hazel sighed. She put the necklace down and picked up the earrings. "I see a little girl running and running. She is turning around and waving. Such a beautiful smile. Even with the braces."

Disappointment seeped into her mother's bones.

Joshua's eyebrows rose into a question as he mimed braces. Emily shook her head. He was tempted to gloat but could see she was crestfallen.

"Is something wrong?" Hazel looked uncertain.

A fierce rush of resentment and anger swept over Emily's mother. For a moment, she didn't know who she was angry with or why. Wild, unruly thoughts spun round and round. "Is Emily ignoring me, even in death? Is she with her father?" She stood up, knocking her purse from her lap.

"Dear, have I upset you? Please take a seat." Hazel picked up the purse and gave it to her.

Emily's mother sat, her chest hard and tight. She didn't want to have a panic attack in front of this woman. *What was I thinking, coming here?*

"I'll get us some tea." Hazel patted her shoulder. Emily's mother heard the soft thud of her Crocs as she made her way to the kitchen. Mr. Oxford whimpered and scampered alongside Hazel.

Emily crouched beside her mother. "Mom. Mom, I'm here. It's okay. I'm okay. You need to know how much I loved you. I will always love you. You did your best. I don't know why I closed off my heart. Maybe I blamed you for Daddy's death. I know that's crazy …" She curled her hand around her mother's. "We should have talked."

Emily's mother closed her eyes and let out a long, slow breath. A gentle peace swept through her. For the first time since Emily had died, her body relaxed.

"Is there anyone else you want to see?" Joshua spoke quietly.

Emily didn't answer. She laid her head on her mother's chest. Arms cradling herself and Emily, her mother began to hum "Somewhere Over the Rainbow." Emily closed her eyes, but her shoulders were shaking.

"Are you laughing?!"

"Can't you hear her? She's absolutely tone deaf! Oh, I've missed this." She nestled in deeper.

Joshua turned away from the intimate scene and headed for the kitchen. Mr. Oxford let out a yip and a yelp.

"I don't know who you are," Hazel said without looking up as she set cups on a tray, "but I know you're with Emily. The only thing I have to say to you is be good to her. She's a sweet girl. Understand me?"

Hearing the confident tone in his mistress's voice, Mr. Oxford growled a big-dog growl.

"Fuck, this is bat-shit crazy." Joshua turned back to find Emily. She was standing up, and her mother's face was open and serene. For the moment, her vast and terrible grief was gone.

"I think it's time to go, Joshua. Ready?"

"Are you fucking kidding me? Let's go!"

Hazel passed them in the short hallway. She poked a finger in their direction. "Behave yourselves."

"Joshua, do we have some time?"

"Not much. What do you want to do?"

"I don't know. Maybe just fly around this beautiful red island. Come on, it'll be fun. I'll show you around."

"Still can't believe my brain," Joshua muttered.

Trees, lush green farm fields, fertile red soil, sand dunes and shorelines flashed by.

"Oh look, there's my old school." Without waiting for him, Emily swooped down. When Joshua caught up with her, she was standing in front of a gray, institutional door decorated with graffiti.

"And, who are we haunting now? If, that is, we were actually ghosts or—"

"Just want to check if someone is still teaching here." Emily zipped through the door.

"Hold on. Why so fast?"

"I'm assuming we don't have much time," she called over her shoulder.

Joshua followed her to the second floor. She had a slightly wild look in her eyes.

"Are you okay?"

Emily nodded and moved through the classroom door. Inside, a breeze through an open window clacked the vertical blind.

"Joshua, stand by the window and make the wind stronger. I know you can do this. No questions. Please?"

"Aye, aye, sir." Joshua saluted and hurried to the window.

"Ha ha! Look what I can do!" As Joshua waved his arms, the blind clattered and pitched. A few students put their phones on papers to keep them from flying away.

Emily walked up to the teacher, who wore a "cool teacher" black turtleneck and sat on the edge of his desk as he listened intently to a pretty teenage girl talk about a recent assignment. Nodding his enthusiasm, he walked over to her desk, rubbed her shoulder briefly and continued down the aisle.

"Bastard! Rotten prick!"

"Whoa, Ms. Christian girl! I don't want to have to change my cherished assumptions about you. What the hell is wrong?"

Emily didn't answer. Instead, she went to the teacher's desk and yanked open a drawer. She grabbed the contents and tossed them into the air. Scattered over the floor were dozens of condoms, a picture of his wife and son, and a porn magazine opened to a photo of two naked teenage girls wrapped around each other.

Gasps were followed by nervous laughter followed by snickers followed by "Holy shit!"

"This is an outrageous set-up! Who put this stuff in my desk?" It was hard to tell from his crimson hue whether he was angry or embarrassed.

"Our job here is done. Let's go!"

Joshua was laughing. "Sure thing, but I really need to hear the back story to this scene."

It was time. Their pendants were glowing.

Through inky skies, past millions of ancient stars living and dying, they ascended. They could hear music. Was it the Ugly Brown Birds? All they had to do was surrender to the music and they were back.

They appeared together in the Great Unnamed Room.

Susan put her arm around Emily, leading her to a café table. "Come, tell us all about your experience in the lower realm."

"Susan," Reinhardt said, "I believe we should continue to call it the world, or earth. That's how I feel." He sat down with a backward glance at the Great Green Sanctuary.

"Well, I don't know if I bring this out in them," Joshua jabbed a thumb in Susan and Emily's direction, "but another 'revenge contact' has been accomplished."

"Ah ... my story, I think?" Emily motioned to Joshua to sit down. In sharing the story, she included a brief account of her own experiences with the teacher.

When she finished, Susan was beaming. "Atta girl, show the bastard!"

Reinhardt simply shook his head. Sunita rose and walked over to Emily, putting an arm around her shoulder. Khalid's hands were balled into fists.

Joshua stood up. "Time for me to pay a visit to the Great Green Sanctuary."

Reinhardt raised his eyebrows and nodded encouragingly.

A wide circle of light swooped around the Great Unnamed Room. The opening notes of an anthem poured out of the throats of the Ugly Brown Birds.

"Looks like a searchlight." Khalid's eyes followed the citrine-yellow light.

Gabriel was back. On screen.

20: Gabriel Gives a Pep-Talk

Gabriel stood tall and handsome in an immaculately tailored tuxedo. He was on the other side of a red rope. Beautiful people avoiding the cameras and beautiful people seeking the cameras wove in and out of others who were there to support and others who were there seeking support. Gabriel stood in back of the crowds wearing a faint smile. People walked past him, unaware of his presence.

"Gabriel, you look marvelous," Susan said with wonder. "Could it be? Are you attending an awards show? Is it, could it be, the Oscars?"

A man rushing to help a beautiful woman who had tripped over a camera cord rushed through Gabriel. The man stumbled, looked around, recovered and lunged to grab the woman. It wouldn't do for her to be photographed face down on the red carpet. Gabriel kept smiling his faint smile and brushed the jacket sleeve where the man had made contact. Dress after glorious dress walked by. Some of the glorious dresses were accompanied by perfect suits. Jewels glittered. An earnest-faced celebrity was giving an interview, offering his concerns about the ravages of famine.

"What are you doing there?" Emily asked.

Joshua arched an eyebrow. "What do you think he's doing there? He obviously has an appointment."

"Oh my! Is it anyone we know, Gabriel? Somebody important? Look!" Susan screamed, "There's someone wearing one of my couture fairy dresses!"

"Honestly, Susan if you weren't already dead—" Joshua broke off, laughing. Gabriel chuckled, picking up a fluted glass on a passing tray held aloft by a handsome young man. A commonly agreed upon standard of good looks was being meticulously observed.

"Susan, you know I cannot tell you. If there were another place or time to send you this message, I would have chosen differently. I will be back soon, but these instructions are time sensitive."

"Gabriel, I really have to know. This person you have an appointment with, will they be joining us? If they will, and I'm assuming it's someone of great importance, perhaps we should prepare a special welcome." Susan peered hopefully at him.

Joshua hit his palm to his forehead. "Give it a rest, Susan, for G—" he caught Emily's stare and stopped.

"I don't understand this fascination with celebrities." Reinhardt scratched his chin. "They're people who are simply trying to wake up to themselves. It's the same for all of us."

"You will be happy to know that I have a theory about this fascination with celebrities," Gabriel said with another chuckle. "Your so-called modern world needs gods and goddesses. Not needs, exactly, but each of you is born with an ancient coding that craves drama, complete with heroes and heroines. In other words, myths with gods and goddesses. Celebrities, movies, even tabloids fill that ancient need. We have not yet figured out why this is so, but the moment we do, your need to idolize these imitators of gods and goddesses will simply vanish!"

Gabriel scanned the group to see if they were pleased. It was hard to tell.

"So you're finally coming back here?" Joshua said. "I guess that's good news. We have these missions to accomplish, but none of us really knows what'll happen after they're completed." He looked startled hearing his own words but hurried on. "Well, except for yours truly, of course! My beautiful brain will cease spinning out this crazy, and I'll fall into the big black."

"So you've miraculously emerged from your coma?" Khalid murmured. "You're back to the dying brain story?" At the next table, Emily coughed politely, eyes bright.

"First things first, Joshua. Is that how you say that?" Gabriel didn't wait for a reply. "As I mentioned, I have some instructions, although I prefer to call them suggestions. Much nicer. This need for absolutes has given you and your world a lot of trouble."

A striking redhead in an off-the-shoulder black gown handed Gabriel her glass as she strolled by.

"Wait a minute! Can that lady see you?" Emily leaned forward.

"Hm? Oh. I have adjusted my vibrations. Some will see me, others will not." Gabriel checked his tie and shot his cuffs. "Let's get on with the business at hand, shall we? I want you to consider love."

Khalid lifted his shoulders. "If I were a cursing man like our infidel friend, there are words I'm sure he'd use to express his disdain at the idea of considering love."

"Ah, not sure where you're going with this, man. I'm not against love, for fuck's sake."

The screen froze. Gabriel's eyes filled the screen. They were terrifying. The screen unfroze, and once more beautiful people dashed urgently here and there. "Yes. Love. I want all of you to think about love, your talents and your path. That's it!" Gabriel smiled pleasantly. "The Room of Reflection is an excellent place to contemplate these things, but the Wall of the Seven Heavens will open you up to vastness and possibilities, the aspirational you! Feel free to ask the Ugly Brown Birds to give you an inspiring song. They love that."

His voice softened. "My dear ones, this is important. Do your best to connect with your best. Know you have something the world needs right now. See you soon. Cheers and blessings."

Chapter 21: Kitchen Talk

Joshua stood at the entrance to the kitchen, waving a piece of parchment. The rest of the group were already seated at the long table, eating their evening meal and talking quietly.

"Lookie here! Guess what I found slipped under my door?"

Susan set down her cup of green tea. "Oh, I hope it's details of our spiritual missions!"

"Not exactly."

"So, are you going to keep us guessing?" Emily said.

"And good evening to you, Ms. Impatient. Okay, sit back. Things are about to get real fucking hokey."

He unrolled the parchment. "Hear ye, hear ye …" Joshua looked up. No one was laughing. "Okay, here, we go. For real."

My dear ones (Joshua read), *it has been suggested that a nice chat about what each of you loves about your religion is in order. This suggestion is not meant to open up discussions or debates. Give a simple statement about what you love: nothing more, nothing less. This includes you, Joshua. We wish for each of you to better understand the heart behind the path. For our future missions, collaboration is essential. Breaking down or even, dare I hope, removing your biases toward any other path will be immensely helpful in these all-important endeavors! Cheers and blessings, your Navigator Gabriel.*

He sat down and began digging into a plate of pasta with Chorizo sausage.

"Joshua, do you mind if I say a word or two?" Reinhardt said.

"Go ahead!"

"May I suggest that all of us practice listening with our hearts?" Reinhardt spoke with soft intensity.

Joshua waved to the group. "Did everyone hear that? Reinhardt wants everyone to listen with their dead, shriveled hearts. Got it?" Reinhardt stared at him in disbelief.

"I was going to ask who would like to begin but have decided to choose. Anyone have a problem with that?" Joshua pushed his plate away. When no one objected, he muttered, "This is so fucking lame."

Emily snorted. "So much for listening with the heart. I heard you, and so did everyone else."

"Okay, I'll try harder. Sunita, why do you love your religion?" Joshua's lips stretched into a car-salesman smile, and he leaned over to Emily. "Better?" Her expression tightened.

Sunita stood and offered a bow to all at the table. "What makes me happy to be a Hindu? I love the vastness, the spaciousness of Hinduism. Hinduism encompasses many religions. I love that it is so utterly immense that a label of religion is too narrow. When I offer devotions, I feel connected. I feel more. To me, being a Hindu means I strive to be a better person. I love the timelessness. There is no beginning, no one person who began Hinduism. I feel a great sense of belonging to a lineage and tradition that offers such wise guidance. I love what our beloved Mahatma Gandhi said: 'If we shatter the chains of egotism, and melt into the ocean of humanity, we share its dignity.' Rituals are powerful and have the energy to charge and change life. I love performing rituals, with all the incense, offerings and …" Sunita laughed and looked around the table. "I have so much more to say, stories about the great goddesses and gods, but perhaps you have an idea of my love for this great religion." She sat down.

"Great, Sunita, you sold me! I'm going to become a Hindu," Joshua said. "Alter, would you like to say what you love about being Jewish?"

Alter struggled to his feet and gripped the table. "I have never thought about it before. Loving your religion? I love God and his plan, but loving being Jewish? What makes me happy to be a Jew?" He fingered his beard and was quiet for a time. "I love the Sabbath," he said at last. "The lighting of the candelabrum. I love the prayers. When I pray, which is all the time, I feel I am talking to God. I love the commandments, all six hundred and thirteen of them. I love—" he paused in thought. "Yes. Yes. I love when the cantor sings and leads the rest of us to sing God's praises. I love the community and the way they accept me, old Alter, just as I am. And I love the practical advice God has given us to live a life pleasing to him. Is that enough?"

"Thank you, Alter, that will do nicely. Susan, you're up." Joshua bit his cheek to hold back a comment.

Susan took one more sip of green tea and placed the cup carefully on its saucer. She stood up, threw back her head and raised her arms. Slowly lowering them again, she spoke in a clear, ringing tone. "Where do I begin? The path of a genuine spiritual seeker is not easy, but I would not change a thing. I love the diversity and the adventure. And I absolutely love having no spiritual authority other than the universe. I love no rules or boundaries. I can explore whatever takes my fancy or wherever my spirit directs me. I love not having to follow a doctrine written by old men who are long dead. I love the mysterious, and this spiritual path offers mystery after mystery. I love that my feminine energy is honored. There is no judgment; I am allowed to be me." She pressed her hands to her heart, then opened her arms wide. "I could go on and on—"

"I think we get the picture, Susan, but let's hear from Reinhardt. Reinhardt, why do you love being a Buddhist?"

A few crumbs fell to the floor as Reinhardt rubbed his hands together and scraped back his chair. "Form is emptiness, emptiness form."

Joshua groaned. "Existential Buddhism?"

"This is a quote from *The Heart Sutra*, and I believe we are to be silent and listen!" Reinhardt's face filled with fury; his visible eye twitched.

Sunita spoke quietly to the group. "If Reinhardt and the rest who have not shared their passion for their path agree, perhaps we can share later today or tomorrow?" She avoided looking at Joshua, who was avoiding looking at anyone.

Heads nodded. Reinhardt strode out of the kitchen. Alter's faded brown eyes rested on Joshua. "Joshua, you need to try harder."

Emily, Sunita and Khalid were playing cards at a café table. Emily had found a deck wedged between two books in the library, and the images on the cards portrayed warriors through the ages. Each person had to choose a warrior to represent them throughout the game, but after that they made up the game as they played.

Joshua sauntered by and stopped to watch, but they made no effort to coax him to join. Reinhardt and Alter had already made their way up the stairway to their own rooms, and Susan was gazing into the Great Green Sanctuary, which day by day was growing larger. Feeling wretched, Joshua decided to head up to his room. *Perhaps tomorrow all will be forgiven. Or forgotten. Or whatever.*

The card players decided to call it a night. "Susan, you are the last. Would you like to walk with us to our rooms?" Sunita called over her shoulder.

Susan hustled to catch up with them. "You know, I feel bad for Joshua. He's an ass, but he's not a malicious ass."

Gondolas bobbed in the brown waters of the Lido canal. Gabriel could not tell what century it was, never mind what year. Silence, the darkness of a moonless midnight and the dank smell of the canal wearied him. He had been here many times.

A couple leaning on each other, laughing and walking unsteadily, told Gabriel this was the twenty-first century. The young woman's high-heeled shoes sounded on the centuries-old cobblestones. He would go to the cemetery.

Gabriel recalled how much of this cemetery had been appropriated and become overgrown with Cypress trees and tangles of vegetation. He was relieved that where Alter might be was a tenderly restored, dignified place. But what if he were not here? Gabriel tried not to panic. When he'd been alerted that one of the seven was missing, he thought it would take only moments to find him and return to his mission. He was wrong, and he was angry this had happened at all. His warnings had not been heeded.

Alter stood back after placing a stone on top of his wife's tombstone. He was unaware that his daughter, grandson and everyone he knew lay beneath the ground nearby.

"It is time, dear Alter." Gabriel touched the wide sleeve of the old man's coat. Alter reluctantly nodded.

Joshua drummed his fingers soundlessly on the table. His breakfast plate was untouched. Emily and Khalid wandered in, nodded in Joshua's direction and kept on talking. Sunita joined them, offering Joshua a small smile; he was surprised how grateful that made him. Reinhardt hurried in, as though trying to escape Susan, who was talking rapidly and walking as close as possible to the big German.

"Did anyone notice that Alter is not here?" Joshua's voice was tinged with fear. The words were barely out when Alter shuffled into the kitchen and hesitated in the doorway. Conversation trailed off as everyone turned to him.

"Sorry that I am late. I had a long dream last night. I was back in Venice. My home is no longer. Venice has changed since …" He rubbed a hand over his eyes. "So I walked the streets. I even walked the streets outside the Ghetto. It felt unsettling, strange. This dream, it was very real. I will ask Gabriel about this dream. He was there. Now I feel tired, as though I have been travelling."

Joshua helped Alter to a chair. "It is good to see you, Alter." Once Alter was settled, Joshua straightened and spoke to the group. "Now, I wish to make what is likely to be an awkward apology." He turned to Reinhardt. "I am deeply sorry for my behavior yesterday. As Alter suggested, I will try harder." Joshua sat down.

"Bravo, man. Good for you," Khalid said.

Reinhardt left what remained of his breakfast and lumbered to his feet to hug Joshua. His big arms encircled and disappeared through Joshua, who reddened and grinned ruefully. "It is good to recognize and acknowledge our neuroses. Your interruption stirred up memories when I was ignored by my parents and teachers."

"I am curious. What were the schools like in postwar Germany?" Khalid leaned back, tilting his chair.

Reinhardt laughed. "Well, we did have some Stasi teachers." He went quiet, unaware the rest were waiting for him to continue. He blinked and looked around. "The Stasi were the secret police. The teachers at the pudding school were probably the worst."

Emily spit out her tea. "The pudding school?"

Reinhardt's head was bent over his plate, focused on schnitzel. He looked up. "Yes, before it was a school, it was a pudding factory. Apparently, they were especially busy during the war."

Khalid banged his chair down and slapped his knee. "See now, most people don't consider things like Nazis enjoying their puddings!"

Sunita patted her mouth with a square of linen. "Some of us have not shared our passion for our paths. I propose we meet in the central court and begin with Reinhardt." She rearranged one end of her scarf and left the kitchen.

Alter took in the Great Unnamed Room as though seeing it for the first time. The old man appeared to be out of sorts. Joshua pulled a chair out for him, and he hung onto the younger man's arm as he got the chair under him. Then Alter tilted his head to look up at the dome. The light was unusually vivid, and planets and clusters of stars drifted through indigo skies. Joshua hitched a chair beside him and placed an arm around his thin shoulders.

Reinhardt stood in the middle of the semicircle of chairs. He glanced at the massive cages where the Ugly Brown Birds were keening a lament.

"I was a musician and played in several bands. My aunt, who played first violin in the Berlin Symphony, began to teach me when I was eight years old. Improvisational, classical, folk, all of it. I've never shared this with any of my fellow practitioners, but the chants pull me into a rhythm that's very comforting and reminiscent of my days as a musician."

He straightened up. "In the dark times we left behind, Buddhism helped me and many others to hold our ground, to remain sane. I love practicing compassion. I enjoy sitting on a cushion, allowing things to arise. I love being in the moment. I make every effort to offer myself to others, treating them as guests. I love losing my fixations, my clinging onto. I love being part of a sangha, my community of Buddhists, of our shared purpose of an enlightened society. I love practicing being brave, noble and honorable. I love burning big branches of juniper to make a good lhasang, our smoke ceremony that clears obstacles we collect right down to our pores, allowing us to connect with elemental beings. And I love losing my attachments to all of the above." Reinhardt's eyes were serious but warm.

"Thanks, Reinhardt. Emily, why don't you give it a go? Tell us what you love about being a Christian?"

Emily laid a hand lightly on Reinhardt's arm as they exchanged places. Fair and slim, she was dwarfed by the solid, bear-like man. "You know, Reinhardt, we recently began meditation classes at our church. People seem to really like it." He patted her hand and sank gratefully into a chair. Emily stood in the middle and surveyed the diverse group. "Okay, my turn, eh? Why do I love being a Christian? I love feeling supported. And I love knowing that I'm always loved, no matter how rotten I can be. Jesus loves me. I love being part of a religion that encourages brotherhood and charity. I love Christmas. I love Easter as it gives us a chance to remember the great sacrifice of Jesus Christ, our Lord. And I love the smell of church—old wood and old books and candle wax and sometimes greenery or incense. But forgiveness is key. I love knowing I'll be forgiven, no matter what I do. There's more, but I'll be charitable and give someone else a chance."

Joshua yawned. "Wow, I didn't know I could yawn in this cheery afterlife thingy. At this point, I would like some acknowledgment of my admirable lack of commentary."

Reinhardt began to clap and the rest joined in. And although their claps could not be heard, Joshua smiled and waggled his fingers.

"Okay, I'll say a few things about why I love being an atheist. For one thing, I love logic and I love reason. I love evolution and I love that I have no mythical beings hovering around me taking notes. I love knowing that my actions matter now and not in some promised or wished-for green, flower-filled field in the sky. And I love approaching all problems knowing that solutions are entirely up to me. Personal responsibility. I love it. I love being understood as a clear-thinking person who is not influenced by ancient writings or booming voices from the sky. And also, if I hear a voice, I will not be under any foggy illusions. I'll know I'm crazy." Everyone except Emily laughed. She narrowed her eyes as though she'd figured out why he was an atheist.

"Yes, I know that was brilliant, and all of you are now dying— sorry couldn't resist—dying to be atheist, but now it's time to hear from our Muslim. Ready, Khalid?"

Khalid air-punched Joshua's arm as they passed each other.

"I love being part of a great faith that teaches equality. Rich, poor, healthy, ill, Allah tests all of us. I love the sound of the muezzin calling us to prayer. I love kneeling with my brothers in prayer. I love the poetry of the Holy Qur'an. I love fasting at Ramadan and how it makes me feel more compassionate toward the poor. I love the mercy of Allah. And I love the pluralism of Islam and that I'm included in the great lineage of Abraham. May I offer you a quote by a Muslim convert? His name was Ahmed Holt." The others were listening intently. Khalid looked at Reinhardt and asked more softly, "Are you listening with your hearts?"

He took a soundless breath. "Okay, here's what Ahmed Holt said: 'The sword of Islam is not the sword of steel. I know this by experience, because the sword of Islam struck deep into my own heart. It didn't bring death, but it brought a new life; it brought an awareness and it brought an awakening—as to who am I and what am I and for what am I here?'" Khalid stood silent for a moment. "We have a shared spiritual heritage found in our scriptures and in our desire to be of help to others."

"Okay, so maybe I'll give Islam a try. Beautiful, man." Joshua pretended to wipe a tear from his eye. Khalid laughed and reached to punch him again.

"This was insightful and I believe, helpful," Reinhardt said. "Thank you, Joshua, for facilitating."

"No problem. I still want to hear how a German became a Buddhist. But another time. Okay, guys, that's it. Not sure if another set of instructions will be delivered via creepy stalker angel-being, but I will keep you up to date."

"You know, I'm struck by our similar feelings about our beliefs," Emily said.

Joshua stood to leave. "Oh please oh please oh please! Let's not get all mushy."

"Let me finish, you oaf. I know we're not to comment on other people's beliefs or anything, but, uh, Susan?"

Susan regarded Emily coolly. "Yes?"

"How can you say you've learned to be non-judgmental? You're very judgmental of Joshua."

"Coming from a Christian! Well, that's rich." Susan sniffed.

"Maybe something to work on, Susan?" Reinhardt said. "All of us have stuff to work on."

Susan ducked her chin once but glared at Emily.

Alter shifted and cleared his throat. He was always so quiet that, whenever he spoke, the others gave him time and space. It was by silent but communal agreement that, given the time he came from, his perspective was one the others often overlooked.

"Miss Emily is right. We share many similarities. There is one thing. One thing each of us said. We used different words, but it all means the same thing, I believe. Each of us, when speaking from our heart, said we loved that our religion or path made us feel included. Isn't that one of our great, painful struggles? One of our great desires? Each of us wants to be understood, to be accepted and included. That is very nice, I think."

Chapter 22: Angel Boot Camp

"Father issues?" Susan lifted her eyebrows at Reinhardt as she spooned more quinoa onto her plate.

Reinhardt shook his head, chewing hard to swallow a mouthful of bratwurst. It was his turn to choose music, and Mozart's Requiem was accompanying the clinks of lunch. He swallowed again and wiped his mouth. "Why do you say I have father issues?"

"Anyone who enjoys Mozart's Requiem has father issues."

Across the table, Joshua buttered a chunk of bread so hard that it broke into pieces. "For Chrissake, let's not turn this lunch into a hippie-dippie therapy session."

Reinhardt caught Joshua's eye and raised his glass. Joshua wiped butter off his thumb.

"This music *is* kind of dreary, though. Music is like all art forms. It's powerful in how it affects our emotions and moods." Susan paused to stab at a kale leaf. "Raises or depresses our vibrations. I've had chakra music that was composed by someone who channeled the music from a sphere that mystics through the ages have tried to connect with. She's very talented. It's been rumored that this sacred gift came to her after she had a near-death experience when she was hit by a logging truck in Texas. The story goes that when the paramedics were tending to her, her spirit body was taken by a group of light beings who gave her the gift of this music. She was a noted cellist before and played with a symphony out of Austin. After she recovered, she quit the symphony and began to create chakra music. The light beings never left her side while she composed."

Joshua set down his fork and spoke slowly. "You do know that researchers, *science* researchers, have posited that these," he flung his arms open, "spiritual revelations are caused by temporal lobe epilepsy? Your cellist-turned-hokey-spiritual-music-maker probably had a brain injury."

"It's really sad how little you know, Joshua."

"You're probably right. Anyway, I want to know about angels." Everyone but Susan looked relieved at the change in topic.

"Where in the world—" Susan giggled and flapped a hand. "I mean, where in *heaven* did this sudden interest come from? Naturally, I can tell you lots as I have been to many, many angel workshops and even designed a special—well, all of them were special—fairy dress for a well-known angel expert. And of course I have my own personal angel." Susan poked at her quinoa and tried to look modest.

"Where is this Shining One, Susan?" Sunita asked.

"I love how you people call angels Shining Ones!" Susan leaned over to clasp Sunita's hand.

"Not all of us do," Sunita said, slipping her hand away but giving Susan's a pat. "But I wish to know where this angel is now that you are dead?"

Joshua coughed. "Can we get back to me and my questions about angels?"

"Hah!" Emily pointed her lobster roll in his general direction. "Now I really have seen it all. You asking about angels? I wasn't sure if miracles happened here, but I guess they do."

"I'll have you know that before I died I launched an angel app."

"Man, I wish I was still alive," Khalid said. "An atheist creates an angel app. Now *this* would make an original routine. No one would believe it, and not my usual stuff, but man, it'd be funny. What would you like to know? A belief in angels is the second article of faith for Muslims, so we are obligated to believe. And I do."

"Okay, so what are they made of? How many of them are out there?" Joshua twirled a hand upward.

"In the Holy Qur'an, it is said that Allah made the angels from light. How many? Whew … too many to count, brother. It's estimated that over seventy thousand angels visit the Kaaba in Mecca, and as soon as they leave, another seventy thousand arrive." As Khalid grew more animated, his words sped up. "When the Prophet Muhammad, peace be upon him, was taken on his night journey through the heavens, he was shown that for every four human fingers, there is one angel."

"Thanks, man. That's a lot of information. But what's the point of all these angels?"

"They praise Allah."

"Holy fuck, that's it? They praise Allah?"

"And there's the Joshua we've all come to only mildly dislike," Emily said. Khalid lightly punched her shoulder, and she pretended to fall over. Joshua glared.

"Okay, if it helps, I'll give this a go," Emily continued. "I'm not an expert, but from what I've been told, angels play a variety of roles. Some watch over us while we're alive, some come to our aid when we're in trouble. Angels brought the Virgin Mary a message telling her she'd give birth to the Son of God. I believe all of us have angels."

"O-kay," Joshua said. "If each of us has an angel stalking us while we're alive, what happens when we die? Do they lose their jobs, or do they find some other schmuck to hover over? What happens? If I'm to be an angel, I need to know, goddammit!" He pounded the table.

Emily, Sunita and Khalid laughed. Susan scowled. Reinhardt and Alter had their heads together.

"Joshua, you really are terrible, you know," Sunita chided. "God made angels. I am sure God would direct them wherever they are needed."

"Muslims believe there are two angels who test us while we're in the grave."

"And? Is that happening, Khalid? Do you have two angels who are testing you this very minute?"

"Yeah, brother, that's probably what's happening. I'm being tested to see how long I can put up with an arsehole like—"

"Hold on." Reinhardt half stood up. Beethoven's "Ode to Joy" was beginning, and he hoped the music would shift the energy at the table. "Each of us has beliefs that are important. In Buddhism, we have devas and other elemental beings. Some are protectors but not, I believe, how Christians see—"

Unexpectedly, Alter cut in. "We Jews believe angels give God some distance from what happens on earth. Problems or worries that people have are dealt with by angels. I am happy to say that Jewish angels can debate. They can even debate God. Imagine, debating with God! I don't think I could do that."

"So, your God doesn't like to get his almighty hands dirty?"

Alter rose, his slight frame rigid with anger.

"I'm very sorry, Alter. Please forgive me. I'm being an asshole."

"Yes, he does this asshole thing very, very well," Susan said sardonically.

Sunita ignored the unpleasantness. "We have similar beliefs as the Buddhists, but then Buddhism originated from Hinduism."

"No, I'm sorry, Sunita, it's not that simple. Hindu people like to think Buddhism is an offshoot of Hinduism, but it really is not that simple. And naturally there has been more insight ..." Reinhardt stared into the distance.

"I guess what I'm getting at is, well, even though I still believe this whole situation is part of my dying brain gasping its last, is this whole thing a training ground?"

"A training ground? What do you mean, a training ground?" Susan leaned over the table to look directly at Joshua.

"Last night I was thinking maybe Gabriel is training us to be, you know, angels."

"Ode to Joy" was approaching its extravagant end.

"A kind of boot camp for angels." It was clear he was embarrassed. "So, if this fucked-up stuff by the remotest possibility is real, what if this Gabriel dude is training us to be angels?"

"Wow, How cool would that be?" Emily glanced around to see if anyone shared her excitement. "While we wait for eternal paradise, we get to be angels!"

"Gabriel talked about a mission, some mysterious mission for all of us to participate in," Joshua said. "What if this mission is actually a kind of training to become some kind of angel? Since I have no clue what an angel does, I wanted to know what each of you thought they did, what they looked like and so on."

"I wish to be reunited with my Hannah and perhaps, if God sees fit, my ancestors as well. But an angel? I don't want it," Alter said. Almost as an afterthought, he added, "No offense to God."

"Interesting, but I doubt it," Reinhardt said. "Gabriel seemed to be quite interested in our professions. How would our professions have any bearing on being angels or devas?"

"However Allah wants to use me is fine by me. I happily submit. An angel boot camp. I love it." Khalid opened his hands and offered them upwards.

"Hey, Khalid, I didn't have in mind a jihad-ish angel boot camp." Out of nowhere, Khalid stood in front of him, fists balled. Joshua raised his hands in surrender. "Sorry, man. Bad joke?"

Khalid slouched back to his chair but continued to cast sullen looks at Joshua.

"I wish one of my spiritual groups could see me now. An angel in training." Susan sighed.

"Hold it, I'm not saying that's what's going on, but I'm suspicious. Why does he want us? Is there a greater demand for angels in the fucked-up world we left behind? What sane person would believe such a thing? Really, what's the story?"

"Joshua, I can understand why they would choose the rest of us. Maybe, if you're right, they want angels that represent some of the major faith traditions. But why choose an atheist?"

Sunita stood to leave and carefully pushed her chair in. "Maybe they want an angel to convince atheists there is a heaven, that there is a God or higher beings."

"An atheist angel, why not? Massive wings that blot out the sun, swooping down to give some poor sap comfort. Tell 'em not to worry, everything will be peachy keen, and all that crap."

Sunita had walked over to stand by the massive stone fireplace, tracing the pattern on one of the stones with her fingers. "Who would you watch over, Emily?"

"This is wonderful. Imagine being an angel. I'd have to give it some thought. Off the top of my head, I'd watch over my fiancé and my mom. But there are so many people who could use protection and guidance or anything else I could offer as an angel."

Joshua moaned. "Oh, crap. It's just a theory. Or, to be more accurate, a momentary break in my sanity. Mission? I don't know, but I suspect it's a waste of time to get our wing fittings just yet."

"Best thing to do is come straight out and ask Gabriel when he makes his next appearance." Reinhardt stood up and tossed his napkin onto the table.

Susan floated up, a starry look of wonder in her eyes. "I'm going to be an angel …" She trailed out of the kitchen, arms outstretched. Tremulous notes of "In the Arms of an Angel" trailed after her, slightly off key.

"Oh fuck, what have I started?"

Chapter 23: The Plight of Angels

"No! No? Just like that? No?" Susan's voice bordered on the hysterical. The Ugly Brown Birds flapped and squawked.

In the morning, a cowbell had summoned the group to gather and wait for a message from Gabriel. Susan had bounced on the edge of her chair, eager to be the first to ask Gabriel if they were going to be angels. His abrupt answer left her stunned.

Emily, tucked in a corner, sagged in disappointment.

"Fine, then," Susan said coldly. "I would have thought that we, specially chosen for these missions you talk about, would deserve divine recognition. A designation of angel seemed appropriate."

"My dear Susan, being an angel is not what it's cracked up to be. Look at the average day of an angel! They follow people around …"

Joshua snickered. "See, even Gabriel admits that angels stalk. Stalking angels. How the hell could you guys think this was a good thing?"

"You are damned for hell, man." Khalid grinned.

"DO NOT FORGET I CAN HEAR YOU!"

Six of them jerked up straighter. Alter just nodded thoughtfully. The Ugly Brown Birds broke into a ragtime tune in five/four time.

More softly, with a slight smile, Gabriel continued. "Susan and all of you, as I was saying. Being an angel is not as glamorous as it may sound. Following you people around, trying to guide you more smoothly in your earthly life, it is a challenge." He paused, considering.

"Take the miracle of love. People say they are looking for love. If they had love, they proclaim, all would be right in their world. And yet …" Gabriel held up one elegant finger. "Even as we try to guide them to those whose hearts are of a similar vibration, they turn stubbornly away. Some of you have a fixed picture in your mind of how love should be and will think your way out of love. Others ignore every opportunity their angel offers them to find love." He exhaled. "It becomes tiresome."

The Ugly Brown Birds had settled their feathers and were singing more gently. Out of the corner of his one good eye, Reinhardt noticed a few new trees in the Great Green Sanctuary. He brightened, but in an instant his expression became bleak.

"Would you like to hear a brief story on how frustrating and painful it is to be an angel?" Gabriel saw the skepticism on their faces. "Yes, angels feel pain! They feel pain when their loved ones turn away. Let me tell you about someone who was so caught up in what they hoped for that they lost a golden opportunity for love. Do you remember, Susan, when you were asked to give a talk for that group? Now what was the name? Oh yes, Aspire Spiritual Sisters, or A.S.S." Gabriel shot a warning glance to Joshua. "Do you remember, Susan?"

"Yes, it was a lovely gathering. This wonderful group of spiritual ladies are based in Saint Paul, and they asked me to fly there and talk about my fairy inspirations. They were very excited. But what does that have to do with—"

"In the taxi from the airport, do you remember a street barricade you insisted the driver ignore?"

Susan nodded, frowning.

"You were angry with the driver and pounded on the headrest when he tried to take another route. Earlier, when you mentioned you wanted a latte, he'd suggested a quaint coffee shop. But you were determined to go down the barricaded street because there was a shoe store you wanted to visit. So the driver lifted the barricade and took you to the store."

"Yes, I remember. And I do feel bad. I may have been a little stubborn with the driver. I did buy a pair of shoes there, though. Rotten things fell apart at a black tie dinner party a few weeks later."

"Your angel was trying to get you to that coffee shop, Susan. At a corner table sat a man who had just returned from an amazing retreat in Thailand. A mystic, whose own angel had whispered in her ear, told him that when he returned to Saint Paul, he needed to go to that coffee shop at that exact time. There he would meet a woman from out of town who had fairies all around her and would be the love of his life."

Susan's eyes were round in horror.

"I hope you enjoyed those shoes before they fell apart. I would like to take you through the steps involved in our heavenly attempt to unite your heart with this man's. First, we had to ensure he got on the plane and flew to Thailand—something he'd never done before. Next we had to arrange for him to meet the mystic. Then we consulted with the mystic's angel, who agreed to pass on the message. Yes, we often work with other angels and sometimes with angels from other orders. The president of A.S.S. was inspired by her angel to invite you to talk. And your driver had to receive his message as well. A great number of angels were involved with what we called Operation Fairy Love. We consulted your angel as well, and he said he tried his best. In the debrief after Operation Fairy Love failed, your angel gave us a thorough recounting of all the ways he tried to guide you to the coffee shop. Do you remember how you tripped over someone's luggage at the airport and hurt your ankle? That was placed there by your angel. He knew you'd want to stop at a shoe store, so he thought if your ankle was sore, you would postpone shopping. Norman, your angel … I know you have always called your angel 'Cosimia,' a Greek girl's name meaning 'of the universe,' but your angel's name was actually Norman. We teased him every time you called out what you thought was your angel's name."

Susan was twisting a corner of her dress; the others sat enthralled. Gabriel knew he'd been blunt. These days, angels were encouraged to present information with a softer touch, especially when dealing with Americans and, to a lesser extent, with Canadians and Italians. Gabriel thought it strange that people today seemed crueler, more cut off from their emotions, yet required more sensitive handling. Dealing with the world could be draining.

"You are not the only one, Susan, who ignores their angels. Most people do. All of you have ignored us and made your lives more difficult as a result." Gabriel's voice was so low that they had to strain to catch his words. "You have missed miracles, my dear ones."

Fiery reds, oranges and yellows flared from the screen. A remnant of body memory caused everyone to flinch. Gabriel was gone. An unsettling hush descended over the Great Unnamed Room. The luminosity of the Wall of the Seven Heavens dimmed. The trees and plants in the Great Green Sanctuary drooped.

The group was motionless, each cocooned in their own world. Reinhardt was the first to emerge. He leaned over to Susan. "Sometimes I feel I can see better with this." He pointed to his Ashe eye patch. "What I see now is a woman who was scared. I'm sure there were many times when I didn't see—"

Gabriel was back. "My dear ones, before we leave this subject, I would like to offer another example of ignoring a personal angel. Joshua?"

Joshua tried to arrange his face to reflect both respect and nonchalance. The result was a pained combination of fake piety and a twitching eyelid.

In her attempt to stifle a laugh, Emily spluttered. "Sorry!"

Gabriel ignored her. "We and the angel assigned to you knew that an occasion might never arise on which you would tune in, so to speak. You might say that your angel drew the short straw. She did not have heaven-high hopes that you would listen. In fact, she was fairly certain you would attribute any thoughts or feelings that seemed 'external' to being overworked, overtired, or undernourished due to a faulty balance of nutrients in your overcautious diet. The big *why* you would turn away or ignore us was that you were afraid. You were afraid you might be crazy."

Joshua shifted in his chair and surreptitiously rubbed his eyelid.

"Do you remember the time you had food poisoning?"

Joshua grimaced, nodding imperceptibly.

"Your angel, Marta, thought this was her big chance. Mind you, it was not a major life pivot, when people naturally have more than the usual fears and other neurotic emotions acting as barriers. It was a minor event in which, if you began to listen to her, you would become more receptive. So, when the opportunity arose to prevent your food poisoning, she pulled out all the stops."

Joshua lounged in the chair, arms folded.

"When you were online looking for an elegant place to eat and found this one restaurant, Marta swept in and removed the restaurant site from your computer. Undeterred, you used your phone and called the same restaurant. Faster than the time between two heartbeats, Marta rearranged the phone lines, which is why you kept getting Tony's Tailoring. Still you kept on. You walked to the restaurant to personally arrange reservations. Remember how the sidewalks were extra busy, people crammed together, and more than one person bumped into you on the way? And how rain began to pour, and you without an umbrella? When you got to the restaurant, a notice taped to the door read, 'Due to unforeseen circumstances, we had to close early today. Thanks.' Our Marta may not be a wordsmith, but she cares. The restaurant was indeed open. The notice was gone as you squelched angrily away, sopping wet. Marta was exhausted. She'd had to operate on several vibrations, some of them unfamiliar, like your computer. So, after your many attempts to contact the restaurant, Marta missed the call you made to a friend, who made the reservation for you. For three days after your scrumptious repast, you thought you were going to die."

Gabriel moved to one side. Beyond him, the seven could see a small grove of olive trees. Children, their brown feet indistinguishable from the dust, played on parched earth, tossing and kicking around an overripe gourd. A thin yellow dog, desperate to join in, yelped and skidded into skinny ankles. Overhead, the sky was blue-white, streaked by the odd wisp of cloud left by a storm that had brought too little rain to matter.

"In the beginning of your beautiful world, humans and angels walked together. Creation was new and soft, and the path between heaven and earth was wide open. It was a time of enchantment, when the supernatural was natural. The world you left so recently is far, far less vibrant, and it is losing its vibrational frequencies that keep us—humans and angels—connected."

In the distance, a boom sounded, sending dust spiraling up and the children running for cover. The dog darted after them.

"We have seen this coming, but humans seem intent on hurrying it along. Dear ones, heaven and earth are losing their ancient connection."

Chapter 24: Q and A for Gabriel

Question night (or Gabriel's inquisition, as Joshua referred to it) had finally arrived. The evening meal had been polished off more quickly than usual, and Susan felt cheated. It was her turn to choose music, and she'd hoped everyone would be enchanted by the ethereal New Age singer Fiona Nebula. But there had been time for only three songs. On top of that, she'd had to give an abridged account of when she'd met the acclaimed decoder of the secrets of the universe, Mans Unbridge. No one seemed impressed. Instead, table talk had centered on the anticipated question night. As they gathered in the Great Unnamed Room, Susan was still grousing.

The grand arches were festooned with garlands of red, purple and yellow flowers that spilled out onto the stone floors. An aquamarine, magenta and sea-green cloud of baby stars shimmered near seven chairs, radiating their light toward the Wall of the Seven Heavens. All but Susan were awed. She muttered to herself and bustled over to Joshua to grab his arm.

"Really, I don't see the point of this," she said. "As project manager, you should speak with more authority and tell him for a change what *we* want to—"

"What the hell, Susan. Who cares? Let's see what he says. He said some of the answers may help us on these so-called fucking missions." He shook her off and hurried to catch up with Sunita, Emily and Khalid, who were strolling together past the Room of Reflection.

"If it helps to move us from this realm …," Reinhardt said distractedly to Susan as she glared after Joshua. Reinhardt wandered, entranced, through the swirling vaporous, riotously colored clouds of the star nursery. He sank into a chair but continued to delight in the cosmic spectacle.

"Do you have your questions ready?" Emily asked Khalid. To her own ear, her voice sounded insubstantial.

"I guess. They sound daft, though. This," he gestured, "this is so big, and my questions seem so small and stupid."

"No such thing as a stupid question," Susan sang, oblivious to the enchantment.

Joshua looked heavenward and shuddered. "I hope he's on time."

"I am right here." Gabriel stood in a space that a moment ago was a space.

"In person! This is wonderful." Sunita clapped enthusiastically, while Emily sank lower into her chair.

"Yes, yes, here I am! To show how valued all of you are, I made an extra effort to be here in person. Don't disappoint me! I want to hear some real, how do you Americans say it, head scratchers? Did I get that right, Susan? Joshua?" They nodded. "Alter, would you like to go first?"

Alter turned slowly to left and right, contemplating the others. The Ugly Brown Birds were singing a hopeful song but with some minor thirds to convey hints of sorrow. Trees in the Great Green Sanctuary were swaying. "Questions? No, Gabriel. I have no questions."

Gabriel's convivial mood slipped but regained its footing. "If you are sure, Alter? Very sure?" Alter ducked his chin.

"Emily? What is your question?" Gabriel moved closer to the group, pausing to give the Ugly Brown Birds a short, clipped applause. A shadow of panic crossed Emily's face, and her voice wobbled. "May I have two questions?"

"Go ahead, my dear." Gabriel disappeared into the stars.

"What happens to the soul of a baby who has been aborted? And what kind of music were the Ugly Brown Birds singing?"

Gabriel reappeared. "Quaint expression, soul. The soul, or spirit, comes in when it is time, usually near or during a lunar eclipse. If a woman terminates her pregnancy, the soul knows this and does not enter. It is not the time for the soul or spirit to unite with the mother and all the other beings the new human would encounter. So, no harm is done to what you call the soul." Gabriel looked thoughtfully at Emily. "To answer your second question, the Ugly Brown Birds were sending out music to be used in a commercial."

"A commercial?!" With the exception of Alter, who looked confused, the group wore identical startled expressions.

"Yes, a commercial. This particular one is for those special shoes you humans run in. The company is donating money to a charity that helps children who have no shoes at all. The person tasked with composing music that would inspire people to buy or donate to the charity was having, oh my, here I go again. What is that expression?"

"Writer's block?" Joshua suggested.

"Yes, thank you, Joshua. So, we helped this songwriter. She should have the song when she wakes up. Right now, I believe she is drunk. Were my answers helpful, Emily?"

"Thank you, yes they were." Emily's face had cleared.

"Khalid? Questions?" Gabriel paced slowly in a small circle near Khalid. Khalid's eyes were greener than usual, the color of freshly mown grass in spring.

"I also have two questions. Why is sex or sexual preference such a big deal? And why are there cultural biases?"

Gabriel paced with his hands clasped behind his back. "Yes, very good, Khalid. I assumed you would ask such questions. We have lots of laughs here about sex. Don't ask me why it is so feared or seen as taboo. For heaven's sake, you cannot have life without sex! Yes, it has been distorted and even used as a terrible weapon, but sex between adults is beautiful. The benefits are immeasurable." The Ugly Brown Birds stopped singing and the trees in the Great Green Sanctuary stopped swaying.

"Some of us believe the reason sex took on such importance in your spiritual literature is that it scared people. The power it holds is natural but can overwhelm. Sadly, during the early days of major religions, demonizing sex was a way to exert power over others. Sex is meant to bring pleasure, raise your vibrations, and improve health. And if the two people involved are a man and a woman, sometimes a child is the result of all this power. Sex is not meant to make victims out of anybody. I cannot stress that strongly enough. Khalid, sex scared the hell out of humans, so they put rules and restrictions in place to subdue its power." Gabriel threw his head back and exploded into laughter. Everyone held onto their chairs, which had begun to rock. The bird cages swung wildly; the diaphanous orb of stars expanded. On earth, a sudden whirlwind barreled through a prairie ghost town, ripping a rusted sign off an empty gas station.

"To summarize, Khalid, sex is a wonderful, magical gift for humans. And as with so many wonderful, magical gifts, humans have—how would you put this, Joshua?—oh yes, fucked it up. Even worse, they attributed all these restrictions to one holy book or another. Okay, what was your second question?"

Khalid laughed. "My second question is why we have cultural biases."

Gabriel stopped pacing. "Khalid, when you first came here, did you have any biases toward any of our wonderful group?"

"Yes, yes, I did. I may still have some."

"Why do you think that is?"

"We have certain cultural habits and—"

"Exactly. You are right, my dear Khalid. Certain cultural habits, mannerisms and neuroses are imprinted on every culture on earth.

And what, may I ask, is wrong with that? Nothing. Unlike sex, cultural biases are not something we laugh at here. In fact, they pain us. Why not rejoice in these differences? Why not celebrate them? Become curious, or as my friend Howard suggests, invoke your 'holy curiosity.' The answer to your question, Khalid, is fear. That is all. Fear and a depressing lack of curiosity. This fear of the other is very old and may have served humankind once, but no longer. Your world today cannot survive without embracing your differences."

"May I go next?"

"Yes, of course, dear Sunita. How may I help you? What questions have troubled or perplexed you?"

"Thank you, Gabriel, for doing this. I have only one question, and it is from my heart. Will my parents ever be happy again? I mean in the life they are currently living. I cannot imagine how painful my death is for them."

"Yes, they will be happy. As a matter of fact, they are close to being happy now. They will always love and miss you, but they have found a treasured place to put those feelings and have been able to alchemize their deep feeling of grief to one of gratitude for you as a daughter. But, if I can take a side road for a moment? Quite frankly, we do not understand this human obsession with happiness. Constantly and desperately seeking happiness takes people away from growing as humans. The first step toward happiness is to stop looking for it. But back to your beautiful question, Sunita. When you died, you left behind love, and your parents will feel the exquisiteness of your love for the rest of their lives. The love you bequeathed them will always, always push aside the hurt. It is very simple. Love is stronger than pain."

Sunita stood and bowed deeply. Gabriel bowed even more deeply in return.

"Joshua, do have questions for me?"

"Nope, I'm good." Joshua slouched, arms folded, a look of calculated boredom on his face.

"Come now, Joshua, you are the project manager. You must have some questions."

"No, really, I can't think of a thing. Thanks, though."

Gabriel studied his hands. A frisson of anxiety ran through the group. "Susan!" His smile was sunny. "I am sure you are ready with your questions."

Susan squared her shoulders. "Thank you, Gabriel. I'm wrestling whether to replace my second question with one that just this minute came to me. I don't want to waste my questions, so I'll make a statement." She swiveled toward Joshua and stabbed a finger at him. "You should not be our project manager!" She scanned the room for support, but Reinhardt was focused on the Room of Reflection, Emily was staring at the Ugly Brown Birds, and Sunita was examining the Wall of the Seven Heavens. Khalid and Alter seemed to be dozing. Susan harrumphed and turned back to Gabriel.

"Very well, on with my questions. First, where is my dog, Raj? And second, why do we have so many religions?"

"Thank you, Susan. Those are good questions. Raj is well and on another realm that is neither above nor below this realm in terms of importance or value. Raj, like all animals who die, is happy in this other realm. In some cases, animals are reunited with their owners. For now, we need you here, but he sends his regards." Gabriel smiled brightly.

"Your second question is of course a doozy! Now, I hate to place the blame on humans, but the divisions in religion are similar to biases in culture. Why not celebrate differences, we ask! For heaven's sake! A very long time ago, a time when time was not measured, at least in the way it is measured now, and boy is it measured now—" Gabriel convulsed in laughter. "Forgive me. Whenever I use the word *time*, it cracks me up. Where was I? Ah, yes. A long time ago, it was believed that offering a variety of wisdom traditions and religions would help people. Amazing stories, myths and beliefs, all coming from a universal love beyond human comprehension, would empower people and help them to evolve more quickly. Each tradition holds a piece of the universal truth. Spirit-hearts confined within human bodies would create beauty and radiate love. The hope was that all these rich and varied beliefs would inspire people to explore. Some in our realms believe this ancient experiment still has value. Others think the whole thing has become distorted and self-serving, and it's time to pull the plug. I hold onto hope that people will some day pause and breathe in the beauty found in every religion. Call me a romantic or an idealist, but these religions were created from love, after all."

Susan staggered to her feet. "So no religion or spiritual tradition is greater than another? And they were created to offer people beauty and wisdom? Am I understanding this correctly, Gabriel?"

"Yes, that was the original intent."

"Uh …" Susan looked dazed. "I'd better … I'll just …" Tottering toward the Room of Reflection, she bumped into a potted plant, muttered *sorry*, and kept going.

"Reinhardt, are you ready with your questions?"

"Yes. Will all sentient beings be enlightened? And," he looked down at his big hands, "will I be reborn to a Buddhist family?"

"Yes, that is the idea for you Buddhists, isn't it? For everyone to become enlightened. The short answer is yes, there will be a time. The missions you are all about to carry out will help. A bit. We hope. I do not mind telling you, my dears, we are in a bind. But any opportunity, no matter how insignificant, helps move people forward. As for your next rebirth, how about a nice Catholic family in Boston?"

Reinhardt inhaled sharply, his face blank.

"If you could see yourself, Reinhardt!" Gabriel's laughter boomed. This time, only a remote part of the Indian Ocean was impacted by the vibrations. No ships capsized.

"I am teasing you, Reinhardt. I am not authorized to share with you details of any future rebirth. Well, everyone, I guess that is a wrap. Our brief Q and A—is that how you say it, Joshua?"

Joshua nodded glumly.

"I trust your questions have been answered to your satisfaction." Gabriel prepared to leave. The stellar nursery was gone, leaving only a shimmering blue and purple afterglow.

"Wait!" Joshua called. "Ah, I may have a question after all."

"Is that so?"

"Yes, for one thing and, again I'm just trying this out, because I still believe my dying brain is severely fucked up, but suppose, out of curiosity, that I entertain this—"

"Joshua, if you have a question, ask. I do not have all the time in the world." Gabriel was about to break into another round of laughter but stopped. The realm was now in line with Barcelona. Too big a city. Too beautiful. Tapas would be under way.

He regarded Joshua, who was clearly putting an effort into maintaining his *I don't give a flying fuck* attitude.

"My question, that is, one of my questions, has to do with suicide. From what I understand about the glorious wisdom of Islam and Christianity, both Emily and Khalid would have us believe someone who commits suicide will fry to a crisp in hell. I'm not sure what Jews believe." He looked anxiously at Alter. "I suppose you go through some cleaning process and—"

"It is the same as murder." Alter's voice was dry as November leaves in a deserted park. "Your life is not yours to take. It is given by God."

"Okay, uh, thanks, Alter. I don't know what crazy fairy people think, and Buddhists probably believe someone who offs himself is reborn as a rabbit."

"That's not true, Joshua," Reinhardt said with some impatience.

"Enough!" Gabriel's face darkened. "Ask your question."

"I guess that's my question. What happens to a person who commits suicide?"

Gabriel puffed out his cheeks. "I hope you understand there are some things we cannot share with you. But I can share this. Some people are born with too little protection. Most people are born with a protective covering, but those who commit suicide have little or none." Calm brown eyes looked inquiringly into anxious green ones. Gabriel's voice softened. "They also absorb pain and trauma, and it becomes trapped. So, my dear ones, they are given a pass."

"A pass? What is this protective covering? Absorb pain?" Susan, who was still looking fragile, had returned. "Has anyone else heard of this? I never came across it in any of the—" Joshua held up a palm to shush her. "Please don't do that, Joshua. You remind me of my ex-husband."

"Happy to give you fond memories of—"

"Joshua?" Gabriel's expression was mild. "I am afraid my visit here is almost done. You had one more question?"

"Crazy people. Why?"

Emily gasped. "So crude, Joshua. And so heartless. Do you have any idea how much pain and torment people who struggle with mental illness endure?"

"Do you have any idea how flipping much family members suffer who live with a crazy person, especially a parent?"

"Joshua," Gabriel said again. "Focus, please. A considered response will take too long, but I will say this. Sometimes a person who is deemed crazy is tuned into vibrations or energies that do not fit the parameters of what is deemed normal. Sometimes such a person is a brilliant architect of something the world is not ready to receive. They are born with a wild energy, and there may not be a place to safely use it. And there are indeed sad and painful situations in which all suffer. But I have overstayed. Adios!"

Gabriel was gone.

Gabriel was back.

"I almost forgot. We knew you would have questions. The reason I was here in person is that answering your questions and eliminating concerns frees up space and elevates your vibrations. If only humans on earth realized this truth. When knowledge is satisfied or a fear eliminated, your vibrations increase. *Mata ne!*"

Now Gabriel really was gone.

"Mata ne? What does that mean?" Emily said.

"It means 'See you later' in Japanese." Reinhardt pushed himself out of his chair and headed for the Room of Reflection.

Chapter 25: Gabriel Explains the Tellings

"I wonder what poor bastard he's tapping now?" Joshua strolled in to join the others in the Great Unnamed Room. They were waiting for Gabriel to appear, and most had agreed the summons sounded like the bell of an ice cream cart. The only holdout was Alter. He'd said it was unfair to use this bell, as he had no idea what ice cream was, let alone an ice cream cart.

"Okay, Mr. New York, how do you know Gabriel's on earth?" Emily said.

It was just before their morning meal, and Reinhardt was feeling hunger pangs. Despite the discomfort, he felt pleasantly surprised at being able to feel anything physical. He shifted in his chair. "I have a sense Gabriel can only move between this realm and the earth realm. So, if he's not here, I think we can safely assume he's somewhere on earth."

"I can't stand it!" Joshua yelled. "All this fucking talk about realms! I never expected dying to be this complicated—I just want to slip into the big black!"

Using the cajoling tone one hopes will coax a bad-tempered cat from under the sofa, Susan said, "Joshua, do all atheists believe in this *big black*, as you call it?"

Her tone irritated Joshua, but he was determined not to let her see it. "I have no idea what other atheists call death," he said more reasonably. But he couldn't resist adding, "Unlike people who follow some fucked-up religious path, we think for ourselves."

Sunita spoke quietly. "That is a little insulting, Joshua. With the exception of you, all of us here have followed one path or another, and all of us felt a devotion and commitment to our chosen path. Each of us, in our own way, was onto something bigger than ourselves. Our world began in mystery, and our paths led us to explore these mysteries."

As though he'd been listening, Gabriel appeared on screen. Those on their feet quickly moved to an armchair in the semicircle.

"Good morning, I trust you rested well. I won't keep you long, as I know some of you would like to enjoy your morning meal."

Khalid whispered to Reinhardt, "It looks like he's in the desert."

"Yes, yes, I am traveling through one of your deserts. Please remember I can hear you."

He was back to wearing the white tunic and wide-legged pants. The gleaming white against the sepia backdrop of endless sand created a soothing effect that was only disturbed by a snake of thick black smoke in the distance.

"Not to—". A juddering thud interrupted him. Within seconds, another plume of black smoke rose, and the image wavered. "Not to rush, but I do have things to do and people to see."

The seven glanced at one another uneasily.

"No worries, no one you know. But on to the business at hand. We don't usually do this, but your group is in a special situation." Gabriel thumbed the crease between his brows. "It has been decreed that each of you will participate in the Telling. That is, each of you will share your life story." This statement was met by exclamations and murmurs.

"The rules are straightforward," he continued. "We suggest you spread the Tellings over a few days, and you may decide among yourselves who goes first. Each of you may choose where you wish to share your life story—here in the Great Unnamed Room or in the kitchen or library. You may choose to tell the story yourself or use a narrator. Now, you might be curious. I do love that about you humans, your curiosity. Even though it has got you into some sticky situations, it never fails to delight me. So I imagine you are curious as to why the Tellings should happen. What is their importance? Why share your life story with the others? It is simply this. The Tellings will give you an opportunity to get to know one another better. And we need you to trust one another." He waited, but the group was silent.

"Dear ones, this is absolutely essential. Through centuries and millennia, we have observed that humans make assumptions about one another, and often these assumptions are wrong. They lead to judgments, and these judgments in turn have led to some disastrous consequences. The Tellings will help you to understand one another. When people understand one another's histories, they are less likely to form assumptions and judge one another harshly."

The group shifted in their seats and looked at one another awkwardly. In their vast cages, the Ugly Brown Birds sang a few tentative notes, as though for themselves. On the screen, skies empty of birds were streaked by black smoke. Gabriel stood in absolute stillness as thuds shook the ground.

"As project manager, I think we could forgo these Tellings, as you call them. We've spent a good deal of time together. I think the rest will agree that we've gotten to know each other fairly well."

"Joshua, you seem to have forgotten the word *decreed*. It has been decided. If you hope to slip into your big black sooner rather than later, I suggest you cooperate. Who knows," Gabriel added, "it may be fun. I look forward to hearing all about it. Cheers and blessings!"

"I really, really don't want to do this." Emily's shoulders were hunched, her hands twisting in her lap.

"I'm with you," Joshua said. "Hey, let's stage a revolt. You know, an Occupy thing."

Khalid laughed. "Occupy Heaven? Oh, man, let's just get on with it, so we can—"

Reinhardt heaved himself out of his armchair. "Let's discuss this further at breakfast."

Without a word, Alter pushed himself up and made for the kitchen, deep in thought. The others followed, discussing what Gabriel had said.

Somewhere out of sight, a lyre was playing. Alter's heart lifted to hear music he knew. He hoped the others would enjoy it.

"This music is delightful, Alter," Sunita said kindly. His lined face broke into a rare smile.

"What does everyone think about having the first of the Tellings in the kitchen?" Emily glanced over the rim of her mug of tea to gauge the others' reactions. "Perhaps at the morning meal?"

"In Jaipur and in other places in India, some people, especially couples, would sit under a Banyan tree and talk." Sunita spoke with a reminiscent smile. "Many Banyan trees throughout India hold many confidences, whispered secrets and ancient stories."

"Yes," Reinhardt added. "The Banyan tree is sacred to many cultures. It was the Banyan tree the Buddha was sitting under when he achieved enlightenment."

"I'd love to hear more about Banyan trees," Susan said warmly. "One of my gurus lived near Goa in your beautiful country. I would usually go straight to the ashram from the airport, but I remember the driver pointing out those trees to me on the way."

"There are no Banyan trees here, so I believe that wraps up this talk." Reinhardt said.

Joshua grinned. "I love you Germans. Straight to the point!"

Reinhardt laughed.

"So," Joshua said. "Let's recap. Gabriel suggested we have only two Tellings a day. Susan will offer hers after lunch today in the Room of Reflection. I'll go next in the kitchen. Reinhardt will go first thing tomorrow after breakfast?" Reinhardt nodded. "And his Telling will take place in front of the Great Green Sanctuary. And Emily after lunch tomorrow here in this," he waved a hand around the kitchen, "this heart of our home."

Emily stuck out her tongue at Joshua. His stomach flipped, which brought him to a standstill. Was he attracted to Emily? How could he feel his stomach flip when he was dead? He cleared his throat uncertainly and carried on.

"The lovely Sunita will have her Telling first thing after breakfast the following day near the birds. Khalid, would you like to go after Sunita?" Khalid lifted a shoulder and nodded.

"Khalid will give his Telling under the Arabic writing at the Wall of the Seven Heavens. And Alter in the library. Do you mind going last? I can change with you if—"

"I am fine to go last."

Susan announced, "Well, I better prepare for my Telling."

"Not the Oscars, Susan, not the Oscars." Joshua deadpanned.

Alter headed out to the library.

"Nice to see Alter enjoying the library so much," Sunita remarked.

"Yes," Emily said. "It's the most magnificent room I've ever seen. I suppose you've seen grander?"

Sunita took Emily's arm. "It is true, especially in India, I have seen remarkable monuments and palaces. But this library is the most beautiful. One thing I love about beauty is that it is indefinable. And it takes an open heart to see it."

Emily's eyes were on Alter's retreating back. "I fear I wasted time." She unlinked her arm from Sunita's and shivered, her face desolate. "Sunita, I focused too much on my sadness. And on wants that were so stupid! I fear I missed all the beauty and love."

"Oh my dear." Sunita crooked her arm again, and after a moment Emily took it. Together they walked across the Great Unnamed Room; the Wall of the Seven Heavens radiated light in their direction. Khalid nodded to them as he turned in to the library after Alter.

Joshua stood by the bridge in perfect stillness watching Sunita and Emily, who were now talking, heads together, on a cushioned bench.

"Which one are you attracted to?"

Joshua jumped back and sputtered. "Susan, in case you haven't noticed, we're all dead. Dead people don't fall in love with other dead people."

He stormed off but stopped. He didn't know where to go. With as much purpose as he could muster, Joshua headed into the library and found a chair in a shadowed corner. He needed time to think.

PART II: THE TELLINGS

I'm staying indoors today. On such a chilly, dirty afternoon, even my dog doesn't care to go outside. He seems grumpy. Here I sit in the kitchen with scrolls and scrolls to read and write out. I walk around them to get to the counter to make tea. Or whatever.

Gabriel says I'm doing well, but I think he's being nice.

So our seven are getting to know one another better. Gabriel says it's important that, until they do, not much happens. It would upset the balance or something. But he's anxious about how fast the connection between heaven and earth is weakening and tells me I don't know the half of it. Whenever we get around to talking about it, he sips more gin and becomes quite gloomy.

Yesterday the rain was falling hard, bouncing off the front walk. He was sitting watching it splash and was quiet for a bit. Pensive, you might say. He looked at me with those eyes of his and said, "Mrs. Potts, you are a fortunate human being." Then he left, but he left heavy with something.

Today it's so windy even the birds have the good sense to stay out of the sky. I wonder sometimes about this strange group of seven, wonder if they're stirring up the wind.

Anyways, this next part is called the Tellings. Everyone decided to use a narrator to tell their story. Susan was going to tell hers herself—Lordy, that woman loves drama. But in the end she went along with the others. She hustled to the front of the line, though. ~ Mrs. Potts

Chapter 26: Susan

A few more strokes and he'd be done. It wasn't often she was commissioned to paint a fairy picture for a straight man, but his wife of thirty years had sought her out. And they had money. Her paintings were selling for forty thousand dollars, and the price was rising.

What would it feel like to be with someone for thirty years? Would she be bored? Or would it be a comfort to be with someone who knew you well and loved you anyway? Susan rubbed her neck and stood up to stretch into a Crescent Moon pose. Raj, her Tibetan spaniel, opened one eye to see what was going on. She came out of the pose to rub his ears.

"What do you think, Raj? Is it finished?" He got up from his brocade pillow, turned around three times, and collapsed again with a snuffle and a deep sigh. After a moment his paws were twitching.

"Chasing rabbits?" Raj was good company for the solitude of painting. Susan picked up a palette knife and laid a miniscule twist of Gold Ochre on the canvas. It was just over fourteen years since she became the Fairy Lady. She'd been dabbling with fairies for years, but it wasn't until one of her husband's patients had seen a painting hanging in his office that her career had taken flight.

Her then husband.

Tim had reluctantly agreed to hang her fairy depiction of one of their children in the waiting room of his upscale clinic. He was the go-to plastic surgeon for aging actors, actresses and politicians. The clinic was discreetly situated on a quiet street just outside Seattle. Front-pagers would fly in, have their work done, and recuperate in some serene out-of-the-way location nearby.

It had happened fast. An actress client of Tim's, on the talk show circuit peddling her latest movie, had gushed about Susan's fairy paintings and how lush, ethereal and powerful they were. She described how Susan used several photos spanning years of her subject's life, plus a personality description and a selection of personal belongings, to create her masterpieces. (When the talk show host enquired if Susan was the wife of the famed plastic surgeon, the actress claimed not to know.)

After that nationwide plug, Susan was inundated with orders. Her modest rates skyrocketed, and soon, satisfyingly, she was earning as much as her husband.

Her latest venture was a women's and children's clothing line featuring fairy designs and styles. Wild fiery designs, subtle earthy designs, translucent watery designs and filmy airy designs made of chiffon, silk or light cotton were imprinted on dresses, pants and tops. They were selling like crazy in seventeen countries. She'd also been approached to launch a line of perfumes that reflected the four elements of fire, earth, water, and air. They were still in the experimental stage, but she was excited.

She took a few steps back from the painting and eyed it critically. She'd portrayed him as an Earth Fairy, with thick layers of deep russets, desert tans and multiple shades of green serving as the painting's base. The background atmosphere felt ominous and agitated. From this moody chaos, the subject emerged, virile and solid. Dark, leathery wings, edged with hanging moss, opened wide to surround his body. The moss was so vivid you could almost smell the musky scent of rotted earth and feel its lush wetness. Bold splashes of yellows, reds and oranges mingled, played and clashed in a celebratory dance in the foreground. There was nothing delicate here. He stood, feet apart, a defiant but playful look on his face. Susan had embedded bits of twigs into his salt-and-pepper hair and beard. She was pleased and a little in love; Susan fell a little in love with every subject. His bio had moved her. In a rare handwritten letter, his wife wrote that he had recently sold his shares in a chain of home and garden stores. And he was in remission. During his illness and recovery, they had rediscovered their love for each other and for long, aimless walks in the woods. He was ready, said his wife, "after a lifetime of business, to believe in a bit of magic and even miracles." Susan had already chosen the feather that she embedded into every painting.

At a sun-dance ceremony years ago, a Native American elder had told her that eagle feathers symbolized courage. Susan gently blew on the feather and placed it near his feet.

As the desert sun began its descent, she poured a glass of pinot noir to toast the painting, the subject and his story. Then she opened a sliding door and stepped onto the adobe patio to toast the departing sun. Raj stirred and trotted outside with her.

A few years ago, looking for a new place to live, she had driven realtors in three states crazy before finding this 1920s adobe house with its pueblo style courtyard and vast view of Taos Mountain. Light! How did she ever live without the New Mexico light?

Her spiritual adviser, who was also a skilled numerologist, gave her full approval. A well respected feng shui expert in Taos did a room-by-room Flying Star analysis and an Eight Mansion reading, then created a chart for the year of the house and for any year when there might have been significant renovations. In a detailed report, he carefully outlined the ideal spaces for creativity, relaxation and her altar room. Susan scrupulously followed his sacred recommendations. She kept her condo in Seattle for when she craved the ocean.

She loved the altar room, which she adorned with icons from every faith. The status of these icons rose and fell according to her mood, current guru, and the latest spiritual trends. She attended classes and workshops around the country and even abroad to follow a particular spiritual person of note. On this day, the altar room reflected shamanism. To honor this path and pay homage to where she lived, she had placed Hopi Kachina figures on the highest spot to act as sentries. Angels, the previous occupants of this prized placement, were relegated to a lower shelf. She swiped a finger along the shelf; it needed dusting.

As dusk gathered, Susan headed indoors and switched on a light.

"What'll we have for supper, Raj?" She was pouring a second glass of wine when the phone rang.

"Susan? Hello?"

She attempted to breathe out her resentment and anger. Breathe. Release. Breathe. It wasn't working. "What do you want, Tim?"

"Susan, are you sitting down?" She stood up straighter and gave him the finger with the hand that wasn't holding the phone. "Susan, I'm very sorry to be the one to tell you, but your mother has passed away. She died in her sleep this morning."

It wasn't as though she wasn't expecting the call, but she was taken aback to hear her ex-husband's voice. Why hadn't her brother or sister called, or even one of her daughters?

"I'm just surprised that you're the one to call me, Tim. As you know, my mother was close to all of us. When this day came, I expected to hear from one of ..." Her voice trailed to silence. From the other end of the phone line, she heard an exhalation of air.

"The family thought it best for me to make the call. Will you be all right? Can you come?"

"What a question. I loved my mother dearly. Of course I'll come." Tim gave her the funeral details and rang off.

Susan's mother had been ill for a long time, and Susan flew to San Diego as often as she could to visit her in the nursing home. It was always exhausting and sad. Her mother no longer recognized her, but before that light had dimmed, she'd made it clear she thought Susan had made a mistake divorcing Tim and that she intended to keep a close relationship to her son-in-law.

An astrologer who specialized in past lives told Susan that her mother and Tim had shared many past lives and had old business together. "Okay, so maybe this is part of their old business," she told Raj. After supper, she'd speak to her sister, brother and daughters. She didn't want to give them the satisfaction of knowing she was hurt or angry. She was far too spiritual for that.

Glass in hand, she headed back out to the patio, limping slightly. She really must lose weight; her knees weren't getting any younger. Lightning forked across the deepening dark of the desert sky, answered by a deep rumble of thunder. Or was the mountain speaking after eons of patient silence? Is this what a mountain would sound like? Susan rubbed her eyes. Her fingers came away wet. "Damn," she said to the silence and the dark. She eased herself into a chair.

The air felt strange. Years ago, she'd been top of the class when she took a course in symbolism, how to read everyday signs and the secret messages encoded. It annoyed her now that she couldn't read the messages and signs she felt were clearly present. Tomorrow she would fly to San Diego and hold herself together. The long awaited death of her mother and all the fleeting drama that had led up to this end. I *should offer a Christian prayer for Mother,* she thought. *St. Clare? That won't work—she's the patron saint of television. St. Rita? Hah. She's the patron saint of impossible cases, difficult marriages and parenthood. The secret lives of mothers ...*

How well have you loved?

Susan's head jerked up, and she peered into the darkness. She wasn't afraid. Her house and its surroundings had received the spiritual stamp of approval.

How well have you loved?

This time, her stomach lurched. Perhaps this was finally a sign from one of her guides, angels or messengers from a higher frequency. It was about time. She'd been taught that when there is a death of someone close, our own vibrations are raised and thus able to connect with higher beings.

"So this is it. I am ready," she said to the empty dark. Thunder growled and lightning flashed, illuminating a slice of desert. Raj slept on.

Her breath quickening, Susan felt a pull down a tunnel. For a moment, she feared her round body would become stuck. Her high, nervous laughter echoed. She let herself go and surrendered to whatever psycho-spiritual epiphany might be revealed.

If she was expecting to visit other realms in this spontaneous vision quest, she was disappointed. It all felt very present. She could almost feel the cool ceramic blue and white tile beneath her feet and smell the bitter aroma of the last of the morning coffee. She and Tim were having "the divorce talk." She felt part of the scene being played but oddly disconnected. *Just like my marriage.* He stood silent. Even now, she could feel her chest tighten with fury at his impassivity.

"You wouldn't understand. It's spiritual!" Susan was telling Tim about her lover. He turned and walked out the door. When Susan told her lover she had ended her marriage, he ended their affair the same day.

Another pull, another scene.

Her grade seven history report on women in World War Two was due in a week. Her dad had been a pilot in the air force, but her mom? They had met during the war, but neither talked about it much. She had to know.

Sunday's chicken dinner. Her father carved, her mother spooned green beans and mashed potatoes onto plates.

"Mom, Dad, I know you guys met a long time ago in the war." Susan looked anxiously at them both and carried on with a rush. "But, Mom, what were you doing? You guys want me to get good grades, and I'm writing a history report. Everyone talks about the brave men, but what did the women do? Knit socks? Sit and wait?" She looked from one to the other.

Her mom smoothed her apron and spoke quietly. "I was a Fly Girl, a WASP."

"WASP? I don't understand. White Anglo-Saxon—?"

"I was a Women's Air Force Service Pilot."

"You flew planes?!" Susan had read about these pioneering women. More than twenty-five thousand applied, and fewer than eleven hundred were accepted. And her quiet, home-making PTA mother had been one of them, flying dangerous missions and ferrying planes, goods and ammunition around the country.

"That's how we met, Pumpkin," her father said. "I was stationed in California, and your mother was flying a plane from Arizona. When I saw that slip of a girl climb down from the cockpit, carrying a parachute that was too big for her, I was smitten."

"Susan, it may be hard for you to imagine, but I was the daredevil in the family. My mother was dead set against me doing something so foolish and risky, but Dad gave me the money for the training, and I was off to do my bit." Susan's mother started to clear away dishes.

"Did you love it, Mom? Were you scared? Did you almost die? Do you miss it? Did you kill anybody? Why did you stop?"

Her mother glanced at her father. She set slices of peach pie in front of Susan and her father and brought a cup with the dregs of the coffee back to the table. "I'll tell you what you need for your history report, but that's all," she said firmly.

How well have you loved?

Dawn. The lightning and thunder had stopped. Raj was on the end of the bed looking oddly at her. Susan felt unnerved.

As she turned to shut off the soft bells of her Zen-inspired alarm clock, she looked gritty-eyed at the photo of her mother on the bedside table. Walking with the confident briskness of youth and beaming broadly at the camera in her aviator jacket, her mother with two other Fly Girls strode away from an airplane. They appeared happy, carefree and proud. Susan thought, not for the first time, that she wished she'd known that woman. For a moment she wondered what it would feel like to be a Fly Girl, to feel so sure about what you were doing in life.

"Come on, Raj. You and I have a plane to catch."

Susan packed quickly. Dressing carefully in her newest fairy dress, she picked up a disgruntled Raj in his crate and walked out into the cool desert morning. Everything looked the same, but it felt changed. She shivered.

As the sun rose, the air began to thicken with heat. Susan turned on the air conditioning as she pulled out of the driveway. This drive, with its beautiful light and the juniper and piñon pines dotting the dry hills, always reminded her why she loved it here. She hummed along with the generous notes of "Return of the Angels." Three stories kept running through her brain. She turned the music up in hopes of singing these thought-stories to sleep. It didn't help.

The first story was called *Mother*. The second was *How well have you loved?*, the uncanny experience of the previous evening. Susan pictured herself telling that story to her spiritual group and being greeted by awe and jealousy. There she was, radiant in her Air Fairy purple dress, speaking in a hushed voice, recounting her strange story. The group would love it. They would spend months picking the story clean. Susan smiled to herself. At that point, when there was nothing left to analyze, they would urge her to see a hypnotherapist to uncover anything else that would illuminate a deeper spiritual meaning.

The third story was *Family Issues*. God, she was sick of the word *issue*. But how else to describe the years of unresolved tensions, miscommunication and mistreatment at the hands of her family? And Tim was at least partly to blame. Would her mother's funeral be the stage for the last scene in this tired old drama? Susan pulled into the airport parking lot.

Susan and airports did not get along. Lost luggage, bad-tempered personnel, security problems, lost boarding passes, food poisoning (the airline disputed this), foul smelling seatmates—every time, and in every airport, something always happened. A spiritual adviser had told her that her particular vibration would never work well with any airport. But here they were and all was well. She was a little spooked about how smoothly everything had gone. She was seated comfortably in first class. A tall, good looking flight attendant appeared with a breakfast tray. The plane dipped suddenly. He smiled and the plane righted itself. Susan knitted her brows together but smiled warmly at him as he set the tray in front of her. There was something a bit off about him, but his smile was charming. When he came back to take her tray away, he bumped her elbow and gave her another dazzling smile. Gold wings were attached to his uniform with *Navigator* engraved in bright blue.

"What kind of name is Navigator?" Susan asked, her voice teasing. She was glad she'd taken a minute to put on lipstick before she boarded. He smiled again but did not speak. He seemed to be exclusively serving her. She would definitely use this airline again.

The Greenwood cemetery was perfect. It was also the only thing the family had agreed on. Susan briefly offered up an Inuit prayer for her mother. She hated the moment when the casket was about to close but managed to slip the picture of the three Fly Girls inside.

Her sister, brother and their spouses stood at a distance from Susan; Tim and his new wife stood with them. Tim's eyes held an odd mixture of sadness and reproach when he looked at her. Susan practiced her "shield of emotional armor" without much success. The whole stupid situation hurt. If Alexa and Dana had been able to come, they would have served as buffers. Not that Susan and her daughters were close, but they were adept at peacemaking and had inherited the family trait of denial. *I don't want to talk about denial,* Susan thought with an awkward half-grin that quickly faded. They had called her when they got word of their grandmother's death, but both had cited busy career moments as to why they could not attend the funeral.

As they stood among the palm trees and the safely dead, Susan reflected on the choice of cemetery. The famous pioneer female aviator, Marvel Crosson, was buried here. Mother would have loved being in the company of such an amazing woman. Or, at least, the Fly Girl mother, the woman she was before marriage and motherhood had somehow drained her of possibilities.

Susan tried to tune out the minister and gently feel her mother's presence, but she felt nothing. *Of course.* Her mother was a Fly Girl. She knew how to lift off, to leave the earth behind.

Back in her hotel room, Susan stretched out on the bed and fell instantly asleep. Hours later, as the California sun slid into the Pacific, she woke.

How well have you loved?

Susan felt a strange combination of fear and excitement. Raj stretched in his crate and shook himself.

"Okay, your highness. I've had a bit of a day. Gimme a minute," she croaked. For a moment she was surprised at the sound of her own voice. *No wonder. I've spent the day surrounded by emotional vampires.* Emotional vampires. She knew what she had to do. She would clear herself of the negative energies she'd absorbed from her family.

Returning from a short walk with Raj, she spooned food into his dish and went online.

No success. Her trusted and favorite shamanic retreat centers were either full or not running programs right now. Her cherished shaman was in Paris with his wife and kids.

"What now?" Raj looked at her as though he'd been through this before. Susan went back online.

Within an hour, she had booked a flight and a week at an unfamiliar shaman center in southern Mexico, near the Guatemalan border. The website and its glowing testimonials impressed her. The center wasn't on her shaman's approved list, but she felt adventurous.

As the plane took off from San Diego, she settled into her seat. Again, there had been no glitches at the airport. Feeling a little foolish, she looked around for the strange flight attendant from the earlier flight. She tried to visualize what this center and the experience would hold for her. Maybe she would have a romantic encounter? It had been a long time.

Standing in the doorway of her red clay hut, her face bathed in the fading light of dusk, Susan breathed in the heavy scents and rising nighttime calls of the rainforest. *Erotic*, she thought. Her disquiet eased.

She and Raj had been picked up at the airport in a jeep with the words *Manuel's Jungle Safari* in bright orange on the side. Her usual shamanic haunts had their own vehicle and more discreet signage. Susan climbed in with more confidence than she felt. When they arrived, she was initially dismayed at the state of the buildings. Most could use a good carpenter and painter, but she reasoned that this made the experience more authentic. Staff seemed to be scarce, and the grounds were unkempt. Susan focused on the rainforest. It always made her feel wild and brave. Raj had loved it, running around the undergrowth at the edge of the clearing, chewing on roots and plants. He'd been lethargic when she left him to join the others, but maybe he was just tired after their travels.

Now, sitting in a circle with five other people, Susan scanned her fellow participants' energy fields. All she could pick up was their newness in this experience and hence their nervousness. Throughout the day, they had peppered Susan with questions on what to expect. They made her feel like an elder, and she was pleased at their perception of her as wise. She was the only one who was going to try the Fly Agaric.

In German, Fly Agaric is *Glückspilz,* or lucky mushroom, and represents one of the five symbols of good luck. In Mayan dialect, it is known as *Kukulja,* thunder. While searching online, Susan had discovered that this center claimed special expertise in Fly Agaric ceremonies. She was excited at the prospect of adding it to her spiritual resume. The center's shaman had reportedly spent years working with the rituals and sacred properties of this mushroom.

Susan was thrilled. It was Fly Agaric that opened the doors of ordinary perception to allow access to worlds of elves, little people and … fairies! Darkness deepened. As she and the others lay down on their mats, chants and drumming swelled to obscure the cacophony of the nighttime rainforest.

For a brief moment after Susan ingested the sacred powder, she thought she saw the strange flight attendant. "I want to see the fairies," she whispered. He spoke to her, but she could not make out the words.

Her head was swimming. She wanted to get up and dance, but fairies were holding her shoulders and laughing, the sound like tinkling crystals. Such beautiful, beautiful faces, and those wings, beating ever more slowly … How had she not known the colors in those wings? She could see … she could almost see …

To Susan it felt like a second, maybe two. She felt all her energies gather around her heart in a sweet loving lightness.

A brilliant burst of light. She was flying …

Never had she felt such love. Love for herself, for her children, for her brother and sister, for Tim (even for Tim), for her friends, for her whole world ... And yes. Yes. For her mother, who knew how to fly.

She could not contain this love. Her body could hold it no longer. It was time to surrender. As she soared, her vision was limitless. She could see the world below her, the heavens around her, and ... a cell phone?

Chapter 27: Joshua

It wasn't until the third night that Joshua became unsettled by the voice. On the first night, he'd told himself he was overtired and had drunk too much wine. On the second, it was stress from the looming project deadline.

How well have you loved?

There is a quiet mystery to 3:00 a.m. that romantics, poets and unstable people understand. But Joshua didn't believe in mysteries, and he knew he was no romantic. As for his poetry, it always stalled after "Roses are red." He turned over gingerly so as not to wake Gillian.

How well have you loved?

The voice was becoming insistent.

Joshua lay still, listening to his rapid heartbeat even as he tried to slow his breathing. He had worked hard to create order in his world. Whenever fear showed up, he would chase it away with more work or wine or running. Fear had been his companion since childhood. And now this damned voice was peeling back the thin layer of protection he'd built to cover that fear.

Okay, I'll go to the yoga class Gillian's been after me to try. He knew a promise made at 3:00 a.m. was unlikely to be honored. She'd said it would help relieve the constant stress of his work. If he made this promise, would the voice fade? He felt ridiculous. If Gillian hadn't been asleep beside him, he'd have been shouting back at the voice. He loved Gillian, but he loved his alone time almost as much. Even so, tonight he was grateful she was curled beside him. She was staying with him while she was in New York on business.

Finally, Joshua slipped back into a dreamless sleep.

At the shrill sound of the alarm, Joshua's eyes snapped open. Even as his mind went straight to the project, Gillian lazily rolled toward him and draped her arm over his chest. He gave her a quick dry kiss and swung his legs out of the comfort of the silk duvet.

"Time to seize the day. Carpe diem, and all that crap."

Whenever Gillian stayed for a few days, Joshua wished for a second bathroom. Not that she was messy, but the thought of someone else's hair and skin flakes in his space made him a bit queasy. He kept an antiseptic spray bottle and cloths tucked under the vanity and always insisted she shower before him so he could clean up after. He loved his condo and was proud he'd made it this far. This far and moving farther and farther away from the past.

The sun was making an early morning promise of warmth, a promise that would be broken by noon. Joshua and Gillian sat at the kitchen counter sipping coffee and eating bagels. He never tired of the view into the living room, with its clean modern furniture and artfully placed minimalist sculptures and American hyperrealism prints depicting future workplace environments. A memory of the voice echoed in his head. He took a deep breath and directed his thoughts toward the day's work.

Gillian looked up from her iPad. "Are you okay?"

"Sure, I'm fine. Why, do I look weird or something?"

"Oh, for God's sake, Josh. You look fine. A bit buttoned up, but considering who your clients are today, your look is fine."

"I'll be very happy when this project is done. It's strange ..." Joshua wasn't sure where that thought was going. He picked up his laptop. "We should get going. You have meetings and I have—"

"What's strange?"

"Nothing. It's all good." Joshua bent to give her another dry kiss on the top of her head. Gillian didn't push it. They'd been together three years, back and forth between states, negotiating time together. They knew each other fairly well. Now Gillian's company had offered her a position in a few states including here in New York, where Joshua's business was solidly rooted. Would they take the next step?

They both loved his condo in Battery Park. The view of the Hudson and the Statue of Liberty was breathtaking, and Joshua took pride in showing off the view to friends. Not to his family—they'd never been there. He'd never invited them.

Joshua loved her but rarely said *I love you*. There was no talk of marriage or even commitment. Gillian was okay with that for now, but she struggled with Joshua's tendency to shut down. She knew why he did that, but it didn't ease her pain. Gillian had grown up in a loving, hardworking family. Work and community were central to her parents' life, leaving them little time to spend with her, but she learned early on that doing well in school or achieving a goal that received outside recognition would elicit hugs and praise from her parents. Her grades were good, and for three years in a row she won the Outstanding Youth Community award.

Gillian's family loved Joshua, and he got on well with them. The notion of a small-town Midwestern boy making good in the big city appealed to her hardworking parents. They also liked his traditional views. Those views at times ran counter to Gillian's, but she felt with time he would relax them. She'd heard that people who held rigid views were often fearful and insecure. She worried about what her parents would think if they knew Joshua was an atheist. Or, as he put it, a devout atheist.

On one of their early dates, he had asked Gillian if she knew what the restaurant's name, Dharma Sushi, meant. The fact that she'd enjoyed a Comparative Religion course at university seemed to amuse him.

"For Buddhists, the dharma meant body of teachings from the Buddha, and for Hindus it conveyed a number of meanings, but one notable interpretation is natural order," she said.

"So do you believe any of that? You know, God, Buddha, elves, angels, spirit in the sky stuff?" He tried to sound nonchalant.

Gillian looked thoughtful. "I was brought up Christian, but like a lot of people I've questioned my faith. I haven't gone on any existential quest, though."

"So you're an agnostic?" he asked hopefully.

"I don't know if I'd say that. My friends have all kinds of beliefs. It seems to me that all the different belief systems have their points. For some people, believing seems to give them comfort. I'm reluctant to completely give up on my Christian upbringing."

To Joshua, this answer could only come from someone who'd had the luxury of a good and sane family. Gillian waved her chopsticks. "I don't think any belief should be imposed on anyone. Who am I to judge or know what's out there?"

Joshua didn't reply. Though the light was dim, they could read each other's face. The clatter of dishes set down in front of diners or cleared away, the clack of cutlery dropped on the bamboo floor and even a cringe-worthy version of "Happy Birthday" at a far table provided the backdrop to the lull in their conversation.

When a couple know there's something important that could create a rift in their relationship, they have three choices. They can let the issue go. They can risk the rift and talk it out. Or they can bury it to sit among their other hidden, buried resentments.

When Joshua was helping Gillian on with her coat at the end of the meal, he said, "I think it's fine to have differences. It would be boring as hell to agree on everything."

Gillian laughed and grabbed his arm. That evening they walked happily back to Joshua's condo, both feeling they'd survived a minor setback. Neither realized they'd chosen option three.

This sunny New York morning, he stopped on the sidewalk at the front of the building and kissed Gillian before they each departed for the day.

"Good luck!" called Gillian as she walked briskly in the opposite direction. Joshua was about to point out that luck was nonsense and his success would be due to his efforts, but Gillian was already out of earshot. He reached for his cell phone and started texting his business partner, Edison.

Joshua and Edison played well together. They had met in college and had dreamed up their business venture, "Up & On," after a night of drinking tequila in their dorm room.

Edison was born relaxed. He walked through life with the confidence of one whose family is at ease with itself. They neither looked for nor created drama. The only trauma had been when Edison's uncle died in Vietnam, but even that was before Edison arrived. His dad had wrapped up his sorrow and placed it on a high shelf, but when Edison came along, they named him after his uncle, and he was proud to bear the name. Edison was happy growing up, but like carrots or olives that require the deprivation of moisture or nutrients to grow, Edison didn't have "strive to thrive" energy until he met Joshua.

Edison was the first person Joshua told about his past. He was an unlikely therapist but listened without judgment and often without comment. This was foreign territory to Edison; he had assumed Joshua was a golden boy who got good marks with little visible effort, attracted girls, and was disciplined about diet and exercise. Sometimes his obsession with the right clothes and how things looked struck Edison as uptight, but Joshua could be thoughtful and kind.

Once Joshua knew it was safe to share his past with Edison, he opened up without reservation. The tequila made it easier.

"Things were never, you know, normal but Dad was a manager at an insurance company, and Mom ran a daycare. We had a nice house, and our small town was kind of typical. Everyone knew where they fit. I remember later hearing rumors that Dad's family were a bit, you know, off." Joshua spoke with hesitation, but he was determined to get the story out.

"It was my fifth birthday, and Mom had organized a party. Dad's job was to pick up the cake. It was a Transformers cake, and I was really excited. But he was really late. By the time he arrived, his nose was bloody and he was waving a Bible. He started babbling about how a squad of bad angels with black-tipped wings were after him and we all needed to be saved. He'd been told Mom and I were being enlisted to join the squad, and he had to save us because he loved us so much. Mom was trying to stop him, and kids were crying, but Dad had already crashed into his own dark world."

"Oh, man." Edison poured them both another shot.

"Yeah, well. Later Mom found my birthday cake half melted in the back seat. I think she was hoping to find a bottle of booze. Mom cleaned everything up, and after a few days Dad seemed to be mostly okay. He was still talking about God a lot and hearing voices. It seemed like overnight his eyes changed. The way he walked changed. Mom tried to hold things together and bring as much 'normal' into our daily routine as possible. But Dad crashed again. Fuck. At five years old, all I knew was that my birthday party had been ruined and my dad was now a scary guy. Our neighbors started to avoid us, and Mom's clients pulled their children out of the daycare. Dad was missing work, and when he did go, he'd fire off crazy accusations at his staff and co-workers. One night, I awoke to a loud crash. Dad had broken a window and was throwing out dishes, pots and pictures. He was yelling that ants were crawling on them and they were cursed. Mom tried to stop him, but he kept yelling for her to get out of the way. A neighbor called the cops. He spent a few weeks in hospital." Joshua took a deep breath.

"The diagnosis was paranoid schizophrenia. Mom took him to specialists in the city. With proper medication, they said, Dad could function well and live a normal life. Yeah, right. How the fuck was that going to happen? With neither of them working, we had to sell our house and moved to another neighborhood. Dad didn't always take his meds. Mom began to drink. I think that's when I began to act 'super normal.' They loved me, but it was like living on the edge. I never knew when Dad would start talking out loud to God or aliens. Sometimes I'd stand in front of a mirror and chat with an imaginary friend so I could make sure I looked and sounded normal. Pretty soon I stopped doing that because I was scared it might be crazy. I started to watch what I ate and how I dressed. In my teens, I read only nonfiction, books with knowable edges, because besides not wanting to be crazy, I didn't want to be stupid. I also had a plan. Stay sane. Avoid all religions. Get good marks. Get the hell out of here. Go to a college far away. Never, ever trust authority. I wrote this when I was nine years old, and so far it's still working." Joshua drained his glass and held it out.

"Dad is now a resident of a mental health facility in upstate New York. Sometimes he thinks he's their religious advisor, sometimes he's the social coordinator. No one corrects him. Mom stopped drinking and became a psychotherapist. Seeing as how she had all this experience with crazy people and all. Fuck."

By 2:00 a.m. the tequila bottle was nearly empty. They were lying on their cots staring up at the ceiling.

"Hey!" Edison said woozily. "I have an idea what we can do after college."

"What?" Joshua's mouth felt like sandpaper, and he reached under the bed for a bottle of water. He brought out two and pointed one at Edison, who shook his head.

"We could start a company, go into business together."

Joshua swung his feet onto the floor and steadied himself. Edison did the same. Joshua had a hunger and drive that were morphing into a passion for marketing. Edison had a gift for technology. They tossed around ideas and wrote company names on scraps of paper; they filled a bowl of water and threw the scraps in.

Whichever one floated the longest would be the name. This made perfect sense to their alcohol-soaked brains. "Up & On" won. It was Edison's idea but Joshua liked it. Edison's dad used to say it whenever someone was determined to be miserable. "Up and on" became the family catch-phrase for "Let's turn that page." By dawn they were talking about a company that would offer marketing and sales with web design and social media.

Fresh, eager and naive, they hit the ground at a gallop. The start-up of Up & On shredded nerves but excited them. As different as Joshua and Edison were, they shared a strong work ethic, and neither of them needed to learn lessons twice.

After ten years, Up & On was New York famous. Smaller, hungrier companies were nipping at their heels, and they knew they had to keep moving forward and faster. They had a motivated staff of fifteen and were looking to expand. Their business now included smart phone apps.

A rich online church with millions of followers worldwide approached Up & On with an idea for an angel app. A lucrative contract followed. Joshua thought the whole idea was ridiculous but decided to have some fun with it. He would manage this project himself.

Edison warned him to behave. While they were working on the app, Joshua let slip that he was an atheist. This got the Christian clients buzzing. They said they'd pray for him and offered him VIP seats at an upcoming Christian gathering that featured an A-list inspirational speaker. Politely, Joshua declined. After every meeting, they'd leave a pamphlet that only confirmed Joshua's biases.

The day the angel app launched, Joshua was surprised at how proud he felt, but he had worked on some of the creative elements himself. He ran through its features.

1. Choose your personal angel from a selection of hundreds. 2. Awaken to the sound of angels with the special alarm clock. Choose between the sound of angel wings or heavenly harps, or have your

personal angel speak your name (example: *Thomas, Thomas, this is your angel calling you. It is time for you to begin your blessed day.*). 3. Receive an angel message of the day with a blessing from your personal angel. We encourage you to share these and become a living angel! 4. Listen to an angel song of the day. These songs have been inspired by People of the Book. 5. Use our angel sightings map to explore the world. Press a button and discover where known angel sightings have occurred. A brief history of the location is offered with opportunities to do some angel traveling (member discounts). 6. Share in new angel encounters. A bell gently rings and a halo of light shows on a world map to indicate where the encounter has taken place. Whoever has had the blessed encounter has the option of having a photo of themselves featured. 7. Choose a loved one to be your personal angel. Your dearest ones may be watching you. This feature allows you to upload a picture and even sound recordings of your loved one. They will appear as your personal angel, and their loving voice will bring your daily message. 8. Name that angel! Beautiful pictures of known angels flash on screen. You have thirty seconds to guess the angel. Fun for you and your family. In no time, you will become an angel authority!

Number seven was Gillian's suggestion. Joshua was against it, but she and Edison said they knew lots of people who felt their deceased loved ones were watching out for them. Joshua found the idea preposterous until Edison outlined all the marketing opportunities. And if a deceased loved one was trying to send the user a message, the button feature would light up with the uploaded picture of their loved one, a bright golden halo over their head.

"Over their dead head?" Joshua asked between heaving gasps of laughter. "How the hell will that work?"

"Be nice, Josh," Gillian said.

The app's background color was a pearly white with peacock blues and golden yellows. Two large, folded angel wings opened to reveal a glorious heavenly scene with cherubs running around a meadow. It was going to make them all very rich.

The morning after the launch, Joshua was walking and talking on his phone as usual when he passed the bird man, a homeless guy who always had bits of bread and seeds in his pockets.

"God's little angels," the bird man sang out as he threw crumbs to the gathering pigeons. He gave Joshua an extra-long look that unnerved him.

"Who's that?" Edison's voice in the phone was muffled.

"Just some nutter. Are you eating, man?"

As Joshua swung around to eye the bird man, he crashed into a massive backpack. "Fuckin' watch yourself!"

Joshua and the owner of the backpack were sprawled on the sidewalk. People stepped around them, staring at their own phones. Joshua grabbed his phone, which had landed near the curb.

"What's going on?" shouted Edison.

"Some idiot just knocked me down to the sidewalk," Joshua said, giving the backpacker a dirty look.

"Are you okay?" Edison said.

"Yes, I'm fucking fine. Hang on, will you?" Holding onto his phone and dusting off his clothes, he glared at the owner of the backpack. He was about Joshua's age and could have been Asian, Italian, Middle Eastern ... Joshua had a sudden urge to get away from him, yet there was something oddly compelling about him. The backpack was covered with travel patches, and a pair of baby shoes dangled from one of the straps. Joshua realized he was still sitting on the sidewalk. Edison was yelling, "Josh, buddy, are you there? What's going on?"

"Yeah man, I'm okay. Just a second."

Backpacker man gave Joshua a big smile and said in a surprisingly strong, unaccented voice, "I will help you." A name tag on the front of his shirt read *Gabe*. Time seemed to slow down.

"I'm okay, just leave me alone," Joshua snapped but then felt bad. "I'm fine. Thanks."

Carefully dusting himself off, Joshua watched Gabe disappear into the crowd. He returned to his phone. "This has got to get better, man," he said. He could hear Edison breathe out with relief. "See you soon."

They were already waiting in the airy, open concept offices of Up & On when Joshua arrived.

"Son, as a small token of our faith and appreciation, we would like to give you, Joshua, plane tickets to California to witness our Miracles in Motion program. But not only that,"—he paused and boomed with a wide-mouthed grin—"we have arranged for you to go bungee jumping! Once a year, we round up a bunch of youngsters from good Christian households and, to test their faith in the good Lord, we head to California and take them bungee jumping. Because you know what they say ..." He paused for some response from Joshua, whose jaw was slack. "There are no atheists bungee jumping! Anyone who gets ready to take that big leap believes in some higher power!" He laughed uproariously. "Son, this could be it! Are you up to our little challenge?"

Joshua was leaning away until the word *challenge* made him straighten up again. "Mr. C., it has been an honor working with you. I will happily accept the challenge." Joshua would have preferred to say *Fuck you, Mr. C., and your little game of trying to convert me, you stupid asshole.*

"Oh for Chrissake," Gillian said that evening when Joshua told her. "Why did you accept? I thought we were going to Lake Placid."

"Well, there's potential for more business from this organization, and they've got well-heeled friends. I'll make it up to you. It's just a weekend. Oh fuck it, I'm pissed off at myself for being goaded into this. Come on, let's go to dinner." He held out her jacket.

The day of the jump was clear, cool and sunny after a restless night. The voice had interrupted his sleep again. *How well have you loved.*

As Joshua pulled up to the jump area, he could see they'd already started.

"Praise Jesus," bellowed Mr. C. as one teenager took the leap. Everyone looked as though they were having a great time. Mr. C. spotted him and ran over.

"Are you ready, son?" He was out of breath, and his eyes were bugged out. Joshua hated being called *son* but managed a smile. "Can't wait. Up and on, as we say."

At the platform, Joshua thought he'd be happy to jump just to get away from Mr. C.

"Remember what our Holy Book says, son," Mr. C. bellowed into a sudden warm gust of wind. "Therefore the children of men put their trust under the shadow of thy wings."

As the helpers were attaching the ankle harness, it seemed to Joshua they were paying more attention to Mr. C. than to the job they were doing. He asked them to check the harness again. Perhaps they didn't hear him. Perhaps they thought he gave them the okay to go.

It only took a second. Or maybe a minute.

With his arms wide open, Joshua leaped. The ankle harness came undone, and the cord swung lazily as he plummeted.

Crazy. He didn't feel scared. He knew what was happening. The joke about the optimist falling from the top of the Empire State Building flashed through his mind. Passing the tenth floor. *So far so good …*

He laughed, the sound whipped away by the rushing air. He felt wildly free and happy. He couldn't remember feeling this happy in his entire life.

All his being was centered in his chest. He was surrounded by light. He felt love and insistent separation, no longer falling but soaring higher and higher, faster and faster, and the pull was uncontrollable but he had no desire to resist. On he soared.

A rush of brilliant blues and blinding light and stars and planets and ... a *dorje*? A Buddhist *dorje* thing?

Chapter 28: A Brief Debrief

"So far so good? That's what you were thinking? Blimey!" Khalid's face reflected shocked admiration. The group were pouring tea and coffee and grabbing fruit and pastries. Joshua piled two cheese Danishes and a handful of grapes onto a plate.

"Popped into my head on the way down. Hungry work, these Tellings. Who's up next?"

Reinhardt, concentrating on a slice of strudel, waved a hand. "Tomorrow," he said.

"And after that, Emily will have her little kitchen party complete with Onward Christian Soldiers playing in the background?"

"Piss off, Joshua." Emily's color was rising. "You know very well what Gabriel said. No judgments, no prejudice. That means, Mr. New York, that you do not make fun of my religion or Reinhardt's or Khalid's or Susan's or anyone's. Do you hear me?"

Joshua threw his hands up. "Okay, okay. God, can't you Canadians take a joke? Or maybe it's the Christian part of you that-"

"Why are you so scared?" Susan stretched a hand to Joshua.

"Oh for fuck's sake. Let me guess. A weekend workshop on conflict resolution with a big dose of spirituality?"

"As a matter of fact, yes. It has helped me deal with all I've had to deal with. Too bad you didn't explore that when you were alive, Joshua."

Alter set down his cup with shaking hands and drew his coat closer. His eyes crept longingly toward the doorway. Reinhardt and Khalid exchanged glances. Quiet music from the Ugly Brown Birds drifted in, a counterpoint to the crackle of the fireplace.

"Let's get back to the business at hand," Reinhardt said. "Emily, the kitchen is still where you want to present your Telling?"

"Yes, it's sort of homey." Emily flashed Joshua an ironic look. "You know what they say. The kitchen is the heart of the home."

"And tomorrow morning I'll present mine beside the Great Green Sanctuary," Reinhardt said.

Joshua clapped his hands. "So we're set for tomorrow. That's a wrap." He pushed back his chair and sauntered out.

Chapter 29: Reinhardt

Mothballs. Reinhardt's nose wrinkled. He looked around to locate the source and met the glassy stare of a tiny fox head bouncing along on a fur collar whose wearer was weaving her way down the narrow aisle of the lurching train. He shifted to get more comfortable, but comfort was in short supply on these thin, communist-era train seats.

Although Reinhardt endeavored to stay in the present, he was alert to triggers that could illuminate wounds or traumas deeply buried. He knew that unknown, unresolved traumas keep people stuck in *samsara*, the endless cycle of birth, death, rebirth, birth and death. He wrapped his moss green pashmina scarf around his thick shoulders and sank lower, stretching his long legs out. He was happy to be alone.

Irritated, sad, vulnerable, claustrophobic … These were the feelings that arose when he caught a whiff of mothballs. Time to do some psychological sleuthing. That's what Deborah called it. Reinhardt inhaled deeply, capturing a lingering scent of mothballs.

He was six years old, crouched in the back of his Oma's massive walnut armoire. It had acquired the nickname "The Unconquered," because it was the sole piece of furniture to survive the bombing of the house during the war. Scratchy, heavy wool dresses, hat boxes and fur jackets took up more than half the space. The cloying smell of mothballs permeated everything. The murmur of muffled voices filtered in, along with the clink of cutlery and dishes being moved about. He had a decision to make: he could stay in this suffocating, dark space or leave it and face the strange, starvation-thin great aunt. Reinhardt's family had gathered to welcome her back. After enduring ten years in a Gulag, first in Russia and then East Germany, she had been released.

The family had owned a small shipping business in Rostock. When World War Two ended, Russia and the United Stated began divvying up a shattered Germany, and companies such as theirs were often taken over by one country or other. Most people did not argue. The shame, shock and devastation following the war ran deep. When Reinhardt's great aunt, whose husband had been killed in the war, saw Russians dismantling equipment and shipping parts off to Russia, she told the Americans at the military base in Wiesbaden. The Americans asked her to acquire more information. When she did, the Russians caught her, and the Americans disavowed all knowledge. The great aunt was sent away, along with her two barely grown sons.

Reinhardt crawled out of the armoire, hoping no one had noticed his absence. Especially not his father, whose harsh criticism and shaming could shrivel his insides. Beyond the smell of mothballs, he caught the delicious scent of roasting beef. This was a rare treat. Ration cards made meat a luxury.

He wandered down the galleried hallway and slipped into the room, trying to mix nonchalantly with the others gathered. Besides his gregarious sister, he was the only child there. He brightened to see another aunt, who was first violinist for the Hamburg Symphony and had promised to tutor him when he turned eight. He sidled closer to her while the rest talked softly. The Gulag great aunt sat quietly, a ghost in her own life.

Reinhardt stirred. The train was slowing. He recalled that his great aunt had lived only long enough to see her two sons released.

Suitcases were being heaved and dragged with mumbled curses. The train was finally lumbering into Hamburg Hauptbahnhof, the central train station. He straightened his cramped body and grabbed his unopened laptop. As a sought-after environmental activist and advocate, he had taken the train from Prague to Hamburg in hope of writing an article on the seven-hour journey. Fatigue and reveries had sidelined that.

The next few days would be busy. Deborah was flying in from Nova Scotia to spend time with him, and he was juggling a number of projects.

"Oh my God, you look like Che Guevara!" Deborah handled the worn, faded photograph with care. "You were so skinny. And that hair! All the way down to your bum. My hair was like that back then." She took another sip of wine and stretched out her toes. They were sitting together on a long, well-used sofa in Reinhardt's front room. Even though spring had arrived, the nights were chilly, and a fire in the stove warmed the small house. "That joint was fatter then you! Where was this taken?"

Reinhardt liked the Che comparison. "Alex and I were roaming around Kathmandu. I told my mother I was going to visit friends in southern Germany and ended up there." In the photo, the Himalayas stretched endlessly. The sky was an eye-watering icy blue and Reinhardt was laughing, holding a joint.

"Your poor mother. My God, what a nightmare you were." She finished a cracker topped with stinky Limburger cheese and drained her glass. "The quintessential hippie. Was this when you first felt a connection to Buddhism?"

"Would you like some schnapps? I've got plum and pear." He held up two bottles.

"Mm. I'll try the plum."

He filled two small glasses and handed her one. "Yes and no. After Alex hurt his foot and had to leave, I fell asleep one afternoon and woke to those long horns making that crazy sound." His hands formed the shape of the Dung Chen as he badly imitated the low, moaning sounds. Deborah laughed. Dung Chen meant dharma trumpets, and like everything else in Buddhism, their primary function was to wake up your *bodhicitta*—your enlightened heart. Reinhardt leaned back and extended an arm around her shoulder.

"The crazy thing was, there were these monks in a dingy, dark shrine room sounding the Dung Chens and I started to cry. I sat outside the shrine room crying."

Reinhardt's hemp house was tucked into the dark comfort of the spring night. Situated in what used to be a small town but was now on the outskirts of Hamburg, its wooded lot was an ideal spot to build. The house was the realization of a longstanding dream of building a home out of hemp, and it was his first home. For someone who'd roamed the world, the house felt like a refuge. Hand-painted stones with Buddhist iconography lined the walkway. In summer, a small garden would be a lovingly tended riot of herbs and vegetables. Prayer flags hung over the doorway, waiting for a breath of wind to stir them.

Inside was a collection of art he had fallen in love with in his travels. Some Buddhist pieces were afforded high status. Elegance and intensity were reflected by the King Gesar of Ling thangka in the foyer. King Gesar's heroic task was to overcome dark forces, inner and outer, that bring war and hardship and obscure the spiritual path. Hanging in monasteries and temples, the thangka is a teaching tool and helps meditators to focus. On the wall of the room adjacent to the kitchen hung an Earth Protector thangka, its colors so vivid they seemed to encourage the plants in the garden solarium to wake up and grow. A treasured calligraphy of his guru, Chögyam Trungpa Rinpoche, hung in the office. The scroll of rice paper adorned with thick black brush strokes was placed above a bookcase, an orchid still in bloom nearby. When Deborah asked what the calligraphy meant, Reinhardt was quiet for a moment. "Elegance overcomes aggression," he said at last.

Now he was looking at her to see if she was following his words. "When I heard those horns, I thought how crazy all this was. Still, I felt something old and familiar stirring."

"Where exactly did you fall asleep? Next to a mountain goat? A Sherpa?" Deborah stretched her legs across his legs and leaned against the arm of the sofa.

He placed a hand on her legs and took a sip of schnapps. "No, I was staying at a kind of inn at a Tibetan refugee camp."

"Wow, sounds luxurious. An inn at a refugee camp?"

"You could look out and see this huge rhododendron forest. The camp was in Pokhara, near Kathmandu. It was mostly Tibetans and Buddhists but some Swiss and Aussie hippies as well. When Alex hurt his foot, I thought of going home with him but felt the need to stay. Some of the hippies were heading out to other parts of Asia through Afghanistan. They asked me to come along, but I needed to be alone. I needed to follow something … But those Buddhists." He shook his head. "I thought they were crazy."

"How old were you?"

"I must have been twenty-six. This was in nineteen eighty. I knew I had to follow something but I didn't know what."

"Why?" Deborah swung her feet down and reached for the schnapps bottle. Leonard Cohen's "Bird on a Wire" was playing, and it looked as though they'd still be up when the birds woke up and started hunting for worms.

"Why did I have to follow something? Call it a deeper knowing. I knew." Four soft gongs sounded from the hallway.

"My God, it can't be that late, or early." He touched her knee and stood up. "Time for bed. Thank you for listening." He bent down to kiss her.

"I love hearing your stories. Can I hear the rest tomorrow? Make that today."

"Sure, let's go to the Elbe this afternoon. We can watch the ships come in. There's a tea shop that has incredible cake."

The next day, on the trip to the Elbe, Reinhardt drove with uncharacteristic slowness through his childhood neighborhood, pointing out landmarks. "And there's my old school. We used to call it the Pudding School."

Deborah laughed. "My God, why the Pudding School?"

"It was a pudding factory before the war, and then they turned it into a school."

Reinhardt and Deborah sat at a table near the water but far enough away not to be deafened by the recorded music. Each ship that made its way into port was welcomed by its national anthem and the ship's statistics broadcast in German. People chatted and ate cake, watching the ships from all over the world sail up the Elbe.

"Before the war, a live orchestra played the anthems," Reinhardt said. They were sitting with red wool blankets over their knees, digging into slices of hazelnut torte. "Where was I? Do you want to hear more of my stories, or are they too boring?"

"You're kidding, right? I'm curious as to how you came to Buddhism. You've spent over twenty-five years ...." She wanted to say more but was afraid he would go silent.

"Do you mean why, after all this time meditating, am I still neurotic? Okay, let's hope they have enough cake at this establishment to last the rest of the story."

Deborah laughed and threw cake crumbs to some plump sparrows.

"For a few years, I'd been helping Alex run his business, and it included many trips to India. I was ready for a good long vacation by myself."

"And this time you told your mother, right?"

He laughed. "She knew it was always a dream of mine to travel through the United States, but of course she worried. When you're a mother, worry is part of the package." He drained the last of his tea and stared into the distance. It had taken him years to understand the impact of his mother's sorrow after his father left. Top of the list were a pervasive, anxious feeling of needing to stop others from feeling pain (plus a niggling belief that perhaps he was responsible for their wellbeing), and a desire to avoid close relationships. The acceptance he felt from Deborah was like a balm.

An anthem played notes that sounded like screeching cats competing with clashing cymbals. All around them, people were making faces and laughing. Reinhardt twisted in his chair to see if he could identify the country flag.

"Must be the Dutch," he said. A waiter came over, shaking his head at the ship. He said something in German to Reinhardt, who threw his head back and laughed. They ordered more tea and another round of cake.

"What did he say?" Deborah pressed her fork into the few crumbs left on her plate.

"It must be the Dutch."

She kicked him under the table. "What do you guys have against the Dutch?"

"Ow. It's just a joke, a silly stereotype." The waiter set down the fresh tea and cake and took away the empty teapot.

"So, where do I begin? I landed in New York. Did I ever tell you of the lama who was invited to give some talks in New York? He lives in a monastery in …" He paused and scratched his chin. "Can't remember the name right off the top. Anyway, at that point, this lama had never been to the U.S., or to any western country for that matter. He flew in at night, and the next morning when he woke and looked out the window of his hotel, he cried. He looked at all the people rushing around, and he cried. He thought it was the saddest thing he'd ever seen."

Deborah was quiet.

"Are you sure you want me to continue?"

"Of course. But perhaps a libation would help you with your story?"

He laughed and called the waiter back. Within minutes, the waiter returned with two glasses of red wine. "Cheers," he said in English, bowed slightly and left.

"Is this when you went to Boulder?" Deborah asked.

"Colorado, yes, that's right. A friend had invited me to stay. She'd moved to Boulder to attend Naropa University. It's liberal arts—nonsectarian but Buddhist-inspired. She'd planned to get her MA in psychology but changed to the Buddhist and Visual Arts program."

"Was Allen Ginsberg there at that point?"

"Yes, he was. You know about the Disembodied Poetics?"

Deborah almost choked on her last sip of wine. "Holy hell, what a name! The Disembodied Poetics!"

Pleased he had surprised her, Reinhardt grinned. "I felt at home there. It was ... a new feeling." He looked out to the water. "Anna, the friend at Naropa, invited me to a talk at the Buddhist center. Right away, I thought of the refugee camps in Kathmandu, the robes, those crazy trumpets. But I decided to check it out. When Chögyam Trungpa Rinpoche— his name means Earth Protector—when he walked into the shrine room, I knew."

"You knew." This was the longest he'd ever talked without taking a detour or lapsing into a big pause. Deborah was treading lightly. "What was that knowing like?"

His eyes met hers, and he smiled faintly. "So hard to explain. But this deep, sure feeling spoke to me. It wasn't my mind speaking to me but rather a feeling speaking to my brain. And Chögyam Trungpa Rinpoche was authentic. You felt he could see straight through your bullshit."

Reinhardt let out a slow breath and stared at the water again. Emotions, some dusty and old, were resurfacing with the stories.

They sat in silence, and after a time he suggested they make their way back to the house. He needed to be alone.

Deborah kissed his cheek before heading to the garden with a book. Reinhardt meditated in his shrine room and then took a long, solitary walk in the woods. Deborah's return flight was the next morning.

At the airport, they checked in, then made their way slowly to security. The dreaded goodbye was approaching. Despite his deep need for solitude, Reinhardt hated to see her go. The strange dance of attachment and detachment was being performed.

"Another trip across the big water," he said. "Say hello to all the folks there." He pulled her closer. "And I'll see you on the other side."

"The other side? Right, my side of the Atlantic." She looked up at him. "Just four weeks." He continued to hold her as people flowed around them, rushing to go through security.

"I have a good feeling about the hemp project I proposed to some of the Sangha, my Buddhist community. It looks like the land centers in Nova Scotia and Virginia are trying to work out how we can make it happen. I should have a better idea when I have face-to-face meetings with them." He gave her another squeeze.

"Yeah, maybe you'll have to stay in Nova Scotia for a while. Know anyone who'll put you up?" He scoffed and tickled her.

He pointed to the line that was now snaking around the corner. "You better see if they'll let you through." He opened his jacket to hug her heart to heart and then stood watching until she disappeared. His cheek was wet.

"The Ashe symbolizes confidence without attaining anything or doing anything. Most of us feel confident when we accomplish something or get something, maybe money. This confidence exists without those things." Reinhardt looked down at the small boy who had asked the question. *These open houses were a good way to connect with communities near the land centers, which were in rural areas, mostly in Canada, the U.S. and France. The boy shrugged and moved closer to his father, who stroked his head. The boy slipped away from his father and picked up a dorje, a ritual object whose name, translated from Sanskrit, means the thunderbolt of enlightenment. Reinhardt gently took the dorje away, explaining its significance. The boy's eyes widened. A loud bell announced lunch, and the boy grabbed his father's hand to tug him away from the shrine room.*

Reinhardt's eye opened. Where was he? He'd been dreaming about Dorje Denma Ling, the center in rural Nova Scotia. Slowly, he got up from his chair in the study and went to the kitchen. The bright green *Kachelofen* was nicely warm, and Reinhardt placed a small saucepan on top, throwing in a handful of sage for tea. He loved this old-fashioned tile stove and its central place in his kitchen.

Tea was brewed, leaving a pleasant fragrance of sage in the kitchen. Reinhardt took a seat beside the *Kachelofen* and began to make notes of what he had to do over the next few, busy days. A sense of disquiet enveloped him. After a short while, he laid the notebook down, picked up his mug of tea and walked down the short hallway to his shrine room.

A hand emerged from the thick cloud of incense to pick up a bell. Reinhardt rang the bell and continued with his chants. He held a dorje in one hand and turned a page of a text with the other. It had been over an hour since he sat down on his meditation cushion. He paused a moment and breathed deeply. His chest felt tight. He briefly acknowledged this and returned to his meditation practice. "Great eastern sun," he continued. "Ki ki so so, victory to the gods."

The next morning, after qigong, meditation and a light breakfast, Reinhardt dug into preparations for the rally. Who would have thought Blackpool, home of bucket-and-spade family holidays and donkey rides on the beach, would become an epicenter for global protests on fracking?

"When you're open to awareness, then energy will power this openness. If you're reactive, then energy will power the reaction. With that in mind, or at least in my mind, will this rally be reactive in nature?" Reinhardt looked enquiringly at the familiar face on his laptop. His friend Andre was organizing the rally. "I'll be happy to speak," he went on, "but I want you to know where I'm coming from. It's easy to come from a place of reaction to all the fucked-up fossil-fuels stuff, but I want to offer an opening for people to see what can be done. I believe this will be more effective. This way the energy is directed toward solutions. And if the energy is directed toward the openness of these proposed solutions, then—am I being too preachy?"

"No, you're not being too preachy," Andre said. "I get it. But I can't guarantee there won't be people who are there to fight. This is one big bullshit thing on top of a long series of big bullshit things that the government is trying to get away with. We really want you there. You have a name that'll attract people from all different backgrounds."

Reinhardt smiled in acknowledgement. "I know you can't control every aspect of this rally," he said as he leafed through his datebook. "I have to fly to Paris, but I could stop there for a day. Will the second of May work for you and your posse?" Reinhardt loved American westerns.

Andre brightened. "Perfecto. There's a slot mid-afternoon. Could you be here then? We'll try and keep the Nazi-type protestors away. Oh, sorry!"

Reinhardt laughed. "Don't worry about it. See you May second. Feel free to Skype or email beforehand."

"Okay man, will do. See you later."

Reinhardt clicked the hang-up icon. Once, long ago, he'd been that young. His advice on the futility of reactionary words or actions was unlikely to gain traction. Young men seemed to think anger was a solution to injustice. He'd been no different in his younger days. *Righteous rage.* It could justify everything at that age.

Before responding to emails and preparing for the afternoon's meetings, Reinhardt took a moment to reflect. The Buddha taught that violence breeds more violence and that only love can stop the cycle. Our four-hundred-thousand-year-old brain tells us to fight or flee, but our dharma, the sacred Buddhist teachings, tells us to stand our ground. From the heart, always from the heart, look for the wisest and most compassionate action possible. *Our enlightened heart.* At the thought, he burst out laughing. The last time he'd gone on retreat, Deborah had teased, "So is it Enlightenment or Bust?" He'd pretended to be annoyed but was privately concerned she was thinking he wasn't paying enough attention to her. This was a real issue for them both. Both had heavy workloads. Both were passionate about their work. And there was the little matter of the Atlantic Ocean between them. *One way or another, things will work out*, he thought.

Reinhardt studied his datebook. Even if he juggled a few meetings, his schedule would still be full. From the kitchen, the potent aroma of brewing ginger tea drifted in. He leaped out of his chair, sending the datebook to the floor. He'd been so absorbed in his usual game of trying to squeeze more minutes from his schedule that he'd forgotten the tea. As usual. He often underestimated how long things would take. The charge, the thrill that some meeting or project could possibly make a difference, and Reinhardt was dashing to the finish line. If anyone mentioned pesky issues like logistics, budgets, or that old devil, time, he brushed them aside. *They see obstacles, not opportunities*. Or a personal favorite, *They lack vision.*

As a result he was always rushed, and his many projects never quite wrapped up as neatly as his original vision had played out in his mind. Now and then he tried to change this habit, but he quickly fell back to his usual ways.

As he stirred a spoon of honey into the ginger tea, he recited his schedule to himself. It was going to be tight. The invitation to speak at the fracking protest in Blackpool was important, and he was honored to be included, but it ate up the last space in his schedule. Mozart's Requiem began to play. It was Mozart's last masterpiece, his magnum opus left to an understudy to complete after his death. *Death*, thought Reinhardt, *interrupts*. He carried his tea back to his study. An old friend always teased him that whenever he listened to the Requiem he thought of his father. And, as if on cue, memories of his father flooded in.

Intelligent and aloof, his father had embodied the ideal postwar German professional man. After marrying, he had continued his studies and become a professor of German Literature. Reinhardt's mother, a nurse, supported her husband and young family while he pursued his goals.

Reinhardt's expression softened as he lifted the teacup to his lips. He remembered his mother as a soft, emotional woman. Had she tried too hard to please a man who seemed determined not to notice her efforts? The more disconnected his father became, the harder she tried, but to no avail. When Reinhardt was eight, his parents separated. One day, his father announced, "I do not want to live in this house any longer." He left, even though emotionally he'd never really been there.

Reinhardt's mother crumpled. Divorce was shameful in the sixties, and the shame struck her like a blunt force. The trauma of her broken marriage piled on top of the trauma of the war left her shattered. Reinhardt would come home from school to find her lying on the couch in the same position as when he'd left in the morning. Years later, after she had gathered herself together, she followed Reinhardt to the United States when she became concerned about his involvement in Buddhism. He was in a Buddhist seminary then.

To the surprise of both of them, it was not long before she herself turned to Buddhism, eventually becoming a nun.

At the age of nine, Reinhardt was involved in a rugby tackle and ended up on the bottom of a heap of boys. One boy, struggling to free himself, accidentally stuck a finger in Reinhardt's eye. His mother rushed him to hospital, but the doctors were unable to save it; the retina was detached and the iris had collapsed. Reinhardt started to draw rugby balls on his first eye patches. In his teens, it was the peace sign. When he took his Buddhist refuge vows, it was the Ashe symbol. At first, he was determined to turn the new disability into a declaration of strength and resilience. Later, Reinhardt welcomed the chance to present the symbol, which means basic goodness, to other people.

After his father left, Reinhardt did not speak to him again until he was twelve. Even then, their conversations were cerebral. For years afterward, he would dig around in his memory to recall any talks that had involved feelings. Nothing. There was nothing.

Reinhardt rubbed his face. His hand came away wet. His half-drunk tea was cold, and the Requiem was nearing its stirring end.

Boop-beep. A Skype call was coming in. He'd forgotten Deborah wanted to connect before he left. Reinhardt clicked the icon, and Deborah's face appeared onscreen.

"Is everything okay?" She peered closer.

"How are things in beautiful Nova Scotia?"

"Nice try. Everything's fine here. What's wrong? Is that the Requiem I hear?" He nodded. "Your father?" Another small nod. She leaned in to the screen and kissed him. "So, are you all packed? Wait, I know the answer. My psychic guides are telling me he'll pack. Or maybe throw things in a bag as he's running out the door." Her eyes were round and innocent. "Are my psychic guides right?"

Reinhardt threw a damp tissue at the screen. Deborah laughed.

"How are you doing, sweetheart? Must be near time for you to go to bed."

"Yes, but it's fine. Nice to connect with you before you march out to save the world."

They were quiet, gazing at each other. "I'd better get back to work," he said. "You take care of yourself, and we'll talk in a few days."

"*Gute nacht.*" She leaned in to give him a virtual kiss, and he leaned in to receive it. "You take care of yourself, too, Reinhardt."

"Good night." He clicked the red button and shut down the computer.

Reinhardt waited at the curb outside Blackpool Airport. There was no sign of Andre. After three stops to get here, Reinhardt wanted to get away from airports for a while. A chill crawled up his neck, and he spun around. A young monk stood close to the entryway, a small bowl in front of him. It looked as though he was asking for alms. *What is a monk doing in a touristy town like Blackpool?* Reinhardt dug into his pocket and found a few Euros. When he walked over to place coins in the bowl, the monk covered the bowl with a hand and shook his head.

"I want to offer you alms."

The monk smiled but said nothing. *Perhaps he doesn't understand English.* He tried a few other languages. "*Willkommen.*" No response. "*Hosgeldiniz.*" No response. "*Witamy.*" No response. *Welcome* in German, Turkish and Polish. The young monk nodded slightly at Reinhardt's bag. Reinhardt reached in, and the first item he touched was a small package of saffron he'd brought for a small ritual he hoped to perform at the land center in France. The young monk held out his hand, and Reinhardt handed over the saffron. The monk placed it deep inside his robes, then bowed. Reinhardt bowed. The monk reached his hand out and touched Reinhardt's heart. He flinched and felt tears spring to his eye. Just then, he heard Andre beep the horn.

Weaving around horse-drawn carriages, bicycles and milling tourists, Andre got them to the Blackpool Tower with minutes to spare. Reinhardt had never been to Blackpool and wasn't prepared for the noise, smells and energy of people trying hard to have fun. He and Andre were happy to see a good crowd gathered at the Tower but even happier to see TV crews. Visibility is what they wanted and why they were meeting at this landmark.

Andre showed the necessary papers to the police officer who stopped them, and they hurried through the sign-waving crowd to the podium in front of the Tower. Chants of "Frack off! Frack off! Frack off, you Frackers!" echoed. Young people sitting cross-legged and strumming guitars reminded Reinhardt of his hippie days. He cleared his throat. The chants grew louder and the signs were hoisted higher.

"Good morning," he said into the microphone.

The crowd cheered. Someone shouted, "It's 2:00 p.m., mate!"

Reinhardt paused for effect, scanning the crowd. "I say good morning because it's time to wake the fuck up!"

People went crazy. Reporters spoke with a rushed urgency to their cameras as the crowd shouted back, "Good morning! It's time to wake the fuck up!"

Reinhardt raised his hands to silence the crowd. "I am Reinhardt Krogoll." Again the crowd cheered to hear such a high-profile environmental advocate.

"My fellow humans, it has been a nice sleep. But there are those who have taken advantage and continue to do so. Wake up, and wake up everyone you know. Tell them there are people who want to rape our world. Tell them not to believe the lies that this is clean energy, that the risk to the environment is low, that we have no choice. We have a choice. Tell people there are other ways. Tell them fracking is dangerous. Tell them other countries do not permit this. Tell them—" He stopped, and the crowd held its breath. He spoke quietly, but every word was clear. "Tell them this is their world. Tell them our earth is fragile. Tell them it is time. Tell them *Good morning*."

The crowd shouted back, "It's time to wake the fuck up!"

"I am Reinhardt Krogoll and I came here today to join you," he reached down and picked up a sign that read *We are all Earth Protectors*. "Show them. Lead them toward protecting our oceans, our earth."

Out of nowhere a tall, dark-haired man rushed the stage. Somehow, the large green leaf covering his nether regions stayed in place as he sprinted across the stage. He stopped to give Reinhardt a hug, then dashed to the exit, where he paused and looked out at the cheering crowd. The crowd grew quiet. He smiled, bowed and disappeared.

People snapping photos were disappointed and mystified that the images showed only a white mist. Those watching at home saw a blur cross the stage with an odd, rushing sound.

Startled, Reinhardt quickly recovered and quipped, "Be willing to get off your ass. Or show your ass! Whatever it takes!"

He fell asleep on the short flight to Paris. Before returning home, he had meetings at Dechen Chöling, a Shambhala meditation center in central France.

How well have you loved?

He half woke up. Had a flight attendant spoken? His mild curiosity was overtaken by the delicious descent into sleep.

How well have you loved?

This time, he sat up and looked around. Was someone playing a movie? He heard only the quiet conversations of passengers around him.

At the airport, he waved to the friend who was driving him to the center. "Jim!" The two men hugged in greeting. They'd gone to seminary together in Virginia, and Jim now lived at Dechen Chöling. Once they were away from Charles De Gaulle and the airport traffic, the drive would take about four hours. Plenty of time to catch up.

Now exiting the airport parking lot, Jim told Reinhardt about the latest projects and developments at the land center. Rain spattered the windshield in the late afternoon gloom.

"Looks like Dechen Chöling will need a new director soon. Would you be interested?"

Reinhardt turned, his face registering surprise. "I'd love to, but I have other irons in the fire right now."

"Do you mean the eco-refit in Virginia?" Jim swerved to avoid a cyclist, beeping the horn and raising a middle finger. "You could do that here, you know. Why don't you throw your name into the hat? We've been looking at your plans. It's time, and the Sakyong wants us to green up our retreat centers. Just think, Reinhardt, you could lead Dechen Chöling into a new phase of spiritual and eco development."

Reinhardt watched the windshield wipers sweeping the rain. To the west, the sky was clearing. "It's tempting, but I don't know. Deborah lives in Canada. I'm not sure she'd move here." He gnawed his lip. "Do you have any good chocolate?"

Jim guffawed. "I was waiting for you to ask. Talk to her, Reinhardt. Perhaps she'd jump at the chance to live here. This part of France is beautiful, and the food, the culture ... Dechen Chöling needs a leader with heart and vision. We could really use you."

Reinhardt attempted to stretch out his long frame. "I'll give it some thought."

"It doesn't hurt to think about it, but the deadline for applying is next week." The car pulled smoothly into the passing lane and accelerated. "It would offer a tremendous opportunity. Not only to Dechen Chöling. It would serve as an example of how important it is to bring eco-spirituality to the forefront."

"Doesn't hurt to put my name forward, I suppose."

Jim grinned.

After the noise and hustle of Blackpool, waking up to the quiet, gentle energy in the rolling hills of the land center was a relief. He had three meetings lined up, but there was plenty of time for a good long practice before they began. He knew many people here, and he looked forward to catching up with them. Along with all the Sangha members scattered throughout the world, they were his family. After a few days, Reinhardt knew he would add his name to the list of potential directors. He'd talk with Deborah as soon as he got home.

"Move to France? You know I love you, but move to France and live with Buddhists twenty-four seven?" Reinhardt had not thought the Sakyong would make his decision so quickly. He'd hoped they could ease into this possibility slowly, with long, loving conversations. He didn't want to choose, but he felt it was his duty to accept the directorship. His heart ached.

"Could you try it for a while?"

"My whole life is here. With the exception of you." From the dazed look on her face onscreen, it was clear she'd been thrown by this sudden shift in her world.

"I'll be back to Nova Scotia in a few weeks. Perhaps we can talk about you visiting Dechen Chöling with me. It's beautiful there." He added hopefully, "You could do your writing." Deborah groaned. "Sweetheart, you know my kids and work are here."

"But they're adults." One look at Deborah and he knew he'd overstepped. She had raised her children on her own, and the ties were still close.

Deborah tapped her fingers on the desk in front of her. "Right, well … So let's have a good talk when you come over." She sighed. "Oh, Reinhardt, this is not what I'd imagined."

"I'll give you lots of warm hugs and hot kisses," he teased, trying to lighten the mood. "I love you, *mein schatzi.*"

Deborah laughed but groaned again. "I love you, too, my darling. I'm going to have a big glass of wine and howl at the moon."

Now it was Reinhardt's turn to laugh. "I am sorry, sweetheart. You get a good night's sleep. We'll talk again in a few days." They leaned in to the screen for a kiss and signed off.

He was deeply troubled. While he didn't want to lose her, he felt a profound sense of rightness about this posting. A little nightcap and a little reading would be just the thing after these past few days, followed by a good, long sleep.

It did not go well. Reinhardt tossed and turned. The full moon fiercely shone her ancient light through the window. At one point, he thought he heard the voice from the plane.

How well have you loved?

Finally, he threw aside the bedclothes and got up to do a short practice.

The shrine room felt unusually cool. A thick wool blanket was draped on a chair, and he spread it over his knees. He lit a stub of white candle and a bit of juniper incense. As he settled on his cushion, a strange sensation radiated across his chest. He noted the feeling. Determined to ignore it, he deepened his breath. A sharp pain. His determination deepened, and he focused on his out breath. Tingling pinpoints travelled up and down his arms. *Stress.* He attempted to breathe it out. He felt removed from his body.

Enlightenment. Could it be? Enlightenment?

There was nothing.

But then there was something. His Oma's armoire. Inside was a small violin, his father's diplomas, his mother's nursing cap. He was small and he was inside the armoire but then he was big and he was outside. Flying, floating. His house, the woods, the neighborhood, the whole country, the continent, the world … Above and beyond the world …

Lights. Brilliant lights. And love. Love his body could not contain. Love too big for one person. *Love and lights. Love and lights!* He had no body. He was heart and vision. And, oh, the visions. His beloved guru. Mountains in the heavens more majestic than the Himalayas, the sphere behind the moon glowing, glowing … and a Christian cross?

Chapter 30: Emily

"Dancing queen … Oh yeahhhh."

Stephen was having trouble keeping his mind on the road as he listened to a cassette tape of five-year-old Emily squeakily sing one of "their" songs with all the passion she could muster.

"Do you like that one, Daddy?" her hopeful voice on the tape asked.

"Oh yes, sweetheart, I love it, and you more than anything," Stephen said to the darkness. He wiped his newly shaved face clear of the tears of laughter. For a moment, he thought he heard the cassette tape whir. He pushed a few buttons on the car's audio system, and her voice spoke again.

"What about this one? You are my sunshine …" Stephen joined in loudly, his off-key singing accompanying her sweet, high-pitched words.

"No, you cannot sleep with the window open. It's freezing cold, and it may snow tonight. You'll see your father in the morning. Now get to sleep this instant, young miss."

"But, Mommy, I want to hear him drive in." Emily kicked her legs under the blankets. "I've been practicing a new song for us to sing, and I want to remember it for him." Tears rolled down her round cheeks as she pushed her feet down hard. "You don't even care!"

Were children born knowing these tricks? Heather smiled inwardly. "Okay, what's the new song?"

Emily sat up and began to sing "Somewhere over the rainbow" but trailed off. More tears welled, and her bottom lip was square. In every village, town and city the world over, 8:00 p.m. is the recognized deadline for parental patience when progeny is under six years old, and now it was 8:23.

"Why are you crying?" Heather tried not to sound as exasperated as she felt.

"I'm scared a dragon is gonna eat Daddy!" Emily had tried hard all day to keep the thought to herself, but now it spilled out.

"Oh sweetheart, your daddy will be fine. I Mommy Promise you, there are no dragons on Prince Edward Island."

As Heather reached down to tuck Emily in again, she said, "Let's say prayers again, and you can ask God to take extra good care of Daddy."

Emily almost landed face down on the bedside rug as she scrambled out of bed, one foot tangled in the blankets. Heather helped to free the small foot, and they knelt down together. The room was chilly. In November, it was impossible to keep the century-old farmhouse warm.

"Come on, Mommy! We have to ask God to keep the dragons away from Daddy." The prayers acted as a kind of surrender, and minutes later, Emily was asleep.

"My only sunshine ..." Rubbing his eyes, Stephen continued to sing. His bones ached with fatigue. Grimly, he thought of the conversation he'd be having with Heather. War with Iraq was almost certain, and he'd be returning to base sooner than planned. His gut knotted at the thought of leaving his wife and daughter.

"You make me happy!" shouted Emily.

Stephen laughed. "She's really givin' it."

The car swerved on black ice. Stephen eased his foot off the gas and steered through it, feeling the reassuring grip of dry road again. "Just this last stretch and I'm home." He turned off the music and rolled down the window. Cold air rushed in. He'd waited months to hear this silence, this stillness. The darkness beyond the headlights was total. A brief shudder rippled through him. *Must be the cold. More music will do the trick.* He switched on the well-used cassette tape.

More black ice. The back end started to drift. Without thinking, he touched the brake.

Strange. Outside the car, everything was spinning out of control, yet his perception slowed. *Heather. Sweet Emily.* Even after the car slammed against the tree, the music went on. *You'll never know, dear ...*

Silence. Golden light. Emily was holding her father's hand. He was staring at something in the distance that Emily couldn't see. She leaned in closer to him and peered ahead but still couldn't make out what he was looking at. Dark silence lay behind them, light and faint singing ahead of them.

"Daddy," she whispered. They stood at the entrance of a tunnel. Emily looked around for dragons. The tunnel glowed with light and warmth.

"Darling, I have to go now," her father whispered. "You go back to Mommy. You can't come with me." Emily was clinging to his hand, but he was slipping away. His voice was barely an echo. "Know how much I love you."

"Daddy!" She was still screaming when she woke up.

"How often does he hit you?" Emily reminded herself to maintain a calm voice. The young woman sitting across from her wearing a bubblegum pink track suit was about her age. Purple bruising had nearly closed her left eye.

God, she's so angry and sullen. "Miss, how often does your pimp—"

"He's my boyfriend, you cunt!"

Emily's notepad slipped out of her shaking hands, landing on the balding gunmetal gray carpet. She bent quickly to pick it up, biting her tongue and squeezing her eyes shut. Cheeks aflame, she recovered and faced her client again. The young woman smirked and went on with her story.

"Only once a week or so. I dunno, maybe less or more. Why the fuck does that matter? This is the first fucking time he hit me in the face. He knows fucking better than to do that."

"Excuse me? What do you mean he knows better?"

The woman in pink opened her mouth and then shut it. She looked at Emily speculatively. "Ya know, you look just like her."

Here it comes. If I had a dollar for every time someone said—

"Anne of fucking Green Gables. Everyone thinks this goddamn island is as lily-white innocent as Anne of Green fucking Gables. And we both know that's not true. I bet you're not so innocent, either." She folded her arms and twisted a long strand of purple-streaked hair.

Emily shifted in her chair. "Please, I have to file this report. The sooner we can finish, the sooner you can go. Where else does he hit you?"

The woman's eyes widened. "You don't know, do ya? Let me spell it out for you. Because he is my *boyfriend*," she shot Emily a warning look, "and I *love* him, I give him some of the money I make fucking men. When I piss him off, he holds me down and punches me in the armpits. That way, Miss Anne of fucking Green Gables, my customers don't see and it don't hurt my business. Everyone knows that. He punches me for as long as it takes …" she trailed off when she saw the expression on Emily's face. "Oh, for Chrissake, that's nothing."

"Okay, we have dates and times. You can go for now, but please keep your appointment next week. We've got lots to talk about." Emily practiced her new professional smile.

The young woman in pink tilted her head and narrowed her eyes. "You're kinda young for this, aren't you? The last one I saw was an old bag. Do ya know what you're doing?"

Emily got up from her desk, walked around to open the door of the windowless room and escorted the young woman to the front entrance. After the door closed behind her, Emily scanned to see if anyone in the office was looking at her. No one. She exhaled and leaned her slim body against the door, offering up a prayer for strength in her new role as counselor to women and youth at risk.

She's right, I don't know. Who would think prostitution was so prevalent on good old Prince Edward Island? First aid. Most often Emily and the other counselors at Victim Services felt this was all they were able to do. Manage the pain, bandage the wounds and send them on their way.

With God's help, someday I'll be able to do more. Oh heavens, that felt pious and arrogant!

Driving home after work, she mentally unpacked the day's hard stories. Doing that helped to clear up space. Although Charlottetown was the provincial capital, it was a small city of under forty thousand people. Even with traffic, the trip home took only ten minutes. Emily loved her apartment, especially the English-style garden at the back. In late spring, a few delicate Lady's Slipper wild orchids would appear in a mossy corner. Mornings when the weather was fine, she would carry her tea into the garden and sit on the small stone patio, mulling the previous night's dreams. Sometimes *that* dream would come to mind, but after more than twenty years it was still too painful to sit for long in that memory.

But there are other wounds, shameful wounds, that need healing. The late July evening was warm, and she was in the kitchen. She caught herself rubbing her brow like Daddy used to do. The message light was flashing. She slipped off her shoes, rubbed her feet and picked up the receiver. One message was from her mother asking her to come to dinner on Sunday to celebrate her creepy stepfather's birthday. The message was curt, almost demanding. Her mother knew Emily didn't like her husband but still asked her to call him Dad. Emily would never call him Dad. Never.

The next message was from her friend Katie. Light and breezy, Katie was asking Emily to come to a barbecue to meet her cousin, who was visiting from Montreal. Families on Prince Edward Island often played host to just about every twig on the family tree during summer. Katie had spoken about the cousin before, and Emily smelled a set-up. Katie was always playing matchmaker, and Emily was always resisting. She'd have to meet this cousin or risk hearing Katie go on and on about how picky she was. Katie had been dropping hints about the cousin ever since he'd broken off an engagement. She'd even tried showing Emily pictures of him on her phone, but Emily just looked away.

"You're impossible! I swear if you were Catholic you'd be a nun."

"Yep, you're right. That would've been perfect for me."

"I will simply not allow my best friend to dismiss at the very least an introduction. My God, he's almost as Christian as you, Em!" Katie's efforts at matchmaking had redoubled since her own engagement. Emily would be her maid of honor next summer when the next round of family descended.

Emily phoned Katie back. "Okay, I'll come on Friday. What can I bring?"

"Wear the blue dress. You know, the one that shows off your eyes and your hot bod."

"Katie, don't be so bossy. I'll wear a potato sack if you keep this up."

"Okay, okay, I was just making a suggestion, sweetie. Oh, and Mom said not to bother bringing anything. She's been baking for weeks. We could feed half the Island."

While they were chatting, another message came in. *Busy evening.* Emily said goodbye to Katie and checked the new message. It was one of the ladies from the prayer group reminding her of Thursday's special prayer meeting for Canadian military who had just left for the Middle East. *My father, who art in heaven ...* When Emily was six, her Sunday School teacher had corrected her over and over to say *Our Father.* Emily had been convinced they were talking about her daddy.

Katie. As Emily mixed penne pasta with fresh tomatoes and basil, she thought about Katie with both affection and irritation. She loved her, but Katie loved to get in her business.

"Why don't you ever date? Are you one of those Christian lesbians?" But Katie knew why.

A crack of thunder set the neighbor's beagle into a long howl. Emily was jolted from her reverie. Uninvited and unwelcome thoughts brought her back to the young woman with the black eye. Something about her reminded Emily of herself. She made a mental note to be smart about setting boundaries with her clients.

Dammit, I was only sixteen. It wasn't my fault. In desperation she recounted the reasons she didn't need to feel guilty or ashamed. *He was 32. He was married. He was my teacher.* Her hands were clammy. *More! I need more reasons!* Then the familiar thought crawled in, the one she dreaded. *But you liked it, didn't you?* She knew what the psyche books said. She knew the physiology of a sixteen-year-old body. All those raging hormones and primal instincts fully loaded with no place to go.

Best girl. Emily wanted to be the best girl. After her father died, she felt she couldn't count on anyone. Well-meaning people tried to get close, including her grieving mother, but Emily became self-determined, independent and very, very smart. She would not need or want or love again; she would be self-sufficient. Except for God. God the Father. She studied hard and had a small but loyal group of friends. She knew some kids snickered behind her back, but she didn't care. At sixteen, she was studious enough to earn mostly A's. She was also naturally and unselfconsciously pretty. And until grade ten, most of her teachers were women. In grade seven, she'd had a male substitute teacher for a few weeks. She found herself trying extra hard for him, but then he was gone.

"Did you see him?" Katie hurried to catch up with Emily on their way to English class. Emily picked up her pace and pretended she didn't hear.

"Emily!" Katie grabbed her arm. "Did you see him?"

There was no way around it. "To which *him* are you referring, my dear Katherine?" replied Emily in a near-perfect seventeenth century American accent.

"Oh stop it! You know who I mean. What's with the accent? Oh, I get it, you're trying out for *The Crucible*. Which part? How about Sarah? You could play nutty really well."

"Har-de-har. I'd like to get the part of Betty." Emily hoped that sightings or reports of *him* had been forgotten. No such luck.

"Back to important news!" Katie was considering a career in journalism. "Did you see our new history teacher? His name is Mr. Spencer and he's thirty-two years old and he used to play soccer professionally and he's married with two adorable kids and he's totally handsome!"

"Thank you for the update, Lois Lane, and yes I've seen him." Emily shrugged. "I don't think he's that handsome."

Katie rolled her eyes. "Can't wait for our first history class!"

Studying Canadian history is as rousing as watching a croquet game. Perhaps it's to do with Canadian understatement and the national pastime of comparing themselves to their more boisterous neighbors to the south. But Mr. Spencer intended to change that in his class. He stood at the front watching the rush of new students streaming in, looking for desks to claim and colonize. Who was that girl with the froth of red-gold hair and the startling blue eyes? When Emily glanced at him, his eyes met hers for a long moment.

"See, I told you he was handsome." Katie spoke more loudly than she intended, and everyone laughed including Mr. Spencer. Emily was mortified. Katie blushed and gave a big smile.

Mr. Spencer sat on the edge of his desk and rolled up his shirtsleeves.

"Anyone here ever time travelled? If you could, when and where would you go? Think about it. Would you go to the year 1759 to fight on the Plains of Abraham in a battle that would decide the fate of our country? Or would you go back to 1606 and join Samuel de Champlain for drinks in the long winters in Port Royal? Maybe join in a few plays?" He went on but his gaze kept returning to Emily. "Let's do some time travelling here today. Someone toss out a year."

They decided to start in Port Royal. Mr. Spencer opened a cardboard box and carried it around the room, handing a miniature sand hourglass to every student. "You can either hold it in your hands as you slow down your breath and close your eyes, or you can stare at the piece on your desk, breathing slowly."

He began by describing the sky, the trees, the tantalizing smells wafting on the cold night air, the warmth and light indoors, the texture and taste of the food. With their eyes closed, he had them imagine their hands and then their feet. Soon, each of them was with Champlain and the Order of Good Cheer, snug indoors on a bone-chilling night in December 1606. After the session, he asked them to quietly write down all the details. The class was enchanted.

Forty minutes later, heading to the cafeteria, Katie said, "Who knew Canadian history could be so sexy? We're a sexy, exciting people after all."

"Get ahold of yourself, girl."

"Let me guess, Betty's father in *The Crucible*?"

"Let's change the subject, shall we?"

"Okay, then. So Emily, how's your stepdad?"

Emily groaned. "Please don't ask." For once, Katie left it at that.

Emily did get the part of Betty. Her mom and stepdad came to the performance, as did most of the teaching staff, parents and community. Mr. Spencer sat in the front row. Katie later breathlessly reported that there was no wife in sight. The next history class, Mr. Spencer applauded as Emily walked into class.

"Bravo, Miss Emily, you did a brave job. Shall we time travel outside our country just for today? To, let's say, Salem, Massachusetts?" The class yelled out their approval and got out their miniature sand hourglasses. Even the toughest, disengaged kid enjoyed this part.

After class, Mr. Spencer asked Emily to stay behind. Katie tossed Emily a look that said, *I want absolutely every possible detail and don't forget anything.* Emily smiled to herself and nodded.

"Is anything wrong, Mr. Spencer?" She was surprised her voice sounded so shaky.

"No, no, I just want you to know—" His eyes strayed to her left shoulder, and without thinking he picked a thread off her sweater. Emily felt a thrill ripple through her body. Usually when she had such feelings, she could shut them down. That didn't seem to be working. Mr. Spencer reached out and pushed a lock of her hair behind her ear. For the first time, she realized "weak at the knees" wasn't just an expression.

"Emily, I want you to know I'm here for you any time. I want to be more than your old history teacher. I understand you have a stepfather you're not crazy about. I know how important it is to have a dad. Emily, my dad died when I was quite young as well. I guess you and I have more in common—"

A knock at the door made them both jump. "Mr. Spencer, your four o'clock appointment is here early." The teacher's aide frowned slightly, his eyes moving from one to the other.

"Thanks, Derek. I'll be there shortly." Mr. Spencer stepped back, and Emily reached for her book bag.

"Thanks, Mr. Spencer, but I'm fine. I better go. I have choir practice at the church." She hurried past Derek, not meeting his eyes. *I will never, ever tell Katie anything about this. Ever.*

Yet somehow Emily felt more and more compelled to find reasons to stay after history class. It was as though she were under a spell.

And now it was blizzard season, the middle of January. At midday, with snow pelting the north windows, classes were cancelled. History class had just finished, and the students, including Katie, had literally run from class when the announcement came over the PA system.

"It doesn't look that bad out." Emily wandered over to the window. Mr. Spencer stopped packing his briefcase. The school was emptying quickly. He walked over and closed the classroom door.

"Emily, come here."

She didn't feel her feet as she approached him. Her attempt to push down her feelings was useless. He reached out and brushed her arm.

It must be the snowy silence. Her breath sounded loud; her thoughts were slow and thick.

He moved in closer and placed his hands around her waist. Emily bit her lip and tasted blood. She could feel his warm breath as he closed in and licked the blood off her mouth. Unable to move away, she felt her whole body quaking. The years of holding down her emotions were colliding with her body's need to release passion, and the collision was going to be a big one.

"Stay right there." He went to the window and scanned the parking lot. A sliver of red was all that was visible of his car's right fender, the rest of the car buried in white. There were no other cars. He slowly turned back. He walked toward her before he could change his mind.

"You've been avoiding me," Emily's mother said.

"Just busy, Mom." Emily buried her head deeper in a book, trying not to cry. Her mom stood and waited for Emily to look up, but Emily didn't want her to notice the tears. She took a moment to regain control. It took more time these days to rein in her emotions. Since she and Mr. Spencer had started—. Emily felt her face flush. Since she and Mr. Spencer had started to have sex, she had less and less control over her emotions.

"Emily," her mother said more softly, "is everything okay?"

"So where are you and Dan going this weekend?"

Her mother contemplated her hunched-over daughter. Her intuition had been nudging her for weeks about Emily. Something was wrong, but she let the thought pass. "We've decided to try that new bed and breakfast in Wallace."

"In Nova Scotia?"

"Yes, we'll be leaving Friday evening and coming back late on Sunday. We're going to take the ferry back, just for a change. A nice getaway after the long winter." She looked more closely at Emily, but her daughter's face revealed nothing.

Emily brightened but tried not to show it. This would give her just enough time.

"I solemnly promise never to tell another living soul, but you have to tell me who, Emily," pleaded Katie.

"I will owe you forever, Katie. You're saving my life. But please, please don't ask me again. I can't tell you or anyone ever. Let's get this over with. Oh, Katie, pray with me. I need to be forgiven for so much." Emily looked bereft.

Katie had never seen her friend this way, and she felt sick. She loved Emily. They were sister-friends. Of course Katie knew who it was. When Emily told her she was pregnant, Katie's rage was so fierce she felt dizzy. But she said nothing.

"Come on, you, let's go." She linked her arm through Emily's. "You'll be fine, and I promise to never ask." Katie had made all the arrangements. Since abortions were not available on Prince Edward Island, they had a road trip ahead to New Brunswick.

Both girls were quiet until they were driving across the thirteen-kilometer causeway that joined the two provinces. Below the causeway, the Northumberland Strait was a calm battleship gray.

"Hey, would you like to hear some music?" Katie glanced at Emily, who was staring over the wall of the bridge to peer down at the expanse of water.

"If you don't mind, I would rather not. Is that okay?"

"Sure, sure. You want to talk or would you prefer I continue to show the greatest restraint in my entire life and keep my mouth shut?"

Emily smiled at her friend. "I love you, Katie. You go ahead and talk about anything you want and I will listen. Mostly."

The doctor in the clinic called it "the procedure." Emily tried to think of it like that. Calling it a procedure would put distance between her emotions and what was actually taking place. *A nice Christian girl like me*, she thought bitterly as she lay on the gurney, feet in stirrups. In a matter of minutes it was over. *Weird.* Emily realized her affair with Mr. Spencer was over, too.

For the rest of the school year, she could barely look at him. She had told him, but he'd never asked about it or how she was or offered help. Emily decided she intensely hated cowards and that Mr. Spencer was a very big one. Katie and a few other friends tried to coax her out for parties, but she felt she didn't deserve to have fun. She doubled down on her efforts to be best girl. She was pleased she was again able to control her emotions.

She worked hard to forgive herself and Mr. Spencer; forgiveness was an important part of being Christian. But then, out of the blue, hot and painful emotions would come surging back. Shame and guilt were big players, but anger had a starring role. The intensity made her feel faint, but by force of will she would quench the fire. And she would pray. She joined youth groups at church, and the following summer she volunteered at a Christian camp outside Charlottetown. Days of swimming in the cool Northumberland Strait and leading walks through gentle wooded areas were exactly what she needed. At night, the youth counselors would gather around the campfire and talk. The struggle to be a good Christian in their teen years was a popular topic, but they also discussed future plans and dreams. One girl seemed to be an expert on angels.

For three nights in a row, under the light of a luminous July full moon, angels and their roles in the daily life of a Christian were debated, with most questions directed to the angel expert. Emily hesitated to believe in such powers. She felt comfortable with God the Father. But his assistants? Still, she began to look for signs. The angel expert instructed the group on what signs to look for and how to invite angels into their lives. The group agreed to create an angel game to play with their young charges. Every time someone thought they spotted an angel, or at least a sign, they would shout "Hallelujah!" It was impossibly corny, but it was a fun way to introduce the kids to the idea of looking for the divine and expecting it in their lives. The counselors were surprised at how enthusiastic the kids were. For the rest of the camp, they played the angel game every day.

Emily felt renewed after her weeks as a camp counselor. By now she had changed her goal of becoming a pastor. After her time with Mr. Spencer, she felt she wasn't worthy to lead anyone on a path of righteousness, and until summer camp, nothing else had galvanized her passions. Now she knew she wanted to be a counselor; there were so many wounded women and children.

As Emily rushed into the coffee shop, she spotted Katie at a corner table. She stopped and waved, then executed a small bow.

Katie graciously accepted, her eyes sparkling. "I think there is something you wish to say?"

"Okay, okay, you're right. You, Katie are right. Right, right and right! Happy?" Emily laughed.

"Told you he was cute," Katie said with a smirk. "Hey, we could end up being related! I can so see you and Gavin getting married. After I do, of course. Get it? *I do!*" She chortled.

Emily groaned. "Yeah, I get it, but don't move so fast. We've only had one date. And as you well know, he has to go back to Montreal soon." The sadness in her voice surprised her.

"My aunt, soon to be your mother-in-law, has said over and over how the right girl could encourage Gavin to come back to the Island," Katie said smugly. "Emily, you are the right kind of girl."

And, as time went on, Emily began to feel more confident about this new relationship. Gavin was funny, thoughtful, good looking and ambitious. And he was brave. This quality was top of her wish list for a potential mate, and now there was solid proof. Gavin had been awarded the Medal of Bravery by the Governor General of Canada. He had dived repeatedly in night-time waters to save a mother and her infant son from a car that had gone off the road and was sinking in a lake. Gavin seemed embarrassed, but Emily could tell he was happy and pleased with the outcome. Two years after the rescue, the mother still sent him thank-you cards and pictures of her healthy, growing son.

For the remaining two weeks of his visit, Gavin and Emily saw each other every day. Emily took him to church and even introduced him to her mom and creepy stepfather. They went horseback riding on deserted beaches known only to locals. Each morning, they would pack a picnic and head out to wander. They showed up at Old Home Week holding hands. On the Island, this meant you were either newly married or heading in that direction. Katie was thrilled. On Gavin's second-to-last night on the Island, they were invited to Katie's parents for a lobster boil. A huge old picnic table in the backyard was laden with bowls of potato salad, large pots dented from years of lobster boils, now filled with the fiery red crustaceans, and all the tools needed to crack open the shells.

"I can't believe you talked them into giving you these past two weeks off," Katie whispered loudly to Emily, who sat across from her and beside Gavin. Katie gave a lobster claw a good whack on the side of the table. "And *you*, Ms. Responsibility 2018 taking the time off! What's next, a tattoo?" Katie checked the claw, gratified to have broken it wide open. Digging out the meat with her fingers, she popped the meat into her mouth. Emily laughed. Katie ate lobster like a real Islander. They always had fun watching tourists wearing big plastic bibs and using forks to get at the meat.

"It was totally worth it, my friend." Emily's voice was peaceful. Gavin gave her knee a quick squeeze.

Katie's fiancé, Mark, said to Gavin, "So what's the plan, my man?"

Gavin swallowed a bite of potato salad. "Well, Emily and I have been talking. I'm driving back to Montreal the day after tomorrow. We'll Skype and email, of course, but I, or rather *we* have been talking about—"

Katie's mom interrupted, "You know, Gavin, you have a place here if that's the way this is going."

"Thank you, Aunt Marion. I can do my business from here and fly to Montreal when needed, but I'd like to try my hand at politics here on the Island."

Katie's dad growled, "That will never work, my son. That door closed the minute your parents stole you away to Montreal when you were a baby. Treason! Leaving behind the Island and all our ways, and for what? Some fancy job at a bank? The people of the Island don't forget or forgive easily, and they have very long memories."

"Dad!" Katie was never sure when her father was joking, but then she saw the wink. She laughed and threw a napkin, soggy from lobster, in his direction. Gavin, looking relieved, grinned.

"My son, the Island could use a smart young man like yourself. Too many young people leave for work out west. We're losing our youth and their energy." He tapped the top of his head, where only a few wispy hairs remained loyal to his head. "I lost my youth a long time ago, and this one"—he jerked a finger toward Katie—"sped up the process considerably."

"Oh, Katie, I've been meaning to tell you. You, too, Emily." Katie's mother turned to Gavin. "The girls went to high school together, and they took a lot of the same classes." She wiped her hands on a cloth and started putting lids back on the food. "Remember Mr. Spencer, your grade ten history teacher?"

Emily paled.

"There was talk that he got one of his students pregnant! The RCMP got involved, and the girl's parents sued the school board, but in the end nothing came of it and the case was dismissed—" she stopped when she saw Emily. "Dear, what's wrong?" Gavin turned to Emily, puzzled.

"Emily!" Katie said more sharply than she intended. "Come help me clean up."

Emily stood up, feeling frozen, and followed Katie into the kitchen. Inside and away from the others, they hugged. Katie whispered in her ear, "Let it go." She saw the shock in Emily's eyes. "Yes, I knew all along. Be happy, you're in love. Life is good." Emily nodded.

She and Gavin Skyped, texted, called and used every available means to communicate after he returned to Montreal. They made plans and more plans. It's interesting how people will take something like love, which sits among other miracles, and try to create a container for it. A container like a plan.

"Stupid car," Emily fumed as she kicked the tires.

"It's probably a short in the wiring, nothing serious or expensive," the mechanic said as he wiped his hands for the third time on his coveralls. "Cripes, just leave it with us and you can pick it up tomorrow. Gabe, come out here!" A tall, good-looking young man walked over and unexpectedly touched Emily's shoulder. She was about to give him a dirty look but stopped when she caught his incredible smile.

"Get this fixed for the lady, eh?"

Gabe was whistling what sounded like "You Are My Sunshine." The mechanic said to Emily, "Ya know, every once in a while we get one of those, eh? A whistler. He's new but good. He'll get your car all fixed up." Emily walked home hearing the echo of the familiar tune.

That night after Skyping with Gavin, she slept fitfully.

How well have you loved?

She sat up and looked around the room. Pale moonlight streamed across the foot of the bed. The night was silent except for the swish of cars on the street.

How well have you loved?

"Who's there?" The silence stretched into minutes. *Crazy,* she thought as she sank toward sleep. *I'm in love and I'm going crazy. Great.*

Emily was almost happy her car was in the garage. She could have taken a cab, but the morning was sunny and fresh, and the leaves were starting to change color. In the slanting sunlight of early fall, they glowed. As she walked, her thoughts turned to Gavin. *Premier Gavin McInnis. One day, maybe.* She smiled and walked faster.

It wasn't the most pleasant street to walk in this small city. It was by far the busiest, not only in the city but the entire province. Even so, the occasional tractor would rumble along. She loved this about her Island; you were never far from the land. Up ahead, construction was still going on at the new apartment building. Just then, she saw an old lady with a walker about to walk straight out into traffic. Emily rushed up to her, her strawberry hair bobbing as she ran.

"Ma'am, ma'am!" The old woman slowly turned her head. She was tissue thin with a determined look in her eye.

"Who's your parents?" she demanded. Emily laughed. *Yep, this old thing is an Islander, all right.*

"Ma'am, there's a crosswalk just down the street. Come, I'll walk with you."

"Too far!" The old woman maneuvered her walker off the curb. She ignored the traffic. *Oh damn,* Emily thought. *This old bat's going to kill me.*

"Come on, I'll go with you." Emily placed one arm protectively around the old woman's thin shoulders and held up the other hand, palm out. Drivers slowed and stopped to allow the curious pair safe passage. Relieved they made it across, Emily helped the old woman get her walker onto the curb.

"Whew!" Emily said. She stood waiting for some thanks, but the old woman was hustling away down the sidewalk.

"Duck! Duck!!! Out of the fucking way!"

A steel beam swung in a slow arc. A cable snapped. Workers screamed.

Drivers slammed on brakes in horror. The young woman who moments ago was helping an old woman was flying through the air.

Emily, too, could see her body flying. For a moment, she heard screams and shouting.

And then there was no then.

There was just now.

And more light and joy than she ever imagined. All of her being was centered near her heart. There was not enough room in her body for all the love she felt.

She felt a powerful pull toward ... something. Surrender. Millions and millions of lights.

And there it was. The tunnel. It was okay her daddy wasn't there. She'd see him soon. But what was that? A trident?

Chapter 31: A Clash of Symbols

"What's with all the weird shit we're seeing right at the end? What the fuck does a trident have to do with anything? With me it was one of those Buddhist *dorje* thingies, and I hardly gave Buddhism a second thought until I came here. To be honest, I thought all of you guys"—he waved his fork toward Reinhardt—"wore robes and chanted all fucking day." Joshua stabbed at a sausage so violently it skittered across his plate.

Emily's Telling in the kitchen had lasted into early evening, so they had begun their evening meal.

Sunita's eyes danced. "I know what the trident means. This is amazing and wonderful. The trident is me, or at least it's about me and what I believe. In Hinduism, the trident is the weapon of Shiva."

From the Great Unnamed Room came a few tentative squawks from the Ugly Brown Birds followed by the opening strains of what sounded like Hindu chants.

Sunita lifted her head, listening. Her expression softened. "Do you see what this means? My Telling comes next, tomorrow morning by the bird cages, and these final symbols of our faith are linking us to one another—specifically to the person whose Telling comes after ours. Even at the very moment of our deaths, we seven were interconnected. I believe this means that even the order in which we're doing our Tellings was going to happen."

Emily wiped her mouth. "Like predestination? A Presbyterian friend was telling me about that, but it doesn't seem to be a simple meant-to-be thing or fate. I think it is more about God knowing what's going to happen even if we don't."

Sunita nodded. "Many spiritual paths have similar concepts with different names. For some, it's fate, that what happens to you is your destiny. And many non-religious people believe that things are meant to be."

"In my heart," Susan said, "I know that the universe has guided my destiny."

The small silence following this statement was punctuated by a faint cough from Alter.

"It would seem that God saw fit to bind us together in some way, like different strands in a prayer shawl," he said.

"Joshua," Sunita said, "remember whose Telling came after yours?" He glanced at Reinhardt, who paused with a forkful of potato salad in mid-air and waggled his free hand.

"The *dorje*," Joshua said woodenly.

"A belief in destiny and fate is at the heart of Islam," Khalid said slowly. "Whatever happens is the will of Allah. A believer has free will to obey or disobey Allah, but whatever happens to that person could not have been otherwise. Still, these symbols of our individual faiths feel like something else." He nodded at Joshua. "What do you Americans say? Like something out of left field?"

"Out of left field. Yeah, that about says it. This stuff is plain weird," Joshua mumbled, shoving more food onto his full plate.

"I believe in God's plan for the world and for me," Alter said carefully. "Does God care what word we call his plan? This universe word, or fate, or destiny or some other word man makes up. In my humble studies, I have come to believe all of us see ourselves as part of a plan. Perhaps these final visions are specific to where we find ourselves now, to this realm. And they're a sign from God, or one of his angels, that we are bound together in some way God does not see fit for us to understand at this moment. Perhaps it will be revealed to us but only when God is ready."

Joshua set down his fork and pushed back from the table. "This is heavy shit. It's a wrap for me. Until tomorrow, folks. We'll meet

Sunita by the bird cages after breakfast. Be well. As if any of us could be anything else here, wherever the fuck here is." He flung down his napkin and walked out.

Chapter 32: Sunita

Sunita warmed the stethoscope between her hands and gently blew on it before placing it against her small patient's chest. She listened with care, glancing at the large, unblinking brown eyes. The patient's mother sat very straight on a stool, thin legs dangling over the edge, her child in her arms.

"Is she going to be okay, Doctor Sunny?" the mother said in a small voice. "Maybe you could put the scope on her head."

Sunita caught the eye of the tall woman sitting nearby, her lip twitching, but she quickly assumed a more serious face and placed the scope on her small patient's head. She took the stethoscope off and straightened up to face the patient's mother. "Nahji, I am happy to report that your child will be fine and will live a long and happy life with you."

"Mama, Mama, did you hear what Dr. Sunny said?" Nahji jumped down from the stool and gave her doll a hard hug. Nahji's mother winked at Sunita.

"Thank you, Doctor, for being so kind. Nahji was quite worried about her baby after she dropped her outside the office."

Sunita gave her a warm smile, but when she spoke, her tone was serious. "I will let you know when Nahji's blood tests come back." One glance at the mother's anxious face and she added, "I am sure all is fine."

Sunita wound her bright pink silk scarf round her neck and walked mother and daughter to the door. "Please take good care of your child, Nahji."

"I will, Dr. Sunny." Nahji hugged her doll closer. Sunita shut the door with a sigh. She had delivered Nahji five years ago. Watching the little ones she delivered grow up was something she treasured about her work as a family physician. Watching them get sick was something she hated.

Pray, she reminded herself. Sunita was comfortable with the science of her profession and her devotional practices being mutually supportive. She could not imagine one without the other. She tried not to judge other physicians who did not feel the same way, but to treat the body without considering the spirit was beyond her comprehension.

She sighed once more. Today as on most days, there was no time to allow her mind to wander. A room full of patients was waiting. Most were from the Hindu community in or near her neighborhood of Harris Park, a suburb of Sydney. Some were students from various parts of India who had come to Australia to create a new life for themselves. For most, this was their only chance, and they often did not report street crimes against them for fear it would hurt their immigration process or cost them a prized government job in future. Others were older ex-pats who were delighted to have an Indian doctor. They trusted her. Sunita herself had never known what it was like to make the transition from a homeland so vastly different. She had been born here. Barely.

Her parents, Chahel and Sahasra, had been a young couple, highly educated and highly motivated, when they moved to Australia thirty-one years ago. When they stepped off the plane into the hot Australian sun, Sahasra was eight months pregnant. They were elated to leave India far behind, with its meddlesome families, worn-out customs, and ancient dust of an ancient country. To begin again in this young country felt like a miracle. And they would not make the same mistake as had so many of their countrymen. They would not move to a community that was a Little India. They found the perfect house to begin their lives as Australians and furnished it quickly, poring over western-style furniture magazines to further distance themselves from their past.

As it turned out, they did not have much time. Sunita arrived three weeks early. On the morning she was born, the temperature back in Jaipur was nine degrees Celsius, but in Sydney it was already thirty-seven and climbing.

She was supposed to be called Caroline, a carefully chosen western name. But parental pressure can exert power that effortlessly transcends distance. Chahel's mother insisted, by well-practiced manipulation and not so thinly veiled threats of disinheritance, that the child be given an Indian name.

"After all," she reasoned, "if you two insist on raising my granddaughter in such a reckless culture, it is best that she have a name that will counter that attitude. And as you know, Sunita means well-behaved," she finished firmly.

She won. She also won in having an astrologer draw up the baby's chart. She arranged for a local Vedic astrologer, who had immigrated to Australia years earlier, to visit Chahel and Sahasra a few days after they brought Sunita home from the hospital.

Sahasra was upset, and it was left to Chahel to attempt to appease both his mother and his wife. But Chahel was as bitterly discouraged as Sahasra; they both wanted to leave India behind. Chahel had suggested they could simply ignore the findings of the astrologer. They were, after all, educated people who did not need to believe in such nonsense. Perhaps humoring his mother would silence her? Neither of them believed that for a second.

Sunita was cranky on the morning the astrologer arrived. Chahel and Sahasra greeted him warmly and offered him Chai tea. They had bought it especially for the astrologer but had no intention of keeping any in their home. He got right to business as he laid out Sunita's birth chart with other papers and books. Sipping his tea, he set down his cup carefully and cleared his throat.

"This child, Sunita, will be a gifted healer and a keeper of secrets. She will be beautiful but will not always obey her parents."

At this point he lifted his heavy eyebrows. "You chose a very good name, but the planets are stronger, more powerful."

Chahel spoke up to say that his mother had advised them on the name. Sahasra narrowed her eyes. The astrologer continued, oblivious to the tension. "She will have no brothers or sisters but will maintain close relations with her cousins in India. Sunita and her dadi will have an especially close bond."

At this, Sahasra picked up Sunita and held her tightly. A frustrated tear slid down her face. *All this distance. She cannot possibly have a strong influence.*

Chahel nervously drummed his fingers on his knee. How could his mother, Sunita's dadi, be close? He dreaded the scene that would play out after the astrologer left. He beckoned Sahasra to come sit beside him again and she did so, cradling a fussy Sunita in her arms. The astrologer kept talking, caught up in his own words.

"Sunita will not marry. She is destined for greatness but not in this world."

"What the hot hell does that mean?" Sahasra blurted out. She was proud of how well she was using English. "How can she be great but not in this world?"

The astrologer stood and gave a small bow. "I shall take my leave. Blessings."

After he left, all that remained was the spicy scent of Chai and the mystery of his words. Chahel and Sahasra finally put it down to the irritating need of Indian astrologers to appear mysterious. "Damn them to hot hell," Sahasra added to seal their mutual agreement that Indian astrologers were obtuse.

As she grew up, Sunita was adored by her parents. True to the astrologer's predictions, she had no brothers or sisters. She also grew to be beautiful and smart. To her parents' knowledge, she was rarely disobedient. "Ah ha! So Mr. Astrologer got that wrong," they would say. They looked for mistakes in what he'd said to discount any predictions yet to be played out. They now introduced themselves as Chuck and Sahra.

Sunita's first memory was of elephants. Elephants painted, elephants with embroidered tapestries, elephants with bells. The hem of a brilliant green dress brushed her small leg as the raucous parade swayed through the old city. She could scarcely breathe. Dadi's large old hand swallowed Sunita's small one. Her first memory and her first trip to Jaipur.

Her parents had put off the trip as long as possible, but the threats from Dadi had become more frequent and more dramatic. She was about to die. She was going to sell all the family property. What kind of ungrateful children were they to keep her from her beloved granddaughter? They flew to Jaipur and stayed a month.

Years later, Sunita's first memory-story was always filled with the rich, spicy smells of cumin, garlic and turmeric. Kaleidoscopic colors, gardens that could compete with the beauties of heaven, *devayana*. Columns of trees lining stately streets—and pink. *Pink*. This must be where pink was born. Temples inspired by gods and goddesses, and bright, joyful, abundant love. There were no scars or tears in this story.

She was sitting on her dadi's knee as they swung high on flowered swings, with one of her dadi's henna-painted hands holding onto Sunita, the other holding onto the swing. She stared, mesmerized, at the intricate designs on her grandmother's hands. All around them, women were dressed in dazzling yellows, blues and greens. As the swing swooped down, three-year-old Sunita saw glittering displays of jewelry on ears, hands, wrists, and feet. Some women were singing and dancing in their beautiful dresses, others sat on blankets painting henna on one another's hands. It was the Teej Festival celebrating the goddess Parvati and the return of the rains. At just three, she knew only that she felt at home and was completely, madly, passionately in love. Food, a lot of food. Until she tasted Indian food, she had been a fussy eater.

Sunita cried for days after leaving Dadi, cousins, uncles, aunts and India. Her parents were distraught but more determined than ever to deepen their western ways and ensure their beloved daughter did the same. They bought her Barbies.

As soon as Sunita could print and read, she and Dadi began to exchange letters. Dadi's instructions during one of their crackly phone talks included not only how to address an envelope, place stamps and mail a letter but also how to keep their letters secret. Dadi arranged for a family friend in Australia to give Sunita a package of pretty stationery and overseas stamps for her fifth birthday. She herself sent Sunita a special walnut box with engravings of lotuses to keep her letters in. At first, Sunita was uncomfortable keeping anything secret from her parents, but she was sure Dadi had good and wise reasons for wanting to keep the letters secret. Sunita would stroke the box, humming *O Maa Meri Maa*, and push the box far under the bed. Her parents knew she was receiving letters from India, but the envelopes had an unfamiliar return address, and Sunita told them, as Dadi had instructed, that they were from a pen-pal friend. Dadi reassured her it was not really a lie as they were friends. Were they not?

Stories of beautiful women called goddesses and handsome men called gods were soon fascinating young Sunita. Dadi started with simple stories; as Sunita grew, the stories became more complex. Dadi would quiz Sunita. Who is Brahma? Why is it important to have a statue of the goddess Lakshmi, the goddess of prosperity, in your home? (Or, in Sunita's case, tucked in the top drawer of her bureau.) Sometimes, Dadi would send pictures of beautiful saris with her letters. Sunita would look at them over and over until they were worn thin. Long letters detailing Indian songs, Indian food, Indian history and Indian family life captivated her.

With reluctance, Sunita's parents made the trip back to Jaipur every year, and every year Sunita was beside herself with excitement. On the trip soon after her ninth birthday, when the monsoons had ended and the festivals began, Dadi had acquired another housekeeper.

Dadi's story was that she was being charitable, not that she was an old woman needing help with bathing or getting dressed. The new housekeeper came from one of the more than two hundred slums of Jaipur. This one was called *Kathputli Nagar*, the Puppet Makers Slum. The main source of income for its residents was the crafting of puppets, and Dadi had given Sunita several Kathputli puppets. The new housekeeper had been recently widowed, leaving her with very little income. The housekeeper's case was presented to Dadi at a charity group meeting.

When Dadi was explaining the presence of her new helper to Sunita's parents, she tapped her cane on the ornately tiled floor for emphasis. "You know, one of those aid agencies was nosing around the slum, and our group decided to take matters into our own hands. If someone did not give her some work, she and her boy would starve or die of one of their diseases."

One morning before anyone else was up, Sunita wandered into the kitchen. The new housekeeper jumped up, dropping the knife she was using to chop ginger. Sitting in the corner of the kitchen, a boy not much older than Sunita looked up. The housekeeper tried to conceal him, but it was too late. Sunita, holding one of the puppets, gave the boy a friendly smile.

"My name is Jamal," he said shyly.

"What are you doing here?"

Jamal pointed at the housekeeper. "My mother."

"Do you want to play, Jamal?"

The housekeeper rushed over. "My son is not supposed to be here. I will be in great trouble with your dadi."

"My dadi will not be angry," Sunita said confidently. "I will tell her how happy I am to have a new friend."

And so began the friendship of Sunita and Jamal.

Dadi was aghast that her beloved and high caste granddaughter would be friends with a boy from the Puppet Makers Slum. Even so, Dadi vowed to keep her feelings to herself and hold her tongue. She tried to find ways of limiting their time together, but the two children always found each other. Dadi worried it might be a karmic influence.

Sunita and Jamal spent hours playing school. For Sunita it was play, but for Jamal it was his only chance to learn to read and do his numbers. Sunita even taught him some English. He soaked it all in, eager to learn. Jamal's small, thin body would swell with pride when he corrected Sunita's pronunciation of Rajasthani words.

Walking as elegantly as one can using a cane, Dadi sought them out to see what they were up to. Almost always, she found them sitting shoulder to shoulder, reading or laughing. Jamal even taught Sunita how to make one of the Kathputli puppets. When Sunita proudly showed her grandmother the puppet she had crafted, the old woman felt her heart stop.

After one of these trips, when Sunita was fourteen and sick with longing to be back in Jaipur, she knew she had to talk with her parents, but the thought scared her. Why her parents insisted on not being Indian baffled her. She tried watching them for clues. To make matters worse, her father had started wearing cowboy boots. Sunita hated the sight of them and hid them. Then she felt guilty when her father spent hours hunting for these unsubtle symbols of western culture. When it became clear he wasn't giving up, Sunita dug them out and pretended to have found the ugly, wretched things. Her father praised her and gave her a hug as guilt washed over her. She prayed and made an offering to the goddess Lakshmi.

Finally she could take it no longer.

"Mother, Father, I need to speak with you," Sunita said with more confidence then she felt.

"Sunita, dear, of course. What is troubling you? You may speak to us about anything." Her father folded the newspaper and set down his coffee. Her mother put aside the book she was reading and plumped a cushion on the chair opposite for Sunita. It was a Sunday evening, and golden light from the setting sun filtered through sheer curtains into their tidy living room.

Her parents sat together on the sofa, puzzled but regarding her adoringly. This made it harder. Sunita sat down facing them but, restless, got up again. Before she lost her nerve, she stood up straighter and lifted her chin.

"Mother, Father, I need to know why you don't want to be Indian. I am Indian. I love being Indian. And I want to start Indian dance and go to Temple and wear saris and have an altar in my room." Sunita spoke in a rush, hoping that getting it over quickly would shock her parents less.

It didn't work. Chahel and Sahasra were shocked. How had they failed their beautiful Sunita?

After an excruciatingly long moment, her father said, "We will talk about this in the morning, Sunita."

"But—"

"In the morning."

Her mother got up to kiss her cheek. "Sleep well, dear Sunita. We will chat about this in the morning." Reluctantly, Sunita headed for her room.

After Sunita's door closed, Sahasra turned to Chahel. "This is all your mother's fault," she said bitterly. "The old bat has finally won. All our efforts to shake off the old ways have been for nothing. She has staged every single trip to India!" She rubbed away angry tears.

"Sahra ..." But Chahel did not contradict her. He'd known something was going on, and he suspected that his mother had enlisted the rest of the family in this ruse. Sunita saw only the magnificent palaces, the fabled fortresses, the wealthy neighborhoods. She ate only the best food. Even her cousins seemed to be in on it; they dressed in their best and most vibrant saris when Sunita was around. And then there was Jamal.

Chahel and Sahasra talked long into the night. What would her classmates think? Would they tease her or even bully her? They all wore leg warmers, headbands and neon-colored clothes. One of their mates in a sari? Surely she would be singled out. But in the end, Sahasra put into words what Chahel was thinking.

"Chuck, we are in the west now," she said. "Wouldn't we be hypocrites if we denied her the freedom to make her own choices?"

"It is likely one of those phases young girls go through," Chahel said, groping for reassurance. "She will tire of the novelty."

In the past, Sunita had been quiet and almost sullen. She had a few friends but made little effort to find new ones. While her marks were good, she showed little enthusiasm.

Now proudly, regally, wearing a deep yellow sari, Sunita walked into school that first day. She felt like a princess, and she felt honored to be showing off her heritage in the mostly white school. That morning, while she'd been draping, folding and pleating her sari to ensure it hung perfectly on her slim frame, she imagined the impact her transformation would have.

Of course she would be more popular—maybe even the most popular girl in school. Would all these pale Europeans recognize that she had access to spiritual truths that eluded them? Her spiritual mystique would captivate the other students and even the teachers, and soon both teachers and students would quietly seek her advice on all kinds of issues. With dignity, she would ponder their questions before offering her counsel. After a quiet session with Sunita, the student or teacher would walk away feeling lighter and more confident.

At this point, the fantasy became vague, because she wasn't sure what advice her teachers might seek from her. Still, she was certain her secret spiritual wisdom would give her answers when she needed them.

Reality put a dent in the fantasy.

When she walked into class, she was greeted by applause, whistles and catcalls. Some students asked if she was on her way to a costume party. Others asked if she was trying out for the school play.

She was crushed.

But she persevered. Day after day, she wore a sari to school. Day after day, she answered her friends' questions, who in turn answered their friends' questions, about what wearing the sari meant to her. About India and Hinduism. While kids in the back row still made snide comments, her circle of friends widened. By the second month of this, she was walking into class with a bone deep self-assurance. She was warmer, friendlier and more focused. For the first time in her life, she felt at home in her own body.

Meanwhile, large packages were arriving from India. Sunita was thrilled. Her parents were dismayed. The first package contained all she needed to create her altar. Statues of Lord Shiva and Parvati, richly patterned altar cloths, dainty bells, elegant incense holders, a fine silver tray, a large supply of *kum kum* powder, a *diva* lamp, *mandira*, small bowls and miniature spoons had all been wrapped in cotton and silk cloths. The *Vedas*—Hindu scripture—lay on top.

Christmas had never been like this. Chahel and Sahasra had made a big thing of Christmas in the past, and Sunita had been polite about the presents and celebrations, but her heart had never been in it. Now as they watched her dig into boxes from India, her parents sighed. This was the reaction they had wished for at Christmas: Sunita rapturous with bright eyes and a huge smile.

"Finally, I can do Puja!"

Everything she needed to transform her bedroom to the vivid styles and colors of India came the following week in two more boxes and a crate.

"It isn't even *Diwali*, the Festival of Lights, yet," groaned Sahasra as she leaned against Chahel. Inside the crate was a teak headboard with elephant carvings. Ganesh featured prominently.

"Pink! I am painting my room pink! The same color as Royal Jaipur." When her words were met with blank stares, Sunita looked impatiently from her mother to her father. "You know, the 'Pink City' where you two were born?" She rolled her eyes, and they laughed.

"Sunita! What is this?" Her friend Amber fanned her mouth and reached for a glass of water.

Sunita giggled and handed her a small sauce dish. "*Aloo tikki*, potato fritters, and I spiced them up a bit. Here, try them with this. It's *raita*, a yogurt sauce with cucumber and mint."

She was back from her first solo trip to India and was hosting a sleepover for three school friends, eager to show off her new skills from lessons in Indian cooking. Some dishes were greeted with screams of protest when an unsuspecting friend bit into a spicy treat. Other dishes were swooned over. "Swoon" was a new word for Sunita, one she'd learned watching her first Bollywood movie.

The meal over, the girls settled on small silk rugs in Sunita's room to watch a Bollywood musical on her new DVD player, snacking on crispy vegetable *pakoras* and sipping mango juice.

Sunita laid out her tray of henna supplies on the bed. Dadi had taught her how to apply it, and her friends were longing to try it. While waiting their turn for their hands to be hennaed, they danced to the movie music. Sunita sang along as she worked on a hand, but when *tabla* or *damroo* drums were featured, she laughed and jumped up to join the dancing.

It was just one moment, but one moment can leave a lasting imprint. When Sunita returned to her bedroom with more mango juice, she caught Amber pretending to be Sunita. Horrified and hurt, she watched from the darkened hallway as Amber made fun of her dancing, her saris and her mannerisms. Sunita coughed, and the other girls shushed Amber. Sunita walked into the room wearing a big smile that concealed her searing sense of betrayal. She continued to pretend for the rest of the evening, sending them off the next morning with a cheery smile. This is when Sunita learned the "art of dismissal."

She deployed the art of dismissal when anyone offended or ridiculed her. She offered no path of return. When she cut someone out of her life, they were cast out for good, often without explanation. This left some who wanted to be her friend behaving in a less authentic manner lest they upset her, and they would also be sent to the shadows.

The Monday after the sleepover, Sunita made it clear to the three girls their friendship was over. Sunita knew it would cost her other friendships, and she was fine with that.

Dadi's "India Medical School Campaign" began in Sunita's sixteenth year. Brochures on Jaipur's medical colleges were tucked into packages that included statues of Lakshmi as well as brilliantly colored saris, perfumes and the latest family photos. These always happy photos were taken in front of one of Sunita's favorite Jaipur gardens. She could almost smell the sweet fragrances of the flowers. Chahel and Sahasra desperately wanted her to remain in Australia but also wanted to leave her free to make up her own mind.

"I have been accepted to medical school." On this warm January evening, dinner was tense. Sunita had already told her parents she'd made up her mind and applied, but she had not told them to which school. Every afternoon, she picked up the mail from the hall mat before Chahel and Sahasra got home from work, so they had no idea what she might have received. Sunita had arrived at the table and tucked an official-looking letter under her plate. As she spooned mango chutney on her pakoras, she watched her parents push food around their plates, glancing at the letter. She knew she was being unkind but savored this moment of teenage power. Her parents dropped their forks and looked up.

"Medical school?"

"I applied to Sydney Medical School, and I've been accepted."

In unison, her parents rushed to give her a hug and congratulate her on such a wise decision. Sunita was happy to see her parents' relief but felt guilty she was not telling them about her plans after medical school. Only her dadi knew Sunita intended to come home to Jaipur to practice.

Before university started, she made one more trip to Jaipur. More and more, her excitement over seeing Dadi, her extended family and her beloved Jaipur was eclipsed by her desire to see Jamal. Years before, Sunita had persuaded Dadi to fund Jamal's education to help lift his family out of poverty. Now he wanted to be a lawyer.

"I would like to be a lawyer who helps the people in the slums," he said as they walked together along a tree-lined path by the house. It was almost time for dinner, and soon they would part for the day. Sunita caught his hand and kissed his cheek. Jamal quickly kissed her on the lips.

Leaning on her cane, looking out her bedroom window, Dadi watched.

The next day, Jamal and his mother did not come. Every day, Sunita looked for them. She ate less and less. Dadi deflected her questions, hating to see her unhappy but knowing it was for the best. She continued to fund Jamal's education and paid a small stipend to his mother.

When Sunita boarded the plane for the long journey back, her life had changed. She had lost her best friend.

She met Arun in a dumpster.

Sunita dashed out after a hurried breakfast to attend to last minute errands before medical school began. The past few days had been dour, with unrelenting rain. This morning the sun had returned to take its place of honor in the skies, and Sunita was eager to enjoy a busy day.

She walked quickly, passing neighboring houses shaded by golden wattle and eucalyptus trees. By the time she reached the intersection, she had added two more errands to her growing list. She paused. Her usual route to the shops would be faster, but something nudged her to take the longer route. She smiled, pleased with herself. New life. New route.

She was familiar with the route, but as she slowed her walk, she chastened herself for not going this way more often. Although there was new development, the canopied street maintained a cozy, welcoming feeling. The new condo building, completed a few months ago, fit in well. And then she saw him.

In the parking lot of the new building, a young Indian man was standing in a dumpster, holding up a large manila envelope. She laughed to herself as she thought *Look at that, someone threw out a perfectly good man!*

The sun was now shining with intensity, and Sunita regretted forgetting her sunglasses. She placed her hand on her brow and squinted at him.

"Are you okay? Is there something I can help you with?" As she walked closer, she saw a young man close to her age wearing a turquoise tunic and scowling.

He looked at her, surprised. Cars drove by, dogs barked, a small wind blew bits of litter across the lot, but still he didn't say anything. When he finally spoke, he spoke in Hindi.

"I'm fine, but I believe I threw out an envelope that has some important papers. Immigration papers." Sunita's smile was generous. He lifted his eyebrows. "Can you understand what I'm saying?"

She replied in Hindi, "Perfectly. Did you find them? And do you think it is best to switch to English? It is the language spoken here." She laughed. "Do you know any English?"

He clambered out of the dumpster, extended his hand and then withdrew it, wiping it instead on his tunic. "My name is Arun," he said in perfect, British-clipped English.

She smiled, and while she was adjusting her purse, her feathery soft yellow scarf slipped off and swirled to the ground. Arun hastily seized it and held it in his hands for a few moments. Sunita had a puzzled look and extended her hand to receive it. After a strange, quiet moment, Arun handed her back the scarf.

Sunita was shocked to learn he came from Jaipur and had been accepted to the same medical school.

"Fate," he said with a smile that appeared to be a stranger on his face.

They said their goodbyes, acknowledging they would see each other when university classes began in a few days.

Sunita hurried away, the weight of errands dangling in front of her. She could feel the sun on her face and sense his eyes on her back. She wrapped her scarf more securely and shivered. *Strange man. I will ask Dadi if she knows his family.* She laughed. Of course her dadi would know! This was her area of expertise.

"My darling, you know he comes from a splitted-up family." Sunita laughed through silent tears. Dadi was speaking in English at Sunita's request, but her labored breathing made speaking in any language a struggle. She went on, eager to tell Sunita all that she could while she had breath.

"His parents, shameful thing. Different castes, you know, and they did not even consult an astrologer or their guru. I heard this Arun is very smart and quite good looking." She was panting out each breath.

" Dadi, you sound tired. I better let you get some rest."

"Nonsense, my dear. I am in perfect health. But you sound tired, so I will say goodbye so you can get some sleep."

Sunita leaned her head against a pale yellow wall in the kitchen, tears streaming. Her father walked by and squeezed her arm in understanding.

When she could manage it, Sunita said her goodbye. "I love you, Dadi." She hung up the phone and sank to the floor, repeating, "I love you, Dadi. I love you."

Medical school was exciting and exacting. Sunita loved the intensity of her studies but found she didn't have time for all her rituals and meditations. She made some friends, usually students who were new to Australia. Arun was in some of her classes, but he had some remedial classes to make up. He would smile at Sunita but sit by himself at the back.

Dadi's condition improved a little on new medications, and soon she was up to her old ways. The past two phone calls, she had been after Sunita to invite Arun to dinner. "But I am so busy, Dadi, and you told me he, or perhaps you meant his family, was rather unsuitable."

"Arun, his family, it is the same thing, my darling. Yes, I admit I have heard some rumors, but my dear doesn't everyone deserve another chance? You are so young. Do not become hard."

Sunita could hear the heavy strain as Dadi willed air from her damaged lungs, but she couldn't help muttering to herself, *Even puppet makers' sons?*

It was instant. Sunita's parents detested Arun. They did their best to make him feel at home, offering their best Indian food dishes and warmest hospitality. Arun made an effort. He brought flowers. He was complimentary and gracious. He listened carefully and offered the right responses. He was the perfect guest.

But … They could not identify what it was, but they did not care for him.

Arun began to sit beside Sunita in their shared classes. She was okay with this, seeing it as an opportunity to work out what was off-putting about him. Their conversations mostly centered on their studies. Sometimes Sunita slipped in a personal question about his family or his current social status. He would respond with vague answers and a smile that never reached his eyes.

"Lockdown. This is a lockdown. Please stay where you are and remain calm." It was midday on a Tuesday, and like most days when tragedy strikes, the weather was beautiful. The sun shone sweetly, not with its usual aggression. The temperature hit that rare degree that was pleasant for all. The day was perfect.

Now all faces showed alarm and terror. *Pop-pop-pop* came from the courtyard outside, and without a word spoken, students and the instructor rushed to drag desks to block the door. Sunita was horrified to see Arun slip out the door before the barricade was in place.

More *pop-pop-pop*. Screams. Feet running. Doors slamming. Students cowered on the floor, clutching their cell phones, leaving weeping messages to loved ones. Sirens in the distance. Sirens close. Students praying. Sunita sat by the door in shock—frozen but alert to danger.

Shouts outside. Sunita crouched level with the bottom of the window, looking out. She saw dozens of police cars, emergency vehicles, media satellite trucks, and cars with parents falling out of them. Police held them back from either tragedy or jubilant relief. No one knew anything yet. SWAT teams were in position. Then she saw him.

Just outside a side entrance, Arun was talking to a slight young man who was holding a very big gun. Arun's stance was casual. The gunman was stomping around, waving his gun. A sniper on a nearby roof stood ready. Arun continued to talk with him using calm gestures. Sunita felt faint. She realized she had forgotten to breathe.

The young man dropped his gun and sank to his knees. In an instant, his body was hidden under a swarm of police uniforms. A policewoman guided Arun away, gripping his elbow.

Two weeks later, the school held an assembly to honor the seven who died—five students, a janitor and a professor. Songs, prayers, and speeches were to be offered, and the university president would thank the hero of that horrific day. Arun.

Sunita sat in the front row beside him as he waited to be called. Students rose in unison when he took the stage. Victory signs flashed, and the hall filled with applause. He had been reprimanded by police and university security, but the students hailed him as a hero.

On stage, Arun was asked how he talked the deranged young man into surrendering. "I told him I knew what it was like to feel isolated and different. To be ignored." He paused and looked out at people who a few weeks earlier had ignored him. He smiled. "I knew I needed to do this. It felt choiceless."

Sunita stood with the rest, applauding. When she sat back down, she heard someone seated directly behind her say loudly, "Fucking wog." She flinched.

Sunita and Arun began to date. "So this is what it took for you to date me? If I had known, I would have put myself in front of a crazed gunman sooner." She laughed at his joke.

They were happy, mostly. They were popular and well-liked, including by professors who viewed them as part of a more inclusive Australia. But snickers and loudly whispered insults sometimes accompanied their walks down the hallways and corridors. Sunita ignored or banished anyone who didn't fully accept their relationship.

At times, she tired of covering up Arun's wintry moods and frequent churlishness. But they shared a deep dedication to India, and for Sunita this was rare and treasured.

Dadi continued to astonish doctors with her indomitable life force. When she drew the last, small breath from her tortured lungs, she whispered, "Sunita, come here."

The family in Jaipur delayed time-sensitive rituals until Sunita and her parents arrived. They drove directly from the airport to Chandpole cremation grounds. After the reception, the will was read. Sunita and her parents flew back to Australia wealthy people.

Medical school flew by in a haze of all-night study groups and exams. Internship seemed a breeze in comparison.

"We could both practice here and realize our dreams of making a difference in the lives of our Indian brothers and sisters. I know you have been thinking of practicing in Jaipur, but think about what we could do here, darling." Arun stood with Sunita in the parking lot of a run-down strip mall in Harris Park. A couple of scrawny Indian boys kicked a half deflated soccer ball, using a leaning sign as a goal post.

"Harris Park. My parents would not be happy with this choice." She walked up to the building and peeked through a cracked window.

"You are wrong, my princess. This means you will be staying here. Your parents will be thrilled and," he added hugging her from behind, "we can give them lots of grandchildren."

Sunita turned around to see Arun on one knee with a modest diamond in his hand.

Sunita's father picked up a cloth and wiped the kitchen counter for the third time in as many minutes. "I wish our daughter was ten years old again and we could tell her what to do."

"Please stop doing that, darling." Sahasra rubbed her brow and put her coffee cup down on the now gleaming counter. "We have to support her if we want her to feel safe telling us things. We can be thankful she has insisted on a long engagement."

Chahel poured coffee into a big mug and took a sip. "The money that is being spent on this vanity project! That is what this clinic is, a vanity project so Arun can look like a big, important man. What kind of spell has he put on her? We should consult someone!"

Sahasra chided, "You are sounding like your mother!" She sighed. "Perhaps you are right. But perhaps there is no spell. Perhaps it is simply that he is from her beloved Jaipur."

With the blessings of a Vedic astrologer, the Asha Medical Clinic opened on November first, 2015, at 10:05 a.m. Sunita wiped tears away as the plaque bearing her dadi's name was unveiled. She had sunk most of her inheritance into this clinic. The community embraced the clinic with its central courtyard, a place that quickly turned into a meeting place where gossip and support were exchanged freely. The residents of Harris Park helped with a community garden in the back, providing fresh produce that was often lacking in their diets.

Before long, Arun's dark moods reappeared. His demands for a wedding date were becoming insistent. Sunita was happily busy in the clinic but had begun to dread time spent with him. She found their time alone a chore, and she began arming herself with reasons—or excuses—why a marriage right now would not be a good idea.

Her hands shook as she opened the manila envelope, hot bile rising. This was the third one in two weeks. The threat of an early death was the same, but the accusation was different. This one accused her of having an affair with a patient. Sunita had told no one but Arun about the threats. She did not want her staff to become concerned, and she certainly did not want the gossip that was bound to follow. It could hurt her practice. Arun encouraged her to ignore the letters, promising he would keep her safe. When he found out she had hired a security guard, he was livid.

The new security guard greeted her as she walked into the office after an especially stressful weekend with Arun. His drinking had escalated and he was becoming more verbally abusive. But they were business partners, and everything she had was tied up in the clinic. Sunita felt stuck.

The guard was tall and handsome and appeared to be Indian, although he could have been Spanish or Middle Eastern. Sunita smiled a hello as she walked briskly past patients who were already filling the waiting room. Arun was not in his office, but that was not unusual these days.

How well have you loved?

She bolted straight up. Breathing hard, she listened. Nothing. She thought of the letters and checked in with her intuition. No, this was different. She sank back and pulled the silky duvet up to her chin. Sleep took her traveling to the past. She and Jamal, shoulder to shoulder, reading under a Banyan tree. She and Dadi sipping tea, mid-afternoon in her ornate living room. She and her parents sharing cocoa, watching a Bollywood movie.

How well have you loved?

She remained lying in bed, no longer afraid. Reflections and remembrances flooded her memory. *I hope well. I hope I have loved well,* she whispered to the voice.

The days and weeks were never long enough to see all the patients who needed her help. By week's end, she was spent and looking forward to Friday evenings. However, on this particular Friday, she dreaded what was sure to be a nasty confrontation with Arun. He had not been to the clinic for the past three days. No apology or explanation was offered for the extra work that others had to assume.

Arun insisted they make a picnic and visit Lane Cove National Park. It was clear to Sunita that Arun thought this would be his chance to pin her down to a wedding date and plans. As she was leaving the office, carrying file folders to work on at home, one slipped out of her hands. The guard quickly reached down, picked it up and handed it back to her, touching her hand.

Sunita looked at his name tag. "Gabriel," she said, "Thank you." She could feel in her bones she knew him. *Funny name for an Indian or whatever culture he comes from,* she mused as she hurried out of the clinic. She shook her head. She had other things to concern herself with on this warm Friday evening.

It normally took about thirty minutes to drive from Harris Park to Lane Cove National Park, but to Sunita the evening's drive seemed to take hours. Once they parked the car, though, it felt as if she had just left the office. Sunita was puzzled to find herself thinking of the guard. Arun had been unusually quiet during the drive.

Sunita took a long breath as she stepped out of the car. Still quiet, Arun got the picnic basket out of the back of the car. Impulsively, Sunita touched his arm. "Arun, we need to talk."

She took a step back at the dark look on his face, but he smiled at her and replied, "Of course, my Princess, but let's find our spot."

During their medical school years, they sometimes came here to study and be alone. Arun always felt there were too many people around Sunita and this was the perfect place for them to be together. Alone. Just like now. Sunita spread the blanket on some smooth rocks near the river. Brightly colored pillows from Jaipur were placed near the blanket.

"Arun—"

"Sunita," he broke in. "It's time to consider our future together." His voice was strangely flat. Sunita had her own conversation going on in her head and didn't notice the oddness of his tone.

"Arun," she began again, "I want to end our engagement." She shocked herself. She'd meant to keep those words for the moment in her brain. Arun stood there, looking taller, his expression unchanged. Clearly this did not come as a surprise. All was quiet. Even the evening birds had stopped their conversations. The breeze that had been teasing the trees dropped to stillness.

"I am sorry," she said simply. Sunita stood up and went to Arun to offer him comfort. Her scarf slipped from her neck and Arun caught it. He held one end in his hand and looked up at Sunita. In that moment, looking into his eyes, she knew.

Arun wrapped the soft scarf quickly around Sunita's beautiful slender neck and pulled hard. She continued to meet his gaze. He pulled harder. Life draining out of her body, Sunita thought of her parents and all her loving friends and patients. A clear picture of a smiling Jamal appeared before her. She was not afraid.

Lights flashed, brighter than fireworks at a Jaipur festival. Life draining but heart growing with love, Sunita felt all her energies gather to one point. Love, love, she felt her body could not contain this love. But what was this? A prayer mat?

Chapter 33: Khalid

"And so, Khalid, or should I call you Kaboom? What does the Holy Qur'an say about being a comedian?" Conner March arched her unnaturally high eyebrows in her unnaturally smooth forehead. For this interview, she had ditched her usual low-cut tops and slim skirts for a high-neck blouse and long, flowing skirt.

Khalid took in this picture of faux conservatism and cleared his throat, trying not to laugh. This interview would not make or break him but, as his publicist reminded him, it was still important. Khalid's brand was riding high, and interviews, especially on national television, were vital in keeping it there. He was appearing on the Conner Marches On program to promote his latest DVD, *Growing up Brown in London Town*.

"It is Allah who makes men laugh and weep," Khalid said. "This is directly from the Holy Qur'an. I, Ms. March, am just his humble servant. Another quote that inspires me is also from our holy book: 'Do not lose hope nor be sad.' Again, as his humble servant I offer hope for unity and a relief from sadness. Today you may call me Khalid."

The studio audience applauded. Conner March's smile was dazzling. "You, Khalid, see your comedy as," she sifted through some papers, "as similar to the Art of Protest that is thought to have originated with the blacks of the United States. Is this true?"

Khalid had answered this question in many interviews and considered how to make his answer fresh. "African Americans, yes. And I'm humbled to be part of that tradition. The Art of Protest is a spark that ignites great social changes. It has often been the case that the artist starts the dialogue that galvanizes meaningful change. The artist as an agent of change has been going on for a very, very long time. All of them, including our brothers and sisters in America, have been very brave, and now we Muslims have to carry on, as do our young people and any group who are oppressed by people who—" he broke off and added with a smile, "Humor is a friendly sword that cuts through stupidity and ignorance."

He felt dissatisfied with his response but knew his publicist would be happy he hadn't gone on a rant. The audience, mostly young people, applauded. A few shouted, "You tell them, Kaboom!"

He stood up and gave an exaggerated bow. They laughed again.

"You like to tell people the meaning behind your name. Can you tell our television, online and studio audiences what your name means?" Conner seemed determined to be an agent of change herself and steer the program back to her.

"Again," groaned Khalid and slumped down in his chair. Conner looked at him sharply. The audience laughed.

Khalid straightened up and raised an eyebrow to the audience. "With the help of Allah, my parents chose wisely when they named me. Khalid was a great and mighty warrior who lived in the seventh century. Actually, he's known as one of the greatest warriors in history. His name means eternal, and it's said that anyone who's named Khalid will be amazingly handsome, of high intelligence, compassionate, humorous and, aah, modest." He waited a beat. "Possibly I made that last bit up."

Smiling thinly, Conner asked in a soft voice, "So you were named after … a warrior." She looked into her camera with what she hoped was a concerned look. She'd practiced the look in her make-up mirror prior to the show.

"Yes. And not just any warrior, but one of the greatest warriors. I strive to be a warrior, one who uses humor to cut through ignorance, stupidity and fear. Because ignorance, stupidity and fear keep people apart. I would like to be a great warrior of humor who brings people together." He added, "*In shaa Allah*, God willing."

It was not Conner's audience anymore. Some of them stood up and chanted, "Kaboom! Khalid!" By now, she was only pretending to enjoy herself. Most of her guests had the decency to at least feign gratitude for being on Conner Marches On.

She soldiered on. "So, Khalid, if you are so proud of your name, why do you use the stage name Kaboom?"

Khalid spread his palms. "I wanted to shock people. It's a tragedy what happens in the world in the holy name of Muhammad, peace be upon him. When I stand as a warrior-comedian on a stage, I use the sharpest point of my sword to pierce illusions about what it means to be Muslim. By using the name Kaboom, I'm making fun of stereotypes of young Muslim men, that somehow we're all alike. That's like saying everyone in Britain wants to tuck into a good spotted dick." Another beat. "When everyone knows our national dish is Chinese stir fry. Of course, mine is halal."

"Spotted what?" was heard in a loud quavering voice from the front row. An American coach tour had included tickets to the show in its package.

"Shh, honey. It's a pudding with currants."

The audience erupted.

"Now." Conner was determined to regain control. She winked at Khalid. "I have heard you have a girlfriend. Is this true?" She leaned over to touch his knee. He tucked in his knees slightly.

"God willing, soon," he said with a laugh. "This would make my parents very happy. Sadly, no girlfriend." His head drooped, then he stood up with his arms outstretched. "My beautiful, chaste, intelligent wife is waiting for me! With the help of Allah, find me my wife!"

A man in the audience shouted, "Kaboom, I will give you my sister and three goats." Some people booed, but Khalid said, "My brother, as you can see I have no need for goats. But perhaps you were referring to your other three sisters?"

Even Conner, after a pause, laughed and applauded. *"Growing up Brown in London Town* has just broken another record in DVD sales. I hear there is another movie deal in the works?"

"Yes, all praise to Allah, another movie is in the works. I can't say a whole lot about it, but I will say that my parents are going to be a part of it." Conner went still. This was a scoop. For the briefest moment, Khalid thought he saw a reddish light around her head.

"What?! Your parents will be part of this new movie?" She cleared her throat and continued in a more normal tone, "Your parents. This is big news. I'd heard they were supportive of you but preferred to remain in the background."

"Yes, that's all true. My parents will accompany me on the Hajj, the holy pilgrimage to Mecca, God willing. They agreed to be in this movie because they've wanted me to go with them for some time now."

Conner March was running out of time. She was desperate to catch Khalid off guard, because his popularity ensured that any gaffe would be a score for her. Her trending clips on YouTube would go viral and the Conner March brand would rise even further. One more try.

"Gaza. Share with me and the viewers what has inspired you to go to this violent territory? Is it because it is Muslim? Are you making a statement against Israel? Did the Muslim Brotherhood make a request you couldn't refuse?" She leaned forward confidentially. "Tell me, Khalid."

Offstage, his manager, Abdul, clenched his fists. This was Conner's pattern, asking questions she hoped would trip up her interview subject.

Khalid smiled warmly and pretended to stifle a yawn. He noted the glint of irritation in her eye. "I've wanted to go to Gaza for years. Yes, of course it's dangerous and my parents are worried. Do you have parents, Conner?"

She shook her head and with her eyes urged him to answer the question. The clock was ticking. Then she knew; he was dawdling on purpose. She narrowed her eyes.

"As you may know," he paused and looked around the set, "the good people of Gaza do not get many entertainers. They were among our biggest supporters early on and I feel they deserve a visit to honor their support. Conner, in the beginning of my career, for some it was an act of courage to support me. And, by the way, I don't know anyone in the Muslim Brotherhood as far as I know." Khalid looked at a deflated Conner March and stood up. "Get ready, Gaza!" he shouted. All applauded, including, after a moment, Conner.

"Khalid, it has been a pleasure and an honor to have you on Conner Marches On." She spoke brightly to the camera. "I will leave you," she said to the studio and television audience, "with a clip from *Growing up Brown in London Town*."

Khalid and Conner undid their mics as the clip aired. It showed a confident Khalid striding onto the stage at Up the Creek comedy club, shouting out his usual greeting: "Hellooo infidels and praise be to Allah for the true believers." After the clip ended and the audience filed out, Khalid thanked Conner, reluctantly agreed to a photo, and was met offstage by Abdul.

Abdul had been his manager from the beginning. Khalid still found it hard to believe that his Mullah from his old madrasa—his school—was now his manager.

"*As salaam alaikum!*" Abdul said. "Peace be unto you!"

Khalid returned the greeting and said, "Abdul, when do you think I'll be able to stop answering questions about my love life?"

With his wide, friendly face split into a beaming smile, Abdul said, "Is it any wonder that you are asked this question! Look at your amazingly handsome face!"

Khalid scowled but then kissed him, laughing. "I suppose they will stop asking when I get a girlfriend, *in shaa Allah*."

Abdul looked at his client's tired, young face. "Do not worry; you know it is already written. Allah decided before your birth who you were to marry and what work you would do. And look at you! You are teaching people the true meaning of Islam and making their hearts happier."

"All praise to Allah," Khalid responded. "But who is to say I need a girlfriend or wife?" He took his gym bag from Abdul as they walked toward the exit. "Did you notice if there were many paparazzi outside, or do I need to wear my disguise?"

Abdul laughed. "If you brought it along, it may be a good idea to put it on." He never seemed to mind the paparazzi, but Khalid found them intrusive, unpredictable and scary. Taking a burqa out of his gym bag, Khalid slipped it over his head. Abdul helped him adjust the front veil, chuckling. They were greeted by a dozen paparazzi as they exited the building, stepping into the gray light of a March morning. In the studio parking lot, a chorus of camera clicks met them, but as soon as the reporters registered the burqa, they stopped. Abdul and Khalid walked in silence to their waiting car.

"You did it again, my friend," said Abdul with a laugh as they settled into the back seat of the sleek black Bentley. Their driver signaled and pulled out of the lot. "You fooled the paparazzi. Perhaps it is time for you to look at them a bit differently, though." Then, seeing Khalid, he burst out laughing. "You do look quite ridiculous. If all those girls who swoon over you could see their handsome Muslim now!"

"Hold on, what do you mean, look at the paparazzi differently?"

With a cheerful tone, Abdul said, "You may want to consider them like your angels." He grinned broadly. "They are always with you!"

Khalid groaned. "Oh my uncle-friend, maybe you should start to do my job."

"Ha, no one would want to see a fat, balding old man," he said happily.

As they drove along the busy street, Abdul asked him if he was developing a fondness for his disguise. Khalid gave him a menacing look through the veil. Now that they were safely away from the studios and snaking their way through the London traffic, Abdul slapped Khalid's knee.

"Where would you like to go for lunch?"

"Before lunch, we must find a quiet place for *Dhuhr*, the noon prayer." Khalid said, pulling off the burqa and stuffing it into the gym bag at his feet.

"Driver, up ahead there is a lane. Please stop so we can offer praise to Allah."

The driver, who was also Muslim, quickly turned into an unremarkable lane that was remarkable for being quiet; in London there were few quiet lanes. The three men got out of the car and took their prayer mats and jugs of water out of the car. After washing, the driver determined the direction of Qiblah, toward Mecca, and they set down their mats. Standing with their eyes focused on the place where their foreheads would be later in their prayer, and with their hands raised, they began, *"Allahu Akbar."* Pigeons flew up at the sound, blending with the drab skies.

It was always the same restaurant, the one where they'd had their first business meeting. They both had sentimental feelings about the place, and the food was good. For the hundredth time, Abdul ordered the lamb kebabs. Khalid sat back, tired but relaxed.

"Do you have all the necessary documents?" he asked Abdul. No one paid attention to him here; he was accepted as just another patron. Khalid sometimes wondered if he would actually like being invisible all the time. He had an uncomfortable feeling he wouldn't. He spoke more loudly, unsure if Abdul was going deaf or was absorbed in the kebabs and hadn't heard him.

"Abdul, did you get all our travel papers together?"

Abdul looked up. "Khalid, can't a man finish his food before the business of business has to be discussed?"

Sometimes Khalid felt he was still a student of Abdul's and they were back at the madrasa. Abdul cocked his head, considering Khalid, and put down his food. Wiping the grease off his fingers, he said, "You know me. I have everything all together for our big adventure to Gaza."

Gaza was going to be the last stop on their current tour. "And of course, we will be filming this event," Abdul said when he'd received the invitation. They had successfully toured the United States, Canada, Brazil, Japan and several European countries, but this was the tour date they were most excited over. From the beginning, they knew their most critical audience would be their fellow Muslims. Of course, there were many Muslims in the audiences in other places they'd toured. But an all-Muslim audience in a predominantly Muslim country? Going to Gaza was not only a breakthrough, it also demonstrated to their Muslim brothers and sisters that they were not sucking up to the Zionists as some critics had suggested.

"As you know, my mother is not happy we're going to Gaza," Khalid said.

"Maybe so, but she was happy enough you were appearing on all the big-shot talk shows."

"Come on, Abdul. You know why she feels this way. It's a dangerous place, and she thinks it's especially dangerous for me."

"*In shaa Allah*, we will be fine and they will love you as everyone does these crazy days."

"All Praise to Allah," Khalid said. He signaled the waiter for the bill. "Let's go, Mullah. I want to do some writing."

Abdul's expression softened at Mullah.

"What are you going to write about?"

Khalid scratched his chin and looked thoughtfully at Abdul. "I think I will write about the struggles of a handsome Muslim man in his brave quest to find a suitable girl."

"Really, Khalid?" Abdul looked at him steadily, his expression kindly.

Khalid glowered at him but said nothing. They quickly paid their bill, leaving a generous tip, and joined the driver outside. The driver threw the stub of his Turkish cigarette on the ground and opened the doors.

"I am sure your blessed parents would be more than happy to find you a suitable girl if that is what you want," Abdul said.

Khalid stared out the window at the shabby storefronts. "My blessed parents would match me up with a Bedouin girl at this point."

Just as Abdul reached out to comfort him, Khalid leaned back with his eyes closed. Abdul withdrew his hand, and Khalid maintained this state of emotional hibernation until they reached Khalid's home.

"I'll see you tomorrow, Abdul." As Khalid got out and waved off the car, he saw Harvey the doorman discreetly trying to chase away a street person. The shabbily dressed man was pushing sheets of paper into the faces of passersby, and Harvey had a hand on the man's shoulder to persuade him to move off. The failed attempt became a shouting match.

"Bugger off!" Harvey yelled. The man raised his voice and kept reading what was written on the papers more and more loudly. Harvey stopped shouting long enough to grunt a greeting to Khalid.

"What have we here?" asked Khalid.

"A bloody poet, he says he is. And he"—Harvey jerked a thumb toward the man—"is trying to peddle these so-called poems to every person in the bloody street!" He ended on a shout.

Khalid laid a hand on Harvey's arm and turned to the man. "I'll buy all your poems. In the land of my ancestors, poets were often the most important people in the tribe. They linked the past and the present, reminding people of their dignity. How much do you want?"

The man shuffled closer to Khalid and peered into his face with jaundiced eyes. Khalid flinched at the blast of fetid breath that would wilt sturdy flowers, but he stood his ground. The man made a good try at standing fully upright, weaving as he tried to focus. "Thank you, my good shir. You are a gentleman. That'll be fifteen qu-quid."

Khalid dug out his wallet and gave him twenty.

"Sir, you really shouldn't," Harvey said. "We don't want to encourage his lot. Too many of you good people here."

"*Zakat*, charity, Harvey. It's my duty and honor to help this man's distress."

Harvey opened the door to the building for him and stood back, shaking his head.

The red light was blinking on the phone in the foyer as Khalid walked into the apartment. Only a few people had his home phone number. No doubt his mother had watched the interview and was phoning to offer her review. She hadn't wanted him to do it, citing examples of people Conner March had sabotaged. "Did you see the way Conner tricked that poor young woman, Khalid?" she'd said after showing him a clip on YouTube. But he thought the interview had gone well and hoped he didn't have to listen to an extended commentary when he returned her call. In the meantime, he was tired. He stretched out on the couch.

Moments to himself were rare these days. Lately, it seemed whenever he had time to think his own thoughts, his mind went into rewind.

November in London is seldom cheery, and November 2001 was no exception. There was an added grimness in the air that seemed to pull the gray clouds closer to earth. Khalid's parents had insisted on coming with him to his first day at the madrasa. At eleven years old, he felt sad and scared at this new development in his school life.

"It is all for the best, my son," his father had said. For weeks, his parents had debated the issue. Khalid had been happy at his old school. He had good friends, enjoyed the lunchtime soccer matches and liked most of his classes. Over the years, his parents had discussed the idea of sending him to a madrasa rather than the public school, but Khalid always persuaded them to allow him to remain where he was, promising he would give them better results. Sometimes he felt his parents used this threat to get him to work harder.

Then the 9/11 attacks happened. And everything changed. At first, his friends made excuses for not walking with him or inviting him to join kickabouts with a soccer ball. Favorite teachers ignored his raised hand. Like a lot of Muslims young and old, Khalid was angry, confused and embarrassed. His attempts at hiding his feelings and acting unconcerned were met with threats. Whispered insults in the hallways, obscene phone calls that concluded with promises of a painful death were daily reminders that life had changed. His parents talked about sending him to stay with family in Morocco to finish high school, but Khalid struck a deal. Enrolment had risen in the madrasa, and available space was scarce, but with help from their imam, a place for Khalid was found.

When he saw Abdul for the first time, he groaned. A squat, balding man, Abdul wore a thick and lumpy coat that hung midway down his traditional ankle-length *jubba*. When he saw Khalid, he shouted joyfully, "Masha'Allah, welcome, welcome, Khalid!"

How can he be so happy? Khalid thought. *What's wrong with him? He seems oblivious to this newly shattered world.*

Khalid's parents were relieved. Both the madrasa and Abdul were welcoming. Yet Khalid felt even more alone. It soon became apparent that Abdul believed in happy positives. Of all the newcomers to the madrasa that dark autumn, Khalid stood out for Abdul. He quickly became a favorite guest at Khalid's parents, sharing stories of Khalid's talents for making people laugh. It wasn't long before Abdul was considered an important mentor and uncle.

Now, here it was many years later, and Khalid could not imagine how differently his life would have been without him. *Masha'Allah, God has willed it*, he thought. Even with the drapes drawn and no clock in sight, Khalid could tell it was almost time for afternoon prayer. His thoughts returned to Abdul.

It was from his mother that he'd learned Abdul's story. Born in Iraq, he had moved to London with his young wife, Lina, to accept a teaching position back in the seventies. Lina was a nurse who had yet to qualify with the medical boards in England. Both of them loved children and wanted as many as Allah saw fit to give them. To their great joy, only months after they'd arrived in London, Lina began to experience the symptoms of pregnancy. Elated, they found a doctor who, after examining Lina, decided it was best for her to undergo a series of tests. Abdul would later say it was the darkest moment of his life when the testing revealed that instead of a much-wanted pregnancy, his young wife had cancer. Lina died four months later. Abdul never married again and decided to devote his life to as many children as possible.

"Instead of being a father to one, maybe two, I have had hundreds of children," he exclaimed happily. But Abdul had his crafty side as well. He was an astute business manager who could disarm anyone with his deceptively simple cheerfulness. "All praise to Allah," he would remind Khalid when he successfully concluded a lucrative contract.

All Praise to Allah. Khalid rose from the couch to perform his prayer.

"*Bismillah*, in the name of Allah. We pray to Allah *Jalla Jalaluhu*, may his glory be glorified," Abdul said, nodding vigorously. "Yes, yes, you see this is your quest, your mission, *in shaa Allah*. This comedy competition will be on television throughout the UK! You, Khalid, can inspire Muslims to become more devout, *in shaa Allah*, and teach the nonbelievers that we do not blow things up or hate them or own camels or goats or have ten wives or—"

Khalid was laughing but also worried Uncle Abdul would have a heart attack. Abdul continued more seriously, "This will be a good thing, in shaa Allah, my Khalid. You will, how do you say it? Dazzle them! *In shaa Allah*," he continued, squeezing Khalid's shoulder, "with your charm, good looks and smooth London accent. You will be a hit, *in shaa Allah*."

Khalid laughed. He could not remember when he had heard so many instances of "God willing, *in shaa Allah*." "I'm still only eighteen. Who will take me seriously?"

"Seriously, I hope no one!" Abdul chuckled at his own joke. "Our brothers and sisters will be inspired, *in shaa Allah*, and you will give the young infidels something to think about. You know, Khalid, it is in the nature of young people to rebel. Think of all those nice young British girls and boys. Ha, they will drive their parents crazy, listening to some Muslim kid, *in shaa Allah*. Your parents have already consented. I will pick you up at oh-nine-hundred," he said, consulting his watch as though he were planning a military mission.

Maybe that's exactly what this is, thought Khalid at the time.

"Look Who's Laughing" was the show that launched Khalid's career. Abdul was right. He was a hit and received immediate offers from comedy clubs, radio shows and other television programs. Khalid asked Abdul to be his manager and, to his surprise, he agreed on the spot. At first he kept his teaching job at the madrasa, but he quickly became too busy. Although he was sad to leave his teaching job, after 40 years it was time. Khalid's parents were delighted to have Abdul continue his role as mentor and now business manager.

"With the help of Allah, I make two promises to you," he said one day to Khalid's parents. "One, that I with the help of Allah will keep Khalid safe from harm. And two, that your young man will be a brilliant success, *in shaa Allah*." He was able to keep promise number two.

Kaboom was one of the characters Khalid created for his first comedy series, "Not so Radical." Kaboom was a hapless young Muslim man who tried to fit in with groups who espoused violence to resolve age-old tensions. Wearing traditional Muslim clothing, he tried to stage protests, make outrageous comments and appear menacing, all to hilarious effect. Kaboom was a misfit who came across as both innocent and wildly misinformed as to the teaching of Islam. He was also able to communicate the angst that all young people feel, regardless of race or religion. He was the talk of the talk shows, with pundits weighing in from all sides. The usual experts were invited to offer commentary. Some saw his performances as positive, opening up much needed dialogue. Others, both Muslim and non-Muslim, expressed outrage and demanded Khalid be banned from performing. This resulted in an increase in audiences and security. News organizations worldwide competed to have Khalid on their shows.

"Not so Radical" toured more than twenty countries. Both Abdul and Khalid were delighted, even while concern over safety was growing. Like young people everywhere, Khalid had the audacious belief that no harm could befall him. His parents, like parents through the ages, felt differently but were also proud. He was a hero to many who felt they'd been lied to by those in power, who felt their voices were never heard. This group included many young Muslims and non-Muslims who became protective of this new hero. Liberals adored him but were cautious about their support.

Abdul discovered a talent for business management that included astute financial deals. Cultivating Khalid's image of a young, traditional Muslim who chronicles his struggles to follow his faith came naturally to him. In large part, this was due to the fact that it was true to Khalid's actual life. Endorsement deals, from toothpaste to security devices and even a Khalid doll, created wealth for both of them. Appearances in sitcoms, movies and commercials added even more. They were in talks to create a video game, where the primary market would be young Muslims, but the manufacturers were optimistic the game could sell across other demographics. This game featured the Five Pillars, the articles of Muslim faith, with the hero Khalid encountering situations that challenged his beliefs. Taken from the history of the prophet Muhammad and the rise of Islam, the game had the danger, intrigue, demons and angels that ensured popularity.

Despite the adulation and dizzying success, Khalid was lonely even as marriage proposals flooded in, from farm girls in Iowa to daughters of Saudi billionaires. He was not interested, and his lack of interest disturbed him. He prayed. His mother encouraged him to go to Muslim Marriage events, where professional single Muslims could network and meet potential partners. Abdul suggested they take a small camera crew along. The organizers agreed, in part because it was Khalid. It took cunning to pull this off without paparazzi finding out, but with the help of some retired Scotland Yard men they succeeded.

The film footage became part of his new routine, "Hip in a Hijab," and became an overnight classic.

"Two nights of sell-out crowds, praise God," Abdul said. "This should make you happy!"

They were in their favorite restaurant for a quiet evening meal. Khalid swallowed his last bite of lamb stew. "All praise to God. Yes, I am happy. But Abdul, it is time I married, and I'm troubled."

"*Masha'Allah*," Abdul responded. "God has willed it."

Khalid sighed and said so softly that Abdul had to strain to hear, "Abdul, I believe there is a jinn."

Abdul leaned back, his face ashen. "A ghost? A spirit? Why do you say that, my brother?" His voice was quiet with an edge of fear.

"Last night, I had a dream that wasn't quite a dream. I fell asleep but was aware of my surroundings, like being awake but not being able to move." He looked searchingly at Abdul to see if he understood. Abdul gave a small nod of encouragement. "Then I heard it, a voice. This voice spoke to me, and it said, 'How well have you loved?' I looked around, but there was no one. My heart was pounding, but eventually I went back to sleep. And I heard the same voice again, even louder. *How well have you loved?*"

Abdul looked at Khalid with compassion on his ample, comfortable face. "You have been very tired, my brother," he offered. "There is no power and no strength save Allah, you know this. Some jinns are friendly. I have heard good stories. Perhaps a good one is telling you your intended is near." Abdul examined his kebab and slid a pepper off the skewer.

"*Masha'Allah*," Khalid said woodenly. "God willing. My parents would be happy. But somehow I feel I am to love without the love of a partner."

"That is crazy. And you mean wife, not partner!" Abdul broke into an immense smile. "You need a vacation! Before we go to Gaza, take a trip to the seaside."

"Perhaps," Khalid whispered, more to himself than to Abdul.

Paparazzi had covered all the entrances to the theater. Head down, wearing his traditional *jubba*, Khalid tried to quickly walk past them, but they were onto him. Cameras clicking, a symphony of voices shouting his name, Khalid lifted his head to loud cheers. *Why not? They have to make a living.*

"How many wives, Khalid?"

"Is it true you have an uncle who's a terrorist?"

"When will you see your children?"

"Are you giving all your money to the Muslim Brotherhood?"

Shouted questions tumbled over one another. Khalid stopped suddenly and raised his hands in surrender. His security people bumped into him and tried to push him forward. Khalid whispered to the lead. The security man shook his head but turned and signaled to the others to stand down. Khalid addressed the paparazzi.

"You know, in Islam, we believe an angel is always with you. This angel follows you wherever you go, recording your words and deeds. My friends, today Allah has blessed me with many angels!" he shouted and gestured toward them. Applause, laughter and shouts of "We love you" followed Khalid to the entrance. And then he stopped. His security was losing patience.

"Hold on a minute. Who are you?" he asked a tall reporter. The man met his gaze, looking relaxed. One of the security people grabbed his badge and said, "Gabriel. No last name? What organization is *Another World*?" The tall reporter ignored him and continued to meet Khalid's gaze.

"Let him go," Khalid said roughly, turning abruptly away. He didn't know why he spoke that way, but something about this man unsettled him. He hurried into the theater.

On stage, he was pacing, the energy from the audience buzzing in his head. This was what he was born to do. "Yes, as you can see, infidels and believers, I am a traditional Muslim. My dear parents remind me of this every day. Being a traditional Muslim means I am to marry," he began. Loud cheers and cries of "Marry me!" from women and even a few men rose up from the packed theater.

"Have any of you attended a Muslim Marriage event?" He walked close to the edge of the stage and peered into the darkness. When laughter broke out, he turned in mock horror to see footage of his recent attendance on a huge screen. Onscreen, his bumbling efforts to connect with various eager young women were met by hoots and claps from the audience.

"As you can see, the amazingly handsome Kaboom, ah, fizzled …?"

A good-natured "Nice one, mate!" came from the audience.

"Cheers, mate!" Khalid waved in the direction of the voice. "So, my dear mother found a television show in Jeddah, where four lovely sisters agree to a kind of contest for brides. My dear Uncle Abdul, please roll the clip."

The big screen showed four seated women dressed in identical niqabs that covered their faces. Only their eyes were visible.

"Now, even Allah says we should look for beauty! How am I to do that, I ask you?" The audience erupted with laughter.

"My sisters and brothers, I do want a woman who wears the hijab but she has to look hip."

After the big screen was blank and slid silently into the ceiling, Khalid stood alone on stage. This was the part of his act that people loved best, Khalid telling stories from his life, of growing up Muslim in an Anglo culture. He wrapped up the evening with one about his parents performing the noon prayer in an airport when he was a little boy.

"So here they are, prayer mats laid out between gates 21 and 25. And people are milling around. And they're prostrate on the mats, praying. And along comes this rather well upholstered American woman and she stops to look. And my parents are still praying. And suddenly this woman leans down and yells, "Excuse me, honey, could you look for my earring? It was a gift from my late husband." Khalid did a credible impression of a middle-aged woman with a piercing, nasal voice. "What's wrong with you, honey? Are you all right down there? It has a diamond chip!"

He sketched a quick bow then raised his arms. "Good night, everybody! Don't forget to love each other, my brothers and sisters! *JazakAllah Khair*—may God reward you with the best!"

The audience were on their feet.

How well have you loved?

He woke with a start and looked around.

"Definitely a jinn," he said aloud into the darkness. "I'll talk to the imam tomorrow." He drifted back to sleep.

Dreams tell stories, some true and some not. Khalid had two dreams that night. In one, his parents were preparing for his wedding but couldn't find him. In the other, he was moving his body against another body. Even in the dream, he knew the other body was a man's. And in the dream, he didn't want this other body to be a man's body. He didn't want to feel the passion he was feeling.

For the next night's performance, he decided not to wear a disguise to get in. He approached the same entrance, knowing that his gang of angels would be lying in wait. Would Gabriel be there? His heart knocked as he walked rapidly to a roped-off section. The noise and chaos felt almost soothing. And there he was, in the same place as the night before. Khalid stopped in front of him.

"Do I know you?"

Gabriel reached out a fine-boned hand to touch Khalid. Security rushed in but Khalid signaled them to stay back. "It's Gabriel, right? May Allah reward you for the good." Gabriel's gaze was steady, his eyes somber. Khalid was taken aback, but security pushed him toward the entrance and away from the rain that had just begun to fall.

Now he stood behind the curtains, listening. He stood in the spot where the audience would first see him when the curtains swept open, and he listened to the sounds of humanity. Talking, laughing, coughing, cell phones beeping, all rustle and bustle of settling into seats. Waiting. People looking for their place in the world, searching for meaning and hoping for hope. Race, religion, sex, age—none of it mattered. Some moments feel as though they are the only moments. The emcee was whipping up enthusiasm for louder than loud applause. The audience was chanting.

Slowly, teasingly, the curtains opened to reveal Khalid, the amazingly handsome, top-of-his-game Khalid. Chants turned to cheers. He heard a new sound. A tearing away of metal from metal. A groan above his head a little louder than the cheers.

It was brief. For a moment that seemed like the only moment, he saw the lighting come crashing toward him. *Alhamdulillah*, he whispered, barely a breath. All praise is due to God.

He rose up, seeing the ruin of his body, seeing the stage. Hearing the shocked intake of a thousand breaths.

He felt his heart bursting with more love than a body could contain. Love for all. Love for his parents, for Abdul, for his fans, for London, for each corner of the earth. Faster and faster through darkness and light, darkness and light. Love too vast for one human heart. Vastness beyond concept of vastness. And at the edge of his being, a Star of David ...

Chapter 34: Alter

"What has happened to those pigeons?" Alter rubbed at the grimy window to take a closer look at the empty rooftop across the way. For a moment, he was surprised to hear his old, creaky voice in the empty flat. "Ah, maybe they know there will soon be more exciting places to be than this old Ghetto."

The Carnival would begin in a few days, and Venice beyond the Ghetto gates would be filled with brightly costumed, masked people. *All kinds of people except us Jews*, he thought.

Morning prayers were done and Alter sat, as he did most mornings, staring out the one small area of clean window. The sun peeked through the early morning gray before retreating again behind the low February clouds. Perched precariously above the muddy lane, the flat looked down on the Ghetto where Alter was born and where his parents and grandparents had been born. Being high up kept most noise from piercing the silence of his days. The smells too. Sweet and sour, new and dying; the height of his home protected him from the miasma of the narrow, crowded street.

His people, his community. But Alter liked his solitude and he especially liked his solitude to come without outside smells. Silence. *Ah, this will not be a silent day.* Alter drained the cup of now cold tea. The teacup had been Hannah's. Alter's matching one had broken years ago, and he felt a special comfort in using hers. He examined the cup. He did not remember this fine crack that divided elegant blue flowers from their stems being there yesterday.

It was Sabbath, and his daughter Sarah would be coming by later to collect him. She didn't like her father walking down the steep, broken stairs by himself. Alter didn't tell her that he often walked down by himself. He liked to walk the midnight streets, listening to the hushed sounds of night. Sarah would have scolded him just the way his dear Hannah did, sending a quick, sharp pain of remembrance through his heart.

Even from this height, Alter could still see the goose feathers in the lane. A small dog was licking the cobblestones nearby. How different this enclave had looked the day before. Forgetting it was Thursday, Alter had walked to the Scuola Spagnola Synagogue yesterday to have a talk with the new rabbi. The short walk in the morning was quiet and pleasant. The discussion with the rabbi, however, was neither. Alter was known as an expert on Sephardic laws and customs. Naturally, the new rabbi was as well, but he had new ideas Alter found upsetting. It was in the area of tribal identities where they differed the most. Alter believed it was the solemn duty of every Jew to abide by his ancestral traditions, so his prayers should reach the gate in heaven appropriate to his tribal identity. The new rabbi thought this was not of any spiritual importance whatsoever.

"Now, Alter," he said in an attempt to sound authoritative, "this is the seventeenth century."

To Alter, the rabbi simply sounded arrogant. Even though the rabbi finally agreed to keep this in the liturgy for now, Alter was fuming. He felt he was being pandered to like a child, not respected as a community leader and historian. This new rabbi needed to learn more history, he concluded. *So sad, so sad. We cannot forget our history.*

His head bent, he marched home, carrying on a heated discussion with the rabbi in his mind. Only when something brushed his face did he look up. His street had been transformed. Walking through a storm of goose feathers, he realized he was walking through the frenzied preparations for the Sabbath.

A line of boys sitting on worn stoops, side by side with geese and the occasional chicken slung over their skinny knees, were quickly plucking feathers. The aromatic scents of garlic and cumin drifted through the air, overlaying but not entirely masking the usual rotting odor of the canals.

"Shalom, Alter," Rivka sang out as she swept off her crumbling front step. She paused for a moment and rubbed a cloth that she dug out of her apron to shine the *mezuzah* affixed to the doorpost to declare that this was a Jewish household. When she forgot to kiss the *mezuzah* right away, Alter gave her a dark, reproving look. She quickly touched the newly clean *mezuzah* and kissed her fingers. He nodded in approval.

"Shalom, Rivka." Alter stopped, taking comfort from the chaos around him.

Rivka took a moment from her cleaning duties and bent down to swat the back of her son's head. "Don't play with the goose's head." She turned to Alter. "I heard you had a discussion with our new rabbi." Rivka continued to sweep her now clean step.

Alter exhaled. Of course the entire Ghetto would already know that they had met.

"Nu?" enquired Rivka. "So?" Several other women had joined them, and Alter was sizing up the distance to his own doorway.

"*B'ezrat hashem*, with God's help, all will be good," replied Alter in his most scholarly voice. Rivka and the other women nodded, waiting for more. They were disappointed but not surprised when he didn't offer intimate details of his meeting with the rabbi. Conversations, debates and even arguments between families, friends and neighbors about the new rabbi had been increasing. Even the usual high anticipation of the upcoming celebration of Purim could not dispel the building tensions. Everyone, from the most learned to the uninformed, had an opinion.

Ah, if opinions were as valuable as gold, we would be the richest community in the world.

At the doorway to his own building, Alter touched his *tzitzit*, his fringes, and offered a prayer to God. He looked up to see a young man sitting idly nearby, picking his teeth with a goose feather. Alter did not know him. He glanced back at Rivka and the other women gathered, asking silently who the stranger was. Almost in unison, the women shrugged. The young man lifted his head and offered Alter a slow smile. Alter wondered how someone could sit doing nothing and still look so arrogant. He gave the young man what he hoped was a gravely disapproving look before he touched the *mezuzah* and kissed his fingers. He said another prayer before beginning the long ascent to his flat.

Making the climb took all his concentration. As he ascended each step, he said a prayer. But when he encountered a neighbor, he made an effort to appear faster and stronger. All were busy with their Thursdays. Once inside, he allowed himself the pleasure of surrender. Wrapping his prayer shawl around his shoulders, he carefully lowered his body into a chair. He no longer had to pretend he wasn't an old man.

Ah, God listened to my parents. His parents loved to tell the story of his birth. He was to be born near Purim but seemed determined to arrive early. This determination was a sign of things to come, his parents would say with laughter and love. There were hours left to sleep and dreams yet to be dreamt when Alter's mother woke his father and said, "This one is eager to be born."

"It's too soon!" His father's feet landed on the cold floor. "The midwife said it would be weeks yet. He will die."

Throughout their marriage but especially in times of crisis, it was Alter's mother who took charge and calmed things down. "Don't worry," she said now as sweat poured down her face and blood seeped onto the thin straw mattress, "he will live. I have seen his angels."

She gave her husband a push to fetch the midwife. As soon as they returned, she ordered him to get Psalm 121. Scroll in hand, he ran outside again and read the Psalm until he was hoarse. In the damp cold of this same flat beside the canal, Alter was born a few hours later. It was a Thursday. Not only was he born too early but, as he later learned, he had interrupted his mother's preparations for the Sabbath. Looking at the tiny form, the midwife gently asked Alter's mother if she was preparing to say goodbye to him.

"No, he will live. His angels have told me so," his mother said as she held the barely breathing baby to her breast. The midwife tucked the blankets in and tried to hide her misgivings. "Bring in his father," Alter's mother commanded. He stepped quietly back into the room. It was morning and pigeons were cooing outside the window.

"We shall call him Alter so that he lives to be old," she said. Her face seemed unnaturally bright, and for a moment her husband worried about her mind.

But he answered clearly, "His name will be Alter." *Alter* meant *old age*, and it was the custom to name a sickly baby Alter in the belief that God would know the child was meant to live long.

That Alter's father could speak so clearly after nearly losing his voice reciting the Psalm for hours was seen to be a small miracle from a merciful God. And this, too, became part of the story. It seemed to Alter that his parents needed these small miracles to elevate their daily lives. They were good at looking for signs from God.

God listened to them, Alter thought again. *I am old. Now when can I die?*

Willing death, he closed his eyes but instead slept a deep afternoon sleep. She was making challah. No one could make challah as good as Hannah. It must be Thursday. She had braided the bread, and it was baking over a low, comforting fire. Lentil soup was simmering and the chicken was almost ready to be removed from its cold-water bath. Alter watched the scene, happy to see Hannah move about the kitchen, gossiping with her sister who was sitting at the table peeling garlic cloves. Her sister? Hannah's sister died years ago. Sleep, the cheap substitute for death. He was sleeping and dreaming a dream from long ago ... Now Elijah came running into the kitchen looking to steal some food, hoping his mother and aunt were too busy talking to notice. Alter could feel his scrawny throat tighten with old tears. Elijah also died years ago. What was going on?

How well have you loved?

An unfamiliar voice, but Alter knew the question was for him. Was it one of his angels? He tried to rouse himself from sleep but couldn't move. Hannah and her sister continued to prepare for the Sabbath meal. Hannah was polishing the Kiddush cup and laughing at something her sister said. In his sleep, Alter felt himself strain to listen to their conversation, something he never would have done while they were living.

How well have you loved?

The voice again. Irritation and fear rose up. He wanted to go on watching his Hannah, his Elijah and even Hannah's sister. This voice or angel was asking him a question he had never considered before. It frightened him.

He shivered. He was awake. Alter opened his heavy eyes and, yes, it was his flat. Lasting no longer than a breath, a bluish white light, sharp and clear, flashed and was gone. He shook his head. His face was wet with tears. Old tears. No angel hanging around. Everything was in its place, not that there was much to be in place except his books and papers. These were piled high against every wall.

"Not even space for a mouse, Papa." His daughter Sarah would kiss him in exasperation when she surveyed the too many papers and books.

How well have I loved? For the first time in years, Alter felt deep fear. *What if I have not loved well? What if, when I die, which I hope will be very soon, I am punished? After all my years of waiting to see Hannah and Elijah, what if God strikes me with Kareit and I am cut off from them?* Alter thought with great anguish. "Hear Israel, the

Lord is our God." Alter, touching his fringes, began the Shema, the ancient daily prayer.

On Friday afternoon, Samuel came rather than Sarah to bring him home for the Sabbath. Alter was happy to see his grandson, who at fourteen seemed to stretch a bit taller each time he saw him. Samuel sat down and folded his hands, not quite a man's hands but no longer a boy's, neatly on his lap. Alter was pleased to see him so polite. He was a handsome boy and at times reminded Alter of his own Elijah. By now, though, Samuel was older than Elijah was when he died.

Sometimes, when candlelight caught Samuel's jawline a certain way, or a certain look came into his eyes, Alter called him Elijah. He tried to cover up his mistake, but others around him would exchange looks. Alter saw this and quickly tried to restore his authority by directing them toward a prayer, and they, having kindness in their hearts, followed his lead. Alter struggled with his feelings toward Samuel. At times, he felt his heart open wide with great love. But at other times, when Samuel did something that reminded Alter of his long dead son, he felt his heart close. Throughout the years, he tried to master his feelings, but his heart would not obey his commands.

Dear Elijah. When the day's light faded and Alter was lighting a candle against the darkness, he would pause as the candle flared. Had he thought of Elijah today? On those days he had not, his eyes would fill. If he did not think of him every day, would Elijah cease to have lived at all?

Alter clung to the memory of Elijah at ten years old, just before he got sick. Healthy, laughing at Hannah as she swatted him lightly for teasing his baby sister.

Then this picture memory would fade, replaced by another.

Hannah and Alter had kept vigil by Elijah's sick bed for three days. A frightened Sarah was sent to stay with Hannah's sister to keep her from coming down with the same fever and cough. By the end of the third day, Hannah was weak, pale and exhausted. The doctor had bled Elijah with no relief from his symptoms. He had expectorated him as well, to no avail. There was one medicine that might work, but none was to be had inside the Ghetto gates.

Alter gave Hannah's shoulder a reassuring squeeze before following the doctor out of the flat.

"This medicine. We have to try!" he whispered hoarsely.

The doctor nodded grimly. Alter went back inside to tell Hannah of their plan to leave the Ghetto and get the medicine. It was near midnight, and the chances they would be allowed to leave were slim. Hannah hurried to the other room and knelt beside the bed that she and Alter shared. She pulled a carved wooden box from under the bed and carefully removed a small velvet bag. Inside it was her best necklace, the one Alter had given her on their wedding day.

"Give this to the guard if it helps open the gate." Her voice was strong as she put the bag into Alter's hand and closed her hand over his.

At the Ghetto gates, the guard looked bored and spat on the ground as he listened to Alter's pleas and the doctor's reasoned request. In desperation, Alter reached into his pocket for the necklace and wordlessly held it out to the guard. The guard opened the bag, shook out the necklace and held it up to the torchlight for a better look.

"That's it?" Annoyed, he dangled the necklace briefly from his fingers, then crushed it in his fist and tossed it into the murky canal.

Two days later, Elijah was dead. Alter and Hannah were frozen in grief. When Alter emerged, he was filled with rage. How could God create someone like the guard, who was without a heart? When at last he felt able to return to his devotions, he added the anger of having removed himself from God to the anger that burned within him for the injustices to his people.

Now on this Friday afternoon, here was young Samuel, eager to tell his grandfather about his plans before they set off for home.

"You know how it is with the gentiles at Carnival, Zedie. Even the men on the barge who keep us within our gates at night will be drunk. My friends thought we could even use the costumes we wear at Purim. Just think, Zedie, no one from the Ghetto has ever been to the Carnival." Samuel paused, trying to gauge his grandfather's reaction. "It would be a victory, just like the story of Joshua."

Alter reached out awkwardly and touched his grandson's knee. "My sweet Samuel, save your courage. This is not worthy of you or your ancestors. You would be taking a great risk getting past the guards, and for what? To see a bunch of gentiles, dancing and drinking and wearing all those costumes? Not to mention the other things they will be doing while being covered up? But God will know. God will know ..."

Samuel was attentive, his boy/man hands clasped in front of him.

Alter trailed off, remembering this was his grandson. He was not going to utter a word to him about what he'd heard about the gentiles and how they behaved at Carnival.

"Oh, Samuel, we always want to see what we are not allowed to see. Do your mother and father know about these plans? In the Ghetto, people can smell a secret, and when they do, they talk." He struggled to his feet. "Come, your mother will be getting concerned, and the sun will not wait for us. It will be going down soon. Imagine preparing for Sabbath, and she is also baking for the wedding of Abram and Shosanna," Alter added as Samuel helped him on with his coat. "Just like Hannah, Samuel, your beloved mother is gifted with the graces that a kind God bestows on a woman." Alter's face lit up in reminiscence.

People in the lane were hurrying through doorways, ready to begin their Sabbath. Alter walked more slowly than usual to make this time alone with his grandson last longer. He was happy Samuel had chosen to reveal his planned trip to San Marco Square, but he also shuddered. If any of the group were discovered, there would be nothing anyone could do to help them. The gentiles would not care that these were someone's beloved children, that they were children of God.

To them, we are not people. The boy and his friends do not seem to know this. Reading about the Exodus many times—with discussions after each reading, yes—that should help them to know this truth, Thoughts crowded in on him as he walked. *And extra prayers would not hurt them. Three times a day is not enough for these young men. They need more.* He stuffed his hands into his pockets.

"Shabbat Shalom, Alter. Shabbat Shalom," greeted Abraham, who was walking with his wife toward her parents' home near the canal. Samuel and Alter returned the greetings and were about to step through the doorway of Sarah's home when Alter grabbed Samuel's sleeve. Sitting on a low step next door was the young man Alter had seen the day before. He looked steadily at Alter and gave him that same slow smile.

"Do you know that young man, Samuel?" Alter said in a voice that felt far away.

"No, Zedie, I do not," Samuel replied softly. "But you know how it is these days. People are moving here from all kinds of countries." He sensed Alter's unease.

"Yes, I hear that news of this beautiful, rich place is reaching the ears of people from all over the world," Alter joked, sweeping his arms wide to embrace the tall, crumbling buildings. "My son, have you seen the bags of gold left by the angels on each doorstep?"

Samuel laughed and helped Alter through the small passage.

Once inside, Alter took a breath that did not seem to go all the way in. He put a hand over his chest and fingered his fringes. Sarah came running.

"What took you so long?" she said, looking from one to the other. Worry was etched on her face. Guilt washed over Samuel at the thought of how distraught she would be if he and his friends went through with their plans.

Like most mothers, Sarah had keen eyes that registered the smallest change in her child.

"Samuel," she said, dropping an arm around his shoulder, "are you catching a cold?" He shook his head and squirmed with affection and embarrassment. At that moment, he knew he was out of the Carnival plan, an adventure that the son of the new rabbi had called Jews in the Square.

Sarah looked radiant in her fine wool dress of myrtle green and a matching head scarf. Alter remembered how much his dear Hannah had wanted to buy this for her. Although money was scarce, Alter had not been able to resist his wife's desire to see their Sarah in such rare finery. Hannah almost never asked for anything.

She stood now before the table, which was covered with the traditional white cloth. On the table were candles, ready to light, and two challah loaves under a white napkin. Alter, Sarah's husband Joseph, and young Samuel silently waited for her to begin. She lit the candle that represented remembrance first and then the candle that represented observance. As she circled her hand above the candles, Alter knew she was focusing deeply on her connection to God. She closed her eyes.

"Blessed are you, Lord our God, sovereign of the universe who has sanctified us with his commandments and commanded us to light the lights of the Shabbat." Sarah opened her eyes after saying the blessing and looked at the candles with wonder and respect. She beheld the three men in her life around the table, and her eyes were soft. As she dipped her head in private prayer, Alter's heart was full.

After the prayer and lighting of the candles, they gathered up their coats and left for the synagogue. Outside, Alter was relieved to see that the young man was no longer there.

Alter could not remember when he had heard *Lecha Dodi Likrat Kallah* sung with such passionate devotion. He felt happy to be there with his family, to see his community gathered to celebrate God's love. Even the new rabbi did not bother him too much. He thought about his many blessings. Prayers, more songs and they were on their way back to Sarah and Joseph's house for dinner.

On their walk back, they met the young bride and her family. Obeying custom, the groom had remained out of her sight for several days. Alter was pleased the wedding was taking place on Tuesday. *Blessed be God, it is the best day to get married. Surely this union will be especially blessed,* Alter said to himself. He was accustomed to carrying on long and involved dialogues with himself. *It is written, "it is good," three times in the Torah on the third day of creation. And,* he added to himself, *if this bride is not a virgin, then the groom can complain to the courts when they open the next day.* His talk to himself was concluded. For now.

Sarah tried to move her family of men out of the way of the bride, but the lane was too narrow to get by without having to acknowledge one another. Although it was the Sabbath and they were to be cheerful, Sarah had noticed out of the corner of her eye that the bride's eyes were swollen and red.

"Shabbat Shalom, Shosanna," Sarah sang out warmly to the bride, although her face betrayed concern. The bride's parents, an aunt and a cousin were walking with her. Shosanna did not speak. Instead, her mother took Sarah's arm and pulled her aside.

Esther, Shosanna's mother, whispered in Sarah's ear, "Could your Joseph come by our home later? I know it is the Shabbat, but our neighbor's son Abram needs to be seen by a doctor." Sarah knew Esther would not ask this of her or her husband if it was not serious.

"Abram! What has happened to him?" Sarah asked urgently.

Tears welled in Esther's eyes. "You know, dear, he is often asked to play music for some gentiles. They were supposed to bring him back here—" she broke off and struggled to speak. Sarah pulled her in closer and looked to see who might be watching them. Esther continued, "His father found him this morning outside the gate."

Sarah gasped.

Esther wiped her eyes with an end of her scarf. "He has been sleeping but cannot move his arm, and one of his eyes will not open."

"I will send Joseph to see him at once," Sarah said firmly.

"No, no, dear, it can wait until after your meal," Esther said as she pressed her hand on Sarah's arm. "Praise God he was found in time. He is young and strong."

The women parted, and Sarah rejoined her father, husband and son.

"What was that about, Sarah?" Joseph asked.

"I will tell you after we have our meal," Sarah said as she led the way home.

Back inside, they each washed at the ewer and basin before the meal. Joseph took his place and began the Kiddush prayers. Then he said a prayer over the challah. Alter looked forward to this meal and time every week. Subdued, Sarah dished out the food.

"With God's help, the matchmaker did well." Alter carefully spooned matzo soup past his bushy moustache and into his mouth. Fearing her voice would reveal worry, Sarah nodded.

"It will be a busy time. Purim and a wedding!" Alter's spoon halted in mid-air as he contemplated his unusually quiet daughter.

"A joyous time," she said flatly.

"Do you have your costume ready for Purim, Samuel?" Joseph asked. Samuel's mouth was crammed with bread and chicken.

He nodded and swallowed. "Yes, Father, I am dressing as a gentile."

Joseph laughed. "Now, what would that look like?"

"Enough," Sarah said sharply. Candlelight caught the worry she was trying to conceal.

"I'm sorry," Sarah went on. "Let's talk about what we have to do for Purim and the wedding. Papa, you will join us for Purim and accompany us to the wedding?"

"As it please God, yes, I will be with you."

"Purim and a wedding," Sarah repeated. "Too much."

At the end of the meal, they recited the *birkat hamazon*. As this was the Sabbath, this prayer was said more slowly and with more time to reflect than it was during the rest of the week. To Alter, though, it seemed that Sarah was in a bit of a rush. When at last she shared Esther's sad news with them, he understood why she had been preoccupied.

"Joseph, will you go and help Abram now?" she said.

Shocked by the news, Samuel and Alter offered up a prayer. Joseph gathered his medical bag and ran out the door to see what care he could offer the young man. Alter could see the love and pride in Sarah's face as she watched her husband go. At first, he had not approved of their union.

"Are you sure he is your *bashert*, your soulmate?" he asked her when Hannah was out of earshot. "A doctor, Sarah? Are you sure?"

"Yes, Papa, a doctor. It is an honorable profession, not a disease. He will help people," she said in such a tone that Alter knew this was indeed her *bashert*.

After their meal the family, like most families in the Ghetto, gathered and studied the Torah. Samuel, Sarah and Alter tried for an hour, but they were too worried to be present with God's word. When after a few hours Joseph had still not returned, Samuel walked Alter back to his flat. He had wanted to wait, but Sarah insisted he go home and get a good night's rest.

Early the next morning, Alter was waiting at the front door of the Scuola Spagnola Synagogue, standing as straight as his stooped body would permit. *Is it too much to ask that an old man can have a good night's sleep?* he asked his angels. In between returning greetings of "Shabbat Shalom" to his friends and neighbors, he recalled the night's dreams.

Again, he had woken to that voice, *How well have you loved?* He could only assume the voice belonged to one of his angels. *But why?* he asked himself.

Sarah came rushing up to him ahead of her husband and son. "Shabbat Shalom, Father." Alter took her hands in his. "How is the boy?"

"Joseph says he will be fine," she said wearily. "I worry how these boys will fare in the coming years." Sarah looked around, winding a piece of her scarf into a knot.

For a moment, Alter felt happy. She was like his little girl again, seeking his comfort and guidance. Too often, his lovely daughter seemed determined to become the parent, begging him to leave his flat and move in with her and her family. But neither warnings nor threats could entice him to move away from his memories of Hannah and Elijah. Deep in his heart, deeper than even he knew, Alter felt if he moved from his flat, he would finally be admitting to himself that they were both dead. Dead and buried under the poor soil of the Lido.

People were beginning to turn with looks of anticipation and curiosity, as they stood at the door. It was time to go inside. If you could believe the rumors, the speakers today promised to be especially eloquent.

Their usual spot was taken by a group of gentiles. This was a sign that the speakers were well known. Alter suspected that the gentiles came with curiosity and not the devotion commanded by God. When he discussed these suspicions with Samuel, his grandson suggested that coming to synagogue gave gentiles an opportunity to know them.

The family enjoyed a more leisurely Kiddush in the early afternoon. They said prayers, sang and ate. By the time *birkat hamazon* was finished, it was mid-afternoon. Samuel wanted to read and discuss the parts of the Torah relating to *mal'akhim*, angels.

"Should we see what Daniel has to say?" Joseph said.

"Why angels, my son?" Sarah's tone was soothing in a way only a mother's voice can be. Joseph's sideways glance implied that he thought she was being too gentle. Alter shook his head and remembered that same exchange between himself and Hannah when Elijah was a boy. To his surprise, anger rose in his throat like bile. He swallowed and took a sip of tea.

"Do you have a favorite *mal'akh*, Samuel?" Alter asked, hoping his voice was steady.

Samuel looked at him uncertainly. "Zedie, is it wrong if I do?"

"No, my dear Samuel. It is not wrong. But I think it is time for you to walk your Zedie back home. My books will be wondering where I am."

The days leading up to Purim and the wedding of Abram and Shosanna were busy. No one could remember Purim and a wedding happening so close together. Weeks and even months would go by when nothing significant would happen. Excitement—and worry that something would go wrong—was in the air and in the lengthy discussions and debates.

Doorsteps had never been so clean. With straw brooms swishing, opinions were exchanged on the possibility that Abram would be scarred for life, on how good (or bad) the food for the wedding feast would be, on how drunk the men would get during Purim, on the suitability of the Rabbi's wife's clothing, and even, for light relief, on the best way to mend a prayer shawl. Sarah, like her mother, never took part. By not joining in, she knew she might be singled out as a topic of discussion, but she didn't care. Her Joseph, her Samuel and her father were the most important people in her life.

Alter did not care for Purim, even though it marked yet another time in Jewish history that his people escaped annihilation. The noise, drunkenness and wild celebrations were too jarring. When he heard the light knock at his door, he knew that a timid, hopeful child holding a gift basket of food and candy would be on the other side. He kissed the Book of Esther he was reading and got up to answer the door.

Setting his bloodshot eyes at child height, Alter saw a man's waist. His surprised gaze travelled up. He couldn't be sure—his eyes played tricks on him these days—but the visitor looked like the arrogant young man from a few days ago. The man bowed and held out the gift basket.

"Why are you here? Where is Rivka's grandchild?"

"My name is Gabriel, Alter, and Rivka's grandchild is sick. I offered to deliver this in his place. Rivka is grateful."

Alter reached out and took the basket. He was confused. "Do you want some candy?"

"Yes, thank you."

Alter dug in the basket and found a couple of candies and handed them to Gabriel. There was something about the way this handsome young man wore his shawl that did not feel right to Alter. And yet there was something almost … appealing about him.

"Thank you, Alter. Shalom." Gabriel stepped back into the hallway and quietly closed the door behind him. Alter carried the basket to the table by the window. He sat and opened the basket properly, uncertain of what he might find. Would it be a traditional Purim basket? But inside he found a generous number of *Hamantaschen*, the traditional Purim pastries with a poppy-seed filling.

This is still strange, he thought. *I am going to ask Rivka when I see her at synagogue.*

Alter peered out the window to see what direction Gabriel would take once he had made his way down the long, steep stairs. How long would it take a young man to descend to the lane? He took another bite of pastry. It was feather light, and the poppy seed filling was moist and fragrant. God had blessed Rivka with the best *Hamantaschen* yet, he decided.

Alter waited and watched. He ate another pastry. He waited and watched some more. *He should have been in the lane by now.* The longer he waited, the heavier his eyes became. Still no Gabriel. The day was fading, and Samuel would be coming to take him to the synagogue soon. He shook himself awake and dressed for synagogue, feeling more and more irritated as time passed. Where was Samuel? If he did not come soon, they would be the last ones to enter the synagogue.

Finally, the door opened and Samuel poked his head in. "Zedie, are you ready to go?"

Alter picked up a cane that was leaning against a stack of books. He used it only for special events or when he felt especially fatigued. This evening, both reasons applied.

"There you are, my Samuel. Yes, I am ready."

On their unsteady walk down the dark stairway, Samuel told Alter how his mother had suddenly found many errands for him to do.

"And what were you doing before all these extra errands, Samuel?"

"Zedie, I was sitting on a step talking to Ruth."

Alter squeezed Samuel's hand. His Sarah was a good, watchful mother. "This Ruth comes from good, observant parents?"

Samuel shrugged in the dark stairwell. "I don't know this, Zedie."

Alter nodded to himself. *My Sarah knows.*

As they reached the synagogue, Samuel waved his hand above the crowd that was going in. His parents waved back to indicate where they were. They were talking with Rivka. This was good. Usually if Alter saw Rivka, he would duck into a side street and take an alternate route. In Venice, this was an easy way to avoid being swept up in gossip or endless, meaningless small talk. Tonight was different. Alter wanted to ask her about this Gabriel. But when Rivka saw Alter and Samuel approaching, she left Sarah and Joseph and went into the synagogue.

"Samuel, Father, we have been waiting. What took you so long? Samuel, did you stop and talk to anyone?" Sarah reached up and fixed Samuel's yarmulke.

It did not require fixing, Alter noted with a smile to himself. *So much like Hannah.*

"Come on! The Scroll of Esther will be read already if we do not hurry!" Sarah took Alter's arm, and they entered together. She turned to whisper to Samuel. "Did you remember to bring the noisemakers?"

Samuel thrust his hands into the deep pockets of his coat, a coat that his father used to wear, and pulled out groggers, which the family would twirl and rattle at the right places during the reading.

Although the wearing of costumes had become traditional at Purim, Alter had decided a long time ago his family would not participate. This Purim was no different. He was happy Samuel did not seem to mind but instead enjoyed looking at the effort his neighbors and friends had put into their disguises. Alter agreed with some of the rabbis that this was not how God intended Purim to be celebrated. *It is good to be an observer*, he thought. *This way we enjoy the entire story with all its characters and not from the single-eyed view of a costumed character.* As expected, several people dressed as Esther, Mordecai and Haman.

They stopped inside the doors, looking for suitable seats. Alter was dismayed that their usual places had been taken. As he was scanning for seats, Samuel grabbed his elbow. "Look, Zedie! Do you see that man?"

Alter squinted in the direction that Samuel was pointing. An angel. Alter squinted more to try to see more clearly. Could it be? This angel was dressed in white, like all angels, but there were feathers. Beside him, Joseph said, "He probably used tar to attach the feathers." Alter could only stare. It was Gabriel. But why would he dress like an angel? Alter was not the only one transfixed by this strange sight.

The Scroll was read. The cantor sang. Each time the name of the evil Haman was spoken, the congregation made good use of their groggers and other noisemakers to drown out his name. The sound was deafening. Most of them were well acquainted with the reading and knew when certain passages were about to be read. They yelled, stamped their feet, made any noise they could to obliterate Haman's name. Alter looked to see where the strange angel was sitting but could not find him. Had he disappeared again?

When it was time for Alter to return home, Samuel came with him. Alter was tired. Seeing his fatigue, Sarah had again tried to persuade Alter to come and live with them.

"Papa, you know you'd be welcome with us. And Jacob and I wouldn't worry so much about you climbing up and down those stairs. Please won't you think about it?"

"Dear Sarah." Alter rested his hand on her cheek. The hand was light as a moth's wing.

Sarah knew it was hopeless, but she had to try.

Samuel helped him up the long, steep stairs and saw him into the flat. It took Samuel a few tries to light the small bit of candle on the table. He was surprised at how much light it gave the small room. As he helped Alter out of his coat, he felt the building tremble.

"Zedie, what is that?"

"Nothing to concern yourself with, Samuel. I think I will keep my coat on. It is cold in here." Samuel helped him to put it back on. He leaned down and kissed his grandfather.

"I will come for you tomorrow morning." Alter nodded and patted his shoulder.

As soon as Samuel left, Alter shuffled over to his chair. With an involuntary grunt he sat down more quickly than he'd intended. He got himself straightened and wrapped his coat tightly around his thin body.

Within minutes, he was asleep.

How well have you loved?

Alter emerged from sleep briefly, knowing he was alone. He felt he had no strength to resist slipping back into the dream that was waiting for him, standing at the edge of sleep.

His books were falling. He was falling. He stood at a distance and watched his body struggle against the stacks and stacks of books that were tumbling without end, a cascade of all the books that had been cherished companions through his long, long life.

He could see his body slumped in the chair, coughing. He could see his body striving to breathe. And then there was stillness. *Hannah ...*

Stars. Lights. Indigo, green, red, purple, gold, silver lights.

Vast silence.

Vast light.

Vast love.

Alter was Alter, and Alter was beyond Alter. Beyond. Alter could not contain the vastness, the love.

Chapter 35: Alter's Dream

Reinhardt held Alter's hands in both of his when he told him about the Holocaust. They sat for hours in the library, speaking in low voices. Alter had so many questions. At times, both of them wept. That night, Alter lay awake remembering three dreams from long ago.

The next morning, after breakfast, Alter made a decision. He walked with purpose to the Great Unnamed Room and stood at the bottom of the grand staircase, facing the semicircle of armchairs. Sunita, Khalid and Susan were at one of the café tables, heads huddled close. Reinhardt was coming out of the kitchen with a look of disappointment on his face. Joshua and Emily were walking together toward the café, chatting.

Alter's ancient voice was so low and raspy that he was difficult to hear. But it was so uncommon for him to speak at all, that the others looked up in surprise.

"It was a long time ago. Long ago for me and even longer ago for all of you. I had a dream. When I was alive. When I was a younger man than what you see before you now. I had a dream. It may be important. Please honor this old man, this old Jew, and listen."

Joshua and Emily turned back and came over to the semicircle. Sunita, Khalid and Susan left the café and joined them. And Reinhardt folded his large frame into the chair nearest to Alter, his expression open and warm.

"It was not long after my sweet Hannah died. The night was cold, but it seemed like all nights were cold after she died. The bed we shared every night of our marriage was narrow, but now it felt too big for me. This was a few nights after Yom Kippur. I was tired being around people. I am ashamed to say I was even tired of being around my daughter, Sarah. I wanted to sleep so perhaps I could see Hannah in my dreams. I prayed to God that, in his mercy, he would grant me this one visit from her. I fell asleep. A man who resembled you, Reinhardt, appeared beside me. He was wearing a cloak and a hat that belonged in that time, my time."

Alter stood as straight as his stooped body would accommodate and looked directly at each of the other six, assessing whether they were ready to hear his story. After a moment, he nodded, as if attending to an inner voice. "Now it is time for you to learn about the history of fear. That is what the man in the dream said to me. He took me by the arm, and we flew through a night sky that became bigger and bigger as we flew. I was not afraid, and this surprised me, but I felt a kind of sorrow. In this dream, he showed me many people who were hungry. Their clothes were ragged, and they were so thin that all their bones showed. I asked him, 'Did fear create such hunger?' And the man turned to me and said that other people refused to give them food because they were fearful they would not have enough for themselves. And some of the hungry people were sitting on dust, where nothing could grow. I asked the man, 'How can it be that people sitting on dust is because of fear?' He said that others had dried up their land. They were fearful they would not be able to draw some kind of oil out of the ground, not the kind of oil we cook with or anoint our bodies with, but a kind of oil that is deep under the ground and people pay silver and gold for. And some others wanted water for themselves and took it, even though it left people sitting on dust where nothing could grow."

In the Great Unnamed Room, the only sound was Alter's quiet voice. Even the Ugly Brown Birds were silent.

"All that cold, cold night, this dream continued. He showed me wars between great countries whose names I did not recognize. Wars with more blood and misery than I thought possible. Fields churned to mud and drenched with blood. Cities reduced to rubble."

Alter's voice dropped to a whisper. "He showed me people fighting to the death over a loaf of bread. He showed me people dying of terrible diseases that were like nothing I had ever seen. This man who looked like you, Reinhardt, said over and over how all these terrible, evil events were created by fear."

Alter's faded eyes studied the group. "I do not know why he came to me. I was a poor history teacher living in the Ghetto. What was I to do with what he was showing me? On the second night, I was waiting for him. If anything, it was even colder than the first. I pulled a blanket up to my chin and wore a nightcap to keep my head warm. This time, he did not wait for me to be asleep. He appeared while I was awake, filling every space in the room with his presence. He began by saying, 'Alter, it is time for you to learn more about the history of fear.' That night, he took me to more scenes of terrible suffering. He wanted me to understand how fear creates all the misery in the world. All sadness comes from fear. All anger comes from fear. Prejudice—that is a word I did not know—comes from fear. Religious intolerance comes from fear. This fear, he told me, is ancient. The angels feel it. When they offer help or guidance, fear acts as a barrier, impeding their work. Fear keeps the heart small and the world from becoming a reflection of paradise." He searched his listeners' faces. "Do you understand?"

Small nods. Creaking chairs as people shifted. The atmosphere was somber.

"On the third night, he showed me a small part of what you told me about, Reinhardt, this Holocaust you spoke of. I could not understand it and the man said I didn't need to, but it was part of the history of fear. Yet it was in the future. Most of the history he showed me was in the future. How could that be? How could history be in the future?"

Reinhardt half rose from his chair, but Alter motioned him to sit. "There is a book in the library, which we have all seen," Alter continued. "It is called *The History of Fear*. No single author's name is on its cover, this book that was my dream from so long ago, but if you look on the back of the book, you will see thousands of names, so many that you cannot make out one from the other. And the names come from many different languages. I do not know why I was given these dreams or why there is this book. But I have one question for all of you. You answer me when you feel you have the answer that is true for you." Alter looked into the eyes of each of them. "After all this history, how can you still love?"

He left them then and made his way stiffly to the library.

Silence. Khalid's eyes were drawn to the Wall of the Seven Heavens. He spoke slowly, as if weighing every word. "So beautiful, you know. All this beauty here and on earth. People just want love and acceptance, but we do such terrible things."

Sunita's voice was soft. "Alter's question was how we can still love. After all the violence, with fear fueling violence and poverty, how can we still love? And yet I know I have loved. And I feel the depth of this love even more powerfully now."

"Heavy, man," Joshua said. "But do any of you really believe that it's just fear that creates all the lousy crap in the world? Personally I—"

"Yeah, I believe it is fear," Emily broke in. "This fear keeps us separate and prevents us from fully accepting the divine."

"I agree as well," Reinhardt added. "Fear obstructs the heart. All our neuroses prevent us from seeing the phenomenal world. But to answer his question, how can we still love? We can love because we're all endowed with basic goodness."

Susan nodded vigorously. "I just ignore all the ugly things."

"Wow, what a surprise!"

"Come on, Joshua, that's not very nice," Emily said.

"You didn't let me finish, Joshua. Obviously, I know all the terrible things humans do to one another. I agree with Reinhardt that fear blocks the heart. But the heart is still there, and the capacity to love can never disappear. I'm sure there were times in all our lives when we thought we could never love or be loved. That was fear talking. But our hearts can and do love. It's in our nature, and it's more true to our nature than fear. Yes, there's a history of fear, as Alter reminded us, and this history will be added to." Susan's cheeks felt hot—although she knew that couldn't be right—and she realized she was nervous. She glanced at Emily, who was nodding encouragement. She looked around at the others and was surprised to see respect and thoughtfulness. "We know this is true," she continued more confidently. "Fear will continue and perhaps even grow. I do choose to ignore the ugly, and perhaps it's fear that makes me do so. I'm always afraid that being around fearful energies will bring me down. Reinhardt, you said that it's believed we are entering a dark age, where ignorance will increase. Will the dark lords of fear, hate and all those other Negative Nellies prevail? I've been told they will not." She stood then and pointed upward, emphasizing *not*. "And we'll continue to love. Reinhardt, if you know anything that counters this, please speak up. I believe the world may love less or less fully, but we will love. It's always been this way, and it will continue this way. Our hearts cannot do anything different."

Emily was on her feet and hugged Susan. "Thank you!" She was disconcerted when her arms went through Susan's form, but she recovered and grinned. "Susan, I'm surprised but happy. I hope you'll share this with Alter."

Susan looked startled and pleased. "Of course I will."

"Love and fear. What a strange mixture we are." Khalid stood up and walked toward the library.

PART III

PORTALS

All those Tellings, as Gabriel calls them, each person sharing their story. So much sadness. Although there's love, too. And Alter's dream got me thinking of all the times I allowed fear to stop me. But this is not my story.

Gabriel came by the other evening just as I was wiping the last dish from an early dinner. He stood in the doorway and seemed to be in an angry rush. Perhaps that's the reason his words were so curt. When he said I had to introduce these missions that are about to start, it sounded like a command to me. I pulled myself up and saluted him. For a moment, his face darkened and then he laughed. I don't know all that he is up to these days, but I feel it was good for him to have that laugh.

So, I am told these missions are essential and that others' lives are at risk. Gabriel was blunt and said our seven will very likely encounter dangers as well. Two of these missions include an element of love. You don't need to know my sorry experiences with romantic love. All that gazing into another's eyes. Always been a mystery to me. Kind of like seeing something that you know what it is but haven't had direct experience. Like living where I do and seeing a kangaroo.

Sometimes Gabriel just drops by to chat. He talks about some of his experiences and encounters. His stories are both sorrowful and happy. And I'll admit, some of them are hard to believe. It's sad, some of the things he has to witness.

These days we sit on my old veranda, me on my yellow Adirondack chair and him on the creaky porch swing, sipping brandy. Says it makes a nice change from gin. He always comes just when the evening is giving way to night. Time is strange when Gabriel comes around. A night slips by in a few heartbeats.

Gabriel has let me in on a few secrets our group don't know yet. Mind you, I don't see this as a privilege. From what he told me, this world is in for even more frightening times. ~ Mrs. Potts

Chapter 36: Joshua makes Contact

They had been summoned to meet in the Great Unnamed Room, and as soon as they were together, the screen coalesced in front of them. Onscreen, dressed in white, Gabriel sat with knees crossed on a bright orange Adirondack chair. A white cup and saucer rested on one of the arms. The group leaned in, straining to make out the background. A bright nothing. It looked as though it had been fogged out.

Gabriel glanced up at the clouds and gave a wave, laughing at whoever he was waving to.

"Excuse me, Gabriel but did you want something?" Joshua asked.

Gabriel looked up. "Ah, yes, yes, you caught me musing for a moment. Now is a good time to mention that we will embark on our first mission tomorrow." His tone was casual.

"Tomorrow! Are you kidding me? A little notice would have been nice!" Joshua was fuming. The others sat in stunned silence.

Gabriel smiled and lifted the teacup. "I am giving you notice. Your first mission is set for tomorrow." The screen vanished.

Without any words, they got up one by one and drifted to different areas of the Great Unnamed Room. Alter made his way toward the everlasting stairs. Emily walked over to the Ugly Brown Birds to hear the music. Joshua walked quickly in the same direction as Emily but slowed as he neared her.

In an overly casual tone, he said, "Hey, Emily, do you think you would like to accompany me, you know to, ah, make this stupid fucking contact?"

Emily turned to face him. "Why Joshua, that is the sweetest, most eloquent request I have ever, ever heard!" Recently Emily had launched "Campaign Contact: Joshua Edition." She enlisted an eager Sunita, and the two of them worked the word *resolution* into every conversation where Joshua was present. They talked glowingly of how much lighter and happier they were since their own contact experience. All to no avail. Until now.

"Come on, you know this is hard for me. Give me a break. Please."

"Is it the missions? Is that the impetus? Or are you finally convinced that this is no longer your shriveled-up brain cells sputtering? You know, your brain seems to be taking an awfully long time to shut down. Was it terribly big?" Emily's lips were twitching.

"May I remind you that you and Sunita have been after me to resolve any issues I may have had with Gillian? Which is crazy in itself. Gillian and I were ideally suited. And I can only assume that this curiosity to make contact is just one more part of my brain closing up shop. And yes. For your information, my beautiful, shiny brain was really, really big."

Laughing, she put a hand up. "Okay, okay. Yes, I'll go with you. I assume you want to leave before the mission tomorrow?"

"Yes. Let's go now."

"I didn't expect to feel this way," he said quietly.

"Like what?" Emily was walking around, looking at vases perfectly positioned, pictures arranged in symmetry. Even the utensils in the lab-like kitchen were artfully displayed, although the counter was piled with dirty dishes. She picked up a kitchen towel from the floor and hung it on its hook.

"I don't know. Just, you know, this place." He swept his arms around the condo. "It was so important to me. I felt everything in here reflected who I was and showed me that I'd made it, that I was safe. Safe from crazy, safe from having to depend on anyone, safe from feeling scared. Now I don't feel anything about this stuff. Except, jeezus cripes, what the hell has been going on here since I, since I ...?"

"Died?" Emily added helpfully.

"Look at this place!" He held out a take-out container and made a face. "I think this is beginning to ferment."

He picked up a sweater thrown on the floor, a shoe tossed near a chair, a scarf thrown over a lampshade. Nearby, a half-started painting sat on an easel. The paint palette was dry and crusted, and a dab of red paint had hardened on the floor. In place of the elegant vase Joshua had bargained hard for in Tuscany, an empty vodka bottle kept company with a pair of open nail clippers on a side table. Joshua remembered the purchase of this table and the time spent to find this particular style, never mind the cost.

He ran a hand through his hair. "What the hell is going on?"

"Okay, I take it Gillian wasn't always this, um, messy?"

"No! And when did she take up painting? Or drinking cheap, store-brand vodka?" He looked around, a little wild-eyed. Then he saw the picture of him and Gillian that she had insisted be placed on one of the end tables. It was so rare for Gillian to insist on anything that he'd relented, even though it hadn't really gone with his carefully orchestrated decor. Now it was the only thing in the place that made sense.

Emily saw his growing agitation and touched his arm. "Josh, whether you like it or not, I am sending you love."

He rolled his eyes. "Please tell me it is not gooey, sticky Christian love?"

She stood facing him. She cupped her hands around her heart, closed her eyes and then reached out and placed both hands on Joshua's heart. "Love is love, is love, is love …"

"Okay, so you are aware my heart no longer beats, right?" He stepped away from her and walked to a window-seat that offered a spectacular view of the Hudson River. The sun was about to drop behind the buildings on the far side of the river. He spun around. "You mean like sister love, right?"

"Of course, silly. What else would I mean? Goof! Dead goof!" Their laughter stopped when Gillian walked into the living room, glancing around as if she'd heard something.

Resolution. Joshua had never given the word much thought. He'd thought briefly of Edison but felt there was little unresolved. Could he have shown more appreciation for Edison's work loyalty, care and commitment? Sure, but it always just felt right, uncomplicated. His mother and father came to mind, but he dismissed any thought of resolution there. It wasn't as though he felt nothing for them. It just seemed too broken, shattered into pieces to be swept up and thrown into a bin.

But Gillian. Joshua wished he'd told her how much he valued her, how grateful he was that she could love him. He felt directed. No, that wasn't right. He felt a *passion*, a word he'd considered dangerous while he lived. Now he had a reckless, passionate desire to let Gillian know he truly loved her. But who was this Gillian? The one who drank cheap vodka, cut her nails in the living room and left moldering food containers strewn about?

And now here she was, clutching her iPad to her chest, looking spooked.

Emily gasped. "Oh Josh, she is exquisite."

Even wearing yoga pants, a loose T-shirt and with her long, dark hair pulled back, Gillian moved with the easy grace of someone walking into a five-star restaurant. But her eyes were red and puffy. As she looked around, her gaze passed through Joshua and Emily without a flicker. She pressed a button, and music began to play. "I want you back, I want you back, I want you back …" Jenn Grant's ethereal voice sang words of a heart's loss that transcended time, culture and age.

Joshua squeezed his eyes shut and turned his back to Gillian. "I don't know if I can do this, Emily."

"Turn around and open your eyes, you bastard. This is it. This is your one chance to resolve your unresolved."

He opened his eyes and ran a hand through his hair again. "If I wasn't dead, I would think I was having a panic attack. You remember what Susan said? That if something doesn't feel right, you probably shouldn't move forward? I don't like this."

"Give me a break! Now I know there's something wrong with you. Quoting Susan! Get a bloody grip."

"I may need you," Joshua said quietly.

Emily softened. "I'm right here, Joshua."

He turned toward Gillian, who was now sitting on the loveseat, sobbing and rocking back and forth. Still clutching her iPad, she pressed repeat. "I want you back, I want you back …" Joshua knew her iPad would probably show a photo of him, but he couldn't look. Emily, sensing this, took a look and nodded yes; it was a picture of him. Joshua groaned loudly.

Gillian abruptly stopped crying. Her face swollen and blotchy, she asked the gathering gloom, "Is anyone here?"

"We better get on with it, Joshua."

Joshua nodded with a determination he didn't feel.

A tiny bell on Gillian's iPad rang, signaling that her angel app had a message for her. She had downloaded the app the day it was launched, and although Joshua had laughed at her then, he'd been pleased she'd wanted something he'd created. The bell tinkled happily again.

"Fuck you!" Gillian yelled.

Joshua's anxiety spiked, and he turned to Emily.

"Now or never, and I mean never." Emily gave Joshua a push. She stifled a laugh as her hand went through him.

Snot was trickling down Gillian's face, which she swiped at with the back of her hand. "What is this stupid effin' thing doing?" She opened up the app. "Jesus loves you, this I know" began to play. She turned down the volume but noticed the halo button was glowing. *Number 7: Choose a loved one to be your personal angel.* "This was my idea, and it's fucking up!" She pressed the button. When Joshua's face appeared, she dropped the iPad in horror. She had not uploaded his picture to the angel app.

"Gillian! Gillian, it's me. Please, I have some things to tell you and I don't have much time!"

Gillian fell to her knees and sat on the floor with the iPad beside her slumped body.

"Gillian?"

She was panting. "I want you back. I want you back ..." She pressed stop to silence the music. "I'm going crazy. Joshie? Oh, no, I'm going nuts."

"Gillian, please pick up your iPad." Joshua's voice sounded tinny and thin even to his own ears.

Her iPad lay face down on the carpet. Hand shaking, she slowly turned it over. The image was fuzzy, but it was definitely Joshua. For a moment, Gillian looked as though she was going to faint.

"Don't faint, darling. And no, you are not going crazy. It is me and I am ... well, it's hard to explain, but ..."

"Oh, Josh." She picked up the iPad and hugged it to her chest, sobbing.

"Honey, sweetheart, I don't have much time." His voice was slightly muffled against her chest.

She pulled it away, "You're dead. Josh? Is this a crazy trick? What's going on? What the hell!"

"I am definitely dead." He lifted a shoulder in a small shrug. "I'm sure it's shocking to you and many others that I'm not in hell."

Gillian was sitting up now with the iPad on her lap.

"Ah, this is exactly where I'd like to be."

"Really? You freakin' rise from the dead to flirt with me? You want to be on my lap?"

The halo glowed more brightly, and Joshua's face faded for a moment.

"Wait, don't go! Don't fucking go, you bastard!"

"Gillian, I love you more than you can know. I am so sorry I didn't tell you that more often. I couldn't believe you could really love me. I wish I'd shown you more passion. And I wish most of all that we had time—time to grow our hearts."

"Josh, where are you? Is this for real? You sound like Josh, but some of what you're saying doesn't sound like anything my Josh would say." Gillian's words were coming in gasps as she tried to catch her breath.

Joshua spoke softly. "What can I say? Since, well, dying I have learned a few things. Right now, I need you to know that you were the most important person in my life." Gillian put her head in her hands and cried.

"Please, sweetheart. There's nothing to cry over. Really, it's all kind of amazing. Wish you were with me. Oh, God, no—I mean I love you. My heart is filled with love for you. I want you to know how grateful I am that you shared part of my life. Your heart was able to love this stupid, self-absorbed bastard. Gillian, you need to really, really know this. Love means everything. Everything else is bullshit. Live your life. Love as fearlessly and fiercely as you can. Do you understand?"

Hiccupping, tears flowing again, she nodded.

"My love for you will live on in your heart, but don't keep it contained there. Be reckless, give it away. I love you, Gillian. But, hey, Gillian? When did you start drinking and painting and being, ah, casual?"

"Oh, Josh." Gillian's laughter sounded painful and beautiful. "I've always been this way. I stopped painting when I met you. Remember? You complained about the mess and the unlikelihood of any viable income. I talked to my mom and she agreed with you, but you know parents ..." She took a deep breath. "Well, most parents. They want their children to be safe. My mom knew I'd be safe with you. In accordance with Parent Law Number Two, happy comes after safe. Don't get me wrong. I was happy, Josh."

"Promise me you will love, Gillian."

The app winked out. Gillian thought she was screaming, but the words came out as a whisper. "I promise, Josh."

The sun was long gone, and the condo was dark except for the faint glow of the small screen. Two people wept, one alive and one not. Emily held out her arms to Joshua. Their forms melded together and formed a single orb of blue light. Joshua relaxed his head into the place between Emily's shoulder and neck. He sobbed. Emily whispered, "Let it go, Joshua. Let her go."

With their medallions glowing brighter, they rose, cocooned inside the orb of light.

From a distance, Gabriel watched. New York was still New York: brash, clamoring, exhilarating, like no other city on earth. And here and there, two by two, more people became engaged than had ever done so in a single night.

Chapter 37: First Mission

"Ha!" Emily raised an arm in victory. Arms and legs outstretched, she had jumped in front of a woman to protect her from getting soaked. Cars and trucks were splashing through deep wells of rainwater in the busy street, sending muddy waves over careless pedestrians. The woman stopped and examined her clothes before shaking her head and walking on.

They were in New York, making their way to their first mission. Reinhardt walked close behind Alter, and Sunita had linked arms with the old man. Privately, she and Reinhardt had agreed that Alter would suffer immense shock at the world's version of itself in the twenty-first century.

"How are you faring, Alter?" Out of habit, Sunita picked up a corner of her sari and sidestepped a puddle.

"With God's help and your kindness, I am fine, my dear." Alter's long dark coat dragged behind him. He barely glanced at the skyscrapers and traffic congestion, but every few steps he would stop, stare at something and shake his head. Sunita paid no attention to his muttering and cackling laugh.

Reinhardt stepped from behind and walked alongside them. "Alter, we thought you might be in a state of shock."

"I read more than history, you know." Alter's smile held shadows of sadness. "The books I have been reading are quite correct in their descriptions. My ghetto life was difficult but not as difficult as this world appears to be. Look!" He waved an arm toward a skyscraper. "What are they trying to do? Compete with God?"

Sunlight pierced the remnants of low clouds and refracted off the towering glass monuments to strike car windshields, blinding drivers. Screeching brakes, curses soft and loud added intensity to the morning chaos. Most people had been kept awake by rain and wind lashing bedroom windows. Frowns were deeper, confusions more common, and tempers easily stoked.

"Hey, look what I did!" Emily skipped down the sidewalk and jumped in front of a man, shielding him from a spray of filthy water. He surveyed his clothes and looked around.

"Emily, we are on a mission. Our first mission." Joshua air quoted *mission*. "But where's Sunita? Where's Reinhardt?" Before he could ask about the rest, Emily stopped him.

"Wait a minute, Joshua. It doesn't hurt to help a few people along the way. Sunita is over there." She pointed to a bench where a hunched-over man sat, head in hands. After determining that Alter did not need her, Sunita had stepped away.

"What the hell is she doing?" Joshua moved closer to Emily, in part to keep her from saving every pedestrian in New York from getting drenched.

"She is easing that man's headache. Sunita feels he's been going through a great deal of stress and is at his wit's end. Taking away his physical pain will help."

Joshua practiced page six of lesson one in *Patience for the Chronically Impatient and Perpetually Irritated.*

"And Reinhardt?" His voice sounded squeaky.

"Over there." Emily pointed to a spot farther down the street.

"What the—what is he doing?"

Emily smiled. "It is *so* awesome."

"Emily, only people who are fifteen years old may use the word awesome."

Emily jumped and floated upward. "Oh don't be such a downer. Reinhardt has fixed it so that parked mega-SUV can't drive. The woman inside is furious and talking to her mechanic. Only all the mechanic can hear is blah, blah, blah."

"Smart. But we have this massive mission that may have global consequences." He stopped abruptly and looked around. "So freaking weird. I keep feeling I'll run into someone I know and it'll all be kind of normal. Like I didn't die and—"

As a yellow cab swooshed past, Emily broke away and jumped in front of a man and a little girl, shielding them from getting soaked.

"Must be our lucky day," the man said. "Daddy, it was an angel!" He patted her head as they hurried on.

"Emily, did you hear what I said? We have bigger things to do than stopping gas guzzling motorists, easing headaches and making sure New Yorkers remain dry."

Emily turned back to him. "This is important too, Joshua. One person at a time. Every person we help may pass on their good energy to others. And the others may in turn pass it on, and so on, and so on. Kindness as a superpower!"

Joshua rubbed his temples and muttered page seven of *Patience for the Chronically Impatient and Perpetually Irritated*. "When at your very edge, visualize a field of corn with a late summer breeze blowing the stalks in swaying harmony."

"Sorry, what was that?"

"Nothing. Emily, where's Khalid?" This time his voice sounded so calm he barely recognized it.

"Are you blind?" Emily was laughing.

"No, I'm just dead." Joshua shot back.

"We just passed him."

Joshua looked back. On a bench in front of an office building sat a man in a hoodie and scuffed jeans. His face was barely visible as he stared at the sidewalk, hands hanging loose between his knees. Khalid sat next to him, talking in his ear.

"I don't believe this. Am I to assume he's helping the poor sap?"

Emily nodded happily. "Look at him, Joshua! It's priceless. Can't you hear him?"

"Hee, hee."

"Oh, loosen up, Joshua! Khalid is giving him one of his best routines."

"I assume this man has been depressed?"

"Completely and utterly despondent. Without a sliver of hope. Khalid is not only making him feel good for the moment, he's helping him change how he sees his world. Isn't he brilliant?"

Joshua ran his hand through his hair. Not a strand changed. "Okay, so where's Alter?"

"See that kid sitting on the step over there?"

Joshua wondered what a teenaged boy would think if he knew that an old and very dead Jewish scholar from the seventeenth century was standing in front of him. The kid was pale white and looked as though he had caught a train in from the suburbs.

"So what's the story?" Joshua said.

"Look at him! Look at his clothes! He's clearly trying to dress like someone from the ghetto. A little gangsta. Alter asked me why he was dressed like that. When I explained the kid was trying to fit into a ghetto lifestyle, Alter was outraged. He fixed the kid's iPod so all it'll play is the history of ghettos. The poor kid tried to take out his earbuds, but Alter has them stuck there until he hears the entire history of the Venetian Ghetto."

"Two questions for you, Miss Emily. One, how did Alter learn to fix tech devices? And two, why is it okay for everyone else to get angry but not me?"

Emily closed the gap between them and stood nose to nose. "Really, Joshua those are your questions?"

Sunita came rushing up to them, her eyes sparkling. "That was so much fun. A woman was in dreadful pain with her menstrual cycle, and now she is feeling perfectly fine. And that child"— she pointed to a little boy in a bright blue T-shirt who was walking in a line with other children, holding onto a rope—"his stomach is much better."

"Peachy," Joshua said tonelessly. Emily and Sunita looked sharply at him. "It is time, I believe. Oh, cripes. Where's Susan? Dare I ask? Never mind. I don't think I want to know."

Emily put her hand on his arm. "No problem, Joshua. There she is."

Susan stood in front of a building that had deteriorated to such a state that it was soon to be demolished. A bitterly contested estate and entrenched battle lines within a family had left the building falling to ruin.

"So what is she going to do, paint a five-story fairy on it?" Joshua glanced at Reinhardt, who had just joined them. The woman behind the wheel of the mega-SUV seemed to be stuck inside her vehicle with Sting's "Fragile" playing at full volume.

"And why would a fairy be a bad idea?" Emily asked.

"I didn't say it would be a bad idea, did I?" Joshua said sharply. "Crap. My stupid mouth." He put an arm around Emily's shoulder. Although she couldn't feel the muscles and bones of his arm, she felt his care and affection.

"Wow, you're really pathetic at apologizing. Let's see what Susan's up to, eh?"

Some people moved around Susan and some moved through her. Those who moved through her felt a shift in their thoughts and in the moods those thoughts inspired. No matter what had been on their minds, all of them without exception felt a focused and passionate need to create something. Some dashed into a nearby flower shop, others into an art supply store. A few began dancing. Susan stood, legs apart and arms akimbo, gaze fixed but soft.

And then the cracked and dirty windows were whole and clean. And then flower boxes that grew herbs rather than flowers appeared under those windows. And then the chipped gray paint that covered the entire sad, neglected building was replaced by soft white with yellow trim. And then the cheap, broken front door was replaced by one of rich oak. And then the worn steps leading up to the front door were replaced by an elegant stone walkway.

The group joined Susan, who now sat on the sidewalk as if exhausted. Some people half tripped over her and looked back to see what had caused them to miss a step. Walks quickened, and focus was shifted to finding beauty.

"Are you okay?" Reinhardt's face held, in equal measure, concern and happiness—two emotions that few people can hold at the same time.

Susan looked up at the others ranged around her. "What do you think? I did a little decorating inside as well. Oh, and Reinhardt, you'll be happy to know I changed all the heating equipment, water, toilets and so on to be more environmentally friendly."

Reinhardt threw his head back and laughed in delight. "Susan, you are *wunderbar*! I have a sense, and you know our senses are heightened, that the family battling over this building will make amends with each other."

Alter leaned down to where Susan sat on the sidewalk. "That's very good, my dear. Families need to get along."

Joshua sauntered up to the front door. "I knew it! I knew you couldn't resist. Look here, everyone."

In the center of the new oak door was a very small etching of a fairy with luxurious, extravagant angel wings.

Joshua blinked and blinked again.

"Hey, man, are you going to cry?" Khalid said.

"No, man. Okay, to be honest, almost. Just about. Nearly. I'm fine." Joshua reached inside his jacket for the scroll that Gabriel had given him.

Emily extended a hand to Susan, but she shook her head, wild hair bobbing, and pushed herself up. "Whew. Okay, Joshua, I'm ready."

"So, Gabriel asked me to read from this paper." Joshua stood in front of the group and checked to make sure they were listening. "No wandering off, okay? As a group," he emphasized *group*, "we are to make our way to the United Nations building. This is my town, so I'll lead."

New Yorkers hustled past them. Some looked behind, sensing something. Some walked straight through the group and shuddered.

Thick, gunmetal clouds had rolled back in, but the air was now heavy and still. All 193 member state flags, plus the U.N. flag, hung limply. The group glided past the security screening and stood outside the entrance to the U.N. Headquarters.

Unfolding the scroll he'd kept bunched up in his back pocket, Joshua read Gabriel's instructions. "Dear ones, you will be attending an urgent meeting called by the Security Council. Right now, the Security Council has to make a decision.

Joshua stopped reading and scanned the group. "Are we keeping you from something important, Khalid? Another appointment, perhaps? Dinner?"

Khalid looked up slowly. "Sorry, I don't see the point in all this. How effective are they anyway? The Human Rights Council is a joke. The biases toward and against certain countries are outrageously obvious."

Sunita moved closer and touched his arm. "You are not wrong, but this is not the time, Khalid."

Khalid nodded slightly. "Go ahead, Joshua. I will try to focus."

Joshua turned around and stood for a moment looking at all the flags. When he turned back, he gave Khalid a nod and continued reading.

"The decision incumbent on the Security Council today is one they are making without all the facts. This in itself is not unusual. However, the missing facts in this situation will lead them to vote against their mandate, which is to maintain peace and security. Welcome to your first mission! Cheers and blessings!"

Joshua rolled up the scroll. "There you have it."

Khalid looked at him with some surprise. "There we have what, exactly?"

"And what is this mission?" Reinhardt pressed.

"I don't know."

"What do you mean, you don't know?" Susan asked.

Joshua tucked the scroll back in his pants pocket. "I don't know for certain, but I would hazard a guess that our first big fucking mission is to disrupt this vote."

"What if this vote is something that I as a British Muslim think is a good idea? What then?"

Reinhardt leaned in. "Or what if voting against this resolution goes against an environmental policy?"

"Or the arts?" Susan demanded.

Joshua waved his hands. "I think we have to go and find out for ourselves. If they're voting for something that goes against what any one of us deems important, than we'll have to opt out. For example, if they're voting in favor of fracking or banning all images of fairies, then we can't complete this mission. I mean, that's my view. Anyone else?"

"Let's create our own vote," Sunita said. "Right now, before we go any further. If this vote goes against any of our cherished ideals, then all of us will agree to opt out of this mission."

Emily twisted her hands. "Wow, this is big. We would be disobeying Gabriel and who knows who else!"

Susan looked at her sharply. "We are not Gabriel's or anyone else's puppets."

"Hear, hear," Reinhardt said in rare camaraderie.

"I don't mean that. It's just, well ... Yes, I know you're right. We should protect and respect each other's values." Emily raised her hand. "I vote in favor of aborting the mission if it doesn't align with any one of our values."

All of them clapped.

"My dear, it is the only way." Alter said. "We stand together."

"This is like herding fucking cats." Joshua drummed his fingers against his thigh. "I hope you know that if we decide not to do this mission, we could end up staying in that realm for who knows how long."

"Are you that anxious for your big sleep or the big black?" Sunita asked gently.

He groaned. "Fuck, I don't know what I want any longer, but aren't all of you ready to move on to your respective places of heavenly fucking bliss?"

"My son, if I could tell you how much I wish to see my Hannah, you would never doubt love. And now that I have learned," he put a hand over his eyes, then rubbed his face. "Now that I know my Sarah and her family are also there, my desire to leave is stronger. I wish to tell my Sarah how sorry I am for being such a stubborn father and for not being happier for her."

A sparrow perched on the tip of his hat, poked at its breast feathers to smooth them, and flew off. People walked by and through them, talking on phones, checking watches, hurrying forward.

Sunita put her hand on the old man's shoulder. "Then, Alter, why will you jeopardize your anticipated reunion with them?"

"You forget, my dear, that being a Jew means I am obligated by God to make things right. This mission is important for me, but if I were not to consider what is of value and importance to the rest of you, what kind of Jew would I be?"

Sunita embraced him, their forms melding together. People walking by saw a wavering light, like heat rising, of blue and gold in a double helix dance.

"Golly gee, I hate to break up this touching scene, but we better get in there."

Inside, the corridors were packed with visitors, diplomats, security officers, assistants and assistants to assistants. Press from around the globe formed their own community.

The seven whooshed past a long, snaking line of people being funneled through a checkpoint to show their security passes. Joshua yelled over his shoulder, "This is out-fucking-standing! When I'm interviewed about my time in a coma, I'll say the absolute best part about the tortured imaginings of my brain was breezing through a never-ending security line-up."

"So, you're back to your coma story?"

Joshua didn't respond to Khalid. All of them stood silent in the Security Council Chamber. They weren't alone. Tech people were doing tech things and security people were doing one last sweep before the council room opened to U.N. members, press and vetted spectators. The mythic Phoenix rising from the ashes dominated the iconic multi-paneled painting by Per Krohg.

Sunita's soft voice was shaking with outrage. "When will they replace that racist painting?"

"What the hell are you talking about? Sure, the symbolism is a bit overdone but ..."

They were now standing directly in front of the painting. A tech person snaked a cord through one of Khalid's legs.

Sunita gestured to the bottom third of the painting, where white people were helping darker-skinned people up from hellish realms. "Please tell me you see what I see."

Joshua grimaced. "Ah. Gotcha."

Assistants in tow, the five permanent members and ten temporary members took their seats at the horseshoe table. A constellation of lights overhead illuminated the room.

Reinhardt whispered, "I find it quite disturbing that the five permanent members of the Security Council are also the largest manufacturers of weapons in the world."

"Don't think we need to whisper, my German friend. Now, what is so important that it took us away from my coma-inspired cozy realm?" Joshua moved down to the centre of the room, and the others followed to see what the Security Council members were doing.

In front of each member, an iPad screen showed details of a vote that was needed to determine if a safe haven should be created for a country that was in grave danger from a heavily militarized neighboring country. Tensions had risen to dangerous levels, and a longstanding border dispute had erupted into armed conflict. It was rumored that the sudden rage was a ruse, since the line of sagging fences and random cairns that stood between the two countries had been contested for decades with only minor saber-rattling and the occasional potshot. Now, it was believed, the leaders of the aggressor country were being richly paid by a consortium of multinationals hungry for resources that the target country was unwilling to part with.

The safe haven would hopefully provide safe passage for those who were in the most peril, allowing the Council to investigate further and de-escalate tensions.

"This is a no-brainer! Of course we'll make sure they all vote for a safe haven. We'll do everything we can to make sure this happens! Right?" Emily bounced on her toes with fists tightly balled.

"Calm down, Miss Prince Edward Island, of course we'll do all we can to make sure the vote is in favor of a safe haven." Joshua leaned over the member from France, who was frowning at his tablet, tapping a pen. With the exception of Alter, who was standing below the mural looking up at it, they moved among the permanent members who sat around the horseshoe table.

With his back to them, Alter spoke quietly, as if to himself. "I do not think a safe haven is wise."

Six heads turned toward him. Susan gasped. "Alter, how can you say such a thing! These are modern times, and we ..." Reinhardt put his hand on her shoulder to shush her. She stiffened, then softened and after a moment reached up to touch his hand.

"Srebrenica." Alter stood small and still.

Reinhardt dropped his head. In the library talk with Alter, their conversation had not begun and ended with the Holocaust. It had ranged forward to more recent tragedies.

"History was never my thing. Can someone explain Srebrenica?" Joshua mangled the name.

"Resolution 819," Khalid spoke in a monotone. "In April 1993, the U.N. voted to declare Srebrenica in the eastern part of Bosnia a safe haven. The villages and towns in this area had been strategically targeted for massacres and artillery shelling for a few years. People, mostly Muslims, who were able to survive made their way through unspeakable dangers and poured into this small mountain town. This gave the Serb forces time to gather what they needed to round up and massacre eight thousand men and boys in 1995. There's more to the story, but I don't want you to get fagged."

Sunita's eyes glistened with unshed tears. "Yes, they passed this resolution but did not provide support to forces who might have implemented measures to ensure its intention."

Joshua threw his hands up and walked away. The member from the Russian Federation stood to speak. Alter moved with surprising swiftness to Joshua and took his arm. The rest divided their attention between the Russian's speech and Joshua and Alter's low voices.

"Sounds as though they're prepared to provide lots of support for this safe haven to remain safe." Emily looked hopefully at the others as Alter and Joshua rejoined them.

Reinhardt folded his arms. "It's clear this area and its people are in terrible danger of ethnic cleansing." He winced. "I hate that phrase. But somehow I don't trust the U.N. will be able to keep them safe in this zone."

The member from France was now detailing the measures taken to stop the violence. He agreed with the Russian that a declaration of safe haven was essential.

"Two of the permanent members have spoken in agreement. Remember if any of those five exercise their veto, the vote is nullified." Reinhardt had moved to stand behind China's representative.

"For Chrissake, we don't have enough time! Do we encourage them to vote in favor or do we do some magic shit to have them vote nay or whatever the fuck the term is?"

"Magic shit?" Susan's eyebrows shot up.

Joshua started to say something but thought better of it. He moved beside Alter and listened as member after member spoke in support of a yes vote. But there was one outlier.

"Looks like your guy may have a problem with this resolution." Joshua thumbed to the U.K. member.

"Pompous ass," Khalid said, "but he's repeating Gabriel's warning that all the facts are not known." Khalid stood beside Susan, who quietly drew a hand to her breast.

"I feel pain coming from you, Khalid. Is it the massacre in Bosnia?"

Surprised, Khalid nodded. For the first time, he smiled at her.

"Okay, let's huddle." Joshua swept his arms for all to gather round. "Sorry, Alter, it's an American football expression. It means we gather close in a circle and work out our next move." Under the mural, the seven huddled, with Alter barely visible in the middle. Reinhardt spoke first, arguing for a vote against a safe haven. A safe haven was a Band-Aid solution, he said, and the global community was likely to become distracted by another crisis and not dig deep for a lasting resolution. Alter, too, spoke in his careful, scholarly way against a safe haven. All of them listened intently. Khalid's face was growing stormier.

"We can't count on any of these arseholes to follow through with their promises to keep the safe haven safe! They're all mouth and no trousers."

Emily whispered loudly and passionately. "Really, we do have to trust. The world is a different place than back in the nineties, right? People will be watching to make sure they do things right this time! We can't just leave these poor people to live in such threatening situations. Think of the children!"

Sunita, who was huddled beside her, squeezed her shoulder.

Khalid looked at Reinhardt and Alter, who wore similar grim expressions. Finally, Joshua broke up the huddle.

"Okay, so what does our vote look like? Logically, a vote in favor of a safe haven looks to be the best option. I agree with Emily that times have changed and we can't leave people in the precarious situation they're in. Am I right? Reinhardt, Alter, my Muslim friend?"

"My gut says no." Reinhardt patted what he used to refer to as his eating muscles. "But as you say, logically it makes the most sense to encourage our friends to vote yes."

Alter, Khalid and Reinhardt walked slowly back to the table and the Security Council members. The rest ran ahead.

Emily pointed toward the table. "Look! They're getting ready to vote! And I think the U.K. guy is going to vote no. Come on, let's hurry!"

"Joshua, fix his tablet with some favorable articles on safe havens." Sunita commanded. Joshua saluted her and got to work.

The U.K. member idly scrolled through the articles but appeared unimpressed.

"He doesn't care!" Emily said. "You're right, Khalid, he's an ass. What's his motivation? Money? Shadow companies where he and his cronies will lose if this area is declared a safe haven? What the hell will change his mind?"

Joshua stood back, smiling. "He will vote yes."

There were three dissenters among the ten non-permanent members, but the five permanent members voted in favor of a safe haven. Reporters scrambled to get their stories out, and spectators began to leave. One woman yelled that the vote was rigged and people would die. Security people were on her in seconds.

"Whew, that was close! Victory is ours!" Emily whooped and ran around the room. Sunita, Susan and Joshua laughed at her, but the smiles that Alter, Reinhardt and Khalid wore were thin. "Come on, let's blow this pop stand and go back," Joshua called out to Emily. Alter and Reinhardt gave him a quizzical look.

Outside, they hugged one another.

"Let's hope this was wise." Alter shuffled toward a baby stroller and leaned in to smile at the well swaddled baby. The baby gurgled back.

"So, mate, how are we getting back?"

Joshua dug into his back pocket and pulled out the scroll. "Says we are to hang right here but remain close together. No wandering off, okay?"

They brushed past inky blue stars. Angels and other beings ascended and descended to earth.

The Ugly Brown Birds were singing a lament. "Now, that's a strange *Welcome back, you guys rock* kind of song!" Emily grabbed a seat and patted the chair next to her for Sunita to sit. "We absolutely need to have a celebratory dinner!"

A deep roar quelled their celebration. The Great Unnamed Room shuddered.

Gabriel stood in the middle of the room, his anger vibrating. Each of the seven shrank from his terrifying scrutiny. His voice filled every space in the vast room.

"You failed."

Gabriel vanished.

They were shattered.

At the morning meal, everyone rearranged food on their plates. No one ate. No one talked. If one of them caught another's eye, both quickly looked away. Near the end of the meal, a somber gong sounded. They all jumped out of their seats but then stood irresolute before walking slowly to the Great Unnamed Room.

Gabriel stood in the central courtyard. When they were all seated, he spoke.

"You failed your first mission." He began to pace, clasping and unclasping his hands. "This leaves us in a difficult situation. Naturally, we have to remedy what has transpired. As I speak, many are involved in doing just that. It leaves us a little short at the moment for answering prayers, pleas and such but …" He turned his back on them and strode away.

They glanced uneasily at one another.

"We thought—" Joshua began.

Gabriel was back.

"Be quiet. I will keep my talk short, and I will not entertain questions. We trusted you. We trusted you to make the right decision and guide the members of the Security Council accordingly. This safe haven declaration is unsafe. It works to the advantage of armament greed. Most importantly, it endangers lives. This will be rectified, but it doesn't bode well for future missions. I will leave you to ponder where you went wrong and—"

"I want to resign my position as project manager," Joshua broke in.

"Not how it works, Joshua." Gabriel looked up at the great dome. The group followed his gaze. Planets, asteroids, and stars drifted overhead, following their ancient paths. He sighed and turned back to the group, a kinder look on his face.

"I will leave you with one instruction for the next mission. Lead with your hearts."

Gabriel was gone. The Ugly Brown Birds began to sing. The notes were tentatively hopeful.

Chapter 38: Mission Refugee

The young woman sat in a corner of the dimly lit tent, where a small tear allowed light to seep in from between the other tents that rested on this barren ground, one after the endless other. Her hand reached up to touch the tender purple and red bruising on the left side of her face. She wasn't the only one in the camp who had cuts and bruises. Some had sustained broken bones while escaping the horrors of what had once been the safe haven of their homes.

Again, she looked behind to see her daughter sleeping on the thin mattress. As she turned her head, she felt the strain in her neck muscles. *Safe, she is safe here*, she thought. Every few minutes she repeated this reassurance. She reached for the small jar of beauty cream her cousin had sent her from Paris and dabbed a finger point of cream to her face, smoothing it on the swollen eye as well. It was silly, she knew, but at this moment she needed to feel that such a small thing mattered.

In the realm beyond earth, bells began to ring.

"Sleigh bells?" Emily glanced up.

The bells jingled again, louder and more insistent, ringing non-stop. The seven raced to the Great Unnamed Room, where Gabriel was standing by the already flickering screen. Even Alter walked rapidly, only a few seconds behind the others.

And now they sat, transfixed by the scene playing out in front of them.

The woman stood up and walked quietly past her sleeping child. She turned a corner of the tent flap to peer out. Although the tent offered some protection from the stench, a wave hit her when she opened the flap. She staggered and doubled over, retching, as the smell of masses of unwashed humans hit her. Shit, urine, vomit, filth and the smell of fear were carried by a small wind that blew in from an unseen valley.

Chastising herself for being weak, she straightened and looked down the corridor of tents that extended into the darkness, thousands upon thousands. The dark was almost total. Even the stars were few. Perhaps they knew this place was too sad; their light would make little difference. A tall woman was walking past the tents, swinging a lantern. Shadows of two women and an older girl played on the dusty side of one tent. The tall woman looked around her and ducked quickly inside.

The young woman closed the flap, wishing for company. There was something disquieting about the tall woman. She pushed away any thoughts that might become attached to her emotions. She knew no one here.

Everything had happened so quickly since that terrible day she had confronted Ahmed.

Filthy from the dust of rubble, fingernails broken from shifting rocks to find anything useful in the ruins of their home, she had screamed at him. "Why! Why stay here? Nothing is left. Our home is gone, our families have left or been taken away or killed. Nothing, nothing, nothing!!"

"Maysa, this is still our home," Ahmed said quietly, his voice much older than his years. Across his lap lay a gun that had been given to him earlier in the day.

"Home! You are staying here to protect stones? Rubble? The rats? It is all gone! Our lives here are finished! You will die. Ahmed, your place is with us, your wife and daughter. It is us you are to protect. Not stones. Not rubble. Us." She was sobbing and holding their daughter tight. The little girl was silent with shock; she had not spoken since the bombing stopped.

"This land," he said as tears ran down his young, gaunt face, "this land has been in my family for generations. This land is my blood. Yes, you are my blood now, but this land"—he stood suddenly and rammed the gun butt on the ground—"what am I without this land? I am no one. This land is my history. This land is me."

Maysa wept, hugging her daughter. She knew in her bones she was defeated. She could not compete with the countless generations who had lived, loved and toiled on this land. Her husband, she knew, would not leave the rubble and dust of what had once been his family's home.

Only a few days earlier, Ahmed was in a state of panic and shock, running up one rubble-strewn street after another in the village. At times, he threw a stone angrily out of his way, yelling at nothing and everything. At times, he stumbled but kept on. As he ran, childhood memories played out. In this house, his best friend had lived, the one his mother disapproved of. In that house, the village seer had lived, frightening all with her uncanny and dark predictions. House after house had a story, a place in his heart and mind. Now gone, obliterated. He ran and ran.

When finally he returned to Maysa, he had news. A truck would come early the next day, before morning prayers, and take her and their daughter to a refugee camp.

At first, she protested, but her voice betrayed how weak and tired she felt. He knew she would think of their daughter's safety first and go in the truck. After her brief protests, they collapsed into each other. Night was coming and so too were increased dangers. Darkness offered immunity to the jackals who took advantage of the misery and vulnerability of those who survived, especially women and children. While Ahmed had been running up one street and down another, trying to find a way out for his wife and daughter, Maysa had found food scraps and rough shelter in a space that had been her aunt's kitchen. As she and their daughter slept on ground they had cleared of stones and debris, Ahmed kept an all-night vigil.

The screen faded. Reinhardt cleared his throat. "Did you know that seventy-five percent of refugees are women and children?" His voice was somber.

Khalid adjusted his shemagh and stood up. Without a backward glance, he walked away from the rest and disappeared into the Room of Reflection.

"I would assume Khalid is angry?" Alter looked around for confirmation.

"Yes, of course he is angry." Sunita's voice was soft. "These are his countrymen. And he may believe, like a lot of people, that this conflict is due to policies in the West."

Reinhardt shifted in his chair. "There is a clear link between this war and climate change. Before this began, Syria experienced its worst drought in history. This caused a forced migration of nearly two million people. The result of this migration destabilized the already unstable and created this nightmare."

Joshua looked unimpressed. "Climate change. Yeah, well ... The talk is so fucking apocalyptic. End times and we are all going to die unless we unplug fucking everything. You know, you guys need a good P.R. person."

Reinhardt shrugged. "You are right. But they speak with such fear because climate change is frightening."

Khalid came back. His face was puffy, and his voice was hoarse as he said, "Any updates?" When Sunita reached her hand toward him, he shifted away. As he lowered himself into his chair, the screen came alive again.

Gears grinding, the truck rumbled and backfired in the inky darkness before shuddering to a stop in the rubble-strewn street. Ahmed, Maysa and their daughter ran toward it from the shelter of a broken wall. Hugging his daughter, Ahmed helped them both up into the back of the truck, each of them clutching a small bundle of clothes that were little more than rags. Maysa had searched all afternoon, digging and clawing through stones, to find their good clothes. The small bundles were the best of the worst. Mother and daughter found a space to sit, crowded together with other women and children. Two young men stood near the cab of the rusty truck with guns over their shoulders. Seeing them made Ahmed feel better. Maysa pulled her daughter's head into her lap. The less she saw, the better; she had seen far, far too much.

The rattling old truck drove over roads that were barely more than paths, through the darkness and into the dawn. The driver was going as fast as he dared. There were more people to pick up once this group was delivered to the camp, and therefore more money to be made. More important, the rebels could descend on them at any moment, killing the lot of them or taking the women and children to use as sex slaves. The women and children being jostled in the back sat paralyzed by fear.

Finally, the truck arrived at the gates of the refugee camp as the sun was rising. In the streaks of early light, a city of tents stretched to the horizon. Mother and daughter scrambled off the truck and joined a serpentine line of people to get registered. As the sun rose high into the sky, some in the line collapsed from heat and thirst. Harried aid workers rushed to keep up with the overwhelming needs of so many. Eventually, mother and daughter were directed to a dusty tent sparsely furnished with two cots, a bucket, and a small wash basin on an upturned crate.

Mornings were especially taxing. If people woke up with hope, that hope was quickly dashed once the rough routines began. They lined up for morning meals that were never enough.

"I am full," Maysa insisted as she passed her daughter what was left in her bowl.

A tall and remarkably clean woman was walking between people and spied the mother and daughter sitting close together.

"Sister, I know you must still be hungry." She pulled a handful of dates out of a big pocket in her dress and offered them to the mother.

Maysa shaded her eyes from the already blazing sun and saw the same tall woman that she had seen the previous night.

"Thank you, but I am fine." She instinctively held her daughter closer.

The tall woman shrugged and smiled. "It is hard, isn't it? Your husband, was he killed, or …?"

Maysa's eyes misted over. "My husband had to stay behind. I am hopeful he will get some sense and join us soon."

The tall woman shook her head. "Oh, sister, that is a story I have heard too often. I pray you are right, but I think it is best if you face reality. It is doubtful he will come."

Maysa narrowed her eyes. "I pray you are wrong. My husband may be stubborn, but he is not a fool."

"That may be true, but life beyond this camp is very dangerous. It is dangerous here, too, especially for such a pretty woman and her daughter. Have you no one to protect you?"

"Protect us from what?" Maysa tucked a thin blanket around her daughter's head, hoping to block out this conversation.

The tall woman noticed this and said, "It is better she hears." She paused and looked around to see if anyone was in earshot. She lowered her voice.

"It pains me to tell you this, but there are rapes." She angled her head toward the girl. "Theft is a problem as well, but it looks as though that would not be a big problem for you. Food is becoming scarcer, and there is talk that the aid agencies may abandon us at any moment as the surrounding areas are taken over by rebels."

Maysa raised her hand to stop the woman from saying more. "But we were told it is safe here."

The tall woman shrugged. "What else could they say? Your husband acted on the best information he had, but"—she looked around—"but I have better information. I know a place where you will have clean water, good food and comfortable accommodations. It is safe and peaceful. Your daughter will be able to continue with her education as well. How does that sound, my sister?"

On Maysa's face, hope was mixed with doubt. The violence and destruction of the past week, the exhaustion, the fears and the grave uncertainties had short-circuited her otherwise good intuition. She no longer knew what to believe or whom to trust.

"I will think about this. My husband believes we are here at this camp. What if he comes and we are not here?"

"That is an easy problem to fix!" The woman laughed, although her cool eyes took the measure of Maysa's anxiety. "Probably the easiest problem I have heard in a long while. We will leave word of where you and your beautiful daughter are living comfortably. Think of how relieved he will be, knowing you are safe and well looked after!"

A tear slid down Maysa's cheek as she stroked her daughter's hair. "Why would you do this for us?"

"Because I have been in your situation." The woman stood up and brushed the dust off her dress. "Please consider your daughter and make your decision quickly. Safe passage is arriving tomorrow."

She strode confidently away. An aid worker was walking in the direction of the mother and daughter but was called away. In the distance, the tall woman stopped to talk to a rough-looking man who handed her a thick envelope, which she quickly tucked into a pocket. She glanced all around, then nodded to the man and moved away, disappearing into a tent. Maysa watched her, frowning slightly, before taking her daughter's hand and starting the long walk back to their own tent.

Emily shot to her feet. "Oh no! I know what's happening. After everything they've lost and everything they've been through."

"What are you talking about?" Susan said.

"The sex trade," Emily said, anguished. "I've read about it. That woman has been targeting women and children—we've been watching her do it, and we saw her being paid off. She and the man must be part of a rebel group. The women and children will be herded onto a truck with a promise of a better life and taken away, but they'll be taken to a place where they'll be sold and used for sex. It's likely they'll never be heard from again. This has to be our mission—to stop them."

Back at the tent, Maysa was surprised to see a teddy bear sitting on the smaller cot. Around its neck was a bright ribbon and a small card that said, "Tomorrow at noon by the fence behind the latrines." Her daughter's eyes were round as she picked it up and hugged it. The presence of the teddy bear unsettled Maysa, and as she looked around, she noticed that one of her meager possessions was gone. She searched under the cots and all around the tent, but a headscarf was missing. Her best and favorite. The one good piece of clothing she had found in her hours of digging that had left her fingernails bloody. Maybe the tall woman was right, that theft was a problem even here. And if she was right about that ...

Maysa settled her daughter, then headed outside to find the tall woman. The woman saw her and let her search for a few minutes to allow Maysa's fear to increase. She finally allowed herself to be seen and pulled up two stools that had been lying in the dust, blown over by the wind. Inviting Maysa to sit, she spoke reassuringly about how much safer and better life would be for her and her daughter.

"Fuck, fuck, fuck!" Emily could not contain her anger. "This is outrageous!"

Her uncharacteristic outburst shocked the others. She was on her feet again, fists clenched. "When do we leave?" Her eyes were bright with rage.

Joshua spoke slowly. "We have to do this right. I'm sure Gabriel has instructions for us. Obviously, we can't go on our own."

The screen lit up, and there was Gabriel. "Emily is right about your mission. Ready, my dear ones, for your instructions?"

Susan wrinkled her nose at the imagined stench. "I'm happy I can't smell."

Sunita shot her a look, but Susan pretended not to notice. They stood in the midst of tents, children, open latrines, stray dogs, and women who were worn down by the ongoing conflict.

"It is endless." Emily looked in vain to see a beginning or an end to the tents.

"Do you mean the tents or the suffering?" Reinhardt asked.

"Both, I guess," she replied quietly.

They passed more than a few people who had infected wounds.

In a desolate monotone, Sunita said, "Bacteria loves blood."

Joshua winced. "The old and alive me would have passed out by now, but never mind. We don't have much time."

"I think I see her!" Emily had left the group to search and now stood in a row of haphazardly placed tents some distance away. These tents looked as though they had been set up quickly to meet the ever more urgent demand. Aid workers were running in and out of larger tents that housed medical supplies and other essentials. Armed guards, no more than sixteen years old, stood stone-faced nearby.

Maysa felt as though she were being watched. Thinking she saw a shadow, she turned and flinched, scaring her daughter.

"Emily, dear, I think you are standing too close to her." Susan called.

Emily stepped back but not very far.

"Are you easing her trauma?" Reinhardt asked gently.

"Trying to, but it feels so big." Emily sounded worried and fearful.

"Take a moment and ease your own fears, Emily. We can only help others when we are okay ourselves," Reinhardt offered. Emily nodded and flashed him a grateful smile.

Sunita crouched in front of the little girl, looking her over. "Something is wrong with her heart, and she is malnourished. But I am confident this can be remedied with care."

Emily stood back as Maysa's tight shoulders began to relax and her breathing slowed.

"Good job, Emily. Easing her shock and trauma will help her regain her intuition, and she will make sounder decisions." Reinhardt looked cautiously pleased.

Joshua looked around for Alter. In the searing, relentless heat of midday, Alter in his long black coat stood apart from the rest. Joshua moved to stand beside him. Alter turned to him with a mournful look.

"Joshua, how can this be? You and the others tell me stories about all the wonderful things the world has done since I died. Miracles even. All the diseases that have been cured, plentiful food, the ways you travel. You have even talked about people leaving the earth and travelling through the heavens and they don't even have to die! And this? How can the world not stop this suffering? Is this not as important as some fancy or clever way of playing games or talking with each other? I don't understand."

"That book we saw, *The History of Fear*? I am afraid there are chapters you have not read, and there are more chapters being written," Joshua said. "Come, Alter, remember why you are here. We'll have a long talk when we get back, okay?"

The old man stepped closer to Maysa and began to send doubts. He did his best to open her mind to see the faults in this new friend. Besides the doubts, he sent questions, important questions for her to ask.

The tall and clean woman approached Maysa. "The truck has come early and is eager to take you and the other fortunate women to safety and comfort. Please get ready now or you will miss your great opportunity."

Maysa quickly packed their few things, including the small jar of beauty cream, into their two small bags. She had believed herself to be fully decided but now felt queasy. "I need a few more minutes."

The tall woman was taken aback. "My friends cannot wait, sister. They are doing you a great favor. The best time for this to happen is during lunch when there is always confusion and noise. I explained this to you yesterday. I will be back for you and your daughter in a few minutes."

Maysa's daughter came out of the tent carrying the teddy bear and rubbed her mother's back with one small dirty hand.

"Susan, she is getting nervous. If she is too scared, she will not resist this woman. I don't fucking know, but some beauty may give her hope." Joshua spoke quickly, trying not to show his anxiety and frustration.

Susan's frantic eyes met Joshua's. "I know the power of beauty, but I'm having a hard time finding any!"

"Send her an image then, but hurry."

Susan sent her a vision of cool waterfalls, flowers and lush green fields with crops ready for harvest. Maysa sat up straighter.

Reinhardt sat beside her and focused on her breath: calming breaths in, fearful breaths out. Khalid directed his attention to the little girl, sending her a picture of a fat, happy kitten chasing a piece of string. She began to laugh. Maysa reached down absently and stroked her hair.

Susan stepped closer and offered hope even in the absence of a reason to hope. Emily and Sunita sent her pictures of her husband, pictures of happy times past and imagined happy times to come. Reinhardt laid his big hand on Maysa's thin shoulder, hoping to convey a sense, an imitation, of her husband's touch.

"She is coming back! I can feel it," Emily cried. "But have we done enough?"

As Sunita reached out to take Emily's hand, Maysa stood up, resolved. "We are not going. We are not coming with you. I thank you for your generous offer, but my daughter and I will remain here."

The tall and clean woman drew a sharp breath, and her expression hardened. "Come, sister, they are waiting, my good and brave friends who have so kindly offered their assistance to you and your daughter."

She grabbed Maysa's hand and pulled.

"Stop! What are you doing?" One of the guards came running up. "Who are you and what are you doing here?"

The guard looked the tall and clean woman up and down. "I think you'd better come with me."

The woman set off at a run. Another guard caught up with her and pulled her off her feet.

"Joshua, was that you? Did you arrange the guards?" Emily asked.

Joshua grinned. "Just in case, I sent a message from my fried and fucked-up dead brain." He tapped his head.

"We did it!" Emily jumped and began to float. Sunita grabbed her hand to bring her back.

"Not quite," Reinhardt said firmly. "There is the little matter of the people, this woman's friends who are waiting near the fence, if I am correct."

They ran to a part of the fence beyond a row of latrines, far from the aid stations. Four men stood just outside a gap that had been cut in the fence. Beyond the fence, a truck idled. Three women and five children were walking toward the men.

"Oh, this has to be stopped," Sunita said. "Send another message, Joshua!"

"I'll try."

"Susan, send them the biggest, most badass mythic beast you can imagine," Joshua said quickly.

Susan squatted in the dirt and scrunched her face. Later, the women and the guards would swear they all witnessed the same thing: a massive, red, bloodied head with a long, purple tongue dragging the earth and eyes that rolled in all directions. The men panicked. They looked back at the idling truck. With guns slapping against their legs, more guards from the camp came running up the path. The men ran to the truck. The women and children stood uncertainly, watching them go. One of the guards stopped and spoke to them quietly, gesturing them to return to the camp.

"Can we stop the truck?" Emily cried.

The men in the truck could see that things were not going according to plan and let out the clutch to drive off. A puffy cloud of black smoke began to curl out of the engine.

"Wow, we are good!" Khalid exclaimed.

The men leaped out of the truck and ran down the road.

Gabriel strolled into view.

"Did you do that or did we?" Joshua asked.

"Does it matter?" Gabriel said with a smile. "Well done! Why don't you go and say good-bye to Maysa?"

"I could cry with happiness." Emily's eyes glistened and then widened. She pointed. "Look!"

Ahmed, filthy with sweat and dust, was running up to greet his wife and child. A smiling aid worker hurried after him, trying to keep up. Ahmed scooped up his wife and child, burying his face in their hair.

Chapter 39: Gabriel Elucidates

The mid-day meal was over, and most of the group were leaning back in their chairs talking. At the far end of the table, Emily and Khalid were playing a game Emily had made up called "Who's That Angel?" Joshua's back was turned to them, but every time they laughed or shouted, he jerked around.

A bell rang.

"And now it's time to play 'What kind of bell is Gabriel using this time?'" Joshua said. He pushed his chair back and stood up, his gaze directed toward Emily and Khalid. "Anyone want to hazard a guess?"

Emily was already sprinting for the door. "Holy heavens, what's wrong with you? It's a fire truck bell," she shouted. The rest were right behind her but bumped to a stop outside the kitchen, scanning the vast space of the Great Unnamed Room. No sign of Gabriel or the screen. Khalid was the first to notice a subtle change near the Wall of the Seven Heavens. Shadows, white and then deeper white became more solid, more Gabriel. It was unsettling. He felt … tentative. They hurried to join him.

"Greetings, my dear ones. Gather near! I thought it would be inspiring to have a chat near the magnificent Wall, which is such a wondrous testimony to humans' desire for meaning and purpose." Gabriel turned away from them, absorbed for a time in the Wall's sacred scenes.

When he turned back to face them, he spread his arms and hands as if offering a benediction. "As you know, there is an article in the very thick manual for the newly departed, written by the Higher Vibrational Council, stating that any mission that is a final mission is not to be revealed beforehand. This rule has never been broken. Until now." Gabriel waited. All stood still as ancient, bone-white statues.

"Before I reveal this final mission, some context is necessary."

Emily stuck her hand up. "Gabriel, this is really big news! Does this mean we'll be leaving here soon?"

A look of panic flitted across Joshua's face as he said to Emily, "Anxious for the sweet hereafter?"

Gabriel raised a hand. "Yes, Emily, it means that you and the rest may leave after this mission. But it is essential that you remain focused on this mission and remain here in mind, heart and spirit. I strongly discourage you from speculating about what comes after the mission. Humanity has not been served well by your annoying habit of looking ahead and thinking about outcomes. It weakens precious energy. And to be successful in this all-important mission, you will need all of your energy." His voice reverberated through the Great Unnamed Room.

Alter took one shuffle step forward. "The library is a good place to talk."

Gabriel vanished.

"Splendid idea, Alter." Gabriel's voice echoed from somewhere within the grand library. As they all headed toward the sound, Sunita took Alter's arm.

"Down the third passageway to your right, take a sharp left, make your way up the next two flights of stairs," Gabriel called. "If you go past the statue of Hermes, you have gone too far."

Alter and Sunita moved slowly behind the others, looking at a multitude of lights suspended from spider-web-thin threads. "Have you been in this part of the library, Alter?" Sunita asked softly. He shook his head.

One by one, they walked through the modest wooden doorway into a circular stone room infused by a rich, amber light that glowed warmly on the arched stone ceilings, walls and floors. Gabriel sat on a straight-backed chair. A semicircle of seven roomy chairs were arranged in front of him. Alter was the first to notice that there were no books in this room.

"Yes, and there is a reason why there are no books, my dear Alter. This room awaits books yet to be written. Yes, books are written every day, but these books will reveal what the world is not yet ready to know. And, given recent events, may never be ready ..." His voice caught, but he continued. "Please sit. I trust you find this room agreeable. My intention was to gather you together in a neutral space, in a room favored by no one in particular. But let's get started. There is much to discuss."

Gabriel could feel the strange and disturbing mixture of anxiousness, curiosity, hope and fear mingling together. Moments like this reminded him how very much he loved humans.

"Your world ..." He looked at Reinhardt. "I believe you Buddhists have talked about an impending dark age. This is correct?"

"Yes," Reinhardt said, "this has been predicted by many for a long time."

Gabriel nodded. "Here it is, my dear ones. The portal between the heavens and earth is closing. We do not know the precise moment when this will happen, but everything points to this happening very soon. It is imminent." He enunciated each syllable.

"You can't be serious! Heaven and earth cut off from each other? What will happen to people? To angels?" Emily asked in whispered shock.

"Do you mean a separation between heart and mind?" Reinhardt, trying to keep his voice calm and reasonable, sounded curt and demanding. He lifted a shoulder in apology.

"That is correct, Reinhardt. In Buddhist-speak, the portal between mind and heart is perilously close to being severed, cauterized."

Susan leaned forward. "In all my studies and wisdom teachings, I learned that we were about to cross a threshold, one that ushers in a New Age. Peace, love—" Gabriel's look silenced her.

"Please," he continued. "Sit back and listen carefully. I will be happy to entertain questions when I am finished."

Gabriel crossed his long legs. "The portal between heaven and earth carries prayers, wishes, miracles, love, artistic inspirations, heart desires, kindness, dignity—and we may even go so far as to include altruistic inclinations. We fly, and you fly, through this portal. In some traditions, this portal represents heart wisdom. When we lead with our heart, then prayers, wishes and indeed miracles occur. Miracles are natural, but the neurotic human mind gets in the way. In the beginning, when creation was still soft and unformed, this portal was not necessary. Back then, we walked with you. Side by side. Together. Angel and human. I remember—" His voice was wistful. "I wasn't there, but the great epics have been handed down. There was a natural communion. The world was an enchanted place. In short, there were no barriers. But things changed. Your world has created many myths to explain this shift, but the truth has never been revealed and will not be revealed now. Nevertheless, it was during this time that a portal was created. You may view this portal as a lifeline. And, I repeat, this lifeline is about to be broken. The mind is dictating, and the heart is withering."

Gabriel paused. The amber light that infused the room dimmed. A moment as brief as half a heart-beat passed as Gabriel looked away to determine the cause. He began to speak more quickly.

"The clarion calls have been sounding for more than a century, but for the past few earth decades the calls have become louder. Shattering, actually. Some of us call this The Great Turning Away. No matter how we try or what we do to open people up to their hearts and see the phenomenal world, they are turning away. And though some have not turned away, their voices are fading, and others are becoming too fearful to hope. Any who still offer up prayers are not asking from their hearts but from their minds. We cannot work with this."

Gabriel unfurled a scroll that rolled out on the stone floor and past their feet. He scanned the list. "There are three hundred and twenty-four signs of this spiritual dystopia on this list, which I will leave for you in the main foyer of our beautiful library. It will be rolled up and placed by the statue of Eris. I advise you to read the list only if you remain unconvinced or confused about the signs. But now I will take questions."

"The dark ages, indeed. Was there a specific catalyst? Another massacre? A catastrophic disaster?" Reinhardt asked.

Gabriel stood up. "Thank you, Reinhardt. Yes, there was a catalyst. One person."

"One person? Are you kidding me?!" Joshua bolted out of his chair.

Gabriel waved him to sit down. Joshua sank back, agitated. "Yes, Joshua. I know this may be hard for you to believe, but every single person in the world matters. It is well known that all who live on earth are interconnected. Each person's actions and feelings matter. This has been true from the beginning. One person tipped the balance. Is that the correct expression, Joshua?"

Reluctantly, Joshua nodded.

"Who is this person? How did they tip the balance?" Emily asked.

Gabriel's smile was warm. "First things first. The person's name is Hope."

"Are you kidding me?" Joshua was on his feet again. "The world is without hope, or nearly, and now you're telling us the person who finally drove the world over the freaking edge, her name is Hope? My fucking everlasting fucked-up brain cells!" He sagged into his chair, head in hands.

"Now this is the Joshua we love," Emily said through weak laughter.

Turning to her, Joshua drawled, "So it's true. You love me. I knew you couldn't resist me for long."

Gabriel held a hand up. "I will tell you the story of Hope later. This situation is without precedent, and time is of the essence. Heaven, all the heavens and earth, depend on this mission. If the portal closes completely, there will be no communication between heaven and earth. After you hear about Hope, then I will offer you details."

"Gabriel, how can we do anything?" Alter spoke hesitantly. "If God cannot stop this from happening, then what can we do?"

"Alter, through the ages we in this realm and other realms have done much to keep the portal open. Besides inspiring open, brave hearts, answering prayers and performing miracles, we have helped in a myriad of ways. Humans—brave humans, humble humans— have contributed immeasurably as well. Some have sacrificed a great deal. Now people are turning away from our vibrations. We need people who have walked on earth, people who still retain a goodly amount of neurosis." Gabriel looked squarely at Joshua and smiled. "Your vibrations will align better than any divine being, given the current conditions. It is believed that you, all of you, stand a better chance of breaking through. But you do have the option of not participating. There is extreme danger in this mission, which I will explain when the time is right."

Gabriel rubbed his chin, a gesture he had seen on a movie once while he was waiting for someone in a theater. "We will continue, but let's take a moment and listen to some music that was inspired by open portals and brave hearts. It is essential, my dear ones, to elevate your energy. All the information you will need will be revealed."

Amid a rustle of feathers, the Ugly Brown Birds began to sing.

Chapter 40: Into the Woods

They were in their bedrooms, slumbering in their states of suspension. Each awoke to Gabriel's voice: "Time for a field trip, my dear ones."

"Is No-Spirit-Land like hell?" Emily sat beside Sunita on a dead tree trunk, her feet kicking at a pile of soggy brown leaves. Sunita gave Emily's shoulder a comforting squeeze. Emily caught the feeling and smiled wanly. If they'd been able to smell, they would have smelled the musky rot of summer's death.

"Not quite the same, no," Gabriel said. "If one is taken into No-Spirit-Land, there is a dim sense of awareness, but you drift endlessly."

They were in the protected zone of Mrs. Potts' territory, in a small hardwood grove not far from her home. Poplars towered over white birches and formed a circle, with birds and small animals active on this late November day. The sun's light was thin. A cluster of dark clouds ranged along the horizon, just visible through the leafless branches, bringing a threat of snow or sleet. Gabriel and the group sat on logs surrounding a well-used campfire. Blackened, cracked chunks of wood lay at the bottom of the pit, with a few empty beer cans scattered nearby. Reinhardt adjusted his eye patch, a habit that arose whenever he saw a slight against nature.

Gabriel had not told Mrs. Potts he was bringing the seven here. When he had considered where and how to tell them about No-Spirit-Land, he had pictured this place, ordinary and grounded.

"In all my teachings, I have never heard of this No-Spirit-Land," Susan huffed. "Is it similar to a person becoming an earthbound spirit or a ghost?"

Gabriel's smile was brief. "No, Susan, if a spirit becomes bound to earth, there is a good chance they will be released at some point to continue their journey. But if a being gets caught in No-Spirit-Land, they remain there. They retain just enough consciousness to know where they are, but there's no escape. No exit." Gabriel cocked his head, listening. For a moment, he thought he heard Mrs. Potts singing in her shaky vibrato. Perhaps she was looking for those mushrooms she mentioned on their last visit. He re-emerged from his reverie and returned to the group.

"So, it doesn't sound very different from my big black, to be honest." Joshua toed a small stone and looked startled when it flew high into the sky. "Not sure what the huge, gripping fear is." Nearby a crow squawked a warning and flew away.

"Let me be clearer, then. This *big black* you have referred to exists but not in the way you may imagine, and one does not stay in it for long. No-Spirit-Land is endless nothingness. There is a dim awareness that you are nothing spinning in nothing. It is harsh, endless, relentless despair with no shred of hope. *Capisce*?"

"Please give us the bigger picture." Reinhardt bent down, grabbing a fistful of dirt, moss and leaves. He brought it to his nose, hoping to smell the familiar richness he remembered. Nothing. Instead, he held onto this forest flesh.

Without hesitation, Gabriel began. "Due to increased harshness of heart, vibrations have dropped to a low never seen before—to such a degree that higher beings now face a new danger when coming to earth. Spirits, angels and devas have always come and gone with little threat. Sadly, this has changed, and the situation grows more dire with each passing moment. We feel this is due to the imminent closure of the portal but concede there could be additional factors."

"Are people who are dying or dead at risk of being taken into this dreadful abyss?" Susan shuddered theatrically.

"It is exceedingly rare, my dear Susan. As I said, higher beings, angels, navigators and so on are at extreme risk." He stood and walked over to a young poplar. "It grieves me to say, but each one of you will be in great peril. Our sources say this is likely due to an increase in your vibrations. This elevated threat of No-Spirit-Land has moved us to offer you the chance to opt out of this mission. Each of you has this choice. For the time being, you will not move on to any other realm, but you will be safe. Unfortunately, we do not have the luxury of time. I need your decisions now. I will take a short stroll through this lovely wood while you talk or contemplate or do whatever you need to do to make your decisions."

"Huddle?" Joshua suggested.

"Rhymes with cuddle." Susan nodded toward Emily. Joshua flushed and glanced away.

Sunita shot to her feet, throwing her scarf around her neck. "I am in. I cannot bear the idea of this happening."

"It is very clear to me as well." Reinhardt said. One by one, each of them stood. Khalid began to laugh. The rest joined in at the absurdity of what they were about to do. Their laughter moved the trees, sending birds scattering into the sky. Gabriel returned, smiling broadly.

"Would you like to discuss your training here in our tranquil wood or back in the bliss of the realm?"

"Oh cripes, training!"

Chapter 41: Apprentice

"While you were on earth, each of you committed yourself to spiritual practices that will add some protection. So, I propose the following. With the exception of you, Joshua." Gabriel playfully wagged a long finger at him. "But never fear, I have a plan!"

"Goody," Joshua muttered.

They were back in the Great Unnamed Room, sitting at the café tables. The prism was glowing red for courage and yellow for dispelling negative thoughts. The Ugly Brown Birds slept, their long beaks tucked into their wings.

"Hey, mate!" Khalid punched Joshua's arm. "It looks like you may have to consider our paths after all and which one offers the most bang for its spiritual buck in terms of protection."

Gabriel stopped, hands on hips, looking at Khalid. After a moment, he turned to Reinhardt. "Reinhardt, I understand that you were well versed in protector practices."

Reinhardt scraped his chair back and stood up as though at attention. "Yes, I practiced them daily."

Gabriel began pacing with his hands behind his back. The seven recognized this as a sign that he was venturing into deep waters.

"Good. I want you to begin sharing these practices with the rest. Even if you do not believe in their value,"—he looked pointedly at Joshua—"please follow dear Reinhardt's instructions."

He turned to Emily. "Emily, you devoted yourself to the idea that miracles, if asked for with humility, can come to pass. I will ask you to teach the others to pray, specifically to pray for and expect miracles. Please begin today."

Emily's eyes were wide. "Yes, of course, I can do that."

"Khalid, you were taught to surrender your will to Allah. Surrender can be a practical and fearless thing to do. Often when we offer up to, or surrender, we lose our grip on something that was out of our control anyway. Some believe we allow more powerful parts of ourselves to emerge when we surrender. By using prayers and reciting some Surah, chapters from the Holy Qur'an, you can teach the rest the fine, wise art of surrender."

"In shaa Allah!"

"Susan, my dear Susan. What can you offer to help protect? I have considered this at length. And then finally!" He snapped his fingers. Susan jumped. "You believe so many wondrous things, but one belief that is relevant in our situation is your belief in elemental magic. I know you are well versed in some practices that help rouse elemental magic. Susan, I want you to begin sharing and teaching these traditions with the others."

Beaming, Susan offered a deep *namaste*.

With his clear, strong voice, Gabriel said to Sunita, "The little space within the heart is as great and as vast as the universe." Sunita stood and moved closer to him; together they continued: "The heavens and the earth are there, and the sun and the moon and the stars. Fire and lightning and winds are there, and all that now is and all that is not."

They smiled warmly at each other. "Sunita, I want you to teach the others how to radiate this energy to all the people you will encounter on this mission."

Sunita bowed deeply. "Thank you, Gabriel. Swami Prabhavananda, the wise monk-philosopher, will be my inspiration."

Gabriel looked at each one in turn as he said, "Sharing this energy and guiding the others to do the same will not only help raise the vibrations of your group but also of people you will encounter on your mission."

His expression softened as his eyes found Alter. "Alter, you have prayers and blessings for everything. Teach the rest of the dear ones to pray for strength and guidance in dealing with obstacles or difficulties you may encounter. And Alter, I have an additional request. Teach them *tikkun olam*, how to repair the world. In other words, teach them to be alert to any problems."

With great gravity, the old man nodded.

Joshua fidgeted, anxious to hear what would be asked of him.

"Joshua, my dear Joshua." Gabriel studied him. "It is clear your heart has expanded. The great release you offered your dear Gillian was the mark of a generous spirit. Although you remain loyal to applied logic and action, we see this as a positive. Joshua, as project manager, you are to remind the ones offering their precious gifts to keep in mind the profound power of belief conjoined with action. I am a big fan of applied theory—it requires connecting mind and heart. While you were alive, you were a lover of logic. Now that you have had, shall I say, certain experiences here, you have been introduced to heart. Joshua, if you decide to go on this mission, you are tasked to teach others to bring into alignment their beliefs and their actions."

Joshua's eyes were wide with doubt. Gabriel reassured him. "You can do this, Joshua. Trust. Trust the others will help you."

"Sorry, mate. Now you'll have to explore all of our paths." Khalid couldn't help himself. "But no worries, we'll support you."

Gabriel took a long drink from a goblet that had materialized in his hand. "There you have it. You have your assignments. I suggest you start straight away. What is at stake is horrifying, and it changes everything. As you can imagine, all the heavens are in a state. Higher-order angels that fly around the earth in four wing beats can no longer do so. Urgent messages meant for humans who are struggling with this or that are not getting through and, oh well, I could go on." He tipped his head back, drinking whatever was in the goblet.

Gabriel walked away, whistling a strange tune. The Ugly Brown Birds stirred and tried to align notes to his but stopped, seemingly exhausted by the effort. They watched him in silence.

He walked back and gave the group one of his old, dazzling smiles. "Thank you, my dear ones. You have your assignments. Remember, fear is no match for noble passion. This is true in all realms including earth."

There were stomping outs. Shouts and tears. Brief and sometimes nasty debates. And hugs and cheers and teasing. Each one of them tried hard to listen without bias. Each one practiced unfamiliar practices that they doubted would work. They acknowledged the doubts and suspended them; Reinhardt suggested this bit of advice. They tried. Something larger than themselves was at stake, and for this they stepped into the unknown.

Teachings took place in the Great Unnamed Room, the library, the kitchen, near the Great Green Sanctuary, by the Wall of the Seven Heavens and in the café. No one claimed any specific territory. They were encouraged by Gabriel to teach where they felt like it, at any given moment.

Alter was a wise and gentle teacher. He taught them to pray for strength and to be alert to wrongs. He was delighted to also teach them about *tikkun olam*—and even more delighted with how quickly they grasped the concept. After his teaching time, he would watch carefully how well they applied the lesson. Susan turned out to be his star pupil. She had a special skill for noticing wrongs or things out of place. Alter tested them by moving books in the library from one section to another and by mixing up the order of chairs. He was in his element. His obvious delight, a word no one would ordinarily have ascribed to him, inspired all of them to direct their best energies to his teachings. Alter also taught them how to nurture the divine spark, elevating worth and dignity. "This," he said, "will bring you closer to the divine."

Sunita's teachings were poetic. She meditated before each teaching and appeared radiant and patient. Yet everyone except Reinhardt and Susan struggled with the idea that the human heart could be so powerful. Standing in front of them, explaining the ways this concept could benefit people, drained her patience, but she persevered. Alter felt the concept lacked humility; Khalid agreed. Sunita read poems and sang songs to inspire them to open their hearts wider and experience the vastness.

Khalid taught, with humor and sincerity, the value and profound importance of submitting to Allah—"or," he said, "you may think of it as losing your ego." He told stories from the Holy Qur'an and shared personal reflections. Like the others, Khalid had them look for opportunities to practice submission.

To the surprise of all, Susan was firm and quite strict. She let them know that only their best efforts would do, and that her subject was essential. Khalid enjoyed the classes and became adept at spotting magical occurrences. (Joshua muttered that this was not too difficult, considering where they were.) It was not lost on them that Susan was more strict with Joshua than with anyone else, often demanding he spend extra time noting extraordinary happenings and report back to her on his findings.

Reinhardt was a well-practiced and heart-centered teacher. Although his talks sometimes wandered off and weren't always clear, his genuine desire for them to become confident with protector practices was evident. Most of them felt these practices could be the very thing that saved them from No-Spirit-Land, so they listened well. He explained that these teachings would help them relate to the lowered vibrations of others they would encounter on their mission. Reinhardt gave them reminders, after his classes and throughout the day, on practicing the practices.

When Emily taught, Joshua sat up front. For once in his life (and afterlife), he didn't care what people thought of him. When they teased him, he just laughed. Emily told stories of miracles recorded in the Bible, but she also told stories of miracles throughout history. She even included stories from people in her own life who felt they had experienced or witnessed miracles. As Emily's teachings unfolded, Reinhardt disputed the notion that some external force would see fit to intervene in the affairs of humanity. Emily gently reminded him to practice his own advice and suspend his doubts. Reinhardt acknowledged that he was applying his old biases about Christianity. Miracles, he said, had always been around. Emily surprised most of them with her knowledge of other traditions that allowed for miracles. She encouraged them to think of all the miracles they had experienced when they were alive—the birth of children, love—but to think about times in their lives that had remarkable turnarounds.

"Ah, yes, we all want turnarounds." Joshua noted ruefully.

Joshua did not teach a class, but he checked in with each teacher to discuss ways of better connecting belief and action, theory and practice.

At the center of the long kitchen table sat a folded piece of paper in the shape of a crane.

"Oh, I think I know what this represents!" Susan gasped. It was the next morning, and they were sitting down to breakfast.

"Do tell." Joshua heaped hash browns onto his plate.

His words were barely out when Susan rushed on. "It looks like origami, the Japanese art of paper folding. The crane is sacred in Native traditions, but there's a story of a little Japanese girl who died of leukemia due to radiation poisoning years after Hiroshima. Her story inspired millions and transformed the origami crane to symbolize peace and hope. Gabriel is sending us a message." Susan reached over to pick up the delicate crane, trailing her sleeve through Reinhardt's platter of sausages. Unperturbed, he shifted the platter out of the way.

"What does it say?" Emily leaned forward.

Susan carefully unfolded the delicate paper and cleared her throat.

"Training is over."

Chapter 42: Gabriel's Revelation

They were scattered throughout the Great Unnamed Room, library and Room of Reflection when the sound of a great gong reverberated, summoning them. Gabriel was standing in the precise center of the room, wearing a safari outfit complete with binoculars dangling from his neck.

"Not a word," he warned. "No time to change. Time is limited these days with so many crises and fewer of us able to do the work. I have been advised to share my human story."

The screen dropped down, pinpoints of blue and white lights sparkling.

Gasps and murmurs sounded as chairs were pulled closer to the screen. The prism pulsed with silver, purple and turquoise, colors that would cultivate spiritual truths and dispel negativity. Images of an ancient city appeared, with majestic domes, spires, and one small, dark-haired boy.

The narrator's voice was clear and crisp as a mountain stream in the Bavarian Alps.

Tonight, young Gabriel would see if there was an empty or mostly empty pallet to sleep on at Jawla's home. Early evening and it was still warm, with the night-scented jasmine sending her sweet perfume to the streets. He stopped running and drew in a noseful of the scent. After a moment's pause, his small legs were moving faster than before down the narrow streets.

A market vendor called out, "Gabriel, do you want some food?"

Gabriel laughed and waved. "Not tonight!"

He raced past narrow houses whose window boxes spilled out flowers and herbs. Dark curls flying, brown eyes sparkling, bare feet slapping the cobblestones, he ran.

He was happy. Today he had found them. The two tiny faces.

Jawla put her finger to her lips as she laid her new baby down on soft blankets. She beckoned Gabriel out of the infant's room to the kitchen.

"We haven't seen you in a long time, Gabriel. Do you want some soup?"

Gabriel nodded and sat down. She ladled soup into an earthenware bowl and set it down in front of him. As he eagerly spooned it up, she smiled. "So, to what do we owe this great pleasure?"

He wiped his mouth on the sleeve of his brown tunic. Jawla made a mental note to stitch extra material to the tunic to accommodate his growing frame.

"I found them, Jawla! I found them! Those two small faces on the medallions at the base of the horseshoe arches." His eyes were round with excitement. "I made a wish for you and for your new baby and for—"

Jawla laughed. "Stop, Gabriel! You mean in the Patio de las Munecas, the patio of the dolls?"

He nodded vigorously. "Yes, I was in one of the halls to listen to a debate and wanted to say hello to someone. Good fortune will be yours soon, Jawla." He tipped the bowl to catch the last of the soup.

"This is exciting news, Gabriel. If it is true that finding those tiny faces and making a wish brings good fortune, then you will have my gratitude for many years. You will stay here tonight." She took his small hand in hers to lead him to a sleeping pallet.

Gabriel didn't remember his parents. He was told they'd died of an illness that killed many people at the time. In rare agreement, his neighbors agreed to take turns looking after him. He loved moving from house to house.

When he was four years old, he began to venture beyond his community. On his first trip, he met Menachem, who, upon discovering he had no parents, took him home. Gabriel stayed with him and his wife, Hasna, for several days. He loved it there and enjoyed learning about the Torah and the small birds in cages Menachem and Hasna kept nestled in the wild foliage on their back patio. Soon enough, Gabriel returned to his old neighborhood, but the idea of a world beyond, with unique smells, foods, accents and ways of worship, excited him. Cordoba in 1018 was a vibrant, progressive city where Muslims, Christians and Jews not only co-existed but enhanced each other's lives.

Gabriel loved the Great Mosque. He spent as much time as he could walking its pillared halls and speaking to people, many of whom would offer him money. He seldom accepted, but if he was staying at a home where money was scarce, he would accept with thanks and pass on the gift to the family.

He enjoyed time in the courtyard, where sometimes a newcomer to Cordoba told him stories from other lands. Stories of people who would take their sick relatives to the graves of saints in hopes of a cure. Stories of people who were not thinking well, being burnt alive. Gabriel didn't know if these stories were true, but he was happy he lived in Cordoba.

Often, he would wander in from the courtyard to a deep sanctuary whose roof was supported by a forest of pillars. He would sit, watching men pray near the Mihrab, the niche in the wall that indicated the direction of Mecca. After, he would ask questions and attend great debates between Jews, Christians and Muslims. People from all faiths indulged him. Many commented that this little boy posed good questions.

He began to stay with a widow who lived near the Great Mosque. Lubna taught Gabriel how to read and write Arabic and Spanish. She introduced him to poetry, reading some of her own to a wide-eyed Gabriel. Often she came home from her work as a secretary to the Caliph at the mosque to find Gabriel reading or weeding her small garden. In the evenings, they cooked together. Gabriel enjoyed the quiet of this home, but soon curiosity about other families and other homes seized him. It wasn't long before he was on his way, although he showed up from time to time to stay for a few days.

The sun was shining, burnishing the tiled roofs a deeper red. Gabriel was running with other boys up and down the serpentine alleys and streets. A bricklayer yelled at them as they knocked a pail over, spilling its contents. All of them ran away except Gabriel, who stood quietly and watched as the man raged. When the bricklayer picked up a tool to throw at Gabriel, he ran home to where he was staying.

Later he came back. The bricklayer was still there, working hard and yelling at other workers while sweat poured down his unshaven face. Gabriel was carrying a jug of water and half a loaf of bread.

"Want some?" He set down the jug, spilling a little of the cool water. The man looked up, ready to rage, but softened when he saw the earnest expression on the boy's face.

They sat together, taking long drinks of water. Gabriel's stomach rumbled, but he refused a bite of the bread. He asked the bricklayer where he lived and if he had a family, thinking he might provide an interesting housing opportunity. The man talked about his family, and Gabriel told him about the ideas he'd heard during a recent debate.

The sun was sinking below the tiled roofs, and workers were leaving the site. Gabriel realized he had better leave if he was going to enjoy some dinner. On his way back to Jawla's house, he took a detour to find the boys he had played with earlier. Up one street and down another, he peered in windows and looked into gardens. It was dark now, and he was tired and hungry. Windows were darkening and doors were bolted. It had never happened before, but Gabriel would have to find a place to sleep.

In a narrow alley empty of flowers or people he found a small shed and crawled in. He soon drifted off to a hungry sleep.

He dreamed he smelled smoke. *Must be incense smoke.* Deeper into the dream, he felt the sun burning his face and body. He gulped smoke, fragrant in the dream like the frankincense in the churches he visited. His throat was gripped by a searing pain and his eyes were too heavy to open. The sun was scorching. His mind searched the Torah, and in the dimness of dreams recalled King Solomon: *A righteous man falls down seven times and gets up.*

Gabriel felt love move his body to rise and rise.

He looked at the shed, from which orange and red flames leaped into the dark night. He rose higher and saw Cordoba. He rose higher and saw countries and oceans he had heard tales of. He rose higher and saw the world.

He turned to see the heavens and a felt a spirit close by.

Follow me.

The narrator's voice faded. Gabriel studied the silent group. "Questions?"

"A million." Emily had unknowingly leaned in closer to Joshua.

"Have you been here in this realm since you died?" Khalid asked with amazement.

"That is correct. My dear ones, I think perhaps the best thing for me to do is share what I can, so we are not here for eternity." He chuckled at his joke. "This will be brief. Some time after I came here, I was extended the rare invitation to become a navigator. They cited my young age and the fact I had nothing to resolve. My easy acceptance of my life, curiosity about the paths and people I encountered, and my open, happy heart were other considerations. The navigator at the time wanted to move on to another realm; she was not unhappy, just curious. It took an earth century, give or take, to train me. I am not at liberty to share these teachings." He paused and met the gaze of each one in turn.

"It wasn't my idea to share my Telling, but others … well, others thought by sharing, it would offer you reassurance that I know what it's like to be human. Mind you, I died as a nine-year-old human. The handsome adult you see before you is the result of a choice I was given. At the time, I felt I might not be taken seriously if I presented myself as a young boy. So I chose to grow up, so to speak."

"Thank you." Reinhardt stood and bowed. The rest followed his example. Emily stifled a grin at Joshua's small, stiff bow.

"I will take my leave now. See you soon, my dear ones. *Kwaheri!*"

"Anyone hazard a guess?" Joshua stood up. The others were already dispersing.

"It's Swahili for goodbye," Emily called over her shoulder as she caught up with Alter and walked with him to the library.

"How the hell do you know that?" Joshua's voice echoed through the now empty room.

Chapter 43: Gabriel's Farewell Feast

It was a feast. Dmitri Shostakovich's String Quartet in C Minor was playing. Music filled all space. If you listened with a careful ear, you could discern the Ugly Brown Birds adding their melodies to the dark, mournful notes. A red silk tablecloth with an intricate mandala in the center, edged in gold, lay perfect on the long table. The symbols embossed on the mandala were indecipherable. Reinhardt commented that some things, sacred messages in particular, require a wisdom teaching to fully absorb their meaning. Susan sniffed her disagreement.

Matching slipcovers clothed the chairs, and tall, moon-silver goblets graced each setting. Deep purple candles were already lit and sending their flames high. Exotic flowers, carefully selected from the Great Green Sanctuary, filled crystal vases. Reinhardt had taken part in the selection of flowers after Gabriel assured him they would grow again. Light glinted off the silverware and the dinnerware, which were placed with mathematical precision.

Susan was more flustered than usual and talking more quickly and more loudly. She had taken it upon herself to coordinate the feast. "A title, this occasion needs a title," she declared. "I know! It will be called A Feast for Angels."

Joshua walked away, keeping a newly made promise to himself to keep quiet lest he upset Emily. As events accelerated, he increasingly feared he would never see her again.

"Do you think Gabriel would like to sit here?" Susan said, indicating a chair at the head of the table that resembled a throne, although one befitting a prince rather than a king.

"Well, Susan, considering it wasn't here this morning, I would assume that is its purpose," Joshua said with a patience that was almost serene. Emily and Reinhardt glanced at each other, concerned about this un-Joshua behavior.

"Are you all right?" Emily asked.

"Sure, sure, I'm fine. Just considering the implications of this so-called portal closure. And, of course, the cryptic message about danger we face on this little escapade."

Emily nodded and adjusted one of the goblets a fraction. "I have no doubt Gabriel will fully explain. This escapade, as you call it, is our big mission. Don't you feel the least bit honored to be chosen for the most important spiritual mission, like, of all time?"

Susan picked up on the conversation. "Well, I'm not surprised that I was chosen for this, but to be honest, I'm afraid."

"I think it is wise to acknowledge your fear, Susan." Reinhardt cast his eye around the room as though inspecting it.

Joshua moved away and stood by the fireplace. His voice carried throughout the kitchen, bouncing off the stone tiles. "Is it just me or does anyone else find it crazy strange that we would be taking the time for this feast? I mean, if the closing of this supposed portal is real, it means the end of heaven and earth! No more angels, fairies, elves or whatever other imaginary magical beings. I mean really, why a fucking feast?" Joshua's pledge to maintain quiet and calm had lasted five minutes.

Emily looked at the others, hoping one would offer up a solid, sensible reply. When no one did, she spoke tentatively. "I'm sure Gabriel has his reasons. He did say we were to elevate our energies, so ..."

Joshua looked incredulous. "Seriously, Emily!"

"Gobsmacked?" Khalid laughed.

A trumpet sounded. All of them jumped.

And then he was standing by the throne-chair.

"My dear ones, welcome to our little feast! Please, please, sit and enjoy what may be our last repast. As you can hear, I have chosen one of my all-time favorite earth composers, Dmitri Shostakovich. He did have a little help, by the way." He swept an arm in the direction of the Ugly Brown Birds, who were now happily asleep in their cages. "Shostakovich's String Quartet Number 8 in C Minor. Appropriate, *n'est-ce pas?*"

Alter leaned in close to Sunita, "What is he saying?" Sunita laid her hand on Alter's bony shoulder.

"Before we get to our talk, let's partake of this sumptuous repast! Susan, as a special treat, this one time only, you may eat food other than that quinoa, kale or whatnot."

Susan looked down at her place setting, and her eyes misted over. Set before her was a chilled mango ginger soup to start. To one side, under a transparent dome to keep everything hot, were perfectly roasted red peppers stuffed with a silky mushroom risotto and garnished with a drizzle of truffle oil. Gabriel poured her wine, a private reserve pinot gris, and returned the bottle to its chilled bucket nearby. She could not speak but nodded her gratitude to him.

"I give up," Joshua said, looking around at everyone eating. "No questions, anyone? For Gabriel? There is a massive elephant in the room, and no one is asking questions?"

Gabriel put his large fork down. "In due time, Joshua, your queries will be properly addressed."

Alter leaned toward Sunita. "What is wrong with our Joshua? Why is he talking about an elephant?"

"It is one of those expressions I told you about. It means people are avoiding something obvious."

Alter shook his head and dipped his spoon into his matzo soup. "Strange," he muttered.

Sunita tried not to look to see what Gabriel was eating but couldn't help herself. He smiled brightly at her. Teasingly, he wrapped a wide sleeve in front of his plate.

Everyone ate their favorite foods and tried to carry on ordinary conversations, but the expectation and uncertainty of what they would be discussing after the feast weighed on them. Sunita told stories of the many festivals held in Jaipur, and Emily talked about the importance of the potato harvest on Prince Edward Island.

"Riveting," Joshua said before taking an extra big bite of his bloody steak.

Gabriel placed his large, white napkin over his plate and tapped his goblet. Then he stood and held the goblet high. "I wish to propose a toast to honor your successful training exercises. Bravo! Bravo!"

All stood and raised their glasses, toasting Gabriel and each other.

"Okay, so I admit it was the hardest thing I ever did, but all's good." Joshua sat back down.

Alter smiled. "My Joshua, you made a very old man happy."

"Yeah, here's to us. But Susan, you were a hard nut."

Susan raised her wine glass. "Why, thank you, Khalid."

Setting down his wine glass, Gabriel tapped his water goblet with a knife. "If everyone is finished with this delightful feast, I suggest we retire to the Great Unnamed Room. If it suits you, you may take along your libations."

Reinhardt picked up his glass of deep red port and grabbed a wedge of Stilton cheese. Khalid carried his fresh mint tea. Susan topped up her wine glass. Sunita took her honey-lemon tea. At Reinhardt's suggestion, Emily and Joshua each carried dainty glasses of schnapps. Alter carried a sturdy cup of milky coffee.

Instead of standing in his usual spot, Gabriel was ensconced in a large red wing chair that had not been there earlier. Although no one spoke, the chair's sudden appearance unnerved them. They had become accustomed to watching Gabriel, in all his theatrics, communicate the latest message, instruction or, on occasion, wisdom, using the screen. Or standing in the room commanding their attention. Sitting in a comfortable chair seemed out of step given the gravity of the situation. They took their seats and mentally braced themselves.

"With the exception of the first mission, each one of you has conducted yourself admirably. And now we come to this mission, which is even more critical than we thought. The feast in which we have just partaken may seem an odd thing to enjoy during the biggest crisis of our time. However, that shared feast reminds us that, even in the bleakest times, we are to continue to take pleasure. Sharing pleasures in elegant surroundings dignifies us. It is that simple and that important. I will leave you with two things tonight. The first is the story of Hope, which will play on our magnificent screen. The second is the following song. My dear ones, no matter what you witness, no matter what pain or harsh hearts you encounter, remember this. Your world is capable of creating this."

Gabriel walked over to the Ugly Brown Birds. He wore white gloves and held a small baton. With a flourish he raised it and began to conduct. Each exultant note of Bach's "Ode to Joy" was extravagantly filled with undiluted heart.

Chapter 44: Hope

Gabriel left immediately after his symphonic performance; his voice echoed instructions to watch the screen to learn about Hope.

Infinitesimal stars and dots burst off the screen and went wheeling through the Great Unnamed Room. A young woman's mahogany face filled the screen, her short black hair haloed by the patchy, slatted sunlight behind her. She wore a blindfold and spoke carefully in an accent that sounded mid-Atlantic.

"My name is Hope Gor. I was born in Kenya and moved with my parents to the U.S. when I was four years old. I am honored by both my mother's and father's ancestors but feel a deep connection to my mother's people. I claimed my mother's name to honor her powerful lineage. Chief Gor was a renowned healer, using magic and the power of miracles from the time he was a young boy. He died a long time ago, but there are days I dream of how he walked and talked. When I was younger and got a scratch, I would stare at the blood that seeped out of the small wound. This was the same blood as Chief Gor! I would refuse bandages or anything that would conceal or stop the blood. My ancestors were very powerful and I carry that same power." Hope glanced sideways and leaned out of view of the camera. "Is that enough?"

"No, that was garbage! What do you think you are doing?" a rough, tobacco-coarsened voice roared.

"I am informing you that I come from a sacred blood line known for producing people gifted with magic, and it may be best for you to let me go." She added, "For your own safety."

The image on the screen pulled back to reveal the interior of a dusty shack. Hope sat on a wooden chair, arms and feet bound with rope. Clustered around her were half a dozen desperate-looking men. All but one of them shuffled back at her words; only the man with the rough voice leaned in. "I don't believe your American lying mouth!" he snarled in her face. Hope tried not to gag at the smell of old sweat and cigarette smoke.

Inside the shack's unlatched door, chickens pecked at hard-packed earth before heading outside into the blazing sun for better prospects. Hope wondered if this shack was used by poachers or drug smugglers. *Maybe they share,* she thought and then mentally called up her lineage, her bloodline. *Magic and miracles run through my veins.* She silently chanted and prayed. Hope and her boyfriend had been wrenched apart as soon as they were captured. Were these men drug smugglers, human traffickers or poachers? Hope supposed it didn't matter in terms of her safety or survival.

"I am not lying to you. Chief Gor was a very powerful man. I carry his blood and his power." She tried to shrug her shoulders to indicate her lack of concern but the binding constrained movement. "Google him. You will see."

"It doesn't matter who the fuck you are or think you are!" he roared, punching Hope in the stomach. Hope muffled a scream and a groan, swallowing acid bile. Behind the filthy blindfold, she squeezed her eyes tight to stop hot, angry tears from escaping.

"What fucking matters is that you know who we are. Yeah, we proudly supply Americans and others in the West who love our drugs. Supply and demand. We supply. They demand. It works very well, sister. But I believe I can try a new profession. How much would your country pay me to get your black ass back? Now what the fuck were you and that pasty-faced man doing near our camp?"

Hope's thoughts were running fast. Until now, she'd had no idea what these men were up to. "As I told you multiple times, Michael and I are here to help those who do not receive proper food, medicines—" A sharp slap across her face silenced her. Hope felt warm blood trickle down from her nose. She laughed.

"This is wonderful! This blood along with my monthly bleed will strengthen my powers. I have to warn you, though. When my powers are peaking, I speak in tongues." Hope heard feet edging away, the creaking open of a door. She still heard breathing, though, and a rustling. Some of the men had remained. A click. She was certain it was the click of a gun, readying to shoot. Her tongue felt swollen. How many hours had it been since she had drunk water? She felt her organs shrivel. Crazy. She needed to act crazy.

Hope began to speak, using small bits of language she had picked up. German, from the time she spent in Hamburg participating in an international studies exchange program. German words collided with bits of mangled Yiddish she was taught on a few drunken nights in Venice. Half-phrases of Hindi and Rajasthani followed, learned during a young women's international summit on reproductive rights outside of Jaipur. Arabic came from her nights in the Moroccan Sahara, camping with Michael and Berber friends who laughed at their attempts to speak the language. She threw in *whack* from New York slang, and *ristra* from New Mexico, the local word for a string of red chile pods. Rolling her head back and forth, she spoke this strange linguistic fusion in a cave-deep tone. She ended with a growl and the highest pitched scream she could manage. Just before Hope passed out, she heard the door slam and feet retreat into silence.

Small fingers tugged at her blindfold, and larger ones loosened the ropes that bound her. The sound of new voices and lighter footsteps joined the touch of small hands helping to free Hope. She blinked and quickly shut her eyes against the sunlight streaming through the open door of the shack. When she felt ready, she opened them cautiously and saw a small child holding her filthy blindfold. A man, perhaps the child's father, was speaking gently in words she could not understand. The room was filling up with more people—men, women and children. Hope was faintly aware of a skinny dog licking her hand. She looked for Michael, but all the faces were moonless midnight black.

It was days later that she learned her beloved Michael had been killed shortly after they were separated. The aid agency bundled her up and sent her back stateside.

"Hold on!" Susan leaped out of her chair and was pointing at the frozen screen, which showed a pixelated image of a stretcher being carefully lifted onto a transport plane.

"Is she one of us? She has been to all the places we lived!"

Stunned looks stared back at Susan.

"I have no clue what any of this means, but I can't wait to meet her," Sunita said quietly.

"We will find out the meaning of this, if there is a meaning, at the appropriate juncture," Reinhardt said firmly. "Now, shall we continue with Hope's story?"

The screen unfroze and a laughing younger Hope filled the screen. She was throwing a football and yelling to the unseen person to catch it this time.

Hope lived her name. She loved her family. And though they had their share of heartbreak, she maintained a happy heart. Her unaffected confidence inspired others to take risks. A young mother struggling against depression went back to school; a neighborhood drug addict went into treatment; a young, idealistic man went into politics. When she was eight years old she started P.O.P., the Power of Possibilities, initially with a squad of three girls she enlisted. Each time they saw a child who was struggling with a problem and was without visible support, they enlisted the child into their squad, gave them a big talk, and found an adult who could help solve the problem. A picture of a gap-toothed, wild-haired Hope holding a school civics award for her first movement hung in her father's study. Her parents alternated between pride and alarm at their only child's lack of fear and utter guilelessness.

One afternoon, when Hope had yet to cross the threshold into her teens, a police cruiser pulled up to their home with a stony-faced Hope in the back seat. A long talk about assumptions followed, after it was learned Hope had assumed someone was being bullied because of a speech impediment. This turned out to be untrue, but stories of her temper followed her throughout her teens. Hope carried on, unfazed, but agreed with her parents and cultivated composure.

Secretly she thought, if there was a divine Creator, when he or she was creating humans they would have done well to stick to black. No other skin color in the world was more beautiful to Hope than black. She could not imagine being attracted to anyone who was not black. Until she met Michael.

They fell fast. Hope and Michael shared many of the same ideals and hopes for the world. They felt a bone-deep commitment to helping others. Hope loved Michael's humor, and occasionally they shared in pranking friends. When the opportunity came up to travel together on an aid mission, they didn't need to discuss it.

Gabriel's voice cut in. "We have been watching Hope for some time. We have marveled at her resilience. Grit, I believe is the word. Other qualities as well, such as her acceptance of her own neuroses. Naturally, she works on them but is unafraid and unashamed to recognize and work with them. Yes, we have given her support on various projects, but Hope simply moves forward on her own heart energy. She has helped far more people than she realizes."

Gabriel told them that after the death of her beloved Michael and her own convalescence at home, Hope began to rally. She knew that returning to her activism would be honoring Michael. And, without any shadowy doubts, she knew he would want her to continue.

And then people stopped listening to her. Throughout her life, Hope naturally attracted others who were passionate about helping others, but now they seemed to be disappearing into sadness: trading activism for cynicism and dead-end, negative comments. People who she used to be able to count on to share her courage were gone. Others appeared to collapse within themselves.

Hope felt alone but, for a time, mustered the energy to remain active on the front lines of social injustice. One night, after a long day with dim prospects for any positive outcome to a project she was working on, a strange feeling came over her. She sat with it. Never had she experienced this feeling before. Depression. Hopelessness. Defeat. Lack of confidence. Root-deep rage—all foreign emotions for her.

For days, Hope tried to shake the feelings. She maintained her meditation, did yoga and took long walks. Nothing helped. In the past, she would watch some news item detailing some tragedy, and her first feeling would be of what could be done. Now she felt hopeless. Her world began to narrow.

In a last-ditch effort to revive herself, Hope flew to Paris. She loved the art, the music, the way Parisians ate bread, drank wine and lived now. Hope needed vibrancy. She knew her impressions of Paris were those of a classic American tourist, but she needed to be someplace she did not have to fix or heal. Outside the Musée D'Orsay, she came to a full stop. The line-up was not as long as in the past, and people were not engaging with each other but simply looking at their phones, colors leached from their faces.

But in the end it was Monet.

Hope loved the impressionists, and this was one of her favorite rooms in the museum. But when she walked in, she halted, appalled. People were walking past the Monets. Without pause except to hold a phone aloft and snap a photo. Walking past the Monets, without wonder.

"Hope left Paris and returned home," Gabriel said. "This is where she is today. My dear ones, Hope is hopeless. We need her back. Without her, the portal will close."

Chapter 45: Finding Courage

It was the evening before their last mission. Each of them was aware of what was at stake but could not fully grasp a world without heaven, a dystopian wasteland.

They were seated at the long wooden kitchen table, and Reinhardt had chosen the music again. For this auspicious occasion, Dvorak's Symphony No. 9, *From the New World*, was playing its wistful, hopeful notes. They tried to eat, but mostly they just pushed food around their plates.

"I am still struggling with the magnitude of our task," Sunita said. "What if we fail?"

"Not an option. We have to show up with our full game on. Gabriel gave us the deep dive. Happy to see no one opted out." Joshua's words tumbled out in a rush.

Reinhardt looked at him and frowned slightly. "Are you okay, Joshua?"

"Sure, sure. Just a bit spammed out. A lot of information, you know."

"Joshua, you are using strange words. Are you frightened?" Alter's face reflected genuine concern.

"This *is* rather epic!" Emily leaned toward Joshua.

"Rather? It is epic. Good heavens, this is our Crucible!" Susan said.

"I feel it is important for us not to view this as our Crucible," Reinhardt countered. "It is indeed a test, but to keep our focus, it is essential we view this as an offering to the world."

"Ah, this is more than an offering. This is a great mission from Allah, and I am honored to be his servant."

"Okay, okay no need to rant and rave. I think we are on the same thread. Plan is to meet at the Wall of the Seven Heavens in the morning. Right? To receive some additional bullshit inspiration or whatnot. And then, *boom!* We go to meat space!"

"Why are you talking like this?" Emily's clear blue eyes looked bewildered.

"Just getting into my natural groove."

Sunita set down her fork and looked around the table. "Do any of you believe that we are each born with a certain quota of courage? That, at some point, we use up our quota and strive to live a life free of risk?"

"Guess we never got the chance to find out, did we? Susan, what do you think?" Joshua said, a knee bouncing with nerves.

Susan ignored him. "Shall we raise a toast?"

"Splendid idea!" Reinhardt raised his glass. He had not noticed the symbol on it before. He smiled to himself, recognizing Lungta, a mythical Tibetan creature from pre-Buddhist times. Lungta represented the combined speed of the wind and the strength of the horse to carry prayers from earth to the heavens.

"In India toasts are not done," Sunita said, "but I have no problem observing."

"It isn't appropriate for Muslims to toast. I think that should be obvious. But," he added, "same as Sunita, I have no problem if the rest of you feel inclined to indulge in—"

"Okay, we get your message." Joshua cut Khalid off. "For Chrissake—oh, sorry, Emily—if we can't even agree on bloody toasts, how the hell are we going to succeed in this mission?"

Alter stood up, raised his glass and, in a voice louder than any of them had heard from him, said, "*Mazel tov!*"

"Ki ki so so ashe lha gyal lo tak seng khyung druk di yar kye," shouted Reinhardt.

Emily stood up. "Bless us and keep us safe, oh Lord. And cheers!"

"Odin, far-wanderer, grant me wisdom. Friend Thor, grant me your strength. And both be with me. Or us. All of us." Susan stood with her arms stretched out, holding her wine glass.

"Ah, Susan, I knew we could count on you!" Joshua laughed.

Susan looked puzzled as the rest also laughed. For the moment, it eased their nervous tension.

Morning. The prism glowed a fiery red for courage. Sunita led the group to the Wall of the Seven Heavens, which was suffused in golds, purples, blues, yellows and red. The colors radiated throughout the Great Unnamed Room. All of them were silent, thinking their own thoughts, but all shared two repeating thoughts.

They might fail.

One or all of them might not return.

Chapter 46: Finding Hope

They were scattered. Tossed. A murmuration of shadows, human and beast, rose up to meet them as they descended through cloud mountains and thin, yellow sunlight. In a one-breath moment, Reinhardt heard an echo of the chorus of chants in large meditation centers. They lost sight and sense of each other, each utterly alone in the towering swirls and spirals of shadows. The murmuring drowned out thought. When would it end? Would it end?

Phrases began to emerge. At first, the murmurs were telling stories. Then came the messages.

You let death kill you.

You can't be a good Muslim and gay.

Information is not wisdom.

You could have done more to help the earth.

Studying spiritual paths doesn't make you spiritual.

There is nothing you can do.

All is lost.

One moment they were in a world of murmuring shadows, and the next they were standing on a small, ordinary street in an equally ordinary American town. Emily stomped her feet a few times on the sidewalk.

"Were those Interlopers?" she said, rubbing her hands on her arms as if to dispel the cold. "I've heard they show up, not so much to block you but to show you how you're blocking yourself. They show you your greatest weakness or insecurities. It's like some kind of initiation."

"Yeah, well, if it was them, they did a fucking good job," Joshua said. "That was disturbing shit. But no time to have a cozy chat. We gotta get to Hope. Stat." He began to stride down the quiet, tree-lined street.

"Wait!" Sunita looked around, worried. "Where is Alter?"

Joshua called Alter's name again and again. Susan scanned the skies. Emily and Khalid paired up to look in and around houses, sheds and the school. Sunita and Reinhardt checked corner stores and the library. When they entered the library, they were so sure Alter would be there that they shared a laugh, imagining everyone's relieved surprise when they brought him back. But there was no sign of him.

Emily and Khalid quickly agreed on how they would search. They first checked the house, then the garage or shed, and finally did a sweep of any shrubs, trees or ponds in the yard. Driven by fear and anxiety, they moved fast. When they had scoured the whole block, they found themselves in front of the house they had first arrived at. They slid down to the sidewalk, defeated. Emily pulled a daisy from the grassy boulevard and began to pluck its petals.

"In the words of our fearless project manager, what the fuck are you doing?" Khalid asked.

Emily dropped the balding daisy and brushed her hands. "Just a childish game. What are we going to do, Khalid? How can we go on without Alter?"

Khalid was silent for a moment. "There are more streets. Time is against us, but we have to continue. Come on." He stood and reached for Emily's hand.

"Wait a minute. We didn't check this house." The paint on the house they'd arrived at was flaking, and the yard was weedy, but there were signs the place had been built with care and once had been loved.

Emily and Khalid ran through the house calling Alter's name. The young man who lived there was engrossed in his iPad but glanced up and gaped when cupboard and closet doors started flapping open. He tossed it aside and ran after them, closing doors and yelling "What the hell is going on?" His voice rose with panic and bewilderment.

Emily and Khalid sprinted to the back yard and stopped.

Alter sat on a swing, his long coat dragging on a well-worn patch of dirt. On the swing beside him, a small boy pumped his chubby legs trying to start the swing. An older girl listlessly kicked a ball around a patch of scrubby grass behind them.

Swirling around Alter was a shadow that churned with the colors of ashes.

Emily and Khalid looked at each other. Wordlessly, they agreed to rein in their excitement and approach calmly.

"Hi, Alter. We're happy to see you. Is there anything we can do?"

Emily thought she'd never seen anyone look so forlorn and hopeless in her life. *Or afterlife,* she noted wryly.

The shadow around Alter darkened and expanded. Emily paled. "What can we do?"

"Emily, I think I hear the others," Khalid said. "I'll tell them where we are and bring them back here. To be honest, I'm clueless."

Emily turned her attention to the children. She was taken aback by how dispirited they were. The little boy had been defeated by the swing and sat motionless on the plastic yellow seat; the girl had abandoned the ball and was scuffing her toe in the dirt. Emily moved closer to Alter, but before she could act, Joshua, Sunita, Reinhardt and Susan arrived. They stopped short when they saw Alter.

Joshua raked his hand through his hair. "Damn! Double damn! Oh, cripes, I sound like you, Emily. Ideas? Now!"

Emily was fading. Tendrils of the shadows enveloping Alter had crept over and were writhing around her feet. Sunita grabbed her hand and pulled her to safety. Although still wobbly, Emily became more solid.

"Remember hearing a shadow say 'You let death kill you'?" she said in a shaking voice. "I believe that was meant for me as well as for Alter. You know how we turned away from some people." Her voice trailed. Sunita squeezed her arm. "I have some ideas why I wasn't totally overtaken, but Alter …" Still weak, she waved a trembling hand.

The children, now wandering through the group, became more animated. Khalid sent them comical images. For a moment, a light flickered in their eyes and smiles twitched. Then a man in the house yelled for them to come inside, and they scuffle-walked up the paint-chipped steps, taking care not to hold the flaked railing in case of splinters.

Alter was rapidly fading in the roiling black shadow-cloud. His ancient eyes, unblinking and frightened, stared back at them.

Susan stood frozen, hand over her mouth. Reinhardt and Khalid wore grim expressions, arms hanging useless but fists clenched. Joshua turned his back and joined Sunita and Emily at the far end of the scrabbly yard, unable to watch the gaunt old man who now shivered violently, wrapped in the thickening shroud.

Sunita, eyes full of sorrow and fear, reached out to comfort Joshua. Emily sat on the patchy grass, knees drawn up. She stared straight ahead, vibrating. Joshua embraced Sunita and whispered hoarsely, "I'm gutted."

Emily spoke, but Sunita and Joshua couldn't make out her words, so they moved closer. The three of them sat together under the dim light of an early evening sky as birds darted hurriedly toward home.

Dazed, Emily looked up at the birds and said in a hollow voice, "I wish we were them. Not aware of this threat. Not seeing someone you love tortured and suffering. Returning home to a nest that smells of summer."

It no longer mattered. It didn't matter if he made a fool of himself. It didn't matter if he was rejected. Joshua leaned in and kissed Emily on the cheek, their forms mingling, creating red and green lights that danced above their heads.

Then Joshua got to his feet. "Enough of this bullshit." With one step, he launched himself through the thick, gray mass of shadow. An instant later, Emily leaped through with Sunita close behind her. The moving shadow was now coal black.

"You're not doing this without me!" Susan yelled. Reinhardt and Khalid rushed in, an orange and purple tip of Susan's dress trailing behind.

The wind held its breath. Silence. The day was gone and a waxing quarter moon drifted across the night sky. Inside the house, the girl gazed with unfocused eyes out a window overlooking the back yard, tuning out the blare of the TV. She tapped a pencil on the sketchbook that lay on her lap. Chewing her lip, she began to draw a massive dark cloud with streaks of light flaring out from its ragged edges. She put down her pencil and stared out the window. A faint silhouette of blue-purple light floated out of the yard. The girl sat back, feeling cocooned and isolated by the night.

Joshua dashed through the front gate and stood on the sidewalk looking frantically for signs of anyone. Cupping his hands around his mouth he called the other six by name. One by one the names echoed back. Nothing. Silence. Utter alienation.

No human could hear his anguished scream. His pain of aloneness reverberated to a multitude of galaxies, to stars newly born and to stars about to die. He didn't feel the rending.

"I blame myself." Alter's raspy words turned into a cough. A corner of his long coat picked up an empty coffee cup as they headed down the littered sidewalk, and a passerby squinted and rubbed his eyes to see the empty cup moving along by itself. "If I had not listened so closely to what the shadow was saying …"

Sunita had taken Alter's arm as they walked. He was still fragile; periodically he faded to resemble a shadow. "Alter, it really could have been any one of us. Those Interlopers show up to reflect our deepest wound or regret. I don't think any of us could know how dangerous they are."

"That's exactly what happened," Susan blustered. "If we'd known, we'd have been better prepared and none of this would—"

Reinhardt interjected, "There's no point looking back. It is of the utmost important for us to raise our *lungta*, our unconditional confidence, and find Hope."

Emily walked ahead of the rest in shocked silence. How could they be so unmoved? She paid no attention to the pretty canopied street with its neat houses and unnaturally green lawns. Then Reinhardt was beside her, matching her steps.

"Have you noticed there are no people outside?" He had joined her in hopes of offering her comfort and encouragement.

Emily didn't look at the big German. "I suppose you're about to launch into an observation of people closing off from each other and turning inward." Her voice was flatter than a prairie landscape.

Susan, who had been directly behind them, leaped in front and stopped, her face stormy.

"Now listen here, Missy. We all miss the stupid bastard but we have to keep going. We have big things to do and you will just have to dig deep and find some grit. Step up, Emily!" Her eyes were bulging and unblinking.

Emily gasped, but when she spoke, her voice was steady. "Back off, Susan. What gives you the fucking right to tell me to dig deep? You want to see grit? I'll show you grit." She took a step forward and Susan rocked back.

"I only meant—"

"Yeah, well." Emily's head was high as she brushed past Susan. "Hope better be fucking worth it."

Sunita released Alter's arm and pulled Reinhardt aside. "I would like to have a chat with Khalid. Please keep Alter safe." Reinhardt nodded and gently took the old man's trembling arm.

"Do you think Joshua landed in this No-Spirit-Land?" Khalid spoke with soft caution.

Sunita slowed her walk to create more distance between them and Emily. "Who knows!" She sighed. "But I agree with Reinhardt. We have to keep our focus on Hope."

Khalid sidestepped a big crack in the sidewalk and then laughed at himself for doing so. "You know, I thought this No-Spirit-Land was a lot of tosh but ... And now Emily. Hope she isn't off her trolley."

"Emily is fine," Sunita said crisply but added more gently, "Khalid, we can't worry if Emily is fine or off her trolley, as you say. We need to feel confident in each other to do our best. I believe this No-Spirit-Land is real, and so we have to remain vigilant."

A gray mass loomed up in front of them, undulating and churning, cutting them off from the others who were by now far ahead. Khalid reached for Sunita's hand; their linked energy generated a small sky-blue orb of light. Sunita looked directly at the mass, her eyes shining.

"*The earth is enjoyed by heroes. I have no fear.* Say it with me, Khalid." Sunita's voice was low and intense.

"Are we enough, Sunita?" Khalid sounded far away.

"Say it!" Sunita stepped toward the dark mass.

They chanted, *"The earth is enjoyed by heroes. I have no fear."*

"Louder!" Sunita shouted as she advanced toward the mass that was towering above them.

The mass enveloped them, roaring out, at supersonic levels of sound, taunts of past wounds and insecurities. The words lashed at them, piercing their hearts, tearing away their carefully crafted layers of courage. Khalid was curled up on the sidewalk but kept chanting. Sunita swayed but remained standing. The deep roaring sound of a volcanic eruption ended thoughts and defenses.

And then there were four.

Susan was calm, serene. She sat on the uneven edge of the sidewalk, legs splayed in front, eyes closed, smiling slightly. Emily, who was pacing in front of her, wanted to smack her.

"You were the closest to Sunita and Khalid. How did you not notice anything!" Emily was livid. Susan continued to sit in her state of near bliss.

Reinhardt resolutely maintained full focus, trying to determine if they were anywhere near Hope. He broke focus briefly to make sure Alter was still close by. A clanging bell rang, liberating a primary school's small occupants for recess.

Susan spoke with her eyes closed. "Clearly *they*, these Interlopers or whoever they may be, are trying to divide us. Weaken us, so we don't succeed on our sacred mission of restoring Hope to the world."

Reinhardt overheard and came over to them, guiding Alter with him. "Susan may be right, Emily. We have to remain united. Let's find Hope."

"I may not have the power to do this for myself, but I will do it for each of you and for Josh, Sunita and Khalid. And please, please, everyone be careful and stick together." Emily lightly touched the others in turn as if to reassure herself they were really there. "This way. I'm sure Hope is in this direction. I felt a twinge earlier."

Sidewalks and streets were busier in this part of town. A middle-aged woman walked through them, ripping off the crucifix she was wearing and tossing it to the ground. The pedestrian behind her simply walked on the necklace and past a man who was weeping. Another woman crashed into a baby stroller, shrugged and kept walking, ignoring the yells of the baby's mother.

"This is grim. Let's hurry on." Emily's voice was tinged with grief.

"Look at that," Susan pointed at a giant screen that flashed non-stop news.

Breaking News, it flashed. *Major religious leaders all over the world are threatening to step down from their positions. Spiritual leaders have been quoted as saying their teachings are being ignored or perverted to such an extent that their positions may no longer be tenable. Speaking from the Vatican, Pope Mark II said—*

"Holy Heavens! Come on!" Emily ran ahead, darting down a side street. Alter, already close behind, was the first to catch up with her. They rushed into a grocery store whose shelves were stacked with prepared meals, snacks, and convenience foods. The store's former life as a co-operative that focused on organic and vegan food was evident only in a tired display of bruised fruits and wrinkled vegetables.

"There she is!" Susan yelled so loudly some customers thought they'd heard a voice. Necks snapped around. Phones were whipped out and checked.

Alter went quiet. He was looking at the vast quantities of food.

Hope strolled a far aisle, earbuds firmly embedded in her ears. She scrolled her phone as she picked up item after item, barely looking at what she was dropping into her cart. Her hair was tossed up in a clip at the top of her head. She reached around and scratched the back of her neck.

"You are too close!" Emily scolded Susan. All four of them were clustered around Hope, with Susan flush against her. Susan stepped back a pace.

Hope pulled out her earbuds as she approached a small old woman who was on tiptoes, reaching for a large bottle of brandy on a high shelf.

"Hey, Mrs. P. Can I give you a hand with that?"

The old woman smiled at Hope over the shoulder of her nubby gray cardigan and lowered her arm.

"That would be lovely, dear. Thank you."

They chatted, clearly familiar with each other. Hope grabbed down the bottle and put it in the old woman's basket. They chatted a moment longer and then Hope waved goodbye, securing her earbuds once again.

"Who is that woman? She feels like someone I should know or remember knowing." Emily looked at Susan and Reinhardt.

"I know what you mean, Emily, but I don't recall her either." Susan inspected the bottle of brandy. "Not a bad choice."

"Let's keep our attention on Hope. We will follow her back to her place and go from there," Reinhardt said decisively.

Each of them gave the old woman one more glance as they followed Hope to the check-out. She looked back at them and chuckled as they passed.

"Did she see us?" Emily clutched Reinhardt's sleeve.

"I doubt it. She was likely laughing at something Hope said," Reinhardt replied, his gaze on Hope as she walked to her car. As she pulled out of the parking space, she ran over a traffic cone, glanced at it and sped off.

"It's on! Let's go!" Emily said. "I wish the rest were here. We really, really need their talents and abilities." She twisted her hands together.

Alter took her hands in his gnarled ones. "My dear, we have to trust God is with us."

The white walls of the apartment were stark and unadorned. Hope quickly put food items away in the galley kitchen, dropped a tea bag in a mug, sat at the table by the window and picked up her iPad. When the kettle whistled, she got up, hitched up her baggy yoga pants and poured water into the mug.

"What do we do now?" Emily whispered.

"For starters, you can welcome us back." Khalid grinned as he and Sunita emerged from another room.

Emily leaped at them, laughing. Reinhardt, Alter and Susan crowded around, their conjoined energy creating a halo of light that bounced around the room. A skinny cat no one had noticed before began to chase the halo.

Emily peered behind Khalid and Sunita, praying Joshua was with them. In the deepest place in her heart, she hoped.

Hope carried her mug of tea to the small living room and sat on a leopard-print chaise longue. She set her tea down and rubbed her forehead. As the halo of light cast an incandescent glow, the room's light constantly moved and changed.

"What ...? Where ...? How ...?" Emily sputtered.

Sunita and Khalid beamed at each other. "We have a story to share with you, but later!" Sunita moved to sit beside Hope, who was watching her cat chasing after air.

"What's up, Zola?" The cat stopped in mid-pounce to turn to her mistress but scampered away again after the orb of light. Hope sat back and closed her eyes. Sunita sat nearer.

"Both of you add exquisite color to this rather drab apartment," Susan said, nodding at Sunita's bright sari and the vivid blue of Khalid's shirt and shemagh.

Reinhardt clapped his big hands together. The luminosity from the halo dimmed and its oscillation ceased as the group moved away from each other. The cat sat down and licked her paws.

Reinhardt stood alert. "I strongly suggest we begin and—"

Emily put a hand on his arm. "Pause and pray? Or take a moment and remember …?" She couldn't finish.

"Joshua," Susan offered helpfully. Emily, not trusting her voice, nodded.

They came back together, forming a circle. Khalid, Alter and Emily bowed their heads. Reinhardt looked straight ahead. Susan threw her head back and mumbled a chant. Remembering what Joshua would say about Susan chanting, Emily snorted. She wiped her eyes.

Hope jumped and looked their way.

"Seems someone is a clairaudient," Susan remarked. She looked at the others and added, "That means she can hear those who have passed over. Made transition. Passed through the veil. Departed—"

Khalid rolled his eyes. "Died, Susan! We died!" He caught Emily's eye and winked. She laughed in spite of herself. "Bloody hell," he muttered.

Hope uncurled her body and walked over to the group. She stepped up to each one and, without knowing quite what she was doing, placed her hands over their faces. Each of them stood still and silent.

She whispered, "Michael, is it you? Or am I crazy-hearing?"

Quietly, Sunita said, "We'd better make ourselves seen. Let's visualize ourselves as solid."

Hope staggered back. In front of her stood a pretty young woman in a sari, another young woman in a flowered dress, an old Jewish man in a trailing black coat, an Arabic young man in a shemagh, a big, older man with an eye patch, and a wild-haired older woman in a flowy dress of riotous colors.

Sunita spoke gently. "I am so excited to meet you. You are such an impressive young woman."

Hope shrank back and scrabbled on the floor for her iPad. "What the hell is this?" She began to punch in nine-one-one.

Khalid reached for the iPad, sending it floating away to another room. "No need to call anyone. We're just here to have a chinwag."

"A chin what? Never mind, never mind." She stood in the middle of the circle they had formed and was turning round and round. "Who are you? What the hell is going on?"

"I know we are a shock to you, especially after all you have endured." Susan's voice was soft and feathery.

Hope narrowed her eyes. "Are you that fairy lady?"

Susan beamed and cast her eyes down modestly. "Yes, most people recognize me by that moniker."

"Wait just a minute! How do you know, any of you, what I've been through?" Hope took a big breath and walked through them to stand outside the circle. She wrapped her arms around herself and glared. Her breathing was rapid. From the other room, a cell phone beeped.

Alter stepped forward. "My dear, it is little wonder you are *fermisht*." The others looked at him quizzically. "Shooked up," he said, searching their faces to see if he got the word right.

Emily nodded. "Hope, this is all going to sound crazy, but we are spirits. Ghosts, if you like. Not long ago, we were just like you. Walking, talking, loving, and at times suffering. And then we died. And somehow found ourselves in a place where …" She cast about for help.

"Sounds crazy?! It *is* crazy." Hope's brown eyes were flashing. "Spirits or ghosts showing up out of nowhere and paying me a visit. What the hell! How long have you been here? Are you ghost stalkers or—?" She swung around as Khalid guffawed, but when she saw the warmth in his eyes, her expression softened. She took a deep breath. "Okay, so if I just relax with this and go along, will you get the hell out of here?"

Reinhardt clapped his hands once. "We will do a quick introduction and then share with you why we are here."

Hope's eyes grew wider with each introduction. "And one of you is missing?"

"Yes, that's right. Our project manager, Joshua, has vanished. For the time being," Reinhardt added quickly, looking at Emily.

"You are the strangest group I have ever encountered." Hope began to laugh. Tears rolled down her cheeks. The group stared as she laughed so hard she began to choke. She grabbed her mug of tea and drank it down, then wiped her streaming eyes and sat on the chaise longue, taking long breaths to settle herself.

"Okay, so here we are. I am spending an afternoon playing host to a crazy, improbable group of dead people." Hope's gaze was intense and unflinching. "Why are you here?"

"Hope, we need you. The world needs you," Emily began.

Hope shot to her feet. "Don't you dare bother me! Go! Leave! Get out now!" Raw fury infused every word. "How dare you! How dare each of you! Damn you to hell! After all I have given, after all I have lost, and you say the world needs me. I say, fuck the world!" Hope's eyes were wide and wild.

Sunita sat on the chaise longue and patted the seat beside her. In a gentle, loving voice she said, "I can't imagine how you feel."

Hope roared, "Don't bother with your bullshit sympathy!"

Susan perked up a vase of nearly dead flowers, blowing on them to send their scent around the room. Emily smiled her understanding at Susan, then focused on Hope's heart, wincing when she felt the pain. Reinhardt concentrated on taking in her pain and giving her comfort. Khalid moved her to recall one of her and Michael's many escapades.

Hope sank onto the chaise longue and allowed Sunita to sit closer.

"Remember, you stand in front of ancestors who were brave and noble," Alter said.

Emily noticed a change of light through the window. "I don't know the signs of the portal closing but ..."

Khalid and the others joined her at the window. "Blimey. This doesn't look good."

The sky hung lower and the colors of the trees, grass and flowers had dimmed.

Susan hurried back to Hope. "Here's the situation, Hope. There's a portal between this world and the heavens. This portal allows prayers, miracles, healing, angels and other divine beings to travel back and forth. People have turned away from their hearts, and their hope has drained." Hope opened her mouth to speak, but Susan rushed on. "There's more, but I'll cut to the chase. If this portal closes, all contact between heaven and earth will cease. You, Hope, have been keeping this portal open. But now that you've closed off your heart and lost hope, the portal will close. You radiated hope to many people, and those you touched have gone on to touch others. In the same way anxiety or anger is contagious, so are love and hope. Hope, we need you back!" Susan dropped into a chair, exhausted by her efforts.

"I believe it is becoming increasingly difficult for us to remain here. The vibrations are becoming too dense." Reinhardt gestured toward the window, where the mid-afternoon light was growing dimmer.

Hope sat stunned. "Really, I can't imagine that I or any one person would have that kind of power." For a moment, she said nothing; then she seemed to make a decision. She walked over to Alter, who stood beside Emily. "Thank you, sir, for reminding me of my blood."

She turned to Khalid. "Were you the one who sent me the story of Michael and me trespassing in the Italian countryside and being chased by a wild boar?"

Khalid smiled. "Yes. If I weren't dead I'd use it in one of my routines."

"I *thought* you were Kaboom! I loved you! Okay, you crazy dead people, what's the plan? I can't stand myself these days. What can I do to help?"

In another time, a time when people's hearts and ears were more open, their whoops would have been heard many miles away. As it was, people in the next street paused, distracted, before returning to their phones.

The six travelers gathered around Hope and instructed her to open her heart wide. The love each of them had felt as they were dying returned now. Love too big for a human heart to contain poured out of each of them. Hope stood and received all this love. She felt her body would fracture into a million shards. The heavens opened up, and she felt herself flying through galaxies, free and weightless. Fearlessness and fierce hope charged through her body.

When Hope came to, they were gone. She was ready.

"Did all of you remember to leave your gifts with Hope?" Sunita asked.

They were cautiously optimistic the portal would remain open, at least for now, although they agreed the opening would likely be narrow. Alter noted that if this were indeed true, people might have to put more heart into their prayers. "And may I suggest that humility and trust would help these people as well," he added, pointing his gnarled finger to the heavens.

"My gift of beauty and art will brighten her heart," Susan said. "And if, as we surmise, Hope is a conduit who is especially capable of influencing others, my gifts will be enjoyed by many."

"I gave her my humor," Khalid added. "I think it's safe to say we all remembered, Sunita." He caught up to Emily, who was walking ahead of the others.

"He was such an asshole," Emily said softly. Her gaze followed a flock of birds ascending higher, returning home on a sepia sunset.

Khalid chuckled. "Agreed. And what a heathen!"

Emily smiled and linked her arm through Khalid's. "I'm not going back."

Khalid broke away. "What are you talking about? You have to come with us! Hey!" he shouted to the others. "We have a problem, a big problem, here!"

As the exchange between Khalid and Emily grew more heated, Reinhardt stepped between them to diffuse the tension. Emily's face was like thunder as she raged about loyalty and friendship. Reinhardt gave her space to vent and then spoke, standing on the cracked pavement with his shoulders back, offering his warrior-heart.

"Emily, your pain is exquisite." He spoke quietly. "It shows another hue in the riotous colors of love. Joshua is not here. If he is to be found, he will not be found here. Our realm offers you the opportunity to move on, to go to your heaven. If you stay here, you risk becoming stuck, wandering like a hungry ghost."

Emily swayed and then righted herself. She was silent for several seconds. "Okay," she said at last.

They passed a colorful wooden house with a veranda at the edge of a field. An old woman sat on an Adirondack chair singing off-key. A small dog ran up the steps, whining.

"The dog senses us. Hey, is that the woman we saw speaking to Hope in the grocery store? The one buying brandy?" Sunita moved closer to get a better look.

"Yes, that's her, all right. I wonder how they know each other?" Khalid said. He listened to the singing. "Can't be from a choir group."

"Time to return. Let's leave from that field. It feels right." Sunita led the way, her sari shimmering over the freshly cut hay.

Chapter 47: The Return

The silence was complete. Suspended in nothingness. Gabriel stood in front of the Wall of the Seven Heavens. Dressed in a long, gleaming white tunic and wide-legged pants, he walked with deliberate slowness, framing what he would say to his dear ones. The Ugly Brown Birds were rehearsing a new song, one that fused euphoria and sorrow. It was a delicate business; Gabriel thought this song might be their most challenging composition yet.

Soon. Soon they would return. He sighed. The trees in the Great Green Sanctuary swayed. The prism dispersed amber, suffusing the room in a warm glow. The vibrations shifted.

They were back.

He smiled.

Gabriel opened his arms wide as though once more offering a benediction to the subdued group. "Well, well done, my dear ones! This monumental feat is to be celebrated, even though you are also grieving."

Emily looked at him with brimming eyes. She was shepherded by Sunita and Reinhardt, and the rest stayed close to her. Emily's sorrow was so raw and open, Gabriel was briefly overwhelmed and turned his back.

"I'm going to my room," Emily said tonelessly and walked over the bridge and up the everlasting stairway. The rest followed, their steps slow.

"I told you, I'm not hungry." It was the next morning, and Emily had come to a halt on the bottom step of the stairway. As Sunita took her by the shoulder and pointed her toward the kitchen, Emily looked longingly back up the stairs. "Really, I'm not hungry. I'm just tired."

"You have to eat something," Sunita urged.

"Or what? It's not like I'll starve to death if I don't."

Sunita laughed. "True. But your spirit may starve without the nourishment of your friends' company. And we are all your friends, dear Emily. Look, there's Alter talking to Reinhardt. And Susan and Khalid are just coming. Please."

As the six approached the entrance to the kitchen, they stopped in confusion. Parachute Club's "Rise Up" was thumping, and cutlery was clinking on glassware in time with the music. Who could have arrived before them? Emily took a step back, but Sunita nudged her into the kitchen. The others were right on their heels.

"Great job, guys. Great job. Susan, did you eat my bacon?" Joshua was tilted back in his chair, feet up, with an upturned glass in his lap and two spoons held mid-air. He swung his feet down and set the glass and cutlery back on the table. The music faded to its conclusion. "I heard you were a tad upset that I pulled a Houdini." His eyes were on Emily.

Emily rushed him and knocked him to the stone floor. Laughing, they scrambled to their feet and were met with unaffected embraces by the rest. Sunita broke into a dance, pulling Khalid and Susan with her. The Ugly Brown Birds launched into a lively Indian song. Even Reinhardt and Alter, moving awkwardly, danced. When the song ended, everyone sat down at the table but were too excited to eat.

"My son, what happened? Where did you go?" Alter's face was creased in a smile no one had seen in centuries.

Joshua returned Alter's smile, then sought out Emily again. "So, my recollection may not be crystal clear, but when I found myself alone—." He shook his head at the memory. "Well, it was pretty freaky being left with no one and no idea what the hell to do. I remember a roar—like the world was splitting into a thousand pieces and I was in the middle of it all. Naturally, I felt I was being pulled into the orbit of this bullshit No-Spirit-Land. To be honest, I think I was. Okay, actually I'm sure of it. Some scary shit went down, but there are big chunks I can't remember. But then I felt a, a … swerve. I don't know how else to describe it. I thought I saw Gabriel and those light-being goons but can't be a hundred percent sure. Next thing I know I'm here in this never-ending brain drama." He reached for Emily's hand, but she twisted away from him and stood up with clenched fists on her hips.

"So while we were risking our lives, basically saving the portal between the heavens and the earth, you were dilly dallying. Here!"

"Emily, dear, he may have more to say," Susan offered.

Joshua shifted uncomfortably in his seat. Emily unclenched her fists and sat back down but turned away, hugging her arms.

"I don't remember coming back here," Joshua said. "Gabriel intimated that I was in rough shape. I've spent my time in a sleep that's different from our usual suspension. Wild dreams, visions, fucked-up crazy stuff. Now I guess I'm back to normal. My normal, anyway."

Emily spun around. "Why didn't Gabriel say anything when we got back? We thought you were gone forever! You have no idea—"

"I'm not sure if Gabriel knew I was going to be okay." Joshua picked up his fork, looked at it and set it down again.

Alter struggled to his feet and shuffled over to Joshua. He placed a bony hand on his shoulder. "You are … okay now, my son."

Joshua's throat closed. After a moment, he cleared it and managed, "Thanks, Alter." The old man patted his shoulder and moved slowly back to his seat. Joshua watched him settle, then said to the group, almost as an afterthought, "Are there any other near misses or apocalyptic shadow kidnappings to report?"

Khalid caught Sunita's eye, and she gestured for him to proceed.

"We told the rest we would share our story," he said. "I will try and be brief. Sunita and I were swept up into this massive shadow. Both of us were chanting *The earth is enjoyed by heroes. I have no fear.*"

Sunita broke in, "Yes, that is a quote by Swami Vivekananda." She signaled to Khalid to continue. "Sorry for interrupting."

"No worries. We kept on chanting even as this thing roared and swallowed us up. I could feel us being ripped apart, but somehow we hung onto each other. Sunita, do you want to tell the rest of the story?"

Sunita sat straighter, the look in her eyes recalling both the terror and the fierceness she felt. "I yelled louder than I thought possible to Khalid that we had to keep our focus on where we wanted to be. It's what surfers do."

"Surfing? You?" Joshua asked, surprised.

"And why not me? Do you forget where I come from?" She paused. "A surfer is aware of his board, or in our case our situation. This is where you are. And a surfer has to remain vigilant to surroundings and make adjustments with their body. I kept Khalid close. When this, this *thing* twisted, we twisted. When it howled, we howled." She looked over at Khalid, who nodded encouragement. "As conditions change, no matter what they are, a surfer maintains focus on the shore. We kept our focus on a miniscule opening that kept appearing and disappearing as the thing moved. This dark, terrifying mass twisted suddenly and we found ourselves right at the opening. We leaped through it together."

"Holy—! That's crazy!" Emily's eyes were wide.

Khalid took up the story. "When we landed, we ran, but I don't think that thing knew we were gone. I thought I glimpsed Alter's coat trailing around a corner. And that's when we caught up with the rest of you. Well, not you, Joshua," he added quickly.

Alter looked happy and content. "We have what matters now. We are all together, and heaven and the world can still talk to each other."

The Ugly Brown Birds sang a sweet lament.

Chapter 48: Transition-Transcend

After the final morning meal, which they did not know was their final morning meal, a bell sounded. And then another, and another, and another, until the air rang with the joyous pealing of bells.

"Ode to Joy," Khalid said in delight, smiling broadly to Joshua and the others. They were still sitting at the table in the kitchen. One by one, they pushed their chairs back and filed out, with Alter leading the way to the triumphant notes of the bells.

Gabriel stood by the end of the bridge, clapping his hands without his hands actually touching. Thousands of small silver stars, barely visible, floated down and carpeted the stone floor. Candles in all colors and sizes blazed throughout the Great Unnamed Room. One towered upward so high it nearly reached the top of the domed ceiling. Rows and rows of lights filled the space.

"My dear ones!" Gabriel swept his arms wide. "Ode to Joy is your song, a poem that celebrates the unity and brotherhood of all mankind! Please gather round, my dear ones. You are being celebrated—here in this realm and in others as well!"

Sunita was the first to speak. "Are those lights spirits?"

"Now, where are my manners? These are some of my, ah … friends who were most anxious to meet you and offer a toast to your glorious victory!"

"Some of these friends of yours feel familiar." Sunita's eyes were filled with wonder. "Is it possible some are our ancestors?"

"Yes, a few are ancestors who are here for a brief time. Dear ones, many from various realms wanted to be here to celebrate. When some ancestors expressed a wish to join, we thought it would be fitting. Each of you stands in front of blood or spiritual lineage— or both!—that has imbued you with altruism, respect for others and courage."

They were startled to find each of them holding a fluted glass in their hand. Gabriel stepped forward.

"My dear ones, it has been my divine pleasure to host and guide you. Your mission has achieved what many thought impossible. Through your success, we have averted disaster. Yes, we know the times are still precarious, but heaven and earth are closer now. More art is being created. Reports of kindness and generosity are pouring in. People on earth will love more bravely and, well, so much more …" Gabriel faltered, his eyes unnaturally bright.

He recovered and raised his glass. "Our dear, brave Hope has stepped up to the challenge of inspiring others to action. Prayers are flowing more freely. As we speak, a small but important miracle is occurring in a town on the coast of Chile. Yes, the portal is open!" Gabriel bowed his head and then raised it again to give them his best and brightest smile. "Bravo to our heroes! And, dare I say, heroes of the heavens!"

Reinhardt winced at the word *hero* but joined the others in cheering and raising their glasses toward Gabriel and the rows of lights, briefly wondering if his guru was among them. The lights were now radiating all colors of the spectrum.

"So, my dear ones, this is it! Your day of departure!" Gabriel beamed. "It is my supreme pleasure to inform you that you have choices that others here have not been afforded. Yes, you have the choice of choices! In a moment—I love that word, *moment*—I will outline these choices. And really these choices are rare rewards."

"Departure? After all this time I may see my Hannah?" Alter found a chair and sank into it. He bowed his head and folded his hands tightly on his lap.

"Yes, Alter you are now free to go. But we cannot promise you will—"

Emily raised her hand with such urgency that Gabriel stopped mid-sentence. "Gabriel, could you outline our choices?" she blurted.

Joshua, who had been subdued and silent, shot her an anguished look.

"Yes, yes, you are quite right, Emily. So, my dearest of dear ones, here are your hard-won choices."

Those of the group who were sitting, leaned forward. Those who were standing, stood straighter.

"First option: you leave. My friends here"—he waved his hand toward the lights—"will escort you to the departure area, and you will move on to where you believed you would go when you died. Second option: you may stay here. In this realm. If you choose option two, you will go on more missions." He waved aside the gasps that greeted this news. "But you will enjoy more freedoms," he hurried to add. "Sad to say, I cannot discuss the nature of these freedoms at this juncture, but I can say you will not be disappointed. My friends who have kindly agreed to join us here today—well, truth be known, they were very excited to meet you in, ah, person—will escort you to the same departure lounge area as those who choose option one. That is, to go, to move on, to—"

"Yes, I think we get the picture," Joshua said impatiently. "My choices include being some angel in training or slipping into a blissful void. Got it." Emily's eyes bored into him but he refused to look at her.

Khalid's face registered shock. "This is rather a surprise. But with option two, do you mean we stay here, right here, until Judgment Day?"

Gabriel laughed.

"Heavens to heavens! Thank you, Khalid, for reminding me. If you, or any one of you, choose to remain in our glorious realm, then before every fourth lunar eclipse you will be given the choice to stay or depart. This was a sensitive issue for us to resolve, but we are pleased with this time frame. There is a lunar eclipse today, which is why we chose to do this now. And why the timing is critical. One more very important item to mention. None of you may disclose your decision. Doing so would interfere with frequencies and could spell disaster of epic proportions."

Joshua glanced around. Why did they look … different? He gave his head a small shake, shut his eyes tightly and opened them wide. Yes, the difference was slight, but the others were fading. He brought his own hands up for inspection. The change was minimal but it was there, a washing out of color. Panicking but trying not to, he studied Emily. Again, slightly but definitely paler. His anxiety-charged thoughts raced. Were the others weakened by their exposure to all the freaky shit crisis? In Susan-speak, were their vibrations losing essence? Would they fade to a vapor?

"What time will you use?" Khalid said. "The lunar eclipse occurs at different times in different time zones on earth." Sunita looked at him curiously.

"We will use the precise moment the lunar eclipse occurs at the exact mid-point in the Atlantic Ocean. After this eclipse, we will use an exact mid-point in the Pacific. Alternating oceans seemed the fairest thing to do. Oh, and before I forget." Gabriel nodded to Reinhardt. "This lunar eclipse timing is beneficial for those of you who will be leaving and reborn. It is not widely known, but the spirits of the unborn connect with their human fetuses during a lunar eclipse. Yes, we have things all nice and tidy!"

"You have presented our choices clearly, but our decision is not so clear," Reinhardt observed. "For me, the option to remain here and help sentient beings without the limitations of the physical body is tempting. However, should I be reborn instead, so I can also help and relate to my own karma? It is possible, of course, that staying here is also part of my karma." He was speaking mostly to himself and was surprised to see others nodding in agreement.

"Reinhardt, you are making me dizzy!" Susan said with a shake of her gray head. She turned to the rest of the group. "I believe I have already made up my mind."

The Ugly Brown Birds were singing staccato, their music heightening the tension. Alter lifted his head and contemplated the birds. He stood up and headed toward the library.

"Do not be too long, my dear Alter. Remember we have a precise time allotted for this transition." Gabriel swept out an arm to encompass them all. "And, regardless of your decision, all of you have to go with my friends to the departure area."

Chairs scraped as people got up and drifted away. Khalid walked over to the Wall of the Seven Heavens and stood there, hands in pockets. This was his favorite place in the Great Unnamed Room. Sunita came to stand beside him.

"Have you made a decision, Khalid?"

Khalid's eyes moved upward to a scene depicting the seven ancient planets and stars so plenteous the spaces between them were difficult to see. Skies that had seen Muhammad on his night journey through the Seven Heavens. Inky blue skies, with a nebula bearing witness. He looked closer and saw a brilliant red heart in the center of the nebula. Khalid laughed. During his many visits and contemplations at the wall, he was certain this heart had not been there.

"Sunita," he whispered, "do you think there are fewer stars now than in the ancient world? I don't remember seeing this many stars in the skies we left behind."

"You may be right, Khalid. Perhaps some stars left for other galaxies." Her expression was soft. "Are you scared, Khalid?'

His laugh was small and tight. "Yes, I am. I thought when we were done here, I'd be released from the torment of the angels who sit at my grave." He smiled at her. "And perhaps that is true. But I'm scared I won't be accepted. And ..." He stopped to consider. "I like it here. I feel good about what we were able to do for people, for the world. Still ..." He gestured to Joshua, who was heading to the library and holding his hand out in front of him, frowning at it. "Who knew

I would be friends with an atheist? Not all the time, maybe, but we have a kind of bond. He can be such a prat!"

"I feel all of us have a bond, a strange one, but ..." Sunita thought about Khalid's words. "Yes, I will be sad to say goodbye. And who knows what will guide our choice in the end? In the end ..." She looked at Khalid. "Perhaps I am disturbing you? I should leave you alone to think."

"No worries. Talking helps. But what about you?"

Sunita gazed at the Wall of the Seven Heavens. "For me, it is easy. I feel at peace with my decision." She smiled warmly at Khalid and walked back to find Gabriel. He was talking to the lights, which were dancing as if they were laughing.

Emily finally cornered Joshua in a remote nook of the vast library. He sat on the floor with his back against a pile of books, Nietzsche's *Twilight of the Idols* open on his lap.

Emily folded her legs and sat on the floor beside him. He seemed unsurprised at her arrival and said quietly, "Are you excited to see your lord and savior? Just think, soon you'll be sitting beside Jesus, petting all those fluffy, blue-eyed lambs that follow him into every photo op."

"I believe you're thinking of Little Bo Peep."

"Damn, I always get those two mixed up."

Emily laughed and punched his arm. "I'm mad at you. A bit. We need to talk, and we don't have much time."

"Emily, I need you to make your own decision." He spoke with a quiet fury, but his eyes betrayed grief. "I may be a heathen, but I have my values. Don't factor me into your choice. Please. I don't want to be responsible for your everlasting damnation or happiness or—"

"Are you daft? I've never met a more presumptuous twit in all my life or, I guess, death."

Joshua shrugged his shoulders, shaking off some embarrassment. "I thought we had a connection. Excuse me if—"

Emily turned his face toward hers and kissed him passionately. A fusion of spirit and heart created a diaphanous circle of pulsating light that expanded with a sensuous slowness. Emily abruptly broke away, and the light vanished. She got up awkwardly and ran, through labyrinths, corridors and winding stairs until she fled through the grand, pillared exit.

In the distance, a trumpet sounded. A clarion call to gather. Joshua sighed, pushed himself to his feet and trudged after her.

In the Great Unnamed Room, Susan smiled happily as the others showed up. "This is so exciting. I love the trumpet. An instrument of the gods' and goddesses' celestial symphony, you know."

"A trumpet? Can this get any more clichéd?" Joshua appeared worn and weary. He looked to see where Emily was.

She stood a little distance away, leaning against Sunita's shoulder. Sunita kissed Emily's head. Although Emily could not feel the kiss, she sensed it and closed her eyes, thinking this might be the last time.

Gabriel raised his hand to silence the trumpet. Two lights flanked him as he stood before the group.

"My dear ones, I trust you have wisely and fully contemplated your decision. It is time for me to take you through the steps that will bring you to the departure area, where you will have a short wait before the lunar eclipse begins. So, first, each of you will return to your room."

"Excuse me? Back to our rooms?" Susan's hand rose to her chest.

"Not transcendental enough for you, Susan?" Joshua spoke while examining one of his fingers. His hands appeared to be even less solid than before. He checked the others; all of them were more translucent.

Gabriel noticed Joshua's alarm and rushed on. "The reason, my dear Susan, is that your room will raise your vibrations to align with the departure area. And"—his words sped up—"to answer any other potential whys of being back in your room, don't forget that's where you began. Entry-exit kind of thing. Second, expect a heavy fog to descend. Don't worry, this is normal. A light will begin to penetrate this fog, followed by nine gongs and, presto! You'll find yourself in the area of departure." He stopped, pleased with himself.

Alter furrowed his bushy eyebrows. Khalid whispered to him the meaning of the word *presto*. His brows furrowed more deeply.

"Can you tell us what the departure area looks like?" Emily asked. She hoped she sounded curious, but even she could hear the anxiety in her voice.

"I do not know."

"What do you mean, you don't know?" Susan's words sounded thin and tinny.

Was Joshua the only one who saw their forms becoming more formless? His brain frantically tried to reason it out. And then it hit him. The leap into the shadow engulfing Alter, and the isolation and utter desolation that followed, had put him on hyper-alert. *No doubt that hellish torment catalyzed this perception*, he thought. Joshua endeavored without success to calm himself even as Gabriel continued speaking.

"Well, my dear Susan, I have never been there. Actually, I will share—" One of the lights floated close to him. Gabriel glanced in its direction and continued. "Apparently we do not have time to explain why I have never been there. Reports do indicate, however, that it is a place of great and unequalled serenity. Once you are there, you will be taken to what we affectionately call the POD."

Gabriel caught the alarm radiating from Joshua and nodded to him, silently acknowledging his reason for being shocked and afraid. Joshua saw in Gabriel's eyes that his suspicions were right. The others were weakened by all that had happened. The risk they might fade to nothing was real. With a steady look, Gabriel transmitted a command to Joshua that they should carry on; if the others knew, fear would further diminish their vibrations. After an almost imperceptible nod from Joshua, Gabriel continued.

"For you, my dear ones, who have not made your decision yet, POD can be thought of as an acronym for Place of Decision. For all others, it will be your Place of Departure." Gabriel ran a hand over his face. "And at the risk of repeating myself, this is the first time since, well, since time was simply a concept, that anyone has been offered this choice. Stay. Leave. It is up to you."

He nodded at one of the lights. "Yes, I am beginning to ramble. Cheers and blessings, my dear ones."

In ones and twos, the seven ascended the stairway. Stars and candles dimmed and winked out. The Ugly Brown Birds nestled in their cages, content to be still. The lights departed. Gabriel stood in the center of the Great Unnamed Room, alone in the dim light.

Two things happened at the same time. Nine gongs sounded, and the most loving moment of the lives they'd lived struck the center of their chests. With no time to ponder, they found themselves sitting on crystal-clear circular benches inside a clear globe suspended in a cosmic night, where night was always night. Shooting stars, a few planets and asteroids flew through the darkness.

"What now? When do we declare our decision?" Joshua was relieved they were all there and together—and that now they were in the POD, all of them looked solid.

"We're in a snow globe!" Susan's laugh was high and stayed suspended for a moment.

"I don't know how I know, but I feel that in a moment there will be no light," Emily said slowly. "And when light returns, whoever remains in this enclosure will return to the realm. Did all of you experience that love memory?"

There were nods and smiles at the memory of this briefest of brief memories.

"Again, I don't know how I know, but I feel that memory empowered our hearts," Emily went on. "And it is our hearts that have made the decision."

Reinhardt tilted his head as he pondered her words, and his broadening smile warmed her. "I believe you are right," he said.

The globe was embryonic. Thoughts flew around, and each of them not only heard the flying thoughts but felt the responding heart.

Emily punched Joshua when he thought what a crazy and curious bunch they were.

Reinhardt smiled his enigmatic smile when Khalid thought how solid and helpful Reinhardt had been.

Sunita leaned into Joshua when he thought how he did not wish anyone to go.

What felt like hours passed in milliseconds.

Joshua said, "So our dead, shriveled hearts have chosen to stay or go. And when the light disappears and then returns, whoever remains in this wacky snow globe will return to Gabriel and the realm?"

"Yes."

The light disappeared.

There was nothing.

Nine gongs sounded.

The light returned.

I vowed to Gabriel not to reveal who decided to remain in this realm.

He said he may require my services soon but won't say why. Going forward, as I've heard some say, I've begun to tend to the gardens here, give the old house a lick of paint and fix the gates. This being a portal for all those heavenly beings, it seems only right for them to travel through a nice place.

Hope comes by from time to time, when she's in the area.

I make sure to always have enough brandy and gin on hand for Gabriel if he's in the neighborhood. I'm thinking it will be any day now.

One odd thing. Gabriel said that because of the tremendous help they had all given—Alter, Susan, Khalid, Reinhardt, Sunita, Emily and Joshua—they are now considered angels. But apparently there's a mandatory probationary period that applies to all of them. Everyone. No exceptions.

And then he smiled that dazzling smile.

Cheers and blessings to all. ~ Mrs. Potts

The End

Acknowledgments

I have done many things in life that some may consider brave. However, writing this book easily ranks as a top contender for the bravest. I am so grateful to those who have offered support, both personally and professionally. For someone who struggles with accepting support I attracted some stellar folks!

Among those who share personal space with me, I would like to express my profound appreciation and love to my partner, Lennart Krogoll, who is the inspiration behind one of the characters. My children, Sarah Young MacDonald and Joshua Young, who gently cheered me on and pitched in with some edits and insights.

Rachel Cooper was heaven-sent! As Editor, Rachel has top notch skills and, with her firm and gentle guidance, moved this novel forward. Her genuine care for the novel was evident and her decision to take on this project, fearless. I will always be grateful to her!

Thank-you to Jeff Brown for a dream cover! Technical skills, artistic vision and patience are a rare combination!

My path has converged with some amazing people; people who have challenged and inspired me. I am grateful to be entrusted with my client's secret sorrows, traumas, joys and leaps forward. It is clear to me that everyone matters. This wild, unruly world needs each of us. Bless unity in diversity!

Cheers and Blessings!